BURY YOUR DEAD

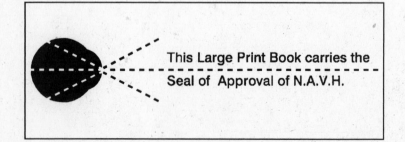

BURY YOUR DEAD

LOUISE PENNY

THORNDIKE PRESS
A part of Gale, Cengage Learning

GALE
CENGAGE Learning™

Detroit • New York • San Francisco • New Haven, Conn • Waterville, Maine • London

GALE
CENGAGE Learning™

Thorndike Press, a part of Gale, Cengage Learning.

Thorndike Press® Large Print Mystery.

The text of this Large Print edition is unabridged.

Other aspects of the book may vary from the original edition.

Set in 16 pt. Plantin.

LIBRARY OF CONGRESS CATALOGING-IN-PUBLICATION DATA

Penny, Louise.
  Bury your dead / by Louise Penny.
    p. cm. — (Thorndike Press large print mystery)
  "A Chief Inspector Gamache novel"—Copyright p.
    ISBN-13: 978-1-4104-3172-1
    ISBN-10: 1-4104-3172-X
    1. Gamache, Armand (Fictitious character)—Fiction. 2. Police—Québec (Province)—Fiction. 3. Murder—Investigation—Fiction. 4. Québec (Province)—Fiction. I. Title.
  PR9199.4.P464B87 2010
  813'.6—dc22   2010027764

Published in 2010 by arrangement with St. Martin's Press, LLC.

Printed in the United States of America
1 2 3 4 5 6 7 14 13 12 11 10

This book is dedicated
to second chances —
Those who give them
And those who take them

ACKNOWLEDGMENTS

Michael and I spent a magical month in Quebec City researching *Bury Your Dead.* Québec is a glorious place, and the old walled city is even more beautiful. I hope I've managed to capture how it felt to walk those streets every day and see not just the lovely old stone buildings, but see my history. Canadian history. Alive. It was very moving for both of us. But Quebec City isn't a museum. It's a vibrant, modern, thriving capital. I hope I've captured that too. But mostly I hope *Bury Your Dead* contains the great love I feel for this society I have chosen as home. A place where the French and English languages and cultures live together. Not always in agreement, both have suffered and lost too much to be completely at peace, but there is deep respect and affection.

Much of the action in *Bury Your Dead* takes place in the Literary and Historical

7

Society library, in old Quebec City. It is a stunning library, and a stunning achievement to have created and kept this English institution alive for generations. I was helped in my researches by the members, volunteers and staff of the Lit and His (as it is affectionately known). Because this is a work of fiction I have taken liberties with some of the history of Québec, and the Literary and Historical Society. Especially as it concerns one of its most distinguished members, Dr. James Douglas. I realize some will not be pleased with my extrapolating, but I hope you understand.

I also need to make clear that I have met the Chief Archeologist of Québec many times and he is charming, helpful and gracious. Not at all like my fictional Chief Archeologist.

The majority of the history in the book concerns Samuel de Champlain. I have to admit, to my shame, I wasn't all that familiar with him before starting my researches. I knew the name, I knew he was one of the founders of Québec and therefore Canada. I knew his burial place is a mystery. No one has found it. And this has confounded archeologists and historians for decades. This mystery is at the center of my mystery. But it demanded I learn about Champlain.

To do that I read a fair amount and spoke with local historians, chief among them Louisa Blair and David Mendel. I was also helped by a wonderful book called *Champlain's Dream,* by Professor David Hackett Fischer, of Brandeis University. Professor Hackett Fischer actually came to Quebec City during our stay and when we heard this Michael and I decided to hear him lecture. It struck us (belatedly) as odd that the venue would be a government conference room. When we arrived we sat at the far end of the large table. A very nice young woman approached and asked, in perfect French, who we might be. We, in not so perfect French, explained that I was an English Canadian writer doing research on Champlain and had come to hear the professor speak. She thanked me and a few minutes later a man came by, shook our hands and escorted us to the head of the table. Then everyone stood and the Minister of Culture arrived along with other high government officials. Finally Professor Hackett Fischer came in and was seated right in front of us.

Way too late Michael and I figured out this was a private briefing of high Québec government officials — and us. When they realized who we were, instead of showing us

9

the door, the government officials gave us the best seats and much of the conference was held in English.

This is Québec. Where there is great kindness and accommodation. But there can also be, in some quarters, great suspicions — on both sides.

That is part of what makes Québec so fascinating.

I'd like to thank Jacquie Czernin and Peter Black, of the local CBC Radio, for their help with contacts. And Scott Carnie for his help on some tactical issues.

For those of you who love, as I do, the poetry of the Great War, you'll recognize that I paraphrase a stunning poem by Wilfred Owen called "Dulce et Decorum Est."

Bury Your Dead owes a great deal to my wonderful agent Teresa Chris and editors, Hope Dellon, Sherise Hobbs and Dan Mallory. Their kind words and critical eyes bring out the best in the book and in me as a writer.

Finally, I'd like to mention that the Literary and Historical Society is a gem, but like most libraries it now functions on little money and the good will of volunteers both Francophone and Anglophone. If you'd like to join, or visit, please contact them at:

www.morrin.org.

This is a very special book for me, on so many levels, as I hope you'll see. Like the rest of the Chief Inspector Gamache books, *Bury Your Dead* is not about death, but about life. And the need to both respect the past and let it go.

ONE

Up the stairs they raced, taking them two at a time, trying to be as quiet as possible. Gamache struggled to keep his breathing steady, as though he was sitting at home, as though he had not a care in the world.

"Sir?" came the young voice over Gamache's headphones.

"You must believe me, son. Nothing bad will happen to you."

He hoped the young agent couldn't hear the strain in his voice, the flattening as the Chief Inspector fought to keep his voice authoritative, certain.

"I believe you."

They reached the landing. Inspector Beauvoir stopped, staring at his Chief. Gamache looked at his watch.

47 seconds.

Still time.

In his headphones the agent was telling him about the sunshine and how good it felt on his face.

The rest of the team made the landing, tactical vests in place, automatic weapons drawn, eyes sharp. Trained on the Chief. Beside him Inspector Beauvoir was also waiting for a decision. Which way? They were close. Within feet of their quarry.

Gamache stared down one dark, dingy corridor in the abandoned factory then down the other.

They looked identical. Light scraped through the broken, grubby windows lining the halls and with it came the December day.

43 seconds.

He pointed decisively to the left and they ran, silently, toward the door at the end. As he ran Gamache gripped his rifle and spoke calmly into the headset.

"There's no need to worry."

"There's forty seconds left, sir." Each word was exhaled as though the man on the other end was having difficulty breathing.

"Just listen to me," said Gamache, thrusting his hand toward a door. The team surged ahead.

36 seconds.

"I won't let anything happen to you," said Gamache, his voice convincing, commanding, daring the young agent to contradict.

"You'll be having dinner with your family tonight."

"Yes sir."

The tactical team surrounded the closed door with its frosted, filthy window. Darkened.

Gamache paused, staring at it, his hand hanging in the air ready to give the signal to break it down. To rescue his agent.

29 seconds.

Beside him Beauvoir strained, waiting to be loosed.

Too late, Chief Inspector Gamache realized he'd made a mistake.

"Give it time, Armand."

"*Avec le temps?*" Gamache returned the older man's smile and made a fist of his right hand. To stop the trembling. A tremble so slight he was certain the waitress in the Quebec City café hadn't noticed. The two students across the way tapping on their laptops wouldn't notice. No one would notice.

Except someone very close to him.

He looked at Émile Comeau, crumbling a flaky croissant with sure hands. He was nearing eighty now, Gamache's mentor and former chief. His hair was white and groomed, his eyes through his glasses a

15

sharp blue. He was slender and energetic, even now. Though with each visit Armand Gamache noticed a slight softening about the face, a slight slowing of the movements.

Avec le temps.

Widowed five years, Émile Comeau knew the power, and length, of time.

Gamache's own wife, Reine-Marie, had left at dawn that morning after spending a week with them at Émile's stone home within the old walled city of Québec. They'd had quiet dinners together in front of the fire, they'd walked the narrow snow-covered streets. Talked. Were silent. Read the papers, discussed events. The three of them. Four, if you counted their German shepherd, Henri.

And most days Gamache had gone off on his own to a local library, to read.

Émile and Reine-Marie had given him that, recognizing that right now he needed society but he also needed solitude.

And then it was time for her to leave. After saying good-bye to Émile she turned to her husband. Tall, solid, a man who preferred good books and long walks to any other activity, he looked more like a distinguished professor in his mid-fifties than the head of the most prestigious homicide unit in Canada. The Sûreté du Québec. He walked

16

her to her car, scraping the morning ice from the windshield.

"You don't have to go, you know," he said, smiling down at her as they stood in the brittle, new day. Henri sat in a snow bank nearby and watched.

"I know. But you and Émile need time together. I could see how you were looking at each other."

"The longing?" laughed the Chief Inspector. "I'd hoped we'd been more discreet."

"A wife always knows." She smiled, looking into his deep brown eyes. He wore a hat, but still she could see his graying hair, and the slight curl where it came out from under the fabric. And his beard. She'd slowly become used to the beard. For years he'd had a moustache, but just lately, since it happened, he'd grown the trim beard.

She paused. Should she say it? It was never far from her mind now, from her mouth. The words she knew were useless, if any words could be described as that. Certainly she knew they could not make the thing happen. If they could she would surround him with them, encase him with her words.

"Come home when you can," she said instead, her voice light.

He kissed her. "I will. In a few days, a

17

week at the most. Call me when you get there."

"*D'accord.*" She got into the car.

"*Je t'aime,*" he said, putting his gloved hand into the window to touch her shoulder.

Watch out, her mind screamed. *Be safe. Come home with me. Be careful, be careful, be careful.*

She put her own gloved hand over his. "*Je t'aime.*"

And then she was gone, back to Montreal, glancing in the rear-view mirror to see him standing on the deserted early morning street, Henri naturally at his side. Both watching her, until she disappeared.

The Chief Inspector continued to stare even after she'd turned the corner. Then he picked up a shovel and slowly cleared the night's fluffy snowfall from the front steps. Resting for a moment, his arms crossed over the handle of the shovel, he marveled at the beauty as the first light hit the new snow. It looked more pale blue than white, and here and there it sparkled like tiny prisms where the flakes had drifted and collected, then caught, remade, and returned the light. Like something alive and giddy.

Life in the old walled city was like that. Both gentle and dynamic, ancient and vibrant.

Picking up a handful of snow, the Chief Inspector mashed it into a ball in his fist. Henri immediately stood, his tail going so hard his entire rear swayed. His eyes burning into the ball.

Gamache tossed it into the air and the dog leapt, his mouth closing over the snowball, and chomping down. Landing on all fours Henri was once again surprised that the thing that had been so solid had suddenly disappeared.

Gone, so quickly.

But next time would be different.

Gamache chuckled. He might be right.

Just then Émile stepped out from his doorway, bundled in an immense winter coat against the biting February cold.

"Ready?" The elderly man clamped a toque onto his head, pulling it down so that it covered his ears and forehead, and put on thick mitts, like boxing gloves.

"For what? A siege?"

"For breakfast, *mon vieux*. Come along, before someone gets the last croissant."

He knew how to motivate his former subordinate. Hardly pausing for Gamache to replace the shovel, Émile headed off up the snowy street. Around them the other residents of Quebec City were waking up. Coming out into the tender morning light to shovel, to scrape the snow from their cars, to walk to the boulangerie for their morning baguette and *café*.

The two men and Henri set out along rue St-Jean, past the restaurants and tourist shops, to a tiny side street called rue Couillard, and there they found Chez Temporel.

They'd been coming to this café for fifteen years, ever since Superintendent Émile Comeau had retired to old Quebec City, and Gamache had come to visit, to spend time with his mentor, and to help with the little chores that piled up. Shoveling, stacking wood for the fireplace, sealing windows against drafts. But this visit was different. Like no other in all the winters Chief Inspector Gamache had been coming to Quebec City.

This time it was Gamache who needed help.

"So," Émile leaned back, cupping his bowl of *café au lait* in slender hands. "How's the research going?"

"I can't yet find any references to Captain Cook actually meeting Bougainville before the Battle of Québec, but it was 250 years ago. Records are scattered and weren't well kept. But I know they're in there," said Gamache. "It's an amazing library, Émile. The volumes go back centuries."

Comeau watched his companion talk about sifting through arcane books in a local library and the tidbits he was unearthing about a battle long ago fought, and lost. At least, from his point of view lost. Was there a spark in those beloved eyes at last? Those eyes he'd stared into so often at the scenes of dreadful crimes as they'd hunted murderers. As they'd raced through woods and villages and fields, through clues and evidence and suspicions. *Adown Titanic glooms of chasmed fears,* Émile remembered the quote as he remembered those days. Yes, he thought, that described it. *Chasmed fears.* Both their own, and the murderers. Across tables across the province he and Gamache had sat. Just like this.

But now it was time to rest from murder. No more killing, no more deaths. Armand had seen too much of that lately. No, better to bury himself in history, in lives long past. An intellectual pursuit, nothing more.

Beside them Henri stirred and Gamache instinctively lowered his hand to stroke the shepherd's head and reassure him. And once again Émile noted the slight tremble. Barely there now. Stronger at times. Sometimes it disappeared completely. It was a tell-tale tremble, and Émile knew the terrible tale it had to tell.

21

He wished he could take that hand and hold it steady and tell him it would be all right. Because it would, he knew.

With time.

Watching Armand Gamache he noticed again the jagged scar on his left temple and the trim beard he'd grown. So that people would stop staring. So that people would not recognize the most recognizable police officer in Québec.

But, of course, it didn't matter. It wasn't them Armand Gamache was hiding from.

The waitress at Chez Temporel arrived with more coffee.

"*Merci,* Danielle," the two men said at once and she left, smiling at the two men who looked so different but seemed so similar.

They drank their coffees and ate *pain au chocolat* and *croissants aux amandes* and talked about the Carnaval de Québec, starting that night. Occasionally they'd lapse into silence, watching the men and women hurrying along the icy cold street outside to their jobs. Someone had scratched a three-leaf clover into a slight indent in the center of their wooden table. Émile rubbed it with his finger.

And wondered when Armand would want to talk about what happened.

■ ■ ■ ■

It was ten thirty and the monthly board meeting of the Literary and Historical Society was about to start. For many years the meetings had been held in the evening, when the library was closed, but then it was noticed that fewer and fewer members were showing up.

So the Chairman, Porter Wilson, had changed the time. At least, he thought he'd changed the time. At least, it had been reported in the board minutes that it had been his motion, though he privately seemed to remember arguing against it.

And yet, here they were meeting in the morning, and had been for some years. Still, the other members had adjusted, as had Porter. He had to, since it had apparently been his idea.

The fact the board had adjusted at all was a miracle. The last time they'd been asked to change anything it had been the worn leather on the Lit and His chairs, and that had been sixty-three years ago. Members still remembered fathers and mothers, grandparents, ranged on either side of the upholstered Mason-Dixon Line. Remembered vitriolic comments made behind closed doors, behind backs, but before children. Who didn't forget, sixty-three years later, that devious alteration from old black leather to new black leather.

Pulling out his chair at the head of the table Porter noticed it was looking worn. He sat quickly so that no one, least of all himself, could see it.

Small stacks of paper were neatly arranged in front of his and every other place, marching down the wooden table. Elizabeth MacWhirter's doing. He examined Elizabeth. Plain, tall and slim. At least, she had been that when the world was young. Now she just looked freeze-dried. Like those ancient cadavers pulled from glaciers. Still obviously human, but withered and gray. Her dress was blue and practical and a very good cut and material, he suspected. After all, she was one of those MacWhirters. A venerable and moneyed family. One not given to displays of wealth, or brains. Her brother had sold the shipping empire about a decade too late. But there was still money there. She was a little dull, he thought, but responsible. Not a leader, not a visionary. Not the sort to hold a community in peril together. Like him. And his father before him. And his grandfather.

For the tiny English community within

the walls of old Quebec City had been in peril for many generations. It was a kind of perpetual peril that sometimes got better and sometimes got worse, but never disappeared completely. Just like the English.

Porter Wilson had never fought a war, being just that much too young, and then too old. Not, anyway, an official war. But he and the other members of his board knew themselves to be in a battle nevertheless. And one, he secretly suspected, they were losing.

At the door Elizabeth MacWhirter greeted the other board members as they arrived and looked over at Porter Wilson already seated at the head of the table, reading over his notes.

He'd accomplished many things in his life, Elizabeth knew. The choir he'd organized, the amateur theater, the wing for the nursing home. All built by force of will and personality. And all less than they might have been had he sought and accepted advice.

The very force of his personality both created and crippled. How much more could he have accomplished had he been kinder? But then, dynamism and kindness often didn't go together, though when they did they were unstoppable.

Porter was stoppable. Indeed, he stopped himself. And now the only board that could stand him was the Lit and His. Elizabeth had known Porter for seventy years, since she'd seen him eating lunch alone, every day, at school and gone to keep him company. Porter decided she was sucking up to one of the great Wilson clan, and treated her with disdain.

Still, she kept him company. Not because she liked him but because she knew even then something it would take Porter Wilson decades to realize. The English of Quebec City were no longer the juggernauts, no longer the steamships, no longer the gracious passenger liners of the society and economy.

They were a life raft. Adrift. And you don't make war on others in the raft.

Elizabeth MacWhirter had figured that out. And when Porter rocked the boat, she righted it.

She looked at Porter Wilson and saw a small, energetic, toupéed man. His hair, where not imported, was dyed a shade of black the chairs would envy. His eyes were brown and darted about nervously.

Mr. Blake arrived first. The oldest board member, he practically lived at the Lit and His. He took off his coat, revealing his uniform of gray flannel suit, laundered white shirt, blue silk tie. He was always perfectly turned out. A gentleman, who managed to make Elizabeth feel young and beautiful. She'd had a crush on him when she'd been an awkward teen and he in his dashing twenties.

He'd been attractive then and sixty years later he was still attractive, though his hair was thin and white and his once fine body had rounded and softened. But his eyes were smart and lively, and his heart was large and strong.

"Elizabeth," Mr. Blake smiled and took her hand, holding it for a moment. Never too long, never too familiar. Just enough, so that she knew she'd been held.

He took his seat. A seat, Elizabeth thought, that should be replaced. But then, honestly, so should Mr. Blake. So should they all.

What would happen when they died out and all that was left of the board of the Literary and Historical Society were worn, empty chairs?

"Right, we need to make this fast. We have a practice in an hour."

Tom Hancock arrived, followed by Ken Haslam. The two were never far apart these days, being unlikely team members in the ridiculous upcoming race.

Tom was Elizabeth's triumph. Her hope. And not simply because he was the minister of St. Andrew's Presbyterian Church next door.

He was young and new to the community, having moved to Quebec City three years earlier. At thirty-three he was about half the age of the next youngest board member. Not yet cynical, not yet burned out. He still believed his church would find new parishioners, the English community would suddenly produce babies with the desire to stay in Quebec City. He believed the Québec government when it promised job equality for Anglophones. And health care in their own language. And education. And nursing homes so that when all hope was lost, they might die with their mother tongue on caregivers' lips.

He'd managed to inspire the board to believe maybe all wasn't lost. And even, maybe, this wasn't really a war. Wasn't some dreadful extension of the Battle of the Plains of Abraham, one which the English lost this time. Elizabeth glanced up at the oddly petite statue of General James Wolfe. The martyred hero of the battle 250 years ago hovered over the library of the Literary and Historical Society, like a wooden accusation. To witness their petty battles and to remind them, in perpetuity, of the great battle he'd fought, for them. Where he'd died, but not before triumphing on that blood-soaked farmers field. Ending the war, and securing Québec for the English. On paper.

And now from his corner of the lovely old library General Wolfe looked down on them. In every way, Elizabeth suspected.

"So, Ken," Tom said, taking his place beside the older man. "You in shape? Ready for the race?"

Elizabeth didn't hear Ken Haslam's response. But then she didn't expect to. Ken's thin lips moved, words were formed, but never actually heard.

They all paused, thinking perhaps this was the day he would produce a word above a whisper. But they were wrong. Still, Tom Hancock continued to talk to Ken, as though they were actually having a conversation.

Elizabeth loved Tom for that as well. For not giving in to the notion that because Ken was quiet he was stupid. Elizabeth knew him to be anything but. In his mid-sixties he was the most successful of all of them, building a business of his own. And now, having achieved that Ken Haslam had done something else remarkable.

He'd signed up for the treacherous ice canoe race. Signed on to Tom Hancock's team. He would be the oldest member of the team, the oldest member of any team. Perhaps the oldest racer ever.

Watching Ken, quiet and calm and Tom, young, vital, handsome, Elizabeth wondered if maybe they understood each other very well after all. Perhaps both had things they weren't saying.

Not for the first time Elizabeth wondered about Tom Hancock. Why he'd chosen to minister to them, and why he stayed within the walls of old Quebec City. It took a certain personality, Elizabeth knew, to choose to live in what amounted to a fortress.

"Right, let's start," said Porter, sitting up even straighter.

"Winnie isn't here yet," said Elizabeth.

"We can't wait."

"Why not?" Tom asked, his voice relaxed. But still Porter heard a challenge.

"Because it's already past ten thirty and you're the one who wanted to make this quick," Porter said, pleased at having scored a point.

Once again, thought Elizabeth, Porter managed to look at a friend and see a foe.

"Quite right. Still, I'm happy to wait,"

30

smiled Tom, unwilling to take to the field.

"Well, I'm not. First order of business?"

They discussed the purchase of new books for a while before Winnie arrived. Small and energetic, she was fierce in her loyalty. To the English community, to the Lit and His, but mostly to her friend.

She marched in, gave Porter a withering look, and sat next to Elizabeth.

"I see you started without me," she said to him. "I told you I'd be late."

"You did, but that doesn't mean we had to wait. We're discussing new books to buy."

"And it didn't occur to you this might be an issue best discussed with the librarian?"

"Well, you're here now."

The rest of the board watched this as though at Wimbledon, though with considerably less interest. It was pretty clear who had the balls, and who would win.

Fifty minutes later they'd almost reached the end of the agenda. There was one oatmeal cookie left, the members staring but too polite to take it. They'd discussed the heating bills, the membership drive, the ratty old volumes left to them in wills, instead of money. The books were generally sermons, or lurid Victorian poetry, or the dreary daily diary of a trip up the Amazon or into Africa to shoot and stuff some poor wild creature.

They discussed having another sale of books, but after the last debacle that was a short discussion.

Elizabeth took notes and had to force herself not to lip-synch to each board member's comments. It was a liturgy. Familiar, soothing in a strange way. The same words repeated over and over every meeting. For ever and ever. Amen.

A sound suddenly interrupted that comforting liturgy, a sound so unique and startling Porter almost jumped out of his chair.

"What was that?" whispered Ken Haslam. For him it was almost a shout.

"It's the doorbell, I think," said Winnie.

"The doorbell?" asked Porter. "I didn't know we had one."

"Put in in 1897 after the Lieutenant Governor visited and couldn't get in," said Mr. Blake, as though he'd been there. "Never heard it myself."

But he heard it again. A long, shrill bell. Elizabeth had locked the front door to the Literary and Historical Society as soon as everyone had arrived. A precaution against being interrupted. Though since hardly anyone ever visited it was more habit than necessity. She'd also hung a sign on the thick wooden door. *Board Meeting in Progress. Library will reopen at noon. Thank you.* Merci.

The bell sounded again. Someone was leaning on it, finger jammed into the button.

Still they stared at each other.

"I'll go," said Elizabeth.

Porter looked down at his papers, the better part of valor.

"No," Winnie stood. "I'll go. You all stay here."

They watched Winnie disappear down the corridor and heard her feet on the wooden stairs. There was silence. Then a minute later her feet on the stairs again.

They listened to the footsteps clicking and clacking closer. She arrived but stopped at the door, her face pale and serious.

"There's someone there. Someone who wants to speak to the board."

"Well," demanded Porter, remembering he was their leader, now that the elderly woman had gone to the door. "Who is it?"

"Augustin Renaud," she said and saw the looks on their faces. Had she said "Dracula" they could not have been more startled. Though, for the English, startled meant raised eyebrows.

Every eyebrow in the room was raised,

and if General Wolfe could have managed it, he would have.

"I left him outside," she said into the silence.

As if to underscore that the doorbell shrieked again.

"What should we do?" Winnie asked, but instead of turning to Porter she looked at Elizabeth. They all did.

"We need to take a vote," Elizabeth said at last. "Should we see him?"

"He's not on the agenda," Mr. Blake pointed out.

"That's right," said Porter, trying to wrestle back control. But even he looked at Elizabeth.

"Who's in favor of letting Augustin Renaud speak to the board?" Elizabeth asked.

Not a hand was raised.

Elizabeth lowered her pen, not taking note of the vote. Giving one curt nod she stood. "I'll tell him."

"I'll go with you," said Winnie.

"No, dear, you stay here. I'll be right back. I mean, really?" She paused at the door, taking in the board and General Wolfe above. "How bad could it be?"

But they all knew the answer to that.

When Augustin Renaud came calling it was never good.

Two

Armand Gamache settled into the worn leather sofa beneath the statue of General Wolfe. Nodding to the elderly man across from him he pulled the letters out of his satchel. After a walk through the city with Émile and Henri, Gamache had returned home, picked up his mail, collected his notes, stuffed it all into his satchel, then he and Henri had walked up the hill.

To the hushed library of the Literary and Historical Society.

Now he looked at the bulging manila envelope on the sofa beside him. Daily correspondence from his office in Montreal sent on to Émile's home. Agent Isabelle Lacoste had sorted his mail and sent it with a note.

Cher Patron,
It was good to speak to you the other day. I envy you a few weeks in Québec. I keep

telling my husband we must take the children to Carnaval but he insists they're too young yet. He's probably right. The truth is, I'd just like to go.

The interrogation of the suspect (so hard to call him that when we all know there are no suspicions, only certainties) continues. I haven't heard what he's said, if anything. As you know, a Royal Commission has been formed. Have you testified yet? I received my summons today. I'm not sure what to tell them.

Gamache lowered the note for a moment. Agent Lacoste would, of course, tell them the truth. As she knew it. She had no choice, by temperament and training. Before he left he'd ordered all of his department to cooperate.

As he had.

He went back to the note.

No one yet knows where it will lead, or end. But there are suspicions. The atmosphere is tense.

I will keep you informed.

Isabelle Lacoste

Too heavy to hold, the letter slowly lowered to his lap. He stared ahead and saw Agent Isabelle Lacoste in flashes. Images

37

moved, uninvited, in and out of his mind. Of her staring down at him, seeming to shout though he couldn't make out her words. He felt her small, strong hands gripping either side of his head, saw her leaning close, her mouth moving, her eyes intense, trying to communicate something to him. Felt hands ripping away the tactical vest from his chest. He saw blood on her hands and the look on her face.

Then he saw her again.

At the funeral. The funerals. Lined up in uniform with the rest of the famous homicide division of the Sûreté du Québec as he took his place at the head of the terrible column. One bitter cold day. To bury those who died under his command that day in the abandoned factory.

Closing his eyes he breathed deeply, smelling the musky scents of the library. Of age, of stability, of calm and peace. Of old-fashioned polish, of wood, of words bound in worn leather. He smelled his own slight fragrance of rosewater and sandalwood.

And he thought of something good, something nice, some kind harbor. And he found it in Reine-Marie, as he remembered her voice on his cell phone earlier in the day. Cheerful. Home. Safe. Their daughter Annie coming over for dinner with her husband. Groceries to buy, plants to water, correspondence to catch up on.

He could see her on the phone in their Outremont apartment standing by the bookcase, the sunny room filled with books and periodicals and comfortable furniture, orderly and peaceful.

There was a calm about it, as there was about Reine-Marie.

And he felt his racing heart settle and his breathing deepen. Taking one last long breath, he opened his eyes.

"Would your dog like some water?"

"I beg your pardon?" Gamache refocused and saw the elderly man sitting across from him motioning to Henri.

"I used to bring Seamus here. He'd lie at my feet while I read. Like your dog. What's his name?"

"Henri."

At the sound of his name the young shepherd sat up, alert, his huge ears swinging this way and that, like satellite dishes searching for a signal.

"I beg you, *monsieur*," smiled Gamache, "don't say B-A-L-L or we'll all be lost."

The man laughed. "Seamus used to get excited whenever I'd say B-O-O-K. He'd know we were coming here. I think he loved it even more than I do."

39

Gamache had been coming to this library every day for almost a week and except for whispered conversations with the elderly female librarian as he searched for obscure volumes on the Battle of the Plains of Abraham, he hadn't spoken to anyone.

It was a relief to not talk, to not explain, or feel an explanation was desired if not demanded. That would come soon enough. But for now he'd yearned for and found peace in this obscure library.

Though he'd been visiting his mentor for years, and had come to believe he knew old Québec intimately, he'd never actually been in this building. Never even noticed it among the other lovely homes and churches, convents, schools, hotels and restaurants.

But here, just up rue St-Stanislas where Émile had his old stone home, Gamache had found sanctuary in an English library, among books. Where else?

"Would he like water?" the elderly man asked again. He seemed to want to help and though Gamache doubted Henri needed anything he said yes, please. Together they walked out of the library and down the wooden hall, past portraits of former heads of the Literary and Historical Society. It was as though the place was encrusted with its own history.

It gave it a feeling of calm and certainty. Though much of old Quebec City was like that within the thick walls. The only fortress city in North America, protected from attack.

It was, these days, more symbolic than practical but Gamache knew symbols were at least as powerful as any bomb. Indeed, while men and women perished, and cities fell, symbols endured, grew.

Symbols were immortal.

The elderly man poured water into a bowl and Gamache carried it back to the library, putting it on a towel so as not to get water on the wide, dark floorboards. Henri, of course, ignored it.

The two men settled back into their seats. Gamache noticed the man was reading a heavy horticultural reference book. He himself went back to the correspondence. A selection of letters Isabelle Lacoste had thought he might like to see. Most from sympathetic colleagues around the world, others from citizens who also wanted to let him know how they felt. He read them all, responded to them all, grateful Agent Lacoste sent only a sampling.

At the very end he read the letter he knew was there. Was always there. Every day. It was in a now familiar hand, dashed off,

41

almost illegible but Gamache had grown used to it and could now decode the scrawl.

Cher Armand,
This brings my thoughts, and prayers that you're feeling better. We speak of you often and hope you'll visit. Ruth says to bring Reine-Marie, since she doesn't actually like you. But she did ask me to say hello, and fuck off.

Gamache smiled. It was one of the kinder things Ruth Zardo said to people. Almost an endearment. Almost.

I do, however, have one question. Why would Olivier move the body? It doesn't make sense. He didn't do it, you know.
Love,
Gabri

Inside, as always, Gabri had put a licorice pipe. Gamache took it out, hesitated, then offered the treat to the man across the way.

"Licorice?"

The man looked up at Gamache then down at the offering.

"Are you offering candy to a stranger? Hope I won't have to call the police."

Gamache felt himself tense. Had the man

recognized him? Was this a veiled message? But the man's faded blue eyes were without artifice, and he was smiling. Reaching out the elderly man broke the pipe in half and handed the larger portion back to his companion. The part with the candy flame, the biggest and the best part.

"Merci, vous êtes très gentil." Thank you, you're very kind, the man said.

"C'est moi qui vous remercie." It is I who thank you, Gamache responded. It was a well-known, but no less sincere, exchange among gracious people. The man had spoken in perfect, educated, cultured French. Perhaps slightly accented, but Gamache knew that might just be his preconception, since he knew the man to be English, while he himself was Francophone.

They ate their candy and read their books. Henri settled in and by three thirty the librarian, Winnie, was turning on the lamps. The sun was already setting on the walled city and the old library within the walls.

Gamache was reminded of a nesting doll. The most public face was North America and huddled inside that was Canada and huddled inside Canada was Québec. And inside Québec? An even smaller presence, the tiny English community. And within that?

This place. The Literary and Historical Society. That held them and all their records, their thoughts, their memories, their symbols. Gamache didn't have to look at the statue above him to know who it was. This place held their leaders, their language, their culture and achievements. Long forgotten or never known by the Francophone majority outside these walls but kept alive here.

It was a remarkable place almost no Francophone even knew existed. When he'd told Émile about it his old friend had thought Gamache was joking, making it up, and yet the building was just two blocks from his own home.

Yes, it was like a nesting doll. Each held within the other until finally at the very core was this little gem. But was it nesting or hiding?

Gamache watched Winnie make her way around the library with its floor-to-ceiling books, Indian carpets scattered on the hardwood floors, a long wooden table and beside that the sitting area. Two leather wing chairs and the worn leather sofa where Gamache sat, his correspondence and books on the coffee table. Arched windows broke up the bookcases and flooded the room with light, when there was light to catch. But the most striking part of the library was the balcony that curved above it. A wrought iron spiral staircase took patrons to the second story of bookshelves that rose to the plaster ceiling.

The room was filled with volume and volumes. With light. With peace.

Gamache couldn't believe he'd never known it was here, had stumbled over it quite by accident one day while on a walk trying to clear his mind of the images. But more than the flashes that came unbidden, were the sounds. The gunshots, the exploding wood and walls as bullets hit. The shouts, then the screams.

But louder than all of that was the quiet, trusting, young voice in his head.

"I believe you, sir."

Armand and Henri left the library and did their rounds of the shops, picking up a selection of raw milk cheeses, pâté and lamb from J.A. Moisan, fruit and vegetables from the grocery store across the way, and a fresh, warm baguette from the Paillard bakery on rue St-Jean. Arriving home before Émile he put another log on the fire to warm up the chilly home. It had been built in 1752 and while the stone walls were three feet thick and would easily repel a can-

45

nonball, it was defenseless against the winter wind.

As Armand cooked the home warmed up and by the time Émile arrived the place was toasty warm and smelled of rosemary and garlic and lamb.

"Salut," Émile called from the front door, then a moment later arrived in the kitchen carrying a bottle of red wine and reaching for the corkscrew. "Smells terrific."

Gamache carried the evening tray of baguette, cheeses and pâté into the living room, placing it on the table before the fire while Émile brought in their wine.

"Santé."

The two men sat facing the fireplace and toasted. When they each had something to eat they discussed their days, Émile describing lunching with friends at the bar in the Château Frontenac and research he was doing for the Société Champlain. Gamache described his quiet hours in the library.

"Did you find what you were looking for?" Émile took a bite of wild boar pâté.

Gamache shook his head. "It's in there somewhere. Otherwise it doesn't make sense. We know the French troops were not more than half a mile from here in 1759, waiting for the English."

It was the battle every Québec school child learned about, dreamed about, fought again with wooden muskets and imaginary horses. The dreadful battle that would decide the fate of the city, the territory, the country and the continent. The Battle of Québec that in 1759 would effectively end the Seven Years' War. Ironic that after so many years of fighting between the French and the English over New France, the final battle should be so short. But brutal.

As Gamache spoke the two men imagined the scene. A chilly September day, the forces under Général Montcalm a mix of elite French troops and the Québécois, more used to guerrilla tactics than formal warfare. The French were desperate to lift the siege of Québec, a vicious and cruel starvation. More than fifteen thousand cannonballs had bombarded the tiny community and now, with winter almost upon them, it had to end or they'd all die. Men, women, children. Nurses, nuns, carpenters, teachers. All would perish.

Général Montcalm and his army would engage the mighty English force in one magnificent battle. Winner take all.

Montcalm, a brave, experienced soldier, a frontline commander who led by example. A hero to his men.

And against him? An equally brilliant and brave soldier, General Wolfe.

Québec was built on a cliff where the river narrowed. It was a huge strategic advantage. No enemy could ever attack it directly, they'd have to scale the cliff and that was impossible.

But they could attack just upriver, and that's where Montcalm waited. There was, however, another possibility, an area just slightly further away. Being a cunning commander, Montcalm sent one of his best men there, his own *aide-de-camp,* Colonel Bougainville.

And so, in mid-September 1759 he waited.

But Montcalm had made a mistake. A terrible mistake. Indeed, he'd made several, as Armand Gamache, a student of Québec history, was determined to prove.

"It's a fascinating theory, Armand," said Émile. "And you really think this little library holds the key? An English library?"

"Where else would it be?"

Émile Comeau nodded. It was a relief to see his friend so interested. When Armand and Reine-Marie had arrived a week before it took Émile a day to adjust to the changes in Gamache. And not just the beard, and the scars, but he seemed weighed down, leaden and laden by the recent past. Now, Gamache was still thinking of the past, but at least it was someone else's, not his own. "Did you get to the letters?"

"I did, and have some to send back," Gamache retrieved the parcel of correspondence. Hesitating for a moment, he made up his mind and took one out. "I'd like you to read this."

Émile sipped his wine and read, then began laughing. He handed the letter back to Gamache.

"That Ruth clearly has a crush on you."

"If I had pigtails she'd be pulling them," smiled Gamache. "But I think you might know her.

"Who hurt you, once,
so far beyond repair
that you would meet each overture
with curling lip?"

Gamache quoted.

"That Ruth?" asked Émile. "Ruth Zardo? The poet?" And then he finished the astonishing poem, the work now taught in schools across Québec.

"While we, who knew you well,
your friends, (the focus of your scorn)

could see your courage in the face of
  fear,
your wit, and thoughtfulness,
and will remember you
with something close to love."

The two men were quiet for a moment,
staring into the mumbling fire, lost in their
own thoughts of love and loss, of damage
done beyond repair.

"I thought she was dead," said Émile at
last, spreading pâté on the chewy bread.

Gamache laughed. "Gabri introduced her
to Reine-Marie as something they found
when they dug up the basement."

Émile reached for the letter again. "Who's
this Gabri? A friend?"

Gamache hesitated. "Yes. He lives in that
little village I told you about. Three Pines."

"You've been there a few times, I remember. Investigating some murders. I tried to
find the village on a map once. Just south of
Montreal you said, by the border with Vermont?"

"That's right."

"Well," Émile continued. "I must have
been blind, because I couldn't see it."

Gamache nodded. "Somehow the mapmakers missed Three Pines."

"Then how do people find it?"

"I don't know. Perhaps it suddenly appears."

"I was blind but now I see?" quoted Émile. "Only visible to a wretch like you?"

Gamache laughed. "The best *café au lait* and croissants in Québec. I'm a happy wretch." He got up again and put a stack of letters on the coffee table. "I also wanted to show you these."

Émile read through them while Gamache sipped his wine and ate cheese and baguette, relaxing in the room as familiar and comfortable as his own.

"All from that Gabri man," said Émile at last, patting the small pile of letters beside him. "How often does he write?"

"Every day."

"Every day? Is he obsessed with you? A threat?" Émile leaned forward, his eyes suddenly keen, all humor gone.

"No, not at all. He's a friend."

"Why would Olivier move the body?" Émile read from one of the letters. *"It doesn't make sense. He didn't do it, you know.* He says the same thing in each letter." Émile picked up a few and scanned them. "What does he mean?"

"It was a case I investigated last autumn, over the Labor Day weekend. A body was found in Olivier's bistro in Three Pines. The victim had been hit once on the back of the head, killed."

"Once?"

His mentor had immediately picked up on the significance of that. A single, catastrophic blow. It was extremely rare. A person, if hit once, was almost certainly hit often, the murderer in a rage. He'd rain blow after blow on his victim. Almost never did they find just one blow, hard enough to kill. It meant someone was filled with enough rage to power a terrible blow, but enough control to stop there. It was a frightening combination.

"The victim had no identification, but we finally found a cabin hidden in the woods, where he lived and where he'd been murdered. Émile, you should have seen what was in there."

Émile Comeau had a vivid imagination, fed by decades of grisly discoveries. He waited for Gamache to describe the terrible cabin.

"It was filled with treasure."

"Treasure?"

"I know," smiled Gamache, seeing Émile's face. "We weren't expecting it either. It was unbelievable. Antiques and artifacts. Priceless."

He had his mentor's full attention. Émile

sat forward, his lean hands holding each other, relaxed and alert. Once a hunter of killers, always that, and he could smell blood. Everything Gamache knew about homicide he'd learned from this man. And more besides.

"Go on," said Comeau.

"There were signed first editions, ancient pottery, leaded glass thousands of years old. There was a panel from the Amber Room and dinnerware once belonging to Catherine the Great."

And a violin. In a breath Gamache was back in that cabin watching Agent Paul Morin. Gangly, awkward, young, picking up the priceless violin, tucking it under his chin and leaning into it. His body suddenly making sense, as though bred to play this instrument. And filling the rustic, log cabin with the most beautiful, haunting Celtic lament.

"Armand?"

"Sorry," Gamache came back to the stone home in Quebec City. "I was just remembering something."

His mentor examined him. "All right?"

Gamache gave a nod and smiled. "A tune."

"You found out who killed this recluse though?"

"We did. The evidence was overwhelming.

We found the murder weapon and other things from the cabin in the bistro."

"Olivier was the murderer?" Émile lifted the letters and Gamache nodded.

"It was hard for everyone to believe, hard for me to believe, but it was the truth."

Émile watched his companion. He knew Armand well. "You liked him, this Olivier?"

"He was a friend. Is a friend."

Gamache remembered again sitting in the cheery bistro, holding the evidence that damned his friend. The terrible realization that Olivier was indeed the murderer. He'd taken the man's treasure from his cabin. But more than that. He'd taken the man's life.

"You said the body was found in the bistro, but he was murdered in his own cabin? Is that what Gabri means? Why would Olivier move the body from the cabin to the bistro?"

Gamache didn't say anything for a long time, and Émile gave him that time, sipping his wine, thinking his own thoughts, staring into the soft flames and waiting.

Finally Gamache looked at Émile. "Gabri asks a good question."

"Are they partners?"

Gamache nodded.

"Well, he just doesn't want to believe Olivier did it. That's all."

"That's true, he doesn't. But the question is still good. If Olivier murdered the Hermit in a remote cabin, why move the body to a place it would be found?"

"And his own place at that."

"Well, no, that's where it gets complicated. He actually moved it to a nearby inn and spa. He admits to moving the body, to try to ruin the spa. He saw it as a threat."

"So you have your answer."

"But that's just it," said Gamache, turning so that his whole body faced Émile. "Olivier says he found the Hermit already dead and decided to use the body as a kind of weapon, to hurt the competition. But he says if he'd actually murdered the man he'd never have moved the body. He'd have left it there, or taken it into the woods to be eaten by coyotes. Why would a murderer kill someone then make sure the body was found?"

"But wait a second," said Émile, trying to piece it together. "You said the body was found in Olivier's own bistro. How did that happen?"

"A bit awkward for Olivier that," said Gamache. "The owner of the inn and spa had the same idea. When he found the body, he moved it to the bistro, to try to ruin Olivier."

55

"Nice neighborhood. Quite a Merchants' Association."

Gamache nodded. "It took a while but we eventually found the cabin and the contents and the evidence the Hermit had been killed there. All the forensics confirmed only two people had spent time in the cabin. The Hermit, and Olivier. And then we found items from the cabin hidden in Olivier's bistro, including the murder weapon. Olivier admitted to stealing them —"

"Foolish man."

"Greedy man."

"You arrested him?"

Gamache nodded, remembering that terrible day when he knew the truth and had to act on it. Seeing Olivier's face, but worse, seeing Gabri's.

And then the trial, the evidence, the testimony.

The conviction.

Gamache looked down at the pile of letters on the sofa. One every day since Olivier had been sentenced. All cordial, all with the same question.

Why would Olivier move the body?

"You keep calling this man 'the Hermit.' Who was he?"

"A Czech immigrant named Jakob, but that's all we know."

Émile stared at him, then nodded. It was unusual not to identify a murder victim but not unheard of, particularly one who so clearly didn't want to be identified.

The two men moved into the dining room with its wall of exposed stone, open plan kitchen and aroma of roasting lamb and vegetables. After dinner they bundled up, put Henri on a leash and headed into the bitterly cold night. Their feet crunching on the hard snow, they joined the crowds heading out the great stone archway through the wall, to Place d'Youville and the ceremony opening the Carnaval de Québec.

In the midst of the festivities, as fiddlers sawed away and kids skated and the fireworks lit the sky over the old city Émile turned to Gamache.

"Why did Olivier move the body, Armand?"

Gamache steeled himself against the thrashing explosions, the bursts of light, the people crowding all around, shoving and shrieking.

Across the abandoned factory he saw Jean-Guy Beauvoir fall, hit. He saw the gunmen above them, shooting, in a place that was supposed to be almost undefended.

He'd made a mistake. A terrible, terrible mistake.

THREE

The next morning, Saturday, Gamache took Henri and walked through gently falling snow up rue Ste-Ursule for breakfast at Le Petit Coin Latin. Waiting for his *omelette,* a bowl of *café au lait* in front of him, he read the weekend papers and watched the revelers head to the *creperies* along rue St-Jean. It was fun to be both a part of it and apart from it, warm and toasty in the bistro just off the beaten track with Henri at his side.

After reading *Le Soleil* and *Le Devoir* he folded the newspapers and once again took out his correspondence from Three Pines. Gamache could just imagine Gabri, large, voluble, quite magnificent sitting in the bistro he now ran, leaning on the long, polished wooden counter, writing. The fieldstone fireplaces at either end of the beamed room would be lit, roaring, filling the place with light and warmth and welcome.

And even in Gabri's private censure of the Chief Inspector there was always kindness, concern.

Gamache stroked the envelopes with one finger and almost felt the gentleness. But he felt something else, he felt the man's conviction.

Olivier didn't do it. Gabri repeated it over and over in each letter, as though with repetition it would be true.

Why would he move the body?

Gamache's finger stopped caressing the paper, and he stared out the window, then he picked up his cell phone and made a call.

After breakfast he climbed the steep, slippery street. Turning left, Gamache made his way to the Literary and Historical Society. Every now and then he stepped into a snow bank to let families glide by. Kids were wrapped and bound, mummified, preserved against a bitterly cold Québec winter and heading for Bonhomme's Ice Palace, or the ice slide, or the *cabane à sucre* with its warm maple syrup hardening to taffy on snow. The evenings of Carnaval were for university students, drunk and partying but the bright days were for children.

Once again Gamache marveled at the beauty of this old city with its narrow winding streets, the stone buildings, the metal roofs piled with snow and ice. It was like falling into an ancient European town. But Quebec City was more than an attractive anachronism, a pretty theme park. It was a living, vibrant haven, a gracious city that had changed hands many times, but kept its heart. The flurries were falling more heavily now, but without much wind. The city, always lovely, looked even more magical in the winter, with the snow, and the lights, the horse-drawn *calèches,* the people wrapped brightly against the cold.

At the top of the street he paused to catch his breath. A breath that was easier and easier to catch with each passing day as his health returned thanks to long, quiet walks with Reine-Marie, Émile, or Henri, or sometimes alone.

Though these days he was never alone. He longed for it, for blessed solitude.

Avec le temps, Émile had said. With time. And maybe he was right. His strength was coming back, why not his sanity?

Resuming his walk Gamache noticed activity ahead. Police cars. No doubt trouble with some hung-over university students, come to Québec to discover the official drink of the Winter Carnival, Caribou, a near lethal blend of port and alcohol. Gamache could never prove it, but he was pretty sure Caribou was the reason he'd started losing his hair in his twenties.

As he neared the Literary and Historical Society he noticed more Quebec City police cars and a cordon.

He stopped. Beside him Henri also stopped and sat alert, watching.

This side street was quieter, less traveled, than the main streets. He could see people streaming by twenty feet away, oblivious to the events happening right here.

Officers were standing at the foot of the steps up to the front door of the old library. Others were milling about. A telephone repair truck was parked at the curb and an ambulance had arrived. But there were no flashing lights, no urgency.

That meant one of two things. It had been a false alarm or it hadn't, but there was no longer any need to rush.

Gamache knew which it was. A few of the cops leaning against the ambulance laughed and poked each other. Across the street Gamache bristled at the hilarity, something he never allowed at crime scenes. There was a place for laughter in life but not in recent, violent, death. And this was a death, he knew that. It wasn't just instinct, it was all the clues. The number of police, the lack of urgency, the ambulance.

And this was violent death. The cordon told him that.

"Move along, *monsieur*," one of the officers, young and officious, came up to him. "No need to stare."

"I wanted to go in there," said Gamache. "Do you know what happened?"

The young officer turned his back and walked away but it didn't upset Gamache. Instead he watched the officers talk among themselves inside the cordon. While he and Henri stood outside.

A man walked down the stone steps, spoke a few words to one of the officers on guard then went to an unmarked car. Pausing there he looked round, then stooped to get into the car. But he didn't. Instead he stopped and slowly straightening he looked right at Gamache. He stared for ten seconds or more, which, when eating a chocolate cake isn't much, but when staring, is. Softly, he closed the car door and walking to the police tape he stepped over it. Seeing this, the young officer broke away from his companions and trotted over, falling into step with the plainclothes officer.

"I already told him to leave."

"Did you now."

"*Oui.* Do you want me to insist?"

"No. I want you to come with me."

Watched by the others, the two men crossed the snowy street and walked right up to Gamache. There was a pause, as the three men stared at each other.

Then the plainclothes officer stepped back and saluted. Astonished, the young cop beside him stared at the large man in the parka and scarf and toque, with the German shepherd dog. He looked more closely. At the trim, graying beard, the thoughtful brown eyes, and the scar.

Blanching, he stepped back and saluted as well.

"Chef," he said.

Chief Inspector Gamache saluted back and waved them to drop the formalities. These men weren't even members of his force. He was with the Sûreté du Québec and they were with the local Quebec City police. Indeed, he recognized the plainclothes officer from crime conferences they'd both attended.

"I didn't know you were visiting Québec, sir," said the senior officer, obviously perplexed. Why was the head of homicide for the Sûreté du Québec standing just outside a crime scene?

"It's Inspector Langlois, isn't it? I'm on leave, as you might know."

Both men gave curt nods. Everyone knew.

"I'm just here visiting a friend and doing some personal research in the library. What's happened?"

"A body was found this morning by a telephone repairman. In the basement."

"Homicide?"

"Definitely. An effort had been made to bury him, but when the repairman dug for a broken cable he found the body."

Gamache looked at the building. It had been the original courthouse and jail, hundreds of years before. Prisoners had been executed, hanged from the window above the front door. It was a place that knew violent death and the people who committed it, on either side of the law. Now there'd been another.

As he watched the door opened and a figure appeared on the top step. It was hard to tell with the distance and the winter clothing, but he thought he recognized her as one of the library volunteers. An older woman, she glanced in their direction and hesitated.

"The coroner's just arrived but it doesn't look as though the victim's been there long. Hours perhaps, but not days."

"He hasn't begun smelling yet," said the

young officer. "Those make me want to puke."

Gamache took a breath and exhaled, his breath freezing as soon as it hit the air. But he said nothing. This officer wasn't his to train in the etiquette of the recently dead, in the respect necessary when in their presence. In the empathy necessary to see the victim as a person, and the murderer as a person. It wasn't with cynicism and sarcasm, with dark humor and crass comments a killer was caught. He was caught by seeing and thinking and feeling. Crude comments didn't make the path clearer or the interpretation of evidence easier. Indeed, they obscured the truth, with fear.

But this wasn't the Chief Inspector's trainee, nor was it his case.

Shifting his eyes from the young man he noticed the elderly woman had disappeared. Since she hadn't had time to walk out of sight he presumed she'd gone back inside.

It was an odd thing to do. To get all dressed for the cold, then not to actually leave.

But, he reminded himself again, this wasn't his case, wasn't his business.

"Would you like to come in, sir?" Inspector Langlois asked.

Gamache smiled. "I was just reminding

myself this wasn't my case, Inspector. Thank you for your courtesy, but I'm fine out here."

Langlois shot a glance at the officer beside him then took Gamache's elbow and steered him out of hearing range.

"I wasn't asking just to be kind. My English isn't very good. It's OK, but you should hear the head librarian speak French. At least, I think she's speaking French. She clearly thinks she is. But I can't understand a word. In the entire interview she spoke French and I spoke English. It was like something out of a cartoon. She must think I'm a moron. So far all I've done is grinned and nodded and I think I might have asked whether she's descended from the lower orders."

"Why did you ask that?"

"I didn't mean to. I wanted to ask if she had access to the basement, but something went wrong," he smiled ruefully. "I think clarity might be important in a murder case."

"I think you might be right. What did she say to your question?"

"She got quite upset and said that the night is a strawberry."

"Oh dear."

Langlois sighed a puff of frustration. "Will

66

you come in? I know you speak English, I've heard you at conferences."

"But how do you know I wasn't mangling the language too? Maybe the night is a strawberry."

"We have other officers whose English is better than mine, and I was just about to call to the station to get them, but then I saw you. We could use your help."

Gamache hesitated. And felt a tremble in his hand, blessedly hidden by his thick mitts. "Thank you for the invitation." He met the Inspector's searching eyes. "But I can't."

There was silence. The Inspector, far from being upset, nodded. "I should not have asked. My apologies."

"Not at all. I'm most grateful you did. *Merci.*"

Unseen by either man, they were being watched from the second-floor window. The window put in a century ago to replace the door. That led to the platform. That led to execution.

Elizabeth MacWhirter, her scarf still on but her coat now in the closet downstairs, stared at the two men. Earlier she'd looked out the window, anxious to turn her back on the alien activity behind her. She sought solace, peace, in the unchanging view outside the window. From there she could see St. Andrew's Presbyterian Church, the presbytery, the sloping, familiar roofs of her city. And the snow drifting gently down to land on them, as though there wasn't a care in the world.

From that window she'd noticed the man and the dog, standing just outside the cordon, staring. He was, she knew, the same man who'd visited the library every day for a week now sitting quietly with his German shepherd. Reading, sometimes writing, sometimes consulting Winnie on volumes unread in a hundred years or more.

"He's researching the Battle of the Plains of Abraham," Winnie had reported one afternoon as they stood on the gallery above the library. "Particularly interested in the correspondence of both James Cook and Louis-Antoine de Bougainville."

"Why?" Porter had whispered.

"How would I know?" said Winnie. "Those books are so old I don't think anyone's ever cataloged them. In fact, they were earmarked for the next sale, before it was canceled."

Porter had glanced at the large, quiet man on the leather sofa below.

Elizabeth was pretty sure Porter hadn't recognized him. She was certain Winnie hadn't. But she had.

And now, as she watched the local police inspector shake hands and walk away she again examined the large man with the dog and remembered the last time she'd seen him on a street.

She'd been watching the CBC along with the rest of the province, indeed the rest of the country. It was even, she'd learned later, broadcast on CNN around the world.

She'd seen him then. In uniform, without the beard, his face bruised, his Sûreté du Québec officer's hat not quite hiding the ugly scar. His dress coat warm but surely not warm enough to keep out the bitter day. He'd walked slowly, limping slightly, at the head of the long, long solemn column of men and women in uniform. A near endless cortege of officers from Québec, from Canada, from the States and England and France. And at the head, their commander. The man who'd led them, but didn't follow them all the way. Not into death. Not quite.

And that image that appeared on front pages of newspapers, on covers of magazines from *Paris Match* to *Maclean's* to *Newsweek* and *People.*

Of the Chief Inspector, his eyes momentarily closed, his face tipped slightly upward, a grimace, a moment of private agony made

69

public. It was almost too much to bear.

She'd told no one who the quiet man reading in their library was, but that was about to change. Putting her coat on again she walked carefully down the icy steps and along the street to catch him up. He was moving along rue Ste-Anne, the dog on a leash beside him.

"Pardon," she called. *"Excusez-moi."* He was some distance ahead, weaving in and out of the happy tourists and weekend revelers. He turned left onto rue Ste-Ursule. She picked up her pace. At the corner she saw him half a block ahead. *"Bonjour."* She raised her voice and waved but his back was to her, and if he heard he would very probably think she was calling to someone else.

He was nearing rue St-Louis and the throng heading to the Ice Palace. She'd almost certainly lose him among the thousands of people.

"Chief Inspector."

It wasn't said as loudly as all her other cries but it stopped the large man dead in his tracks. His back was to her, and she noticed some people giving him nasty looks as they suddenly had to swing around to avoid him on the narrow sidewalk.

He turned back. She was afraid he would look annoyed, but instead his face was mild, inquisitive. He quickly scanned the faces and came to rest on her standing stock-still half a block away. He smiled and together they closed the gap.

"Désolé," she said, reaching out to him. "I'm sorry to disturb you."

"Not at all."

There was an awkward silence. He didn't comment on the fact she knew who he was. That much was obvious and like her, he clearly felt no need to waste time with the obvious.

"I know you from the library, don't I?" he said. "What can I do for you?"

They were at the busy corner of St-Louis and Ste-Ursule. Families were trying to squeeze by. It didn't take much to clog the narrow artery.

She hesitated. Gamache looked round and motioned down the street, against the river of people.

"Would you like a coffee? I suspect you could use something."

She smiled for the first time that day, and sighed. *"Oui, s'il vous plaît."*

They fought their way a block down, finally stopping in front of the smallest building on the street. It was whitewashed, with a brilliant red metal roof and above it a sign. *Aux Anciens Canadienes.*

71

"It's a bit of a tourist trap but at this time of day it might be quiet," he said in English, opening the door. They found themselves in the not unusual situation in Québec where, to be polite, the French person was speaking English and, to be polite, the English spoke French. They stepped into the dark, intimate restaurant, the oldest in the province with its low ceiling and stone walls and original beams.

"Perhaps," Gamache suggested when they were seated and the waiter had taken their orders, "we should also choose a language."

Elizabeth laughed and nodded.

"How's English?" he asked. She hadn't been this close to him before. He was in his mid-fifties, she knew from the reports. He was solid, comfortably built, but it was his eyes that caught her. They were deep brown, and calm.

She hadn't expected that. She thought they'd be sharp, cold, analytical, eyes that had seen so many dreadful things their soft centers had hardened. But this man's eyes were thoughtful, kind.

The waiter brought her a cappuccino and him an espresso. The late breakfast crowd was thinning and they'd been placed in a quiet corner.

"You know, of course, what happened this

morning?" Elizabeth asked. The coffee was fragrant and delicious. She didn't often splurge on good coffees, and this was a treat.

"Inspector Langlois told me a body has been found in the basement of the Literary and Historical Society." Gamache watched her as he spoke. "It wasn't a natural death."

She was grateful he hadn't said murder. It was too shocking a word. She'd been testing it out in the safety of her own head, but wasn't yet ready to take it out in public.

"When we arrived this morning the phones didn't work, so Porter called Bell Canada for repairs."

"The repairman came quickly," said Gamache.

"We're known to them. It's an old building and in need of repairs. The phones are often out, either through some sort of short, or a mouse has eaten through the line. This surprised us, though, since we'd only just redone all the wiring."

"What time did you arrive?"

"Nine o'clock. Gives us an hour to sort books and do other work before the library opens. We unlock the door at ten every morning, as you know."

He smiled. "I do. It's a wonderful library."

"We're very proud of it."

"So you arrived at nine and called Bell

right away?"

"He came within twenty minutes. Took him about half an hour to track down the problem. He figured it was a broken wire in the basement. We all thought it was just another mouse."

She paused.

"When did you realize it wasn't that?" Gamache asked, recognizing she now needed help telling her story.

"We heard him, actually. The repairman. His feet on the stairs. He's not a small man and it sounded like a stampede in our direction. He arrived at the office and just stared for a moment. Then he told us. There was a dead man in the basement. He'd dug him up. Poor man. It'll take him a while to recover, I suspect."

Gamache agreed. Some got over an experience like that quite quickly, others never did.

"You say he dug the man up. Your basement isn't concrete?"

"It's dirt. Used to be a root cellar centuries ago."

"I thought it was a prison. Were there cells there at one point?"

"No, the cells were in the level above, this was the lowest. Hundreds of years old, of course, used for keeping food cool. When the repairman said he'd found a body I thought he meant a skeleton. They're dug up in Quebec City all the time. Perhaps this was an executed prisoner. Winnie and I went to look. I didn't go all the way in, didn't have to. We could see from the doorway that it wasn't a skeleton. The man was recently dead."

"It must have been a shock."

"It was. I've seen bodies before, in a hospital or funeral home. Once a friend died in her sleep and I found her when I went by to take her to bridge. But that's different."

Gamache nodded. He understood. There were places dead people should be, and places they shouldn't. Half buried under a library was where they should not be.

"What did the Inspector tell you?" Elizabeth asked. There was no use being coy with this man, she realized. Might as well come right out with it.

"I'm afraid I didn't ask much, but he confirmed it was a violent death."

She looked down at her now empty cup, drunk without even noticing. This rare treat wasted, just a rim of foam left. She was tempted to stick her finger in and scoop it up, but resisted.

The bill had arrived and was sitting on the table. It was time to leave. The Chief

Inspector slid it toward him, but made no other move. Instead he continued to watch her. Waiting.

"I came after you to ask a favor."

"Oui, madame?"

"We need your help. You know the library. I think you like it." He inclined his head. "You certainly know English, and not just the language. I'm afraid of what this might do to us. We're a small community and the Literary and Historical Society is precious to us."

"I understand. But you're in good hands with Inspector Langlois. He'll treat you with respect."

She watched him then plunged ahead. "Can you just come and take a look, maybe ask some questions? You have no idea what a disaster this is. For the victim, of course, but also for us." She hurried on before he could refuse. "I know what an imposition this is. I really do."

Gamache knew she was sincere but doubted she did know. He looked down at his hands, loose fists on the table. He was silent, and into that silence, as always, crept the young voice. More familiar now than those of his own children.

"And then at Christmas, we visit both Suzanne's family and my own. We go to hers for *réveillon* and mine for Mass on Christmas morning." The voice went on and on about trivial, minute, mundane events. The things that made up an average life. A voice that was no longer tinny in his ears, but living now in his brain, his mind. Always there, talking. Ad infinitum.

"I'm sorry, *madame,* I can't help you."

He watched the older woman across the table. Mid-seventies, he guessed. Slim, with beautiful bone structure. She wore little makeup, just some around the eyes, and lipstick. If less was more, she had a great deal. She was the image of cultured restraint. Her suit wasn't the latest fashion, but it was classic and would never be out of style.

She'd introduced herself as Elizabeth MacWhirter and even Gamache, not a native of Quebec City, knew that name. The MacWhirter Shipyards. MacWhirter paper mills in the north of the province.

"Please. We need your help."

He could tell this plea had cost her, because she knew what a position it put him in. And still, she'd done it. He hadn't quite appreciated how desperate she must be. Her keen blue eyes never left his.

"Désolé," he said, softly but firmly. "It gives me no pleasure to say that. And if I

could help, I would. But . . ." He didn't finish. He didn't even know what would come after the "but."

She smiled. "I'm so sorry, Chief Inspector. I should never have asked. Forgive me. I'm afraid my own needs blinded me. I'm sure you're right and Inspector Langlois will be just fine."

"I understand that the night is a strawberry," said Gamache, smiling slightly.

"Oh, you heard about that, did you?" Elizabeth smiled. "Poor Winnie. No ear for languages. Reads French perfectly, you know. Always the highest marks in school, but can't seem to speak it. Her accent would stop a train."

"Inspector Langlois might have thrown her off by asking about her birth."

"That didn't help," Elizabeth admitted. Her mirth disappeared, to be replaced by worry once again.

"You have no need for concern," he reassured her.

"But you don't know everything, I think. You don't know who the dead man is."

She'd lowered her voice and was whispering now. She sounded as Reine-Marie did when reading their infant granddaughters a fairy tale. It was the voice she used not for the fairy godmother, but the wicked witch.

"Who is it?" he asked, lowering his own voice.

"Augustin Renaud," she whispered.

Gamache sat back and stared. Augustin Renaud. Dead. Murdered in the Literary and Historical Society. Now he knew why Elizabeth MacWhirter was so desperate.

And he knew she had reason to be.

FOUR

Gabri sat in the worn armchair by the roaring fire. Around him in the bistro he now ran he heard the familiar hubbub of the lunch crowd. People laughing, chatting. At some tables people were quietly reading the Saturday paper or a book, some had come in for breakfast and stayed through lunch, and might very well be there for dinner.

It was a lazy Saturday in February, the dead of winter, and the bistro was mumbling along with conversation and the clinking of silverware on china. His friends Peter and Clara Morrow were with him, as was Myrna, who ran the new and used bookstore next door. Ruth had promised to join them, which generally meant she wouldn't be there.

Through the window he could see the village of Three Pines covered in snow, and more falling. It wouldn't be a blizzard, not enough driving wind for that, but he'd be surprised if they got less than a foot by the time it was finished. That was the thing with a Québec winter, he knew. It might look gentle, beautiful even, but it could take you by surprise.

The roofs of the homes surrounding the village were white and smoke curled from the chimneys. Snow was lying thick on the evergreens and on the three magnificent pines clustered together at the far end of the village green like guardians. The cars parked outside homes had become white lumps, like ancient burial mounds.

"I tell you, I'm going to do it," Myrna was saying, sipping her hot chocolate.

"No you're not," laughed Clara. "Every winter you say you will and you never do. Besides, it's too late now."

"Have you seen the last-minute deals? Look." Myrna handed her friend the Travel section from the weekend Montreal *Gazette,* pointing to a box.

Clara read, raising her brows. "Actually, it's not bad. Cuba?"

Myrna nodded. "I could be there in time for dinner tonight. Four star resort. All inclusive."

"Let me see that," said Gabri, leaning toward Clara. Somehow Clara had managed to get a bit of jam on the newspaper, though

81

there was no jam around. It was, they all knew, Clara's particular miracle. She seemed to produce condiments and great works of art. Interestingly, they never found dabs of jam or croissant flakes on her portraits.

Gabri scanned the page then leaned back in his seat. "Nope, not interested. *Condé Nast* has better ads."

"*Condé Nast* has near naked men smothered in olive oil lying on beaches," said Myrna.

"Now that I would pay for," said Gabri. "All inclusive."

Every Saturday they had the same conversation. Comparing travel deals to beaches, choosing Caribbean cruises, debating the Bahamas versus Barbados, San Miguel de Allende versus Cabo San Lucas. Exotic locales far from the falling snow, the endless snow. Deep and crisp and even.

And yet, they never went, no matter how tempting the deals. And Gabri knew why. Myrna, Clara, Peter knew why. And it wasn't Ruth's theory.

"You're all too fucking lazy to move."

Well, not entirely.

Gabri sipped his *café au lait* and looked into the leaping flames, listening to the familiar babble of familiar voices. He looked across the bistro with its original beams, wide plank floor, mullioned windows, its mismatched, comfortable antique furniture. And the quiet, gentle village beyond.

No place could ever be warmer than Three Pines.

Out the window he saw a car descend rue du Moulin, past the new inn and spa on the hill, past St. Thomas's Anglican Church, around the village green. Its progress was slow, and left tire marks in the fresh, fallen snow. As he watched it drew up beside Jane Neal's old brick home. And stopped.

It was an unfamiliar vehicle. If Gabri had been a mutt he'd have barked. Not a warning, not out of fear, but excitement.

Wasn't often Three Pines had visitors unless it was people stumbling across the tiny village in the valley by accident, having gone too far astray. Become confused. Lost.

That was how Gabri and his partner Olivier had found Three Pines. Not intending to. They had other, grander, plans for their lives but once they'd laid eyes on the village, with its fieldstone cottages, and clapboard homes, and United Empire Loyalist houses, its perennial beds of roses and delphiniums and sweet peas, its bakery, and general store, well, they'd never left. Instead of taking New York, or Boston or even

Toronto by storm they'd settled into this backwater. And never wanted to leave.

Olivier had set up the bistro, furnishing it with finds from the neighborhood, all for sale. Then they'd bought the former stagecoach inn across the way and made it a bed and breakfast. That had been Gabri's baby.

But now, with Olivier gone, Gabri also ran the bistro. Keeping it open for his friends. And for Olivier.

As Gabri watched a man got out of the car. He was too far away to recognize, and dressed against the snow with a heavy parka, toque, scarves. Indeed, it could have been a woman, could have been anyone. But Gabri rose and his heart leapt ahead of him.

"What is it?" Peter asked. His long legs uncrossing and his tall, slim body leaning forward on the sofa. His handsome face was curious, happy for relief from the vacation conversation. Peter, while an artist himself, wasn't great at the "what if" conversations. He took them too literally and found himself stressed when Clara pointed out that for only fifteen thousand dollars they could upgrade to a Princess Suite on the *Queen Mary 2.* It was his cardio exercise for the day. Having had it, he now focused on Gabri, who was focused on the stranger walking very slowly through the snow.

84

"Nothing," said Gabri. He would never admit what he was now thinking, what he thought every time the phone rang, every time there was a knock on the door or an unfamiliar car arrived.

Gabri looked down at the coffee table, with their drinks and a plate of chocolate chip cookies and the thick Diane de Poitiers writing paper with its partly finished message. The same one he wrote every day and mailed, along with a licorice pipe.

Why would Olivier move the body? he'd written. Then added, *Olivier didn't do it.* He would mail it that afternoon, and tomorrow he'd write another one to Chief Inspector Gamache.

But now a man was walking, almost creeping, toward the bistro out of the thickly falling snow. In just the twenty yards from his car snow had already gathered on his hat, his scarf, his slender shoulders. Olivier had slender shoulders.

The snowman arrived at the bistro and opened the door. The outside world blew in and people looked over, then went back to their meals, their conversations, their lives. Slowly the man unveiled himself. His scarf, his boots, then he shook his coat, the snow falling to the wooden floor and melting. He put on a pair of slippers, kept in a basket by

85

the door for people to grab.

Gabri's heart thudded. Behind him Myrna and Clara were continuing to discuss whether, for a few thousand more, it might be worth upgrading all the way, to the Queen Suites.

He knew it couldn't be Olivier. Not really. But, well, maybe Gamache had been convinced by all the letters, maybe he'd let him out. Maybe it had been last-minute, like the travel deals, a last-minute escape that instead of taking him away had brought Olivier home.

Gabri stepped forward, unable to help himself now.

"Gabri?" Peter asked, standing up.

Gabri got halfway across the bistro.

The man had taken off his hat and turned into the room. Slowly, as recognition dawned, the conversation died out.

It wasn't Olivier. It was one of the men who'd taken him away, arrested Olivier, put him in prison for murder.

Inspector Jean-Guy Beauvoir surveyed the room and smiled, uncertainly.

When the phone call had come that morning from the Chief Inspector, Beauvoir had been in his basement making a bookcase. He didn't read but his wife Enid did, and

so he was making it for her. She was upstairs, singing. Not loudly and not well. He
could hear her cleaning up the breakfast
dishes.

"You okay down there?" she'd called.

He wanted to tell her he wasn't. He was
bored stupid. He hated woodwork, hated
the damned crossword puzzles she shoved
on him. Hated the books she'd piled up next
to the sofa, hated the pillows and blankets
that followed him around, in her arms as
though he was an invalid. Hated how much
he owed her. Hated how much she loved
him.

"I'm fine," he called up.

"If you need anything, just call."

"I will."

He walked over to the workbench, pausing for breath at the counter. He'd done his
exercises for the day, his physio. He hadn't
been very disciplined until the doctor had
pointed out that the more he did them the
sooner he could get out from under Enid's
crushing concern.

The doctor didn't exactly put it that way,
but that's what Beauvoir heard and it had
been motivation enough. Morning, noon
and night he did his exercises to regain his
strength. Not too much. He could tell when
he did too much. But sometimes he felt it

was worth it. He'd rather die trying to escape than be trapped much longer.

"Cookie?" she sang down.

"Yes, Cupcake?" he replied. It was their little joke. He heard her laugh and wondered how much it would hurt to cut his hand off with the jigsaw. But not his gun hand, he might need that later.

"No, do you want a cookie? I thought I'd do a batch."

"Sounds great. *Merci.*"

Beauvoir had never particularly wanted children, but now he was desperate for them. Maybe then Enid would transfer her love to them. The kids would save him. He felt momentarily bad for them, being dragged under by her unconditional, undying, unrelenting love, but, well, *sauve qui peut.*

Then the phone rang.

And his heart stopped. He'd thought, hoped, with time it would stop doing that. It was inconvenient having a heart that halted every time there was a call. Especially annoying when it was a wrong number. But instead of going away it seemed to be getting worse. He heard Enid hurrying to answer it and he knew she was running because she knew how much the sound upset him.

And he hated himself, for hating her.

"Oui, allô?" he heard her say and immediately Beauvoir was back there, to that day.

"Homicide." The Chief's secretary had answered the phone in the office. It was a large, open space taking an entire floor of the Sûreté du Québec headquarters in Montreal. There were, however, a few enclosed spaces. There was a private conference room with Beauvoir's beloved Magic Markers, and long sheets of paper on the walls, and blackboards and corkboards. All neatly organized.

He had his own office, being the second in command.

And the Chief had a large office in the corner, with windows looking out over Montreal. From there Armand Gamache ran the province-wide operation, looking into murders in a territory that stretched from the Ontario border to the Atlantic Ocean, from the frontier with Vermont and New York to the Arctic Circle. They had hundreds of agents and investigators in stations across the province and special teams that went into areas without a homicide squad.

All coordinated by Chief Inspector Gamache.

Beauvoir had been in Gamache's office discussing a singularly gnarly case in Gaspé when the phone had rung. Gamache's secretary had answered it. Inspector Beauvoir glanced at the clock on the Chief's wall just as the phone rang. 11:18 A.M.

"Homicide," he'd heard her say.

And nothing had been the same since.

A small tapping on the door brought Elizabeth MacWhirter out of her reverie. She'd been staring down at the list of members, putting off the time she'd have to phone them. But she knew that time had already come and gone. She should have made the calls an hour ago. Already messages were coming in from members of the English community, including CBC Radio and the weekly English newspaper, the *Chronicle-Telegraph.* She, Winnie and Porter had tried to be coy, but had only succeeded in sounding secretive.

Reporters were on their way.

And still Elizabeth put off phoning, clinging, she knew to the last moments of anything that resembled normalcy. Of their quiet, uneventful lives, volunteering to be custodians of a dusty and all but irrelevant past, but a past precious to them.

The knocking sounded again. No louder,

but not going away either. Were the reporters here already? But they, she suspected, would pound at the door as would the police. This tapping was a request, not a demand.

"I'll get it," said Winnie, walking across the large room and up the two steps to the door. At their desks in front of the large Palladian windows Elizabeth and Porter watched. Winnie was speaking with someone they couldn't see, nor could they hear her conversation but she seemed to be trying to explain something. Then she seemed to be trying to close the door. Then she stopped, and opening it wide she turned into the room.

"Chief Inspector Gamache wants to speak to you," she said to Elizabeth, almost in a daze.

"Who?" asked Porter, popping up at his desk, taking charge, now that the elderly woman had answered the door.

Winnie swung the door wide and there stood Armand Gamache. He looked at the people, but took in his surroundings. The office had a cathedral ceiling, huge arched windows and was sunken a few steps from the door. It was paneled in wood, with wood floors and bookcases and looked like an old-fashioned, miniature, gymnasium where the activity was intellectual not physical.

"I'm sorry to disturb you," he said, coming further into the room. His coat was off and he was wearing a camel hair cardigan, a shirt and tie, and deep blue corduroy slacks. Henri, his German shepherd, was at his side.

Porter stared. Winnie backed down the stairway. Elizabeth got up from her desk and walked over.

"You came," she said, smiling, her hand out. He took it in his large hand and held it.

"What do you mean?" asked Porter. "I don't understand."

"I asked if he could come and watch over the investigation for us. This is Chief Inspector Gamache," Elizabeth waited for recognition. "Of the Sûreté du Québec."

"I know who it is," lied Porter. "Knew all along."

"Chief Inspector Gamache, let me introduce the head of our Board of Directors," said Elizabeth. "Porter Wilson."

The two men shook hands.

"We don't need help, you know. We're fine on our own," said Porter.

"I know, I just wanted to make sure. You've been so kind allowing me to use your library, I thought I'd offer some of my own expertise in return."

"This isn't even your jurisdiction," Porter grumbled, turning his back on the Chief Inspector. "The separatists are going to have a field day. How do we know you're not one of them?"

Elizabeth MacWhirter could have died. "For God's sake, Porter, he's here to help. I invited him."

"We'll talk about that later."

"Not all separatists wish you harm, *monsieur*," said Gamache, his voice friendly but firm. "But you're right, this isn't my jurisdiction. I'm impressed you know that." Elizabeth watched with some amusement as Porter began to melt. "You clearly follow politics." Porter nodded and relaxed further. Much more, thought Elizabeth, and he'd curl up in Gamache's lap.

"The Sûreté has no jurisdiction in cities," Gamache continued. "The death of Monsieur Renaud is a case for the local Quebec City homicide force. I happen to know Inspector Langlois and he was kind enough to also ask me to join them. After some thought," he looked over at Elizabeth, "I decided I would just have a look." He turned back to Porter. "With your permission of course, sir."

Porter Wilson all but swooned. Winnie and

Elizabeth exchanged glances. If they'd only realized it was so easy. But then Porter's face clouded again as the reality sunk in.

This might not be an improvement. They'd gone from no police to now two forces occupying their building.

Not to mention the body.

"I wonder if I could leave Henri with you while I go into the basement?"

"Absolutely," said Winnie, taking the leash. Gamache also gave her some biscuits for Henri, patted him, told him to be a gentleman, then left.

"I don't like this," he heard Porter say just as the door closed. He suspected he was meant to hear it. But, then, he didn't much like it either.

A uniformed officer was waiting for him in the corridor and together they made their way through the warren of hallways and staircases. Gamache had to admit he was completely lost, and suspected the officer was too. Boxes full of books and papers lined the linoleum floors, elaborate stairways led to grotty washrooms and deserted offices. They came to two huge wooden doors and opening them they walked into a spectacular double-height ballroom that led into an equally spectacular twin. Both empty except for a few ladders and the ubiquitous boxes of books. He opened one of them. More leather-bound volumes. He knew if he picked one up he would be well and truly lost, so he ignored it and instead followed the increasingly frustrated officer down another corridor.

"Never seen anything like it," said the officer. "All this beautiful space, gone to waste. Doesn't seem right. What're they doing with this great building? Shouldn't it be used for something worthwhile?"

"Like what?"

"I don't know. But there must be something someone could use it for."

"Someone is using it."

"Les Anglais."

Gamache stopped. *"Excusez-moi?"*

"Les têtes carré," the young officer explained.

The square heads.

"You will treat these people with respect," said Gamache. "They're no more *tête carré* than you and I are frogs." His voice was hard, sharp. The officer stiffened.

"I meant no harm."

"Is that really true?" Gamache stared at the young officer, who stared back. Finally Gamache smiled a little. "You won't solve this crime by insulting these people, or mocking them. Don't be blinded."

"Yes sir."

They walked on, down endless hallways, past some magnificent rooms and past some dreary rooms, all empty. As though the Literary and Historical Society was in full retreat, regrouping into that one splendid library where General Wolfe watched over them.

"Over here, sir. I think I've found it."

They went down some steps and found a uniformed officer standing bored guard over a trap door. On seeing the Chief Inspector he stood straighter. Gamache nodded and watched his young guide leap down the metal ladder.

Gamache hadn't been prepared for this.

At the bottom the officer stared up, waiting, his face going from eager to questioning. What could be keeping this man? Then he remembered. He walked a few rungs up the ladder and extended his hand.

"It's all right, sir," he said quietly. "I won't let you fall."

Gamache looked at the hand. "I believe you." He carefully descended and took the strong young hand in his.

Jean-Guy Beauvoir sat by the fire, a beer and a steak sandwich in front of him. Peter and Clara had joined him and Myrna and

Gabri sat on the sofa facing the fireplace.

It was Beauvoir's first time back in Three Pines since they'd arrested Olivier Brulé for the murder of the Hermit, Jakob. He looked into the huge, open fire and remembered loosening the bricks at the back and sticking his arm all the way in, right up to his shoulder and rummaging around. Afraid of what he might feel, or what might feel him. Was there a rat's nest back there? Mice? Spiders? Maybe snakes.

As much as he declared himself to be rationality itself, the truth was, he had an active and untamed imagination. His hand brushed something soft and rough. He'd stiffened and stopped. His heart pounding and his imagination in overdrive, he forced his hand back. It closed around the thing, and he'd brought it out.

Around him the Sûreté team had clustered, watching. Chief Inspector Gamache, Agent Isabelle Lacoste and the trainee, Agent Paul Morin.

Slowly he dragged the thing out from its hiding place behind the fire. It was a small, coarse burlap sack, tied with twine. He'd placed it on the very table where his beer and sandwich now sat. And he'd gone in again, finding something else hidden back there. A simple, elegant, beautiful candelabra. A menorah, actually. Centuries old, perhaps thousands of years, the experts later said.

But the experts had told them something else, something more precise.

This ancient menorah that had brought light to so many homes, so many solemn ceremonies, that had been worshiped, hidden, prayed around, treasured, had also been used to kill.

The Hermit's blood and hair and tissue were found on it as were his fingerprints. As were the fingerprints of only one other.

Olivier.

And inside the sack? A carving the Hermit had done. His finest work. An exquisite study of a young man, sitting, listening. It was simple and powerful, and telling. It told of aching loneliness, of desire, of need. It was clearly a carving of Olivier, listening. And that carving told them something else.

Jakob's sculptures had been worth hundreds of thousands, finally millions of dollars. He'd given them to Olivier in exchange for food and company and Olivier had sold them. Making millions for himself.

But that hadn't been enough, Olivier had wanted more. He wanted the one thing the Hermit had refused to give him. The thing in the sack.

Jakob's last treasure, his most precious possession.

And Olivier wanted it.

In a fit of rage and greed he'd taken the Hermit's life, then he'd taken the beautiful and priceless murder weapon and the sack, and hidden them.

Behind the fireplace Beauvoir now stared at.

And once found, the sack with its carving started to speak. It had only one thing to say and it said it eloquently, over and over. Olivier had killed its creator.

Between finding the carving and the murder weapon hidden in the bistro, as well as all the other evidence, there was no question what had to happen next. The Chief Inspector had arrested Olivier Brulé for murder. He'd been found guilty of manslaughter and sentenced to ten years. Painfully, Three Pines had come to accept this terrible truth.

Except Gabri, who every day wrote the Chief Inspector to ask that question. *Why would Olivier move the body?*

"How's the Chief Inspector?" Myrna asked, leaning her considerable body forward. She was large and black. A retired psychologist, now the owner of the bookstore.

"He's all right. We speak every day."

He wouldn't tell them the full truth, of course. That Chief Inspector Gamache was far from "all right." As was he.

"We've been in touch a few times," said Clara.

In her late forties Clara Morrow was on the cusp, everyone knew, of making it huge in the art world. She had a solo show coming up in a few months at the Musée d'art Contemporain, or MAC, in Montreal. Her unruly dark hair was growing lighter with gray and she always looked as though she'd just emerged from a wind tunnel.

Her husband, Peter, was another matter. Where she was short and getting a little dumpy, he was tall and slender. Every gray hair in place, his clothing simple and immaculate.

"We spoke to him a few times," said Peter. "And I know you're in touch." He turned to Gabri.

"If you can call stalking him, 'in touch.' " Gabri laughed and gestured to the half-finished letter on the table then looked at Beauvoir. "Did Gamache send you? Are you reopening Olivier's case?"

Beauvoir shook his head. "I'm afraid not. I've just come for a vacation. To relax."

He'd looked them square in the face, and lied.

"Do you mind, Jean-Guy?" Chief Inspector Gamache had asked that morning. "I'd do it myself, but I don't think that would be much use. If a mistake was made it was mine. You might be able to see where it is."

"We all investigated the case, not just you, sir. We all agreed with the findings. There was no doubt. What makes you think now there was a mistake?" Beauvoir had asked. He'd been in the basement with the dreaded phone. And if he hated the phone, Beauvoir thought, how must the Chief feel about them?

He didn't think they'd made a mistake. In fact, he knew the case against Olivier to be complete, thorough and without fault.

"Why did he move the body?" Gamache had said.

It was, Beauvoir had to admit, a good question. The only slight chink in a perfect case. "So, what do you want me to do?"

"I want you to go to Three Pines and ask some more questions."

"Like what? We asked all the questions, got all the answers. Olivier murdered the Hermit. *Point final.* End of discussion. The jury agreed. Besides, the murder happened five months ago, how'm I supposed to find new evidence now?"

"I don't think you do," the Chief had said. "I think if a mistake was made it was in interpretation."

Beauvoir had paused. He knew he'd go to Three Pines, would do as the Chief asked. He always would. If the Chief asked him to conduct the interviews naked, he would. But of course he would never ask that, which was why he trusted the Chief. With his life.

For a moment, unbidden, he felt again the shove, the pressure, and then the horror as his legs had collapsed and he knew what had happened. He'd crumpled to the filthy floor of the abandoned factory. And he'd heard, from far off, the familiar voice, shouting.

"Jean-Guy!" So rarely raised, but raised then.

The Chief was speaking to him again, but now his voice was calm, thoughtful, trying to work out the best strategy. "You'll be there as a private citizen, not a homicide investigator. Not trying to prove him guilty. Maybe the thing to do is look at it from the other direction."

"What do you mean?"

"Go to Three Pines and try to prove Olivier didn't murder the Hermit Jakob."

So there Jean-Guy Beauvoir sat, trying to pretend he liked these people.

But he didn't.

Jean-Guy Beauvoir didn't like many people and these ones in Three Pines had given him little reason to change. They were cunning, deceitful, arrogant, and nearly incomprehensible, especially the Anglos. They were dangerous, because they hid their thoughts, hid their feelings, behind a smiling face. Who could tell what was really going on in their heads? They said one thing and thought another. Who knew what rancid thing lived, curled up, in that space between words and thoughts?

Yes. These people might look kind and concerned. But they were dangerous.

The sooner this was over, thought Beauvoir smiling at them over the rim of his beer, the better.

FIVE

Once at the bottom of the ladder Gamache looked round. Industrial lamps had been brought down and he could see light flooding from one of the chambers. Like anyone else he was drawn to it, but resisted and instead looked into the gloom, allowing his eyes to adjust.

After a moment he saw what men and women stretching back hundreds of years had seen. A low, vaulted, stone basement, a *sous-sol* in French. No sun had ever reached here, only darkness, interrupted over the centuries by candlelight, by whale oil lamps, by gaslight and now, finally, by blinding, brilliant electric lights. Brighter than the sun, brought down so they could see the darkest of deeds.

The taking of a life.

And not just any life, but Augustin Renaud.

Porter Wilson, for all his paranoia was

right, thought Gamache. The people who wanted Québec to separate from Canada will have a field day. Anything that cast suspicion on the English population was fodder for the separatist cause. Or at least, the more radical factions. The vast majority of separatists, Gamache knew, were thoughtful, reasonable, decent people. But a few were quite crazy.

Gamache and his young guide were in an antechamber. The ceilings were low, though perhaps not for the people who'd built it. Poor diet and grinding conditions had made them many inches shorter. But still, Gamache suspected, most would have ducked, as he did now. The floors were dirt, and it was cool but not cold down there. They were well below the frost line, beneath the sun but also beneath the frozen earth. Into a sort of dim purgatory, a place never hot, nor cold.

The Chief Inspector touched the rough stone wall, wondering how many men and women, long dead, had touched it too as they'd come down to get root vegetables from the cellars. To keep starving prisoners alive long enough to kill them.

Off the antechamber there was a room. The room with the light.

"After you," he gestured to the officer, and

105

followed him.

Inside his eyes had to adjust again though this didn't take so long. Large industrial lamps were positioned to bounce off the vaulted stone ceiling and walls but most were beamed into one corner of the room. And in that corner a handful of men and women worked. Some taking photographs, some collecting samples, some huddled over something Gamache couldn't quite see but could imagine.

A body.

Inspector Langlois stood and brushing dirt from his knees he approached. "I'm glad you changed your mind."

They shook hands.

"I needed to think about it. Madame MacWhirter also asked me to come, to act as a sort of honest-broker between them and you."

Langlois smiled. "She thinks they need one?"

"Well, it's more or less what you asked, wasn't it?"

The Inspector nodded. "It's true. And I'm grateful you're here, but I wonder if we might keep this on an informal basis. Perhaps we could consider you a consultant?" Langlois looked behind him. "Would you like to see?"

"S'il vous plaît."

It was a scene familiar to the Chief Inspector. A homicide team in the early stages of collecting evidence that would one day convict a man of murder, or a woman. The coroner was still there, just rising, a young doctor sent over from Hôtel-Dieu hospital where the Chief Coroner of Québec kept an office. This man wasn't the Chief. Gamache knew him, but he was a doctor and judging by his composure he was experienced.

"He was hit from behind with that shovel there." The doctor pointed to a partly buried tool beside the body. He was speaking to Inspector Langlois but shooting glances at Gamache. "Fairly straightforward. He was hit a few times. I've taken samples and need to get him onto my table, but there doesn't seem to be any other trauma."

"How long?" Langlois asked.

"Twelve hours, give or take an hour or so. We're lucky with the environment. It's consistent. No rain or snow, no fluctuation in temperature. I'll tell you more precisely later." He turned, collected his kit then nodded to Langlois and Gamache. But instead of leaving the coroner hesitated, looking round the cellar.

He seemed reluctant to leave. When Langlois peered at him the young doctor lost some of his composure but rallied.

"Would you like me to stay?"

"Why?" asked Langlois, his voice uninviting.

But still the doctor persevered. "You know."

Now Inspector Langlois turned to him completely, challenging him to go further.

"Tell me."

"Well," the doctor stumbled. "In case you find anything else."

Beside him Gamache felt the Inspector tense, but Gamache leaned in and whispered, "Perhaps he should stay."

Langlois nodded once, his face hard, and the coroner stepped away from the pool of light, across the sharp border into darkness. And there he waited.

In case.

Everyone in that room knew "in case" of what.

Chief Inspector Gamache approached the body. The harsh light left nothing to the imagination. It bounced off the man's dirty clothing, off his stringy, long, white hair, off his face, twisted. Off his hands, clasped closed, over dirt. Off the horrible wounds on his head.

Gamache knelt.

Yes, he was unmistakable. The extravagant black moustache, at odds with the white hair. The long, bushy eyebrows political cartoonists were so fond of caricaturing. The bulbous nose and fierce, almost mad, blue eyes. Intense even in death.

"Augustin Renaud," said Langlois. "No doubt."

"And Samuel de Champlain?"

Gamache had said out loud what everyone in that room, everyone in that *sous-sol*, everyone in that building had been thinking. But none had voiced. This was the "in case."

"Any sign of him?"

"Not yet," said Langlois, unhappily.

For where Augustin Renaud was there was always someone else.

Samuel de Champlain. Dead for almost four hundred years, but clinging to Augustin Renaud.

Champlain, who in 1608 had founded Québec, was long dead and buried.

But where?

That was the great mystery that hounded the Québécois. Somehow, over the centuries, they'd lost the founder.

They knew where minor functionaries from the early 1600s were buried, lieutenants and captains in Champlain's brigade. They'd unearthed, and reburied, countless missionaries. The pioneers, the farmers, the nuns, the first *habitants* were all accounted for. With solemn graves and headstones, visited by school children, by priests on celebration days, by tourists and tour guides. Names like Hébert and Frontenac and Marie de l'Incarnation resonated with the Québécois, and stories were told of their selflessness, their bravery.

But one remained missing. One's remains were missing.

The father of Québec, the most revered, the most renowned, the most courageous. The first Québécois.

Samuel de Champlain.

And one man had spent his entire adult life trying to find him. Augustin Renaud had dug and tunneled and hacked away under much of old Quebec City, following any whimsical clue that surfaced.

And now here he was, beneath the Literary and Historical Society, that bastion of Anglo Quebéc. With a shovel.

Dead himself. Murdered.

Why was he here? There seemed only one answer to that.

"Should I tell the *premier ministre?*" Langlois asked Gamache.

"*Oui.* The *premier ministre,* the Minister for Public Security. The Chief Archeologist. The Voice of English-speaking Québec. The Saint-Jean-Baptiste Society. The Parti Québécois." Gamache looked at Langlois sternly. "Then you need to call a news conference and tell the population. Equally. At the same time."

Langlois was clearly amazed by the suggestion. "Don't you think it's better to downplay this? I mean, really, it's only Augustin Renaud, not the *premier ministre.* The man was a bit of a buffoon. No one took him seriously."

"But they took his search seriously."

Inspector Langlois stared at Gamache but said nothing.

"You'll do as you want, of course," said the Chief Inspector, sympathizing with the man. "But as your consultant that's my counsel. Tell all and tell it quickly before the militant elements start spreading rumors."

Gamache looked past the circle of intense light to the dark caverns beyond the main room.

Was Samuel de Champlain here right now? Armand Gamache, a student of Québec history, felt a *frisson,* an involuntary thrill.

111

And if he felt that, he thought, what will others feel?

Elizabeth MacWhirter was feeling ill. She turned her back to the window, a window and view that had always given her pleasure, until now. Out of it she still saw the metal roofs, the chimneys, the solid fieldstone buildings, the snow falling thicker now, but she also saw the television trucks and cars with radio station logos stenciled to the sides. She saw men and women she recognized from television, and photos in *Le Soleil* and *La Presse.* Journalists. And not the gutter press. Not just *Allô Police,* though they were there too. But respected news anchors.

They stood in front of the building, artificial lights on them, cameras pointed, they lined up like some game of Red Rover, and told their stories to the province. Elizabeth wondered what they were saying.

But it couldn't be good, just degrees of bad.

She'd called the members of the library to give them what little information was available. It didn't take long.

Augustin Renaud was found murdered in the basement. Pass it on.

She glanced out the window again at the quickly gathering reporters and snow, a storm of each, a blizzard, and moaned.

"What is it?" asked Winnie, joining her friend by the window. "Oh."

Together they watched Porter descend the stairs, approach the swarming reporters and give what amounted to a news conference.

"Jesus," sighed Winnie. "Do you think I can reach him with this?" She hefted the first volume of the *Shorter Dictionary.*

"You going to throw the book at him?" smiled Elizabeth.

"Shame no one donated a crossbow to the library."

Inspector Langlois sat at the head of the polished table in the library of the Literary and Historical Society. It was a room at once intimate and grand. It smelled of the past, of a time before computers, before information was "Googled" and "blogged." Before laptops and BlackBerries and all the other tools that mistook information for knowledge. It was an old library, filled with old books and dusty old thoughts.

It was calm and comforting.

It had been a long while since Inspector Langlois had been in a library. Not since his school days. A time filled with new experiences and the aromas that would be forever associated with them. Gym socks.

Rotting bananas in lockers. Sweat. Old Spice cologne. Herbal Essence shampoo on the hair of girls he kissed, and more. A scent so sweet, so filled with longing his reaction was still physical whenever he smelt it.

And libraries. Quiet. Calm. A harbor from the turmoil of teenage life. When the Herbal Essence girls had pulled away, and mocked, when the gym sock boys had shoved and he'd shoved back, laughing. Rough-housing. Keeping the terror behind savage eyes.

He remembered how it felt to find himself in the library, away from possible attack but surrounded by things far more dangerous than what roamed the school corridors.

For here thoughts were housed.

Young Langlois had sat down and gathered that power to him. The power that came from having information, knowledge, thoughts, and a calm place to collect them.

Inspector Langlois, of the Quebec City homicide squad, looked round the double-height library with its carved wood and old volumes and wondered at the people he was about to interview. People who had access to all these books, all this calm, all this power.

English people.

To his right sat his assistant, taking notes. On his left sat a man he'd only seen at a distance before today. Heard lecture. Seen on television. At trials, at public hearings, on talk shows. And at the funerals, six weeks ago. Close up, Chief Inspector Gamache looked different. Langlois had only ever seen him in a suit, with his trim moustache. Now the man was not only wearing a cardigan, and corduroys, but also a beard. Shot with gray. And a scar above his left temple.

"Alors," Langlois started. "Before the first one comes in I want to go over what we know so far."

"The victim," his assistant read from his notebook, "is identified as Augustin Renaud. Seventy-two years of age. His next of kin has been notified, an ex-wife. No children. She'll formally identify him later, but there's no doubt. His driver's license and health card both identify him. Also in his wallet was forty-five dollars and there was a further three dollars and twenty-two cents change in his pockets. When the body was removed we found another twenty-eight cents beneath him, fallen from his pocket we think. They're modern coins. All Canadian."

"Good," said Langlois. "Go on."

Beside him Chief Inspector Gamache listened, one hand holding the other on the table.

"We found a satchel underneath the body. Inside was a map of Québec, hand-drawn by him."

It was on the table in front of them. The map showed areas of the city he'd excavated for Champlain, and the dates, going back decades.

"Any ideas?" Langlois asked Gamache as all three men examined the paper.

"I find this significant." The Chief's finger hovered over a blank spot on the map. A map that only acknowledged buildings and streets significant to Renaud's search. Places Samuel de Champlain might have been buried. It showed the Basilica, it showed the Café Buade, it showed assorted restaurants and homes unfortunate enough to be targeted by Renaud.

It was as though the rest of the magnificent old city didn't exist for Augustin Renaud.

And where Gamache's finger pointed was the Literary and Historical Society. Missing. Not plotted. Not in existence in Renaud's Champlain-centric world.

Langlois nodded. "I'd seen that too. Maybe he just didn't have time to put it in."

"It's possible," said Gamache.

"What're you thinking?"

"I'm thinking it would be a mistake to be

blinded by Renaud's passion. This murder may have nothing to do with Champlain."

"Then why was he digging?" the young assistant asked.

"Good question," smiled Gamache, ruefully. "It would seem a clue."

"Right." Langlois gathered up the map and returned it to the satchel. As he watched Gamache wondered why Renaud had needed the large leather bag to carry just that one slim piece of paper.

"Nothing else was in there?" Gamache nodded to the satchel in Langlois's hand. "Just the map?"

"That's all. Why?"

"He could have carried the map in his pocket. Why the satchel?"

"Habit," said the assistant. "He probably carried it everywhere in case he found something."

Gamache nodded. It was probably right.

"The coroner says Renaud was killed by the shovel sometime around eleven last night," said Langlois. "He fell face forward into the dirt and an attempt was made to bury him."

"Not deeply," said the assistant. "Not well. Do you think he was meant to be found?"

"I wonder how often that cellar is used," mused Langlois. "We'll have to ask. Send in the first person, the head of the board. A," the Inspector consulted his notes, "Porter Wilson."

Porter entered. He tried not to show it, but he was deeply shocked to see this library, his library, occupied by the police force.

He had no rancor toward the French. It was impossible to live in Quebec City and feel like that. It would be a torturous life and an unnecessary torment. No, Porter knew the Francophones to be gracious and inclusive, thoughtful and stable. Most of them. There were radicals on either side.

And that was his problem. Tom Hancock, the minister, kept telling him so. He saw it as "sides," no matter how many years went by, no matter how many French friends he had. No matter his daughter had married a Francophone and his grandchildren went to French schools and he himself spoke perfect French.

He still saw it as "sides," with himself on the out-side. Because he was English. Still, he knew himself to be as much a Québécois as anyone else in that elegant room. Indeed, his family had been there for hundreds of years. He'd lived in Québec longer than that young officer, or the man at the head of the table, or Chief Inspector Gamache.

He'd been born there, lived a full life there, would be buried there. And yet, for all their friendliness, he would never be considered a Québécois, would never totally belong.

Except here. In the Literary and Historical Society, in the very center of the old city. Here he was at home, in an English world created by English words, surrounded by the busts of great Anglos before him.

But today, on his watch, the French force had moved in and were occupying the Lit and His.

"Please," said Inspector Langlois, swiftly standing and indicating a seat. He spoke in his best, highly accented, English. "Join us."

As though Mr. Wilson had a choice. They were the hosts and he was the guest. With an effort he swallowed a retort, and sat, though not in the seat indicated.

"We have some questions," said Inspector Langlois, getting down to business.

Over the course of the next hour they interviewed everyone there. They learned from Porter Wilson that the library was locked every evening at six, and had been locked that morning when he'd arrived. Nothing was out of place. But Langlois's people had examined the large, old lock on the front door and while it showed no signs of tampering a clever six-year-old could have unlocked it without a key.

There was no alarm system.

"Why would we bother with an alarm?" Porter had asked. "No one comes when we're open, why would anyone come when we're closed?"

They learned this was the only place in old Quebec City English books could be found.

"And you seem to have a lot of them," said Gamache. "I couldn't help but notice as I walked through the back corridors and rooms that you have quite a few books not displayed."

That was an understatement, he thought, remembering the boxes of books piled everywhere.

"What's that supposed to mean?"

"Just an observation."

"It's true," said Porter, reluctantly. "And more coming every day. Every time someone dies they leave us their books. That's how we find out someone's dead. A box of worthless books appears. More accurate than the *Chronicle-Telegraph* obits."

"Are they always worthless?" asked Langlois.

"Well, we found a nice book of drawings once."

"When was that?"

"1926."

"Can you not sell some?" Gamache asked.

Porter stared at the Chief Inspector. Gamache stared back, not certain what had caused this sudden vitriolic look.

"Are you kidding?"

"Non, monsieur."

"Well, we can't. Tried once, members didn't like it."

"In 1926?" Langlois asked.

Wilson didn't answer.

Winnie Manning came in next and confirmed that the night was indeed a strawberry, but added that the English were good pumpkins and that the library had a particularly impressive section on mattresses and mattress warfare.

"In fact," she turned to Gamache. "I think that's an area you're interested in."

"It is," he admitted, to the surprise of both Langlois and his assistant. After Winnie left, saying she had to launch a new line of doorknobs, Gamache explained.

"She meant 'naval', not 'mattress'."

"Really?" asked the assistant, who'd made notes but had decided to burn them in case anyone thought he was stoned when he'd taken them down.

Mr. Blake took Winnie's place.

"Stuart Blake," the elderly man said, sitting in the chair offered and looking at them with polite interest. He was immaculately dressed, shaved, his face smooth and pink and soft. His eyes bright. He looked at Gamache and smiled.

"Monsieur l'inspecteur," he inclined his head. *"Désolé.* I had no idea who you were."

"You knew what mattered," said Gamache. "That I was a man in need of this magnificent library. That was enough to know."

Mr. Blake smiled, folded his hands, and waited. At ease.

"You spend a lot of time in the library, I believe," said Inspector Langlois.

"I do. For many years, since my retirement."

"And what was your profession?"

"I was a lawyer."

"So it's *Maître* Blake," said Langlois.

"No, please, I've been retired for years. Plain 'Mister' will do."

"How long have you been involved with the Literary and Historical Society?"

"Oh, all my life in one way or another, and my parents and grandparents before that. It was the first historical society in the country, you know. Pre-dates the national archives. Been around since 1824, though not in this building."

"This building," said Gamache, picking up on the opening. "It has an interesting history?"

"Very." Mr. Blake turned to face the Chief Inspector. "It didn't become the Literary and Historical Society until 1868. This was originally the Redoubt Royale, a military barracks. It also housed prisoners of war, mostly American. Then it became a regular prison. There were public hangings, you know."

Gamache said nothing, though he was interested that this refined, cultured, civilized man seemed to get pleasure telling them of such barbarity.

"Hung right out there." He waved toward the front door. "If you believe in ghosts, this is the place for you."

"Have you seen any?" Gamache asked, surprising both Langlois and the young officer.

Blake hesitated, then shook his head. "No. But I can feel them sometimes, when no one else is here."

"Are you often here, when no one else is?" Gamache asked, pleasantly.

"Sometimes. I find it peaceful. I think you do too."

"C'est la vérité," agreed the Chief Inspec-

tor. "But I don't have a key to get in after hours. You do. And, I presume, you use it."

Again, Mr. Blake hesitated. "I do. But not often. Only when I can't sleep and a question troubles me."

"Like what?" Gamache asked.

"Like what grasses grow on Rum Island, and when the last coelacanth was caught."

"And were you troubled by such questions last night?"

The two men looked at each other. Finally Mr. Blake smiled and shook his head.

"I was not. Slept like a child last night. As Shakespeare said, the best way to peace is to have a still and quiet conscience."

Or none at all, thought Gamache, watching Mr. Blake with interest.

"Can anyone confirm that?" Inspector Langlois asked.

"I'm a widower. Lost my wife eight years ago, so no, I have no witnesses."

"Désolé," said Langlois. "Tell me, Mr. Blake, why do you think Augustin Renaud was here last night?"

"Isn't it obvious? He must have thought Champlain is buried here."

And there it was. The obvious answer, out in the open.

"And is he?"

Blake smiled. "No, I'm afraid not."

"Why would he think Champlain was here?" Langlois asked.

"Why did Augustin Renaud think anything? Has anyone ever figured out his logic? Perhaps his digs were more alphabetical than archeological and he'd come to the 's'. That makes as much sense as any of his reasoning. Poor man," Blake added. "I imagine you'll be digging?"

"Right now it's still a crime scene."

"Incredible," said Mr. Blake, almost to himself. "Why would Augustin Renaud be here in the Lit and His?"

"And why would someone murder him?" said Langlois.

"Here," added Gamache.

Finally Elizabeth MacWhirter entered and sat.

"What is your job, exactly?" Langlois asked.

"Well, 'job' is a loose term. We're all volunteer. Used to be paid, but the government's cut back on library funding, so now any money we get goes in to upkeep. Heating alone is ruinous and we just had the wiring redone. In fact, if it hadn't been done we might never have found Mr. Renaud."

"What do you mean?" Langlois asked.

"When we rewired the place we decided to do the phone lines too. Bury them in the basement. If the line hadn't been cut we'd never have found the body, and he'd have been concreted over."

"*Pardon?*" asked Langlois.

"Next week. The concrete people are supposed to come on Monday to put down the forms."

The men looked at each other.

"You mean, if either Renaud or his murderer hadn't cut the telephone line while digging last night, the whole floor would have been concreted? Sealed?" asked the Inspector.

Elizabeth nodded.

"Who knew this was going to happen?" Langlois asked.

"Everyone." She walked over to a table and returned with three pamphlets which she handed out. There, on the front page, was the announcement.

The wiring, telephones and basement were to be redone.

Refolding the pamphlet and leaving it on the table in front of him Chief Inspector Gamache looked at the slim elderly woman.

"It says the work is to be done, but not the timing. The timing seems to me significant."

"You may be right, Chief Inspector, but we didn't keep the timing a secret. Many people knew. The board, the volunteers, the construction workers."

"Where'd you get the money for all this? It must have cost a fortune."

"It was expensive," she admitted. "We got grants and donations and sold some books."

"So the sale of books was fairly recent," said Langlois. "But we heard from Monsieur Wilson that it wasn't very successful."

"Now there's an understatement," said Elizabeth. "It was a disaster. We sold a few boxes, books that had been sitting for decades gathering dust. A shame. They should be in someone's collection, appreciated, not piling up here. And God knows, we need the money. It was a perfect solution. Turn unwanted books into wiring."

"So what went wrong?" asked Gamache.

"The community went wrong. They decided we were as much a museum as a library and every item ever donated was a treasure. The books became symbolic, I'm afraid."

"Symbolic of what?" Gamache asked.

"Of the value of the English language. Of the English culture. There was a fear that if even the Lit and His didn't value the English language, the written word, then there was no hope. They stopped being books and became symbols of the English community. They had to be preserved. Once that happened there was no fighting, no arguing. And certainly, no selling."

Gamache nodded. She was quite right. The battle was lost at that moment. Best to quit the field.

"And so you stopped the sale?"

"We did. Which is why you see boxes piled in the corridors. If one more elderly Anglo dies, the Literary and Historical Society will explode." She laughed, but without humor.

"Why do you think Augustin Renaud was here?" Langlois asked.

"For the same reason you do. He must have thought Champlain was here."

"Why would he think that?"

Elizabeth shrugged, making even that look refined. "Why did he think Champlain was buried under that Chinese restaurant? Or that primary school? Why did Augustin Renaud think anything?"

"Did he ever come here?"

"Well, he did last night."

"I mean, did you ever see him here before that?"

Elizabeth MacWhirter hesitated.

"Never inside, as far as I know. But I saw him at the front door. Yesterday morning."

The young assistant, so shocked something worthwhile had actually been said, almost forgot to write this down. But then his pen whirled into action.

"Go on," said Langlois.

"He asked to see the Board of Directors."

"When was this?"

"Around eleven thirty. We'd locked the door as we always do during a board meeting."

"He just showed up?"

"That's right."

"How'd he even know you were meeting?"

"We put the announcement in the paper."

"*Le Soleil?*"

"The Québec *Chronicle-Telegraph*."

"The what?"

"The *Chronicle-Telegraph*." Elizabeth spelled it for the assistant. "It's the oldest newspaper in North America," she said by rote.

"Go on. You say he showed up. What happened?" asked the Inspector.

"He rang the bell and Winnie answered it, then came up here with his request. She left him downstairs, outside."

"And what did you say?"

"We took a vote and decided not to see him. It was unanimous."

"Why not?"

Elizabeth thought about this. "We don't react well to anything different, I'm afraid.

Myself included. We've created a quiet, uneventful, but very happy life. One based on tradition. We know that every Tuesday there'll be a bridge club, they'll serve ginger snaps and orange pekoe tea. We know the cleaner comes on Thursdays, and we know where the paper towels are kept. In the same place my grandmother kept them, when she was secretary to the Lit and His. It's not an exciting life but it's deeply meaningful to us."

She stopped then appealed to Chief Inspector Gamache.

"Augustin Renaud's visit upset all that," he said.

She nodded.

"How'd he react when told you wouldn't see him?" Gamache asked.

"I went down to tell him. He wasn't pleased but he accepted it, said he'd be back. I didn't think he meant quite so soon."

She remembered standing at the thick wooden door, opened a sliver as though she was cloistered and Renaud a sinner. His white hair sticking out from under his fur hat, frost and icicles and angry breath dripping from his black moustache. His blue eyes not just mad, but livid.

"You cannot stop me, *madame,*" he'd said.

"I have no desire to stop you, Monsieur

Renaud," she'd said in a voice that she hoped sounded reasonable. Friendly even.

But they both knew she was lying. She wanted to stop him almost as badly as he wanted in.

When all the interviews had been completed Gamache returned to the office. There he found them sitting over a pot of tea.

"Welcome to our little lifeboat," said Elizabeth, getting to her feet and inviting him to join Winnie, Porter and herself. "And this is our fuel." She indicated the teapot and smiled.

Henri rushed over to greet him.

"I hope he wasn't too much trouble." Gamache patted Henri's flank and taking a seat he accepted a cup of strong tea.

"Never," said Winnie. "What happens next?"

"In the investigation? They'll get the coroner's report and start looking into Augustin Renaud's movements, friends, family. Who'd want him dead."

They sat together around the table. Not exactly a huddled mass, but reminiscent of it.

"You said Monsieur Renaud asked to speak to the board," Gamache turned to Elizabeth.

"You told them that?" Porter asked, his voice more clipped than usual. "Now you've done it."

"She had no choice," said Gamache. "You all should have told us. You must have known it was important." He looked at them sternly. "You refused to see him, but would you have listened to him eventually?"

He spoke now to Porter Wilson but noticed everyone looked at Elizabeth, who remained silent.

"Eventually, maybe. But there was no advantage for us, and a whole lot of —" Porter searched for a word. "Inconvenience."

"Monsieur Renaud could be very persuasive," said Gamache, remembering the vitriolic campaigns the amateur archeologist had waged against anyone who denied him permission to dig.

"True," admitted Porter. He seemed tired now, as the full import of what had happened weighed more and more heavily. As horrible as it would have been to have Augustin Renaud dig for Champlain beneath their Lit and His Society, the only thing worse was what had happened.

"May I see your minutes for the meeting?"

"I haven't done them up yet," said Elizabeth.

"Your notebook will do."

He waited. Eventually she handed him her notebook and putting on his half-moon reading glasses he scanned the minutes, noting who was there for the meeting.

"I see Tom Hancock and Ken Haslam were there, but left early. Were they there when Augustin Renaud showed up?"

"Yes," said Porter. "They left shortly after that. We were all there."

Gamache continued to scan the minutes then over his glasses he looked at Elizabeth.

"There's no mention of Monsieur Renaud's visit."

Elizabeth MacWhirter stared back. It seemed clear that when she'd asked for his help she hadn't expected him to ask them quite so many questions, and uncomfortable ones at that.

"I decided not to mention it. He didn't speak to us, after all. Nothing happened."

"A great deal happened, *madame*," said Gamache. But he'd also noticed that she'd said "I," not "we." Was she letting them off the hook? Taking the burden of responsibility herself? Or was it really a unilateral decision?

They might be in a lifeboat, but Gamache now had a clear idea who was captain.

Six

It was early afternoon and Jean-Guy Beauvoir realized he'd already made a mistake. Not a big one, more an annoyance.

He had to return to Montreal and interview Olivier Brulé. He should have done that first, before coming down to Three Pines. Instead, he'd spent the last hour quietly in the bistro. Everyone had left, but not before making sure he was in the best chair, the big, worn, leather armchair beside the fireplace. He dipped an orange biscotti into his *café au lait* and looking through the frosty window he could see the snow, falling gently but steadily. Billy Williams had been by once with the plow, but the snow had already filled in behind him.

Beauvoir dropped his gaze to the dossier in his hand and continued reading, snug and warm inside. Half an hour later he glanced at the mariner's clock on the mantelpiece. One twenty.

Time to go.

But not to Montreal. Not in this weather.

Returning to his room in the B and B, Beauvoir changed into his silk long underwear then layered his clothing strategically, putting on his snowsuit last. He rarely wore it, since he preferred being runway-ready and this suit made him look like the robot from *Lost in Space*. Indeed, in the winter, Québec looked like the staging area for an alien invasion.

Fortunately the chances of running into the editor of *Vogue Hommes* in the woods was pretty small.

He walked up the hill, hearing his thighs zinging together and barely able to put his arms flat to his sides. Now he felt a bit like a zombie, clump, clump, clumping up the hill to the inn and spa.

"Oui?"

Carole Gilbert answered the door and looked at the snow-covered zombie. But the older woman showed absolutely no fright, not even surprise. Gracious as ever she took two steps back and let the alien into the inn, run by her son and daughter-in-law.

"May I help you?"

Beauvoir unwrapped himself, now feeling like The Mummy. He was an entire B-grade film festival. Finally he removed his hat and

Carole Gilbert smiled warmly.

"It's Inspector Beauvoir, *non?*"

"Oui, madame, comment allez-vous?"

"I'm well, thank you. Have you come to stay? I didn't see your name on the register."

She looked behind her into the large, open entrance hall, with its black and white tile floor, gleaming wood desk and fresh flowers, even in the middle of winter. It was inviting and for a moment Beauvoir wished he had booked in. But then he remembered the prices, and remembered why he was there.

Not for massages and gourmet meals, but to find out whether Olivier had actually killed the Hermit.

Why did Olivier move the body?

And the very spot he was standing was where Olivier had dumped the Hermit. Olivier had admitted as much. He'd hauled the dead man through the woods that Labor Day weekend, in the middle of the night. Finding the door unlocked he simply dropped the sad bundle here. Right here.

Beauvoir looked down. He was melting, like the Wicked Witch of the West, his snow-covered boots puddling on the tile floor. But Carole Gilbert didn't seem to care. She was more concerned for his comfort.

"No, I'm staying at the B and B," he said.

"Of course." He searched her face for any sign of professional jealousy, but saw none. And why would he? It seemed inconceivable the owners of this magnificent inn and spa would be jealous of any establishment, especially Gabri's somewhat weary B and B.

"And what brings you back to us?" she asked, her voice light, conversational. "Is the Chief Inspector with you?"

"No, I'm on vacation. Leave, actually."

"Of course, I'm sorry." And she looked it, her face suddenly concerned. "How stupid of me. How are you?"

"I'm well. Better."

"And Monsieur Gamache?"

"Better also." He was, it must be admitted, a little tired of answering these kind questions.

"I'm so glad to hear it." She motioned him into the inn but he held his ground. He was in a hurry and it was his temperament to show it. He consciously tried to slow himself down. He was supposed to be there for a vacation, after all.

"How can I help you?" she asked. "I don't suppose you've come for the hot mud treatment? The Tai Chi class perhaps?"

He noticed her bemused look. Laughing at him? He thought not. More likely poking gentle fun at herself and the services of the spa. Her son Marc and his wife Dominique had bought the run-down place a year or so ago and turned it into this magnificent inn and spa. And had invited his mother, Carole Gilbert, to move from Quebec City to Three Pines, to help them run it.

"I can see how you might think so, since I've worn my Tai Chi outfit." He opened his arms so she could see the full splendor of his ski suit. She laughed. "I've actually come to ask a favor. May I borrow one of your snowmobiles? I understand you have some for your guests."

"That's true, we do. I'll get Roar Parra to help you."

"*Merci.* I thought I'd go into the woods, to the cabin."

He watched her as he spoke, hoping for a reaction, and got one. The gracious woman became glacial. Interesting how a moment before she'd seemed calm, content, relaxed. And now, while hardly anything had physically changed she suddenly seemed to be made of ice. A chill radiated from her.

"Is that so? Why?"

"Just to see it again. Something to do."

She examined him closely, her eyes reptilian. Then the mask descended and she once again became the *gentille grande dame* of the manor house.

"In this weather?" She glanced outside to the falling snow.

"If snow kept me from doing things I'd get nothing done in winter," he said.

"That's true," she admitted. Reluctantly? he wondered. "I don't suppose you've heard, but my husband is living there now."

"Is that so?" He hadn't heard. But he did hear her say "husband," not "former husband." They'd been separated for years, until Vincent Gilbert had suddenly shown up, uninvited, at the inn and spa at almost exactly the same time the Hermit's body had appeared.

"Are you sure you wouldn't prefer a mud wrap?" she asked. "It's quite similar to an hour with Vincent, I find."

He laughed. "*Non, madame, merci.* Will he mind if I drop in?"

"Vincent? I'm afraid I've given up trying to figure out how his mind works." But she relented a little and smiled at the melting man. "I'm sure he'll be delighted for the company. But you'd better hurry, before it gets too late."

It was already two in the afternoon. It would be dark by four.

And when the winter sun set on a Québec forest, monsters crawled out of the shadows.

Not the B-grade movie monsters, not zombies or mummies or space aliens. But older, subtler wraiths. Invisible creatures that rode in on plunging temperatures. Death by freezing, death by exposure, death by going even a foot off the path, and getting lost. Death, ancient and patient, waited in Québec forests for the sun to set.

"Come with me."

Carole Gilbert, petite and refined, put on her bulbous coat and joined the alien army. They walked around the side of the inn and spa, through large soft flakes of snow. In the middle distance Inspector Beauvoir could see cross-country skiers striding across the field on well-marked paths. In a few minutes they'd be inside, sipping buttery rum toddies or hot chocolate by the fire, their cheeks rosy, their noses running, rubbing their feet to get the circulation back.

If they were staying at the inn they'd be healthy and wealthy and warm.

And he'd be heading deep into the forest, racing the setting sun, to a cabin where a murder had happened and an asshole now lived.

"Roar," Carole Gilbert called and the short, squat man in the shed straightened up. His hair and eyes were almost black and he was powerfully built.

"Madame Gilbert," he said, nodding to her. Not in an obsequious manner, but with respect. And Inspector Beauvoir realized this woman would naturally receive respect because she treated others with it. As she did now with this woodsman.

"You remember Inspector Beauvoir, I believe."

There was an awkward hesitation before Roar Parra put out his hand. Beauvoir wasn't surprised. He and the rest of the homicide team had made this man's life miserable. He, his wife Hanna and son Havoc had been the chief suspects in the murder of the Hermit.

The Inspector looked at their former suspect. A man familiar with the forest, a man who'd been cutting a trail, straight for the recluse's cabin. He was Czech. The dead man was Czech. His son Havoc worked for Olivier and could have followed him one night through the woods and found the cabin, and found the treasure.

The Hermit had amassed his treasures almost certainly by stealing them from people in the Eastern Bloc when the walls were crumbling. When communism was crumbling, when people were desperate to get out, to the West.

They'd entrusted their family treasures,

guarded and hidden for generations of communist rule, to the wrong man. To the Hermit, before he was a hermit, when he was a man with a plan. To steal from them. But he'd stolen more than antiquities and works of art. He'd stolen hope, he'd stolen trust.

Had he stolen from Roar and Hanna Parra? Had they found him?

Had they killed him?

Carole Gilbert had left and the two men were alone in the shed.

"Why're you heading back to the cabin?"

There was nothing subtle about this brick of a man.

"Just curious. You have a problem with that?"

They stared at each other.

"Are you here to cause trouble?"

"I'm here to relax. A nice trip through the woods, that's all. If you don't hurry it'll get too late."

Was that Parra's goal, Beauvoir wondered as he put the helmet over his toque and straddled the machine, revving the motors. Was he deliberately going slow in the hopes Beauvoir would get stuck in the woods, after nightfall?

No, he decided. Too refined. This was a man who whacked his enemies on the head.

As the Hermit had died.

With a wave Beauvoir was away, feeling the powerful machine vibrating beneath him. He'd been on dozens of Ski-Doos in the past decade, since joining homicide. He loved them. The noise, the power, the freedom. The bracing cold and snow on his face. His body, insulated by the suit, was toasty and warm, almost too warm. He could feel the perspiration.

Beauvoir gripped the handles and leaned into a corner, the heavy machine following him. But something was different.

Something was wrong.

Not with the machine, but with him. He felt a familiar ache in his abdomen.

Surely not. He was just sitting on the machine, it wasn't like he was doing any real work.

Deeper along the narrow path he went, into the woods. Without leaves the forest looked cold and bare. The shadows were sharp and long as was the pain now, in his stomach, in his side, shooting down into his groin.

Beauvoir breathed deeply but the pain grew worse.

Finally he had to stop.

Clutching his middle he slowly fell forward, his arm folding over the handles of the idling Ski-Doo. His head dropped and rested on his arm. He tried to concentrate on the vibration, on the calming, deep, predictable, civilized sound. But his world had collapsed to a single sensation.

Pain.

An agonizing, familiar pain. One he'd thought was gone forever, but it had found him again in the darkening woods in winter.

Closing his eyes he concentrated on his breath, hearing it, feeling it. Long, relaxed breath in. Long, relaxed breath out.

How big a mistake was this? An hour, perhaps slightly more, until the woods were in darkness. Would anyone sound an alarm? Would he be missed? Would Roar Parra simply go home? Would Carole Gilbert lock the door and toss another log on the fire?

Then he felt a hand on his face and jerked his head up. But the hand restrained him. Not violently, but certainly. Beauvoir's eyes flew open and he looked into very blue ones.

"Don't move, just lie still."

The man was old. His face worn, but his eyes sharp. His bare hand, which had started on Beauvoir's face now slipped quickly beneath the scarf and collar and turtleneck to Beauvoir's pulse.

"Shh," the man said. And Beauvoir shushed.

He knew who this man was. Vincent Gilbert. Dr. Gilbert.

The asshole.

But Gamache, and Myrna, Old Mundin and others claimed he was also a saint.

Beauvoir hadn't seen it. The man had seemed all asshole to him when they'd investigated the murder of the Hermit.

"Come with me." Gilbert reached across Beauvoir and turned the Ski-Doo off, then he put his long arms around Beauvoir and gradually helped him up. The two men walked, slowly, along the path, Beauvoir pausing for breath now and then. He threw up once. Gilbert took his own scarf and cleaned Beauvoir's face and waited. And waited. In the snow and cold, until Beauvoir could go on. Then carefully, wordlessly, they limped deeper into the woods, Beauvoir leaning heavily on the tall, elderly asshole.

His eyes closed, Beauvoir concentrated on putting one plodding foot in front of the other. He felt the pain radiating from his side but he also felt the kiss of the snowflakes on his face and tried to concentrate on that. Then the sensations changed. The snow stopped touching his face, and he heard his footsteps echo on wood.

They were at the log cabin. He almost

145

wept, with exhaustion and relief.

Opening his eyes as they entered he saw, a million miles across the single room, a large bed. It was covered with a warm duvet and soft pillows.

And all Beauvoir wanted to do was make it across the room, so much larger than he remembered, to the bed at the very far end.

"Almost there," whispered Dr. Gilbert.

Beauvoir stared at the bed, willing it to come to him, as he and Gilbert inched their way across the wooden floorboards. Until, finally, finally. There.

Dr. Gilbert sat him on the side and while Beauvoir sagged, his head lolling for the pillow, the doctor held him upright and undressed him.

Only then did he let Beauvoir slowly subside, until his weary head hit the pillow and the soft flannel sheets were pulled snug around him and finally, finally, the duvet.

And Beauvoir drifted off to sleep, smelling sweet maple smoke from the hearth, and homemade soup and feeling the warmth close in around him as out the window he saw the snow piling up and the darkness arriving.

Beauvoir awoke a few hours later, coming back to consciousness slowly. His side ached, as though he'd been kicked hard, but the nausea had passed. A hot water bottle had been placed in the bed and he found himself hugging it, curled around it.

Sleepily, lazily, he lay in the bed and slowly the room came into focus.

Vincent Gilbert was sitting in a large easy chair by the fireplace. He was reading a book, a glass of red wine on the table beside him, his slippered feet resting on a hassock.

The cabin seemed at once familiar but different.

The walls were still log, the windows and hearth unchanged. Rugs were scattered around the floorboards, but no longer the fine, hand-stitched Oriental rugs the Hermit had. These were rag rugs, also homemade, but much closer to home.

A few paintings hung on the walls, but not the masterpieces the Hermit had collected, and hidden here. Now they were modest examples of Québécois artists. Fine but not, perhaps, spectacular.

The glass Dr. Gilbert used looked like any other glass, not the cut leaded crystal they'd found here after the murder.

But the biggest change was where the Hermit had had silver and gold and fine bone china candelabras to provide light, Dr. Gilbert had a lamp. An electric lamp. And on the table next to Gilbert, Beauvoir noticed a phone.

Electricity had been brought deep into the forest to power this rustic little cabin.

Then Beauvoir remembered why he'd made the trek into the woods.

It was to see once again where the murder had been committed. He looked over to the door and noticed a rug there, right where the bloodstain had been. Might still be.

Death had come to this peaceful little cabin, but in what form? Olivier or someone else. And driven by what? As Chief Inspector Gamache impressed upon them, murder was never about a gun or a knife or a blow to the head, it was what powered that thrust.

What had taken the Hermit's life? Greed, as the Crown prosecution and Gamache contended? Or was it something else? Fear? Rage? Revenge? Jealousy?

The treasures discovered here had been remarkable, but not the most amazing part of the case. The cabin had produced something else, something far more disquieting.

A word, woven into a spider's web. Up in the corner of the cabin, where the shadows were the deepest.

Woo.

The word had also been found carved, not well, into a piece of bloodstained wood. It had tumbled from the dead man's hand and ended up under the bed as though cowering there. A little wooden word. Woo.

But what did it mean?

Had the Hermit made the word?

It didn't seem likely, since he was a master carver and the wooden Woo was rustic, child-like.

The prosecution had concluded Olivier had put Woo into the web and carved it in wood as part of his campaign to terrify the Hermit, keep him hiding in the cabin. And Olivier had admitted, finally, that had been his goal, to convince the mad old man that the outside world was dangerous. Filled with demons and Furies and terrible, terrible beings.

Chaos is coming, old son, the Hermit had whispered to Olivier the last night of his life. Olivier had done his job well. The Hermit was well and truly terrified.

But while admitting to everything else, Olivier denied two things.

Killing the Hermit.

And making the word, Woo.

The court hadn't believed him. Olivier had been found guilty and sentenced to prison. It was a case Chief Inspector Gamache had painstakingly, painfully, built against his friend. A case Inspector Jean-Guy Beauvoir had collaborated on and believed in.

And one the Chief now asked him to dismantle and put together again. Only this time seeing if the same evidence could exonerate Olivier and point to someone else.

Like the man in the cabin with him.

Gilbert looked up and smiled.

"Hello," he said, closing the book and getting up slowly. Beauvoir had to remember this tall, slender man, with the white hair and searching eyes was in his late seventies.

Gilbert sat on the side of the bed and smiled reassuringly. "May I?" he asked Beauvoir before touching him. Beauvoir nodded. "I've spoken to Carole and told her you'd be spending the night," Dr. Gilbert said, pulling down the duvet. "She said she'd call the B and B and let Gabri know. No need to worry."

"Merci."

Gilbert's warm, sure hands were pressing against Beauvoir's abdomen.

Beauvoir had been prodded countless times in the past two months, especially those first days. It seemed his new alarm clock. Every few hours he awoke, dazed from medication, to someone else shoving their cold hands against his stomach.

None felt like Gilbert. Beauvoir winced a few times, despite his pledge not to. The

150

pain took him by surprise. As soon as he showed signs of discomfort Gilbert's hands stopped, pausing to let Beauvoir catch his breath, then they moved on.

"You probably shouldn't have taken the Ski-Doo out," Gilbert smiled, replacing the bed sheets and duvet, "but I imagine you know that already. The bullet itself did some damage, but the longer-term effect is from a sort of shock wave the impact creates. Did your doctors explain that?"

Beauvoir shook his head.

"Perhaps they were too busy. The bullet went straight through your side. You probably lost quite a bit of blood."

Beauvoir nodded, trying to keep the images at bay.

"It didn't hit your internal organs," Dr. Gilbert continued. "But the waves from the impact bruised the tissue. That's what you'll feel if you push yourself too hard, like this afternoon. But you're healing well."

"Merci," said Beauvoir. It helped to understand.

And Beauvoir knew then the man was a saint. He'd been touched by any number of medical men and women. All healers, all well intentioned, some kind, some rough. All made it clear they wanted him to live, but none had made him feel that his life was precious, was worth saving, was worth something.

Vincent Gilbert did. His healing went beyond the flesh, beyond the blood. Beyond the bones.

Gilbert patted the covers and made to get up, but hesitated. He picked up a small bottle of pills on the bedside table. "I found these in your pocket."

Beauvoir reached out but Gilbert closed them in his hand and searched Beauvoir's face. There was a long pause. Finally Gilbert relented and opened his fist. "Be careful with these."

Beauvoir took the bottle and shook out a pill.

"Perhaps half," said Dr. Gilbert, reaching for it.

Beauvoir watched Dr. Gilbert skillfully snap a small OxyContin in two.

"I keep them just in case," Beauvoir said, swallowing the tiny half pill as Gilbert handed him clean pajamas.

"In case you do something foolish?" asked Gilbert with a smile. "You might need another bottle."

"Har har," said Beauvoir. But already he could feel the warmth spreading and the pain dulling and any sting there might have been in Gilbert's comment drifted away.

As he dressed, Beauvoir watched the doctor in the kitchen spooning soup into two bowls and cutting fresh baked bread.

"Les Canadiens are playing tonight, aren't they?" Gilbert returned with the food and made Beauvoir comfortable sitting up in bed. "Want to watch?"

"Please."

Within moments they were eating soup, baguette and watching Les Canadiens slaughter New York.

"Too salty," snapped Gilbert. "I told Carole not to put so much salt in the food."

"Tastes fine to me."

"Then you have no taste. Raised on poutine and burgers."

Beauvoir looked at Dr. Gilbert expecting to see a smile. Instead his handsome face was sour, angry. Entitled, petulant, petty.

The asshole was back. Or, more likely, had been there all along in deceptively easy company with the saint.

SEVEN

Armand Gamache rose quietly in the night, putting on his bedside lamp and dressing warmly. Henri watched all this with his tail swishing and the tennis ball in his mouth. They tiptoed down the narrow, winding wood stairs that seemed carved into the center of the old home. Émile had put him on the top floor, in what had been the master bedroom. It was a magnificent loft space with wood beams and dormer windows out each side of the roof. Émile had explained that he no longer felt comfortable on the steep, narrow stairs, worn by hundreds of years of feet, and did Armand mind?

Gamache didn't, except that it proved what he already knew. His mentor was slowing down.

Now he and Henri descended two floors to the living room where the woodstove still burned and radiated heat. There he put on a single light, slipped into his warmest coat, hat, scarf and mitts and went out, not forgetting to take the most crucial item. The Chuck-it for Henri. Henri was in love with the Chuck-it. As was Gamache.

They walked through the deserted streets of old Québec, up St-Stanislas, past the Literary and Historical Society where they paused. Twenty-four hours ago Augustin Renaud lay hidden in the basement. Murdered. Had the telephone cable not been severed while digging the shallow grave the basement would have been cemented over and Augustin Renaud would have joined the countless other corpses hidden in and around Québec. It wasn't all that long ago archeologists discovered skeletons actually inside the stone walls surrounding the city. The bodies of American soldiers captured after a raid in 1803. The authorities had quickly said the men were already dead when walled up, but privately Gamache wondered. After all, why put bodies into a wall unless it was a grotesque punishment, or to conceal a crime? Since Québec was built on bones and irony, the invading soldiers had become part of the city defenses.

Augustin Renaud had almost gone the way of the soldiers and become a permanent part of Québec, encased in concrete beneath the Literary and Historical Society, helping prop up the venerable Anglophone institution. Indeed, Renaud's life was a mother lode of irony. Like the time he'd dug for Champlain on live television only to break through into the basement of a Chinese restaurant. Since Champlain had spent much of his life trying to find China it seemed, well, ironic. Or the time Renaud had opened a sealed coffin, once again convinced it was Champlain, only to have the pressurized contents explode into the atmosphere in a plumb of missionary fervor. The Jesuit inside, turned to dust, was sent to the heavens, immortal. Though not the sort of immortality he'd prayed for or expected. The priest tumbled back to earth in raindrops, to join the food chain and end up in the breast milk of the native women he'd tried to wipe out.

Renaud himself had narrowly escaped a similar fate, coming within hours of forming the foundation of the Literary and Historical Society.

Armand Gamache had hoped that after the initial interviews his obligation to Elizabeth MacWhirter and the rest of the Lit and His would be over. But he now knew that wasn't true. Renaud had demanded to meet the board, the board had refused, then they'd purged the incident from the minutes. When word got out there'd be hell to pay. And it would be the Anglos who had to pay it.

No, Gamache thought as he and Henri trudged out the gates, he couldn't leave them. Not yet.

The snow had almost stopped and the temperature was dropping. There was no traffic, not a sound except Gamache's feet squeaking on the snow.

It was three twenty in the morning.

Every day Gamache woke at about that time. At first he'd tried to get back to sleep, had stayed in bed, had fought it. But now, after weeks and weeks, he'd decided this was it, for now. Instead of fighting, he and Henri would get up quietly and go for a walk, first around their Montreal neighborhood and now here in Quebec City.

Gamache knew that in order to get through the day he needed this quiet time with his thoughts at night.

He needed this quiet time with the voice in his head.

"My father taught me to play the fiddle," Agent Paul Morin said, in answer to Gamache's question. "I was about four. We have some home video of it somewhere. My father and grandfather playing the fiddle behind me, and me in front wearing these great big sagging shorts, they look like diapers." Morin laughed. "I had my little fiddle. My grandmother was on piano and my sister pretended to conduct. She was about three. She's married now, you know, and expecting."

Gamache turned left and walked through the darkened Carnaval site at the foot of the Plains of Abraham. A couple of guards watched but didn't approach. Too cold for confrontation. Gamache and Henri wound along the pedestrian walk, past attractions that would be filled with excited kids and freezing parents in just a few hours. Then the stalls and temporary buildings and rides trailed off and they were walking through thin forest toward the infamous open field and the monument erected where the English General Wolfe fell, and died, on September 13, 1759.

Gamache scooped up a handful of snow and crushed it into a ball. Henri immediately dropped the tennis ball and danced around. The Chief cocked his arm, smiling at Henri, who suddenly crouched. Muscles tense. Waiting.

Then Gamache threw the snowball and Henri raced after it, catching it in mid-air.

He was ecstatic for a moment then his jaws closed, the snow disintegrated and Henri landed, perplexed as always.

Gamache took the tennis ball encrusted with frozen saliva, put it in the Chuck-it and tossed. The brilliant yellow ball sailed into the darkness with the shepherd sailing after it.

The Chief Inspector knew every inch of the Champs-de-Bataille, in every season. He knew the changing face of the battlefield. Had stood there in spring and seen the daffodils, had stood there in summer and seen the picnickers, had stood there in winter and watched families cross-country ski and snowshoe, and he'd stood there in early autumn. On September 13. The exact day of the battle, when more than one thousand men had died or been wounded in an hour. He'd stood there and believed he heard the shouts, heard the shots, smelled the gunpowder, seen the men charging. He'd stood where he believed Général Montcalm had been when he realized the full nature of his mistake.

Montcalm had underestimated the English. Their courage and their cunning.

At what point did he know the battle was lost?

A runner had appeared in Montcalm's

camp, upriver from Québec, the night before. Exhausted, almost incoherent, he'd reported the English were scaling the 150-foot cliffs from the river and were on the field belonging to the farmer Abraham just outside the city.

Montcalm's camp hadn't believed him. Thought the man mad. No commander would issue such an order, no army would obey it. They'd have to have wings, Montcalm had laughingly told his generals and gone back to bed.

By dawn the English were on the Plains of Abraham, prepared for battle.

Was that when Montcalm knew all was lost? When the English, armed with wings, had done the impossible? The Général rushed there and had stood on the very spot Gamache now stood. From there he'd looked over the fields and seen the enemy.

Did Montcalm know then?

But still the battle needn't have been lost. He could have prevailed. But Montcalm, the brilliant strategist, had more mistakes to make.

And Gamache thought about that moment when he'd realized his own final and fatal mistake. The enormity of it. Though it had taken him a few moments to grasp as everything unraveled, fell apart. With such speed, and yet it seemed now, so slowly.

"Homicide," his secretary had said, answering the phone.

Beauvoir had been in his office when the call came through, discussing a case in Gaspé. She'd stuck her head in the door.

"It's Inspector Norman, in Ste-Agathe."

Gamache looked up. She rarely interrupted him. They'd worked together for years and she knew when to handle it herself, and when not to.

"Put him through," said the Chief. "*Oui,* Inspector. What can I do for you?"

And so the battle had begun.

Je me souviens, thought Gamache. The motto of Québec. The motto of the Québécois. I remember.

"I was at Carnaval once," Agent Morin said. "It was great. My dad took us and we even played fiddle at the skating rink. Mom tried to stop him. She was embarrassed, and my sister could have died, but Dad and I took out our fiddles and started playing and everyone seemed to really like it."

"That piece you played for us? 'Colm Quigley'?"

"No, that's a lament. It gets faster, but the beginning's too slow for skaters. They wanted something peppier, so we did some jigs and reels."

"How old were you?" Gamache asked.

"Thirteen, maybe fourteen. It was about ten years ago. Never went back."

"Maybe this year."

"*Oui*. I'll take Suzanne. She'd love it. Might even take the fiddle again."

Je me souviens, thought Gamache. That was the problem. Always the problem. I remember. Everything.

In the cabin in the woods Beauvoir lay awake. Normally he slept soundly, even after what happened. But now he found himself staring into the dark rafters, then at the glow of the fireplace. He could see Dr. Gilbert asleep on the two chairs he'd pulled together. The asshole saint had given Beauvoir the bed. Beauvoir felt horrible, having an elderly man who'd been so kind, sleep on a couple chairs. And he wondered, briefly, if that was the point. Why be a saint unless you could also be a martyr?

Perhaps it was the peaceful cabin, perhaps it was exhaustion after pushing himself too far, or the little half pill, but Beauvoir's defenses were down.

And over the wall swarmed the memories.

"Homicide," the Chief's secretary had said. Gamache had taken the call.

11:18 the clock had said. Beauvoir had

looked around the room, letting his mind wander, as the Chief spoke on the phone with the Ste-Agathe detachment.

"Agent Morin's on the phone." Gamache's secretary appeared again at the doorway a moment later. The Chief covered the mouthpiece and said, "Ask him to call back in a few minutes."

Gamache's voice was hard and Beauvoir immediately looked at him. He was taking notes as Inspector Norman spoke.

"When was this?" Gamache's sentences were clipped. Something had happened.

"He says he can't." The Chief's secretary hovered, uncomfortable, but insistent.

Gamache nodded to Beauvoir to take the Morin call, but Gamache's secretary stood her ground.

"He says he needs to speak to you, sir," she said. "Now."

Both Chief Inspector Gamache and Inspector Beauvoir stared at her, amazed she would contradict the boss. Then Gamache made up his mind.

"*Désolé,*" he said into the receiver to Inspector Norman. "I have to give you to Inspector Beauvoir. Wait, I have a question. Was your agent alone?"

Beauvoir saw Gamache's face change. He waved for Beauvoir to take the other phone in his office. Beauvoir picked up the receiver and saw the Chief take Agent Morin's call on the other line.

"*Oui,* Norman, what's happened?" Beauvoir remembered asking. For something had, something serious. The worst, in fact.

"One of our agents has been shot," Norman said, obviously on a cell phone. He sounded far away, though Beauvoir knew he was only about an hour north of Montreal, in the Laurentian Mountains. "He was checking out a car stopped on the side of a secondary road."

"Is he — ?"

"He's unconscious, on his way to the Ste-Agathe hospital. But reports I'm getting aren't hopeful. I'm on my way to the scene."

"We'll be right there, give me the location." Beauvoir knew not only was time crucial, but so was coordination. In a case like this every cop and every department was in danger of descending and then they'd have chaos.

Across the room he could see Gamache standing at his desk, the phone to his ear, his hand gesturing for calm. Not to anyone in the room, but to whoever he was speaking with, presumably Agent Morin.

"He wasn't alone," Norman was saying, the transmission cutting in and out as he raced through the mountains to the scene. "We're looking for the other agent."

It didn't take a homicide detective to know what that meant. One agent shot, the other missing? Lying dead or gravely wounded in some culvert. That's what Inspector Norman was thinking, that's what Beauvoir was thinking.

"Who's the other agent?"

"Morin. One of yours. He's on loan to us for the week. I'm sorry."

"Paul Morin?"

"Oui."

"He's still alive," said Beauvoir, and felt the relief. "He's on the phone with the Chief Inspector."

"Oh, thank God for that. Where is he?"

"I don't know."

Gamache took Morin's call, his mind racing in response to what he'd heard from Inspector Norman. An agent gravely wounded, another missing.

"Agent Morin? What is it?"

"Chief?" The voice sounded hollow, tentative. "I'm sorry. Did you find —"

"Is this Chief Inspector Gamache?" The phone had clearly changed hands.

"Who is this?" the Chief demanded. He gestured to his secretary to get a trace and make sure it was being recorded.

"I can't tell you." The voice sounded middle-aged, perhaps late middle-aged, with a thick country accent. A backwoods voice. Gamache had to strain to understand the words.

"I didn't mean to do it. I just got scared." And the man sounded scared, his voice rising to near hysterics.

"Easy, softly. Calm down. Tell me what this is about."

But in the pit of his stomach he knew what this was about.

An agent injured. An agent missing.

Paul Morin had been seconded to the Ste-Agathe detachment the day before, to fill in for a week. Morin was the missing agent.

At least he was alive.

"I didn't mean to shoot him, but he surprised me. Stopped behind my truck." The man seemed to be losing it. Gamache forced himself to speak slowly, reasonably.

"Is Agent Morin hurt?"

"No. I just didn't know what to do. So I took him."

"You need to let him go now. You need to turn yourself in."

"Are you nuts?" The last word was shrieked. "Turn myself in? You'll kill me. And if you didn't I'd spend the rest of my life in jail. No way."

Gamache's secretary appeared at the door, giving him the "stretch it out" sign.

"I understand. You want to get away, is that right?"

"Yes," the man sounded uncertain, surprised at Gamache's response. "Can I?"

"Well, let's just talk about it. Tell me what happened."

"I was parked. My truck had broken down. Blown tire. I'd just replaced it when the police car pulled up behind."

"Why would that be upsetting?" Gamache kept his voice conversational and he could hear the stress, the panic, on the other end subside a bit. He also stared at his secretary who was looking into the large outer room where there was sudden, frantic, activity.

Still no trace.

"Never you mind. It just was."

"I understand," said Gamache. And he did. There were two big crops in the backwoods of Québec. Maple syrup and marijuana. Chances were the truck wasn't loaded with syrup. "Go on."

"My gun was sitting on the seat and I just knew what would happen. He'd see the gun, arrest me and you'd find . . . what I had in the truck."

The man, thought Gamache, had just

shot, perhaps killed a Sûreté officer, kidnapped another, and yet his main concern still seemed to be concealing that he either had or worked for a marijuana plantation. But it was so instinctive, this need to hide, to be secretive. To lie. Hundreds of thousands of dollars could be at stake.

Liberty was at stake.

For a woodsman, the idea of years behind bars must seem like murder.

"What happened?"

Still no trace? It was inconceivable it should take this long.

"I didn't mean to," the man's voice rose again, almost to a squeal. He was pleading now. "It was a mistake. But then it happened and I saw there was another one, so I pointed my gun at him. By then I didn't know what to do. I couldn't just shoot him. Not in cold blood like that. But I couldn't let him go either. So I brought him here."

"You must let him go, you know," said the Chief Inspector. "Just untie him and leave him there. You can take your truck and go, disappear. Just don't hurt Paul Morin."

Vaguely, in the back of Gamache's mind, he wondered why the hostage-taker hadn't asked about the condition of the officer he'd shot. He'd seemed so upset, and yet never asked. Perhaps, thought the Chief, he didn't want to know. He seemed a man best suited to hiding from the truth.

There was a pause and Gamache thought maybe the man would do as he'd asked. If he could just get Agent Morin safely away they would find this man. Gamache had no doubt of that.

But Armand Gamache had already made his first mistake.

Beauvoir drifted back to sleep and in his sleep he replaced the receiver, got in the car with the Chief and raced up to Ste-Agathe. They found where Morin was being held and rescued him. Safe and sound. No one hurt, no one killed.

That was Beauvoir's dream. That was always his dream.

Armand Gamache picked up the ball and chucked it for Henri. He knew the dog would happily do this all day and all night, and it held its attractions for Gamache. A simple, repetitive activity.

His feet crunched on the pathway and his breath puffed in the crisp, dark air. He could just see Henri ahead and hear the slight wind knocking the bare branches together, like the fingers of skeletons. And he could hear the young voice talking, always talking.

Paul Morin told him about his first swimming lesson in the cold Rivière Yamaska and losing his trunks to some bullies. He heard about the summer the family went whale watching in Tadoussac and how much Morin loved fishing, about the death of Morin's grandmother, about the new apartment in Granby he and Suzanne had rented and the paint colors she'd chosen. He heard about the minutiae of the young agent's life.

And as Morin talked Gamache saw again what had happened. All the images he kept locked away during the day he let out at night. He had to. He'd tried to keep them in, behind the groaning door but they'd pounded and pressed, hammering away until he had no choice.

And so every night he and Henri and Agent Morin went for a walk. Henri chasing his ball, Gamache being chased. At the end of the hour Gamache, Henri, the Chuck-it and Agent Morin walked back along Grande Allée, the bars and restaurants closed. Even the drunk college students gone. All gone. All quiet.

And Gamache invited, asked, begged Agent Morin to be quiet too. Now. Please. But while he became a whisper, the young voice was never totally hushed.

EIGHT

Gamache awoke to the welcome smell of strong coffee. After showering he joined Émile for breakfast.

The elderly man poured Gamache a cup as they sat at the long wooden table. In the center was a plate of flaky croissants, honey and jams and some sliced fruit.

"Did you see this?" Émile put the morning copy of *Le Soleil* in front of Gamache. The Chief sipped and read the headline.

AUGUSTIN RENAUD MURDERED WHILE
DIGGING FOR CHAMPLAIN

He skimmed the story. He knew enough not to be dismissive of media reports. They often got hold of people and information the police themselves might not have found. But there was nothing new there. Mostly a recap of Renaud's startling hobby of looking for Champlain and the ancillary benefits of pissing people off. There were quotes from the Chief Archeologist of Québec, Serge Croix, speaking glowingly of Renaud's achievements which, everyone knew, amounted to putting holes in the old city and perhaps spoiling some legitimate digs. There was no respect lost between Croix and Renaud, though you'd never know it by the tribute in today's paper.

Except the reporter had been smart enough to also gather Croix's previous comments about Renaud. And not just Croix but a host of other Champlain experts, historians and archeologists. All dismissive of Renaud, all derisive, all mocking his amateur status, while he was alive.

Without a doubt, Augustin Renaud alive had become a bit of a buffoon. And yet, reading the papers, there emerged today another Augustin Renaud. Not just dead, but something else. There seemed an affection for him as for a beloved, but nutty, uncle. Renaud was misguided, perhaps, but passionate. A man who loved his home, loved his city, loved his country. Québec. Loved and lived history, to the exclusion of all else, including it seemed, his sanity.

He was a harmless eccentric, one of many in Québec, and the province was the poorer for having lost him.

That was the dead Augustin Renaud. Finally respected.

The paper, Gamache was relieved to see, had been careful to simply report on where the body was found. While they mentioned it was a respected Anglophone institution they left it at that. There was no suggestion of Anglo involvement, of conspiracy, of political or linguistic motivation behind the crime.

But Gamache suspected the tabloids would be less reticent.

"That's that library, isn't it? The place you've been working?" Émile broke open a croissant and the flakes tumbled to the table. Émile had had dinner with friends the night before so he and Gamache hadn't seen each other since the murder.

"The Lit and His, yes," said Gamache.

Émile looked at him with mock seriousness. "You can tell me Armand. You didn't —"

"Kill him? I could never kill a stranger. Now, a friend . . ."

Émile Comeau laughed then grew quiet. "Poor man."

"Poor man. I was there you know. Inspector Langlois was good enough to let me sit in on the initial questioning."

As they ate Gamache told Émile about his

day, his mentor peppering him with succinct questions.

Finally Émile Comeau leaned back in his chair, his breakfast finished but another appetite piqued. "So what do you think, Armand? Are the English hiding something? Why ask for your help if they aren't afraid?"

"You're quite right, they are afraid, but not of the truth. I think they're afraid of how this looks."

"With good reason," said Émile. "What was Renaud doing there?"

That was the big question, Gamache thought. Almost as big as who killed the man. Why was he at the Literary and Historical Society?

"Émile?" Gamache leaned forward, cupping his large hands round his mug. "You're a member of the Champlain Society. You know a lot more about this than I do. Could Renaud have had something? Could Champlain possibly be buried there?"

"Come for lunch at the St-Laurent Bar." Émile stood. "I'll have some people there who can better answer that."

Gamache left Henri at home, something he rarely did but the place he was going didn't welcome dogs, though privately he thought they should. Dogs, cats, hamsters, horses,

174

chipmunks. Birds.

And yet there were only people at St. Andrew's Presbyterian Church for Sunday service, and quite a few. The benches were filling quickly. He recognized some as reporters, the rest were probably more interested in gossip than God. Most of the day's congregants, he suspected, had never been inside this church, perhaps never even realized it was there. It had been discovered, along with the body.

English Quebec was on parade.

All the pews were built in a semi-circle facing the pulpit and Gamache found a seat on a curving bench near the side of the church. He sat quietly for a few minutes, marveling at his surroundings.

The church seemed filled with light. It streamed through the bright and cheerful stained glass windows. The thick walls were plastered and painted a cream color, but it was the ceiling he couldn't help staring at. It was painted a fresh robin's egg blue and rose above the sweeping, graceful semi-circular balcony.

Something else struck the Chief Inspector. There wasn't a crucifix in sight.

"Lovely, isn't it?"

Gamache turned and noticed Elizabeth MacWhirter had slipped in beside him.

"It is," he whispered. "Has the church been here long?"

"Two hundred and fifty years. We just celebrated the anniversary. Of course, Holy Trinity Anglican is the big church. Most of the English community goes there, but we struggle along."

"Is it affiliated with the Literary and Historical Society? It seems to be on the same grounds."

"Only informally. The minister sits on the board, but that's just coincidence. The Anglican archbishop used to be on the board but he moved a few years ago so we decided to ask the Presbyterian to join us."

"Do you always get this sort of turnout?" Gamache nodded to the people now needing to stand at the back.

Elizabeth shook her head and smiled. "Normally we could stretch out and sleep in the pews, and don't think a few of us haven't done it."

"It'll be a good collection today."

"Better be. The church needs a new roof. But I suspect this lot is only here to gawk. Did you see the article in *Le Journalist* this morning?"

The local rag, Gamache knew. He shook his head. "Only *Le Soleil.* Why? What did it say?"

"It didn't actually say anything, but it did suggest that the English had murdered Renaud to keep our dark secret."

"And that would be?"

"That Champlain is buried under the Lit and His, of course."

"And is he?"

It was his impression Elizabeth MacWhirter had been startled by his question. But the organ had begun and the congregation rose and she was spared the need to answer. He knew what she would say.

Of course he isn't.

He sang "Lord of All Hopefulness" from the hymnal and watched the congregants. Most seemed lost, not even trying to sing, some moved their mouths but he'd be surprised if any sound came out. And about a dozen, he guessed, raised their voices in song.

A young man climbed into the pulpit and the service began.

Gamache turned his attention to the minister. Thomas Hancock. He looked about twenty. His hair was dark blond, his face handsome though not classically so, more the handsome that went with robust health. Vitality. It was impossible, Gamache had noticed, to be both vital and unattractive. He looked a bit, Gamache thought, like Matt Damon. Intelligent and charming.

They prayed for Augustin Renaud.

Then Thomas Hancock did something Gamache would never have thought possible. While acknowledging that Renaud had been murdered only yards away he didn't dwell on it, or on the curiosity of God's Will.

Instead the Reverend Mr. Hancock, in his long blue cassock and his baby face, spoke of passion and purpose. Of Renaud's obvious delight in life. He connected it to God. As a great gift of God.

The rest of the sermon was about joy.

It was an extremely risky strategy, Gamache knew. The pews were filled with Francophones curious about this subculture unearthed in the very center of their city. English. Most Québécois probably never even knew they were there, never mind so firmly ensconced.

They were an oddity, and most of the people in the church had come to stare, and come to judge. Including a number of reporters, notebooks out, ready and eager to report on the official reaction of the English community. By concentrating on joy instead of tragedy, the church, the Anglos, might be perceived as uncaring, as trivializing the tragedy of a life stolen. A man murdered a stone's throw away.

And yet, instead of playing to the crowd, instead of offering a muted apology, of finding appropriately contrite biblical passages, this minister spoke of joy.

Armand Gamache didn't know how it would sound when written up in tomorrow's *Le Journalist,* but he couldn't help but admire the man for not pandering. Indeed, for offering another, a more positive, perspective. Gamache thought if his church spoke more about joy and less about sin and guilt, he might be tempted to return himself.

The service ended with a hymn and the collection followed by a silent prayer, in which Agent Morin told Gamache about his late grandmother, who smoked incessantly without ever removing the cigarette from her mouth.

"Her right eye was always winking because of the smoke," Morin explained. "And the cigarette just burned down. She never tapped off the ash. It hung there, this long tube of gray. We could watch her for hours. My sister thought she was disgusting but I kinda liked her. She drank too. She could eat and drink without once taking the cigarette out."

He sounded impressed.

"Once when she was preparing breakfast

the whole line of ash fell into the porridge. She just kept stirring. God knows how much ash and crap we ate."

"Did the smoking kill her?" Gamache asked.

"No. She choked on a brussels sprout."

There was a pause and despite himself, Gamache chuckled.

Elizabeth looked at him. "Thinking of joy?" she whispered.

"In a way, I suppose," said Gamache and felt his chest constrict so fiercely he almost gasped.

After the service the congregation was invited back to the church hall for coffee and cookies, but Gamache hung back. Having shaken everyone's hand the Reverend Hancock noticed the large man sitting in the pew and approached.

"Can I help you?"

His eyes were a soft blue. Close up Gamache noticed he was older than he appeared. Closer to thirty-five than twenty-five.

"I don't want to take you away from your congregation, Reverend, but I wondered if we might have a talk sometime today?"

"Why not now?" He sat down. "And please don't call me Reverend. Tom will do."

"I'm afraid I can't do that."

Hancock examined him. "Then you may call me Your Excellency."

Gamache stared at the earnest young man, then broke into a smile. "Perhaps I could call you Tom."

Hancock laughed. "Actually, in very formal circumstances I'm called The Reverend Mr. Hancock, but just plain Mr. Hancock would do, if that makes you feel better."

"It does. *Merci.*" Gamache extended his hand. "My name is Armand Gamache."

The minister's hand paused for a moment. "Chief Inspector," he said finally. "I thought it might be you. Elizabeth said you'd helped yesterday. I'm afraid I was practicing for the canoe race. We haven't a hope, but we're having fun."

Gamache could believe they didn't have a hope. He'd seen the famous canoe race across the St. Lawrence River every Carnaval for decades, and every year he wondered what could possess a person to do such a thing. It took huge athleticism and more than a little insanity. And while the young minister looked fit enough Gamache knew from his notes that his teammate, Ken Haslam was in his sixties. It would be, not to put too fine a point on it, like dragging an anvil across the river. Haslam on the team certainly handicapped them.

One day he might ask this man why he, or anyone, would enter such a race. But not today. Today belonged to a different subject.

"I'm glad I was able to help a little," said Gamache. "But I'm afraid it's far from over, despite your sermon today."

"Oh, my sermon wasn't meant to dismiss what happened, but to accept and celebrate the man's life. There are enough people out there," he waved toward the beautiful stained glass windows and the genteel city beyond, "who'll condemn us, I thought I might as well try to be uplifting. Do you not approve?"

"Would it matter?"

"It always matters. I'm not preaching at you, you know."

"As a matter of fact I thought your sermon was inspired. Beautiful."

The Reverend Mr. Hancock looked at Gamache. "*Merci.* It's a risk. I just hope I haven't done harm. We'll see."

"Are you a Quebecker by birth?"

"No, I was born in New Brunswick. Shediac. Lobster Capital of the World. It's a regulation that when you say Shediac you must also say —"

"Lobster Capital of the World."

"Thank you," Hancock smiled and Gamache could see he spoke of joy for a reason. He knew it. "This is my first assignment. I came three years ago."

"How long have you sat on the board of the Lit and His?"

"About eighteen months I guess. It's not very onerous. My biggest job is to remember not to actually suggest anything. It takes a lot of effort to halt time, and for the most part they've done it."

Gamache smiled. "Living history?"

"Sort of. They can be old and cranky, but they love Québec and they love the Literary and Historical Society. They've spent years trying to keep a low profile. They just want to be left alone, really. And now this."

"The murder of Augustin Renaud," said Gamache.

Hancock was shaking his head. "He came to speak to us, you know. Friday morning. But the board refused to see him. Quite right too. He can go through regular channels, like everyone else. He seemed unpleasant."

"You saw him?"

Hancock hesitated. "No."

"Why wasn't Renaud's visit mentioned in the minutes?"

Hancock looked nonplussed. "We just decided it didn't matter."

But Gamache had the impression this had

been news to Hancock.

"I understand you and Monsieur Haslam left early?"

"We had a practice at noon so yes, we left."

"Was Augustin Renaud still outside?"

"Not that I saw."

"Who had access to the basement?"

Hancock thought for a moment. "Winnie would know better. She's the head librarian, you know. I don't think the basement doors were ever locked. It's really more a question of who could find them. Did you go down?"

Gamache nodded.

"Then you know you have to go through a trap door and down a ladder. Not exactly the grand staircase. A casual visitor would never find that basement."

"But renovations were being done and they included the sub-basement, where he was found. In fact, I understand it's scheduled to be concreted over in the next couple of days."

"That soon? I knew the work was being done but didn't know when. Won't happen now, I suppose?"

"Not for a while, I'm afraid."

The Chief Inspector wondered if the Reverend Mr. Hancock realized he'd all but admitted only a member of the Literary and

Historical Society could have killed Renaud. And not a casual user of the fine library, but someone intimately familiar with the old building. The Chief remembered wandering the labyrinthine corridors. It was a warren of hallways, staircases, back rooms.

Would Augustin Renaud have been able to find that trap door on his own?

Almost certainly not.

Someone guided him down there then killed him.

Someone who knew all about the Lit and His.

Someone who knew the sub-basement was about to be concreted over.

Beside him, the Reverend Mr. Hancock had risen. "I'm sorry, I really need to get in to coffee. I'm expected to make an appearance." He paused and looked closely at the bearded man in front of him.

Like every other Quebecker, he was familiar with Chief Inspector Gamache. The head of homicide appeared on weekly talk shows and news reports trying to explain the decisions the Sûreté was making. Often giving information about a case.

He was always patient, thoughtful, clear in the face of questions shouted and not always civil. He never lost his temper,

185

though Hancock had seen him mightily provoked.

But the man he saw now differed from the man he'd watched for the past three years, and it wasn't just the beard or the scar. He was still thoughtful, civil, gentle almost.

But he seemed tired.

"The coffee will keep." Hancock sat back down. The church was tranquil, cool and quiet. "Would you like to talk?"

Armand Gamache knew this young man didn't mean about the case, and he was tempted. Tempted to tell him everything. But Thomas Hancock was a suspect in a murder case and as much as he longed to confide his sins to this young minister, he resisted.

"Go, please. We can talk another time."

"I hope so," said Hancock, rising. "Joy doesn't ever leave, you know. It's always with you. And one day you'll find it again."

"Merci," said Gamache, and sat quietly in the church until the ringing of the man's feet on the floor was silenced, and he was alone with the whispering in his head.

Over at the Literary and Historical Society the library was open again, as were the offices. A yellow police tape, though, was across one door, that led to the trap door that led to the ladder that led to the sub-basement.

And there Inspector Langlois stood.

His team had collected all the evidence, every inch had been gone over, every hair collected, every masticated rat, every bit of cloth. Soil samples had been put in vials. Photos taken, infrared, ultraviolet, black light. Everything.

They'd found, besides the body, a bloody shovel, a satchel with the map, and footprints. All sorts of footprints. Too many, he suspected, to be able to narrow it down.

He had investigators interviewing Renaud's former wife, his friends, of which there were precious few, his neighbors. They were scouring his home, but it was so packed with books and papers and all sorts of crap it could take weeks.

They were all over this case. Because, like Gamache, Langlois knew a frenzy was just beginning. Whipped by the tabloids, and eventually picked up by the legitimate press. The case was being hijacked. It was no longer just about Renaud's body, it had become about another, an older mystery, an older body.

Champlain.

Was he here?

Which was why instead of being at Renaud's apartment sifting through clues, he was in the dim basement, staring at a bucket of potatoes. At least, he hoped that's what they were.

Beside him Québec's Chief Archeologist, Serge Croix, stooped.

Neither man was happy to be there. Both knew it to be a waste of time.

"Well, Inspector, I can tell you for certain, that is not Champlain."

The two men continued to stare at the potatoes.

A trained excavator, brought by the Chief Archeologist, leaned against his shovel. Another held a device and was walking slowly over the dirt floor. Already they'd dug three holes, and in each they found a metal box or bucket with root vegetables. Probably hundreds of years old. Turnips, potatoes, parsnips. But no Samuel de Champlain.

"Bon," said Croix. "That's enough. We all know he isn't here. In fact, if Augustin Renaud believed he was that's just about a guarantee Champlain is somewhere else."

"Wait, I have something over here," said the woman with the device.

Croix sighed but they all trooped to the dark corner. The excavator repositioned the bright industrial lights.

Inspector Langlois felt his heart speed up and around him he could see the others looking expectant, hopeful. Even Croix.

Despite the fact he knew Champlain could not possibly be buried there, Croix could still get his hopes up. Like homicide inspectors, thought Langlois, archeologists dug and dug, and always believed it wasn't in vain. Something important might lie just below the surface.

The excavator put his shovel into the hard earth and loosened it, nudging it deeper and deeper, an inch at a time so as not to destroy whatever was beneath.

And then they heard the tap and the slight scraping. They'd found something.

Once again, the Chief Archeologist for Québec stooped. Bringing out his tools, finer than the rest, he carefully, painstakingly, cleared away the dirt to reveal a box.

Opening it he shone a light inside.

Turnips. Though one did look a little like the *premier ministre*.

NINE

Armand Gamache walked briskly up the slippery sidewalk and into the park known as Place d'Armes, the bitter wind full in his face. Foot paths were worn through the deep snow criss-crossing the park. Horse-drawn carriages, the *calèches,* waited at the top of the park to take visitors around the old city. Behind Gamache was a row of small, picturesque stone buildings, all turned into restaurants. To his right rose the magnificent Anglican Cathedral of the Holy Trinity. Gamache knew this, from experience. But he didn't look at it. Like everyone else, he kept his head down against the wind, only glancing up now and then to make sure he wasn't about to hit a person or a pole. His eyes watered and the tears froze. Everyone else looked just like him, their faces round and red and glowing. Like mobile stoplights.

Losing his footing on some ice hidden

under a dusting of snow he righted himself just in time, then turned his back to the wind and caught his breath. At the top of the hill, beyond the park and *calèches,* was the most photographed building in Canada.

The Château Frontenac hotel.

It was huge and gray, turreted and imposing, and rose as though expelled from the cliff face. Inspired by castles it was named for the first governor of Québec, Frontenac. It was both magnificent and forbidding.

Gamache walked toward the Château, past the large statue in the middle of the small park. The Monument de la Foi. A monument to Faith. For Québec had been built on Faith. And fur. But the city fathers preferred to raise a statue to martyrs than to a beaver.

Just ahead, the Château promised warmth, a glass of wine, a crusty bowl of French onion soup. Émile. But the Chief Inspector stopped just short of the shelter, and stared. Not at the Château, not at the gothic statue to Faith, but to another monument off to the left, much larger, even, than the one to Faith.

It was of a man looking out over the city he'd founded four hundred years earlier.

Samuel de Champlain.

Bare-headed, bold, stepping forward as

though wanting to join them, to be a part of this city that existed only because he had. And at the base of the statue another, smaller, image. An angel, sounding a trumpet to the glory of the founder. And even Gamache, who was no great fan of nationalism, felt wonder, awe, at the unshakable vision and courage of this man to do what many had tried and failed.

To not just come to these shores to harvest furs and fish and timber, but live here. Create a colony, a community. A New World. A home.

Gamache stared until he could no longer feel his face and his fingers in his warm mitts were numb. But still he stared at the father of Québec and wondered.

Where are you? Where did they bury you? And why don't we know?

Émile rose and waved him to their table by the window.

The two men with him also got up.

"Chief Inspector," they said and introduced themselves.

"René Dallaire," the tall, rotund man said, shaking Gamache's hand.

"Jean Hamel," the small, slim one said. Had René sported a cropped moustache the two men could have passed for Laurel and Hardy.

Gamache handed his coat to a waiter, shoving his hat, scarf and mitts into a sleeve. He sat and put his hands to his face, feeling the burning. Extreme cold left its ironic mark. It was indistinguishable from a sunburn. But within minutes it had subsided, and the circulation had returned to his hands, helped along by sitting on them.

They ordered drinks and lunch and chatted about Carnaval, about the weather, about politics. It was clear the three men knew each other well. And Gamache knew they'd all belonged to the same club for decades.

The Champlain Society.

Their drinks and a basket of rolls arrived. They sipped their Scotches and Gamache resisted the urge to take a warm roll in each hand. The men talked casually among themselves, Gamache sometimes contributing, sometimes just listening, sometimes glancing out the window.

The St-Laurent Bar was at the far end of the Château, down the gracious, wide, endless corridor, through the double doors and into another world. Unlike the rest of the mammoth hotel, this bar was modest in size and circular, being built into one of the turrets of the Château. Its curved walls were paneled in dark wood and fireplaces stood on either side. A round bar took up the center, with tables surrounding it.

That, for any normal place, would have been impressive enough but Quebec City was far from normal, and within it, the Château was unique.

For curving along the far wall of the bar were windows. Tall, framed in mahogany, wide and mullioned. Out of them opened the most splendid vista Gamache had ever seen. True, as a Québécois, no other view could ever match up. This was their Grand Canyon, Niagara Falls, Everest. This was Machu Picchu, Kilimanjaro, Stonehenge. It was their wonder.

From the bar he could see up and down the great river, the view so distant it broke into the past. From there, Gamache could see four hundred years in the past. The ships, surprisingly small and fragile, sailing down from the Atlantic, dropping anchor at the narrowest spot.

Kebek. An Algonquin word. Where the river narrows.

Gamache could almost see the sails being furled, men pulling ropes, securing lines, crawling up and down the masts. He could almost see the boats lowered into the water, and the men rowing ashore.

Did they know what they were in for? What the New World held?

Almost certainly not, or they'd never have come. Most never left, but were buried right below them, on the shores. Dying of scurvy, of exposure.

Unlike Gamache they had no Château to duck into. No warm soup and amber Scotch. He'd barely survived ten minutes in the biting, bitter wind, how had they survived days, weeks, months, with no warm clothing and barely any shelter?

Of course, the answer was obvious. They hadn't. Most had died, slow, agonizing, dreadful deaths those first winters. What Gamache saw as he glanced out the window to the river with its gray water and ice floes, was history. His history, flowing by.

He also saw a dot in the distance. An ice canoe. Shaking his head Gamache turned his attention back to his companions.

"Why're you looking so puzzled?" Émile asked.

The Chief Inspector nodded out the window. "An ice canoe team. The settlers had to do it. Why would someone choose to?"

"I agree," said René, breaking up a roll and smearing butter on it. "I can barely watch them, and yet, I can't seem to look away either." He laughed. "I sometimes think we're a rowboat society."

"A what?" asked Jean.

"A rowboat. It's why we do things like that." He jerked his head toward the window and the dot on the river. "It's why Québec is so perfectly preserved. It's why we're all so fascinated with history. We're in a rowboat. We move forward, but we're always looking back."

Jean laughed and leaned away as the waiter placed a huge burger and *frites* in front of him. A bubbling French onion soup sat in front of Émile and Gamache was given a hot bowl of pea soup.

"I met a fellow this morning who's training for the race," said Gamache.

"Bet he's in good shape," said Émile, lifting his spoon almost over his head, trying to get the stringy, melted cheese to break.

"He is. He's also the minister at the Presbyterian church. St. Andrews."

"Muscular Christianity," René chuckled.

"There's a Presbyterian church?" asked Jean.

"And a congregation to go with it," said Gamache. "He was saying he has a teammate for the race who's over sixty."

"Sixty what?" asked René. "Pounds?"

"Must be IQ," said Émile.

"I'm hoping to meet him this afternoon. Name's Ken Haslam. Do you know him?"

They looked at each other, but the answer was clear. No.

After lunch, over espressos, Gamache turned the conversation to the reason they were together.

"As you know, Augustin Renaud was murdered on Friday night, or early yesterday morning."

They nodded, their good cheer subsiding. Three shrewd faces stared back at him. They were of an age, late seventies, all successful in their fields, all retired. But none had lost their edge. He could see that clearly.

"What I want to know from you is this. Could Champlain be buried beneath the Literary and Historical Society?"

They looked at each other, and finally, silently, it was decided that René Dallaire, the large, Hardy-esque man, would take the lead. The table had been cleared of all but their *demi-tasses.*

"I brought this along when Émile told us what you wanted to talk about." He spread out a map, pinning it down with their cups. "I'm embarrassed to say I had no idea there was a Literary and Historical Society."

"That's not quite true," said Jean to his

friend. "We're familiar with the building. It's quite historic you know. Originally a redoubt, a military barracks in the 1700s. Then in the latter part of the century it housed prisoners of war. Then another prison was built somewhere else and the building must have fallen into private hands."

"And now you say it's called the Literary and Historical Society?" René spoke the English words with a heavy accent.

"Quite magnificent," said Gamache.

René placed his substantial finger on the site of the building, by rue St-Stanislas. "That's it, right?"

Gamache bent over the map, as did they all, narrowly avoiding knocking heads. He nodded agreement.

"Then there can be no doubt. You agree?" René Dallaire looked at Jean and Émile.

They agreed.

"I can guarantee you," René looked Gamache in the eye. "Samuel de Champlain is not buried there."

"How can you be so certain?"

"When you arrived at the Château, did you happen to notice the statue of Champlain out front?"

"I did. Hard to miss."

"*C'est vrai.* That's not simply a monument

to the man, but it marks the exact spot he died."

"As exact as we can get, anyway," said Jean. René shot him a small, annoyed look.

"How do you know that's where he died?" Gamache asked. Now it was Émile's turn to answer.

"There're reports written by his lieutenants and the priests. He died after a short illness on Christmas Day, 1635, during a storm. It's one of the few things we know about Champlain without a doubt. The fortress was right there, where the statue is."

"But he wouldn't have been buried right where he died, would he?" asked Gamache.

René unfolded another map or, at least, a reproduction and placed it on top of the modern city map. It was little more than an illustration.

"This was drawn in 1639, four years after Champlain died. It's not much different than the Québec he would have known." The map showed a stylized fort, a parade grounds in front, and a scattering of buildings around. "This is where he died." His finger landed on the fort. "It's where the statue now stands. And this is where they buried Champlain."

René Dallaire's thick finger pointed to a

small building a few hundred yards from the fort.

"The chapel. The only one in Québec at the time. There're no official records but it seems obvious Champlain would have been buried there, either right in the chapel or in a cemetery beside it."

Gamache was perplexed. "So, if we know where he was buried, what's the mystery? Where is he? And why aren't there any official records of the burial of the most important man in the colony?"

"Ahh, but nothing is ever straightforward is it?" said Jean. "The chapel burned a few years later, destroying all the records."

Gamache thought about that. "A fire would burn the records, yes, but not a buried body. We should still have found him by now, no?"

René shrugged. "Yes, we should have. There're a number of theories, but the most likely is that they buried him in the cemetery, not the chapel, so the fire wouldn't have disturbed him at all. Over time the colony grew —"

René paused but his hands were expressive. He opened them wide. The other two men were also silent, eyes down.

"Are you saying they put a building on top of Champlain?" Gamache asked.

The three men looked unhappy but none contradicted him until Jean spoke.

"There is another theory."

Émile sighed. "Not that again. There's no proof."

"There's no proof of any of this," Jean pointed out. "I agree it's a guess. You just don't want to believe it."

Émile was silent. It seemed Jean had made a direct hit. The little man turned to Gamache. "The other theory is that as Quebec City grew there was a huge amount of building work, as René says. But along with it was excavation, digging down beneath the frost line before they put up the new buildings. The city was booming, and things went up in a hurry. They didn't have time to worry about the dead."

Gamache was beginning to see where this was going. "So the theory is that they didn't build on top of Champlain."

Jean shook his head slowly. "No. They dug him up along with hundreds of others and dumped him in a landfill somewhere. They didn't mean to, they just didn't know."

Gamache was silent, stunned. Would the Americans have done that to Washington? Or the British to Henry the Eighth?

"Could that have happened?" He turned, naturally, to Émile Comeau who shrugged, then finally nodded.

"It is possible, but Jean's right. None of us wants to admit it."

"To be fair," said Jean. "It is the least likely of the theories."

"The point is," said René, looking at the map again. "This is the limit of the original settlement in 1635." He twirled his finger over the old map, then swept it aside and found the same place on the modern map. "Pretty much from where we're sitting now, in the Château, to a radius of a few hundred yards. They'd keep it small. Easier to defend."

"And what would the rest have been?" asked Gamache, beginning to understand what they were saying.

"Nothing," said Jean. "Forest. Rock."

"And where the Literary and Historical Society is now?"

"Woods." René brought the old map out and placed his finger on a big blank space, far from any habitation.

Nothing.

There was no way they'd have buried Champlain that far from civilization.

There was no way the father of Québec could be in the basement of the Lit and His.

"So," Gamache leaned back. "Why was Augustin Renaud there?"

"Because he was mad?" asked Jean.

"He was you know," said Émile. "Champlain loved Québec, to the exclusion of everything else in his life. It was all he knew, all he lived for. And Renaud loved Champlain with the same devotion. A devotion bordering on madness."

"Bordering?" asked René. "He was the capital of the state of madness. Augustin Renaud was the Emperor of it. Bordering," he muttered.

"Maybe," said Émile, staring down at the old map again. "Maybe he wasn't looking for Champlain. Maybe there was another reason he was there."

"Like what?"

"Well," his mentor looked at him. "It is a literary society. Maybe he was looking for a book."

Gamache smiled. Maybe. He got up and paused as the waiter fetched his coat. Looking down at the modern map he noticed something.

"The old chapel, the one that burned. Where would it have been on this map?"

René put out his finger one more time and pointed.

It landed on the Notre-Dame Basilica, the mighty church where the great and good used to pray. As the waiter helped Gamache into his parka René leaned over and whispered, "Speak to Père Sébastien."

Jean-Guy Beauvoir waited.

He wasn't very good at it. First he looked as though he didn't care, then he looked as though he had all the time in the world. That lasted about twenty seconds. Then he looked annoyed. That was more successful and lasted until Olivier Brulé arrived a quarter hour later.

It had been a few months since he'd last seen Olivier. Prison changed some men. Well, it changed all men. But externally some showed it more than others. Some actually seemed to flourish. They lifted weights, bulked up, exercised for the first time in years, ate three square meals. They even thrived, though few would admit it, on the regimen, the structure. Many had never had that in their lives, and so they'd wandered off course.

Here their course was clearer.

Though most, Beauvoir knew, withered in confinement.

Olivier walked through the doors, wearing his prison blues. He was in his late thirties and of medium build. His hair was cut far shorter than Beauvoir had ever seen, but it disguised the fact he was balding. He looked pale but healthy. Beauvoir felt a revulsion, as he did in the presence of all murderers. For that's what he knew in his heart Olivier was.

No, he sharply reminded himself. I need to think of this man as innocent. Or at least, as not guilty.

But try as he might he saw a convict.

"Inspector," said Olivier, standing at the far end of the visitors' room, unsure what to do.

"Olivier," said Beauvoir and smiled, though judging by the look on Olivier's face it was probably more of a sneer. "Please. Call me Jean-Guy. I'm here privately."

"Just a social call?" Olivier sat at a table across from Beauvoir. "How's the Chief Inspector?"

"He's in Quebec City for Carnaval. I'm expecting to have to bail him out any minute."

Olivier laughed. "There's more than one fellow in here who arrived via Carnaval. Apparently the 'I was drunk on Caribou' defense isn't all that effective."

"I'll alert the Chief."

They both laughed, a little longer than necessary, then fell into an uneasy silence. Now that he was there Beauvoir wasn't sure what to say.

Olivier stared at him, waiting.

"I wasn't totally honest with you just now," Beauvoir began. He'd never done anything like this before and felt as though he'd wandered into a wilderness and hated Olivier all the more for making him do that. "I'm on leave as you know, so this really isn't an official call but . . ."

Olivier waited, better at it than Beauvoir. Finally he raised his brows in a silent, "go on."

"The Chief asked me to look into a few aspects of your case. I don't want you to get your hopes up —" But he could see it was already too late for that. Olivier was smiling. Life seemed to have returned to him. "Really, Olivier, you can't expect anything to come from this."

"Why not?"

"Because I still think you did it."

That shut him up, Beauvoir was happy to see. Still, there swirled around Olivier a residue of hope. Was this just cruel? Beauvoir hoped so. The Inspector leaned on the metal table. "Listen, there're just a few questions. The Chief asked me to be absolutely certain, that's all."

"You might think I did it, but he doesn't, does he?" said Olivier, triumphant.

"He isn't so sure, and he wants to be sure.

Wants to make certain he — we — didn't make a mistake. Look, if you tell anyone about this, anyone at all, it's off. You understand?" Beauvoir's eyes were hard.

"I understand."

"I mean it, Olivier. Especially Gabri. You can't tell him anything."

Olivier hesitated.

"If you tell him he'll tell others. He couldn't help but. Or at the very least his mood will change and people'll notice. If I'm going to ask questions, dig some more, it has to be subtle. If someone else killed the Hermit I don't want them on their guard."

This made sense to Olivier, who nodded. "I promise."

"*Bon.* You need to tell me again what happened that night. And I need the truth."

The air crackled between the two men.

"I told you the truth."

"When?" Beauvoir demanded. "Was it the second or third version of the story? If you're in here you did it to yourself. You lied at every turn."

It was true, Olivier knew. He'd lied all his life about everything, until the habit became who he was. It didn't even occur to him to tell the truth. So when all this happened of course he'd lie.

207

Too late he'd realized what that did. It made the truth unrecognizable. And while he was very good, very glib, at lying, all his truths sounded like falsehoods. He blushed, stumbled for words, got confused when telling the truth.

"All right," he said to Beauvoir. "I'll tell you what happened."

"The truth."

Olivier gave a single, curt, nod.

"I met the Hermit ten years ago, when Gabri and I first arrived in Three Pines and were living above the shop. He wasn't a hermit yet. He'd still leave his cabin and get his own supplies, but he looked pretty ragged. We were renovating the shop. I hadn't turned it into a bistro, it was just an antique store back then. One day he showed up and said he wanted to sell something. I wasn't very happy. It seemed he wanted a favor from me. Looking at the guy I figured it was some piece of junk he found on the side of the road but when he showed it to me I knew it was special."

"What was it?"

"A miniature, a tiny portrait, in profile. Some Polish aristocrat, I think. Must have been painted with a single hair. It was beautiful. Even the frame it was in was beautiful. I agreed to buy it from him in exchange for a bag of groceries."

He'd told the story so often Olivier was almost immune to the disgust in people's faces. Almost.

"Go on," said Beauvoir. "What did you do with the portrait?"

"Took it to Montreal and sold it on rue Notre-Dame, the antique district."

"Can you remember which shop?" Beauvoir pulled out his notebook and a pen.

"Not sure if it's still there. They change a lot. It was called Temps Perdu."

Beauvoir made a note. "How much did you get for it?"

"Fifteen hundred dollars."

"And the Hermit kept coming back?"

"Kept offering me things. Some fantastic, some not so great but still better than I'm likely to find in most attics or barns. At first I sold them through that antiques shop but then realized I could get more on eBay. Then one day the Hermit arrived looking really bad. Skinny, and stressed. He said, 'I'm not coming back, old son. I can't.' This was a disaster for me. I'd come to pretty much rely on his stuff. He said he didn't want to be seen anymore, then he invited me to his cabin."

"You went?"

Olivier nodded. "I had no idea he lived in

209

the woods. He was way the hell and gone. Well, you know it."

Beauvoir did. He'd spent the night there with the asshole saint.

"When we finally got there I couldn't believe it." For a moment Olivier was transported to that magical moment when he'd first stepped into the scruffy old man's log cabin. And into a world where ancient glass was used for milk, a Queen's china was used for peanut butter sandwiches and priceless silk tapestries hung on walls to keep the drafts out.

"I visited him every two weeks. By then I'd turned the antique shop into a bistro. Every second Saturday night after the bistro closed I'd sneak up to the cabin. We'd talk and he'd give me something for the groceries I'd bring."

"What did Charlotte mean?" Beauvoir asked. It was Chief Inspector Gamache who'd noticed the strange repetition of "Charlotte." There were references to the name all over the Hermit's cabin, from the book *Charlotte's Web,* to a first-edition Charlotte Brontë, to the rare violin. Everyone else had missed it, except the Chief.

Olivier was shaking his head. "Nothing, it meant nothing. Or, at least, not anything I know about. He never mentioned the name."

Beauvoir stared at him. "Careful, Olivier. I need the truth."

"I have no reason to lie anymore."

For any rational person that would be true, but Olivier had behaved so irrationally Beauvoir wondered if he was capable of anything else.

"The Hermit had scratched the name Charlotte in code under one of those wooden sculptures he'd made," Beauvoir pointed out. He could see the carvings, deeply disturbing works showing people fleeing some terror. And under three of his works the Hermit had carved words in code.

Charlotte. Emily. And under the last one? The one that showed Olivier in a chair, listening, he'd carved that one, short, damning word.

Woo.

"And 'Woo'?" Beauvoir asked. "What did that mean?"

"I don't know."

"Well it meant something," snapped Beauvoir. "He put it under the carving of you."

"That wasn't me. It doesn't look like me."

"It's a carving not a photograph. It's you and you know it. Why did he write 'Woo' under it?"

But it wasn't just under the carving. Woo had appeared in the web and in that piece of wood, covered in the Hermit's blood, that had bounced under the bed. Into a dark corner. A piece of red cedar carved, according to the forensic experts, years before.

"I'm asking you again, Olivier, what did 'Woo' mean?"

"I don't know." Now Olivier was exasperated but he took a breath and regained himself. "Look, I told you. He said it a couple of times, but under his breath. At first I thought it was just a sigh. It sounded like a sigh. Then I realized he was saying 'Woo.' He only said it when he was afraid."

Beauvoir stared at him. "I'm going to need more than that."

Olivier shook his head. "There is no more than that. That's all I know. I'd tell you more, if I could. Honestly. It meant something to him, but he never explained, and I never asked."

"Why not?"

"It didn't seem important."

"It was clearly important to him."

"Yes, but not to me. I'd have asked if it meant he'd give me more of his treasures, but that didn't seem to be the case."

And Beauvoir heard the truth in that, the humiliating, shameful truth. He shifted imperceptibly in his seat, and as he did his perception shifted just a little.

Maybe, maybe, this man really was telling the truth. Finally.

"You visited him for years, but near the end something changed. What happened?"

"That Marc Gilbert bought the old Hadley house and decided to turn it into an inn and spa. That would've been bad enough, but his wife Dominique decided they needed horses and asked Roar Parra to reopen the trails. One of the trails led right past the Hermit's cabin. Eventually Parra would find the cabin and everyone would know about the Hermit and his treasure."

"What did you do?"

"What could I do? I'd spent years trying to convince the Hermit to give me that thing he kept in the canvas sack. He promised it to me, kept teasing me with it. I wanted it. I'd earned it."

A whiny tone had crept into Olivier's voice and made itself at home. A tone not often let out in public, preferring privacy.

"Tell me again about the thing in the sack."

"You know it, you've seen it," said Olivier, then took a deep breath and regrouped. "The Hermit had everything on display, all his antiquities, all those beautiful things but one thing he kept hidden. In the sack."

"And you wanted it."

"Wouldn't you?"

Beauvoir considered. It was true. It was human nature to want the one thing denied you.

The Hermit had teased Olivier with it but he hadn't appreciated who he was dealing with. The depth of Olivier's greed.

"So you killed him and stole it."

That was the Crown's case. Olivier had killed the demented old man for his treasure, the one he kept hidden, the one found in Olivier's bistro along with the murder weapon.

"No." Olivier leaned forward suddenly, as though charging Beauvoir. "I went back for it, I admit that, but he was already dead."

"And what did you see?" Beauvoir asked the question quickly, hoping to trip him up in the rush.

"The cabin door was open and I saw him lying on the floor. There was blood. I thought he'd just hit his head, but when I got closer I could see he was dead. There was a piece of wood I'd never seen before by his hand. I picked it up."

"Why?" The word was snapped out.

"Because I wanted to see."

"See what?"

"What it was."

"Why?"

"In case it was important."

"Important. Explain."

Now it was Beauvoir who was leaning forward, almost crawling across the metal table. Olivier didn't lean back. The two men were in each other's faces, almost shouting.

"In case it was valuable."

"Explain."

"In case it was another one of his carvings, okay?" Olivier almost screamed, then threw himself back into his chair. "Okay? There. I thought it might be one of his carvings and I could sell it."

This hadn't come out in court. Olivier had admitted he'd picked up the wood carving, but said he'd dropped it as soon as he'd seen blood on it.

"Why'd you drop it?"

"Because it was a worthless piece of junk. Something a kid would do. I only noticed the blood later."

"Why did you move the body?"

It was the question that hounded Gamache. The question that had brought Beauvoir back to this case. Why, if he'd killed the man, would Olivier put him into a wheelbarrow and take him like so much compost through the woods? And dump him in the front hall of the new inn and spa.

"Because I wanted to screw Marc Gilbert. Not literally."

"Seems pretty literal to me," said Beauvoir.

"I wanted to ruin his fancy inn. Who'd pay a fortune to stay in a place where someone had just been murdered?"

Beauvoir leaned back, examining Olivier for a long moment.

"The Chief Inspector believes you."

Olivier closed his eyes and exhaled.

Beauvoir held up his hand. "He thinks you did do it to ruin Gilbert. But in ruining Gilbert you'd also have stopped the horse trails and if you stopped Parra from opening the paths, no one would find the cabin."

"All that's true. But if I killed him, why would I let everyone know there'd been a murder?"

"Because the paths were close. The cabin, and the murder, would have been discovered within days anyway. Your only hope was to stop the trails. Stop the discovery of the cabin."

"By putting the dead man on display? There was nothing left to hide then."

"There was the treasure."

They stared at each other.

■ ■ ■ ■

Jean-Guy Beauvoir sat in his car mulling over the interview. Nothing really new had come out of it but Gamache had advised him to believe Olivier this time, take him at his word.

Beauvoir couldn't bring himself to do it. He could pretend to, could go through the motions. He could even try to convince himself that Olivier was indeed telling the truth, but he'd be lying to himself.

He pulled the car out of the parking lot and headed toward rue Notre-Dame and the Temps Perdu. Lost time. Perfect. Because that's what this is, he thought as he negotiated the light Sunday afternoon traffic in Montreal. A waste of time.

As he drove he went back over the case. Only Olivier's fingerprints were found in the cabin. No one else even knew the Hermit existed.

The Hermit. It was what Olivier called him, always called him.

Beauvoir parked across the street from the antique shop. It was still there, cheek by jowl with other antique shops up and down rue Notre-Dame, some high end, some little more than junk shops.

Temps Perdu looked pretty high end.

Beauvoir reached for the car door handle, then paused, staring into space for a moment, whipping through the interview. Looking for a word, a single, short, word. Then he flipped through his notes.

Not there either. He closed his notebook and getting out of the car he crossed the street and entered the shop. There was only one window, at the front. As he made his way further back, past the pine and oak furniture, past the chipped and cracked paintings on the walls, past the ornaments, the blue and white plates, past the vases and umbrella stands, it got darker. Like going into a well-furnished cave.

"May I help you?"

An elderly man sat at the very back, at a desk. He wore glasses and peered at Beauvoir, assessing him. The Inspector knew the look, but he was normally the one giving it.

The two men assessed each other. Beauvoir saw a slim man, well but comfortably dressed. Like his merchandise, he seemed old and refined and he smelled a little of polish.

The antique dealer saw a man in his mid to late thirties. Pale, perhaps a little stressed. Not out for a lazy Sunday stroll through the antique district. Not a buyer.

A man, perhaps, in need of something. Probably a toilet.

"This shop," Beauvoir began. He didn't want to sound like an investigator, but suddenly realized he didn't know how to sound like anything else. It was like a tattoo. Indelible. He smiled and softened his tone. "I have a friend who used to come here, but that was years ago. Ten years or more. It's still called Temps Perdu, but has it changed hands?"

"No. Nothing's changed."

And Beauvoir could believe it.

"Were you here then?"

"I'm always here. It's my shop." The elderly man stood and put out his hand. "Fréderic Grenier."

"Jean-Guy Beauvoir. You might remember my friend. He sold you a few things."

"Is that right? What were they?"

The man, Beauvoir noticed, didn't ask Olivier's name, just what he sold. Is that how shopkeepers saw people? He's the pine table? She's the chandelier? Why not? That's how he saw suspects. She's the knifing. He's the shotgun.

"I think he said he sold you a miniature painting."

Beauvoir watched the man closely. The man was watching him closely.

"He might have. You say it was ten years ago. That's a long time. Why're you asking?"

Normally Beauvoir would have whipped out his Sûreté homicide ID, but he wasn't on official business. And he didn't have a ready answer.

"My friend just died and his widow wonders if you sold it. If not she'd buy it back. It'd been in the family for a long time. My friend sold it when he needed money, but that's no longer a problem."

Beauvoir was quite pleased with himself, though not altogether surprised. He lived with lies all the time, had heard thousands. Why shouldn't he be good at it himself?

The antique dealer watched him, then nodded. "That sometimes happens. Can you describe the painting?"

"It was European and very fine. Apparently you paid him fifteen hundred dollars for it."

Monsieur Grenier smiled. "Now I remember. It was a lot of money, but worth it. I didn't often pay that much for such a small piece. Exquisite. Polish, I believe. Unfortunately I sold it on. He came in with a few other things after that, if I remember. A carved cane that needed work. It was a little cracked. I gave it to my restorer then sold it too. Went quickly. Those sorts of things do.

I'm sorry. I remember him now. Young, blond. You say his wife wanted the things back?"

Beauvoir nodded.

The man frowned. "That must have come as a surprise to his partner. The man, as I remember, was gay."

"Yes. I was trying to be delicate. In fact, I'm his partner."

"I'm sorry to hear of your loss. But at least you had a chance to get married."

The man pointed to Beauvoir's wedding band.

Time to leave.

That had certainly, thought Beauvoir once back in the car and driving over the Champlain Bridge, been *les temps perdu*. Except for announcing that his husband, Olivier, had died nothing of significance had happened.

He was almost back in Three Pines when he remembered what had been bothering him after the interview with Olivier. The word that had been missing.

Pulling off to the side of the road he dialed the prison and was eventually connected to Olivier.

"People will begin to talk, Inspector."

"You have no idea," said Beauvoir. "Listen, during the trial and investigation you

221

said the Hermit didn't tell you anything about himself, except that he was Czech and his name was Jakob."

"Yes."

"There's a large Czech community around Three Pines, including the Parras."

"Yes."

"And quite a few of his pieces came from former Eastern Bloc countries. Czechoslovakia, Poland, Russia. You testified that your impression was he'd stolen their family treasures, then skipped to Canada in the confusion when communism was collapsing. You thought he was hiding from his countrymen, the people he stole from."

"Yes."

"And yet, through our whole interview today you never once called him Jakob. Why was that?"

There was a long pause now.

"You won't believe me."

"Chief Inspector Gamache ordered me to believe you."

"That's a comfort."

"Listen, Olivier, this is your only hope. Your last hope. The truth, now."

"His name wasn't Jakob."

Now it was Beauvoir's turn to fall silent.

"What was it?" he finally asked.

"I don't know."

"Are we back there?"

"You didn't seem to believe me the first time when I said I didn't know his name, so I made one up. One that sounded Czech."

Beauvoir was almost afraid to ask the next question. But he did.

"Was he even Czech?"

"No."

TEN

"I beg your pardon?"

It was, by Gamache's rough count, the millionth time he'd said that, or words to that effect, in the past ten minutes. He leaned even closer, risking toppling headlong off his chair. It didn't help that Ken Haslam had a very, very large oak desk.

"Excusez?" Gamache felt his chair tip as he strained forward. He leaned back just in time. Across the chasm of the desk Mr. Haslam continued to talk or at least move his lips.

Murmur, murmur, murder, murmur, board. Haslam looked sharply at Chief Inspector Gamache.

"Pardon?"

Normally Gamache concentrated on people's eyes, but was aware of their entire body. Clues came coded, and how people communicated was one of them. Their words were often the least informative. The vilest, bitterest, nastiest people often said nice things. But there was the sugar the words rode in on, or the little wink, or the insincere smile. Or the tense arm wrapped round the tense chest or legs, or the fingers intertwined tightly, white knuckled.

It was vital for him to be able to pick up on all the signals, and normally he could.

But this man confounded him because the only thing Gamache could see was Haslam's mouth. He stared at it, desperately trying to lip-read.

Ken Haslam didn't whisper. A whisper would have been, at this point, a welcome shout. He seemed, instead, to be simply mouthing his words. It was possible, thought Gamache, the man had had an operation. Perhaps his larynx had been removed.

But Gamache didn't think so. Every now and then a word was intelligible, like "murder." That word had popped out clearly.

Gamache was straining, physically and intellectually. Reaching to understand. It was exhausting. If only suspects realized, he thought, that screaming and shouting and throwing furniture wouldn't wear their interrogators down, but whispering would.

"I'm sorry, sir." Gamache was speaking English with the slight British accent he'd picked up at Cambridge.

Haslam's office was in the Basse-Ville, the Lower Town. The fastest way to get to the Lower Town was the glass-enclosed elevator called the Funicular that swept up and down the cliff-face from the upper to the lower city. Gamache had paid his two dollars and walked into the Funicular. It dropped over the side and descended. It was a short, very beautiful trip, though the Chief Inspector stayed at the back of the elevator, away from the glass and the sheer drop beyond.

Once there he stepped out into Petit-Champlain, a narrow, charming street closed to traffic and filled with snow and bustling people. Pedestrians ambled along, bundled against the cold, stopping now and then to look into the festive windows at the handmade lace, the art, the blown glass, the pastries.

Gamache continued down to Place Royale, where the first settlement had been built beside the river.

There he found Ken Haslam's office. *Royale Tourists,* the sign said. It was well placed, in a graystone building right on the open square. He walked in, spoke to the bright and helpful receptionist, explaining that no, he wasn't interested in a tour but in speaking to the owner of the company.

"Do you have an appointment?" she asked.

"I'm afraid not." Just at the very moment Beauvoir in Montreal was tempted to reach for his Sûreté ID, the Chief felt his hand move toward his breast pocket then stop. "I'd hoped he might be available."

He smiled at her. Finally she smiled back.

"As a matter of fact, he is in. Let me go in and just see if he has a minute."

And so, a few minutes later, he found himself in a quite magnificent office overlooking Place Royale and the Église Notre-Dame-des-Victoires. The church built to commemorate two great victories over the English.

It had taken Gamache about ten seconds to appreciate the difficulty of the situation. It's not that he didn't understand what Ken Haslam was saying, it was just that he couldn't hear it. Finally, when even lip-reading failed, the Chief interrupted.

"Désolé," Gamache put up a hand. Haslam's lips stopped moving. "Can we perhaps move closer together. I'm afraid I'm having some trouble hearing you."

Haslam looked perplexed but got up and moved to the chair beside the Chief.

"I really just need to know what happened at the board meeting of the Lit and His, the one where Augustin Renaud appeared."

Mumble, mumble, arrogant, murmur, couldn't possibly mumble. Haslam looked quite stern. He was a handsome man with steel gray hair, clean shaven, ruddy complexion that looked like it came from the sun and not the bottle. And now that they were closer together Gamache was better able to understand him. While he still spoke below a whisper it was now almost intelligible and the other signals were clearer.

Haslam was annoyed.

Not at Gamache, he thought, but at what had happened. Someone familiar with the Literary and Historical Society had murdered Augustin Renaud. And the fact the lunatic archeologist had asked to see the board on the very day he died, and been refused, cannot be seen as a coincidence.

But Haslam was mouthing again.

Murmur, mumble, Champlain, mumble idiocy, mumble, canoe race.

"Yes, I understand from Mr. Hancock that you and he left early for a practice. You're entered in the ice canoe race this coming Sunday."

Haslam smiled and nodded. "It's a lifelong dream."

The words were spoken low, but clear. In a gravelly whisper. It was a warm voice and

Gamache wondered why he didn't use it more, especially in his job. Surely this was a financially fatal flaw, being a tour guide who didn't speak.

"Why enter the race?" Gamache couldn't help himself. He was dying to know why anyone, never mind someone closing in on seventy, would do this to themselves.

Haslam's answer surprised him. He'd expected the Everest answer, or something about history, which the man clearly loved, since the canoe races re-created the old mail-runs before ice breaking ships appeared.

Mumble, like, murmur, people.

"You like the people?" Gamache asked.

Mumble, Haslam nodded and smiled.

"Can't you just join a choir?"

Haslam smiled. "Not quite the same, is it Chief Inspector?" And Haslam's eyes were warm, searching, intelligent.

He knows, thought Gamache. Somehow this man knows the value of not only friendship but camaraderie. What happens to people thrown together in extreme situations.

Gamache's right hand began to tremble and he very slowly curled it into a fist but not before those thoughtful eyes across from him dropped to them. Saw the tremor.

And said nothing.

Armand Gamache walked slowly back up the small hill, to Petit-Champlain and the Funicular. As he walked he thought about his conversations with Haslam and the receptionist, who had been equally, perhaps even more, informative.

No, Mr. Haslam doesn't do tours himself, he arranges them through emails. Mostly high-end, private tours of Québec for visiting dignitaries and celebrities. He was a little, she said, like a concierge. He'd done it so long people had come to ask for very strange things, and he almost always could accommodate them. Never, she rushed to assure him, illegal, or even immoral. Mr. Haslam was a very upstanding man. But unusual, yes.

Her French was excellent, and Haslam's, when audible was even better. Had his name been anything other than Ken Haslam, Gamache would have thought him Francophone. According to the receptionist, Mr. Haslam lost his only child to leukemia when she was eleven, and his wife had died six years ago. Both buried in the Anglican cemetery in the old city.

His roots went deep into Québec.

Once up the Funicular, forcing himself to

appreciate the magnificent view but gripping the wall behind him, Gamache leaned into the biting wind. His next stop was clear, but first he needed to gather his thoughts. He walked through the little alley called rue du Trésor which even in the bitter cold February day had artists selling their gaudy images of Québec. Bars carved out of blocks of ice had been set up off the alley and were selling Caribou to tourists who would soon regret this lapse in judgment. Once out of the alley he found the Café Buade and went in to both warm up and think.

Sitting in a banquette with a bowl of *chocolat chaud* he pulled out a notebook and pen. Occasionally sipping, sometimes staring into space, sometimes jotting thoughts, eventually he was ready for the next visit.

From the café he hadn't far to go. Just across the street to the great monolith that was Notre-Dame Basilica, the magnificent gilded church that wed, christened, chastised, guided and buried the highest officials and the lowest beggars.

While Québec never lacked for churches they were the satellites and Notre-Dame the sun.

As he walked through the gates and up

the steps he stopped at the board listing the Sunday services. One had just ended and the next wasn't until 6 P.M. Opening the heavy doors he walked in and felt the warmth and smelled the years and years of sacred ritual. Of candles and incense, and heard the echoing of feet on the slate floors.

The church was dim, the chandeliers and wall sconces sending a feeble light into the vast space. But at the far end, past near empty pews, there was a glow. The entire altar appeared dipped in gold. It shone and beckoned, angels pranced, stern saints stood and stared, a model of St. Peter's in Rome, like a spoiled child's doll house sat in the very center.

It was both glorious and vaguely repulsive. Gamache crossed himself, a habit unbroken and sat quietly for a few moments.

"My family wanted me to become a priest, you know," said the young voice.

"Having built up a tolerance for ash and smoke, I suppose," said Gamache.

"Exactly. And I think they figured anyone who could tolerate my grandmother was either a saint or demented. Either way, good material for a life with the Jesuits."

"But you decided against it."

"I never seriously considered it," Agent Morin spoke in Gamache's ear. "I'd fallen in love with Suzanne when she was six and I was seven. I figured that was God's plan."

"You've known each other that long?"

"All my life, it seems. We met in confirmation class."

Gamache could see the young man and tried to imagine him at seven. It wasn't hard. He looked far younger than his twenty-five years. He had a curious knack for looking like an imbecile. It wasn't something Morin tried to do, but he succeeded. He often had his mouth slightly open and his thick lips moistened as though he was about to drool. It could be either disconcerting or disarming. One thing it never was was attractive.

But it had grown on Gamache and his team as they realized what his face was doing had nothing to do with his brain or his heart.

"I like to just sit in our village church after everyone's left. Sometimes I go in in the evening."

"Do you talk to your priest?"

"Father Michel? Sometimes. Mostly I just sit. These days I imagine my wedding next June. I see the decorations and picture all my friends and family there. Some of the people I work with." He hesitated. "Would you come?"

"If I'm asked, I'd definitely be there."

"Really?"

"Absolutely."

"Wait 'til I tell Suzanne. When I sit in the church mostly I see her coming down the aisle to me. Like a miracle."

"Now there is no more loneliness."

"Pardon?"

"It's a blessing Madame Gamache and I had at our wedding. It was read at the end of the ceremony. *Now you will feel no rain, for each of you will be shelter for the other,*" Gamache quoted.

Now you will feel no cold
For each of you will be warmth for the
   other
Now there is no loneliness for you
Now there is no more loneliness
Now there is no more loneliness.

Gamache stopped. "Are you cold?"

"No."

But Gamache thought the young agent was lying. It was early December, cold and damp and he was immobile.

"Can we use that blessing at our wedding?"

"If you'd like. I can send it to you and you can decide."

"Great. How does it end? Can you remember?"

Gamache gathered his thoughts, remembering his own wedding. Remembering looking out and seeing all their friends and Reine-Marie's huge family. And Zora, his grandmother, the only one of his family left, but she was enough. There was no bride's side and no groom's side. Instead they all mixed in together.

And then the music had changed and Reine-Marie appeared and Armand knew then he'd been alone all his life, until this moment.

Now there is no more loneliness.

And at the end of the ceremony, the final blessing.

"Go now to your dwelling place," he said to Morin. *"To enter into the days of your togetherness. And may your days be good and long upon the earth."*

There was a pause. But not too long. Gamache was about to speak when Agent Morin broke the silence.

"That's how I feel, that I'm not really alone. Not since I met Suzanne. You know?"

"I do."

"The only thing wrong with my image of our wedding is that Suzanne always faints or throws up in church."

235

"Really? How extraordinary. Why do you think that is?"

"The incense, I think. I hope. Either that or she's the antichrist."

"That would mess up the wedding," said Gamache.

"Not to mention the marriage. I've asked and she assures me she isn't."

"Well, good enough. Have you considered a pre-nup?"

Paul Morin laughed.

May your days be good and long upon this earth, thought Gamache.

"You asked to speak with me?"

Gamache's eyes flew open, jolted. A middle-aged man in a cassock was staring down at him.

"Père Sébastien?"

"That's right." The voice was clipped, efficient, officious.

"My name is Armand Gamache. I was hoping for some of your time."

The man's beady eyes were hard, wary. "It's a busy day." He looked closely at Gamache. "Do I know you?"

Since the priest showed no interest in sitting Gamache stood. "Not personally, no, but you might have heard of me. I'm the head of homicide for the Sûreté du Québec."

The man's face cleared of annoyance and he smiled. "Of course, Chief Inspector." Now he put out a slender hand and greeted him. "I'm sorry. It's dark in here, and, do you normally wear a beard?"

"No, I'm incognito," smiled Gamache.

"Then you might not want to be telling people you're the head of homicide."

"Good suggestion." Gamache looked around. "It's been a while since I was in the basilica. Not since the *premier*'s funeral a few years ago."

"I was one of the celebrants," said Père Sébastien. "Beautiful service."

Gamache remembered it as formal, stilted, and very, very long.

"Now," Father Sébastien sat and patted the wood next to him. "Tell me what you'd like to know. Unless it's the confessional you need?"

"I'm sorry, I'm so sorry," the young voice repeated, over and over. Gamache had re-assured him it wasn't his fault, and assured Morin he'd find him before it was too late.

"You'll be having dinner with your parents and Suzanne tonight." There'd been a pause and Gamache thought he heard a sob. "I'll find you."

Another pause.

"I believe you."

"No," Gamache said to the priest, "just information."

"How can I help?"

"It's about the murder of Augustin Renaud."

The priest didn't look surprised. "Terrible. But I don't think I can be of much help. I hardly knew the man."

"But you did know him?"

Père Sébastien looked at Gamache with some suspicion now. "Of course I knew him. Isn't that why you're here?"

"Frankly I don't know why I'm here, except someone suggested I speak with you. Can you think why?"

The priest became prickly, offended. "Well, maybe because I'm the leading scholar on the early settlement of Québec and the role of the church. But maybe that's not important."

Dear God, thought Gamache, save me from a huffy priest. "Forgive me, but I'm not from Quebec City so I'm unfamiliar with your work."

"My articles are published worldwide."

This wasn't getting better.

"*Désolé*. It's not an area of expertise for me, but it's clearly of immense importance and I desperately need your help."

The priest relaxed a bit, his hackles slowly

238

lying flat. "How can I help?" he asked, coldly.

"What can you tell me about Augustin Renaud?"

"Well, he wasn't crazy, I can tell you that." He was the first person to say that and Gamache leaned forward. The priest continued, "He was passionate and obstinate and he was certainly offensive, but he wasn't crazy. People called him that in order to dismiss the man, take away his credibility. It was a cruel thing to do."

"You liked him?"

Père Sébastien shifted a little on the hard pew. "I wouldn't say that. He was a difficult man to like, not very socially adept. Maladroit, in fact. He had only one goal in life and everything else was trivial to him, including people's feelings. I can see how he'd make a lot of enemies."

"Could someone have hated him enough to kill?" asked Gamache.

"There're a lot of reasons for murder, Chief Inspector, as you know."

"Actually, *mon Père,* I've found there's only one. Beneath all the justifications, all the psychology, all the motives given, like revenge or greed or jealousy, there lies the real reason."

"And what's that?"

"Fear. Fear of losing what you have or not getting what you want."

"And yet, fear of eternal damnation doesn't stop them."

"No. Neither does fear of getting caught. Because they don't believe in either."

"You think it's not possible to believe in God and commit murder?"

The priest was staring at Gamache now, his face relaxed, amused even. His eyes calm, his voice light. Then why was he clutching his cassock in his fist?

"Depends on the God you believe in," said Gamache.

"There is only one God, Chief Inspector."

"Perhaps, but all sorts of humans who see imperfectly. Even God. Especially God."

The priest smiled and nodded but his hand tensed even more.

"I'm afraid we've wandered off topic," said Gamache. "My fault. It was foolish of me to debate faith with such a celebrated priest. I am sorry, *mon Père.* We were talking about Augustin Renaud and you were saying he was dismissed as crazy, but in your view he was quite sane. How did you know him?"

"I found him in the basement of the chapel to St. Joseph. He was digging."

"He'd just started digging?"

"I told you he was monomaniacal. He lost all judgment when it came to Champlain. But he actually found something."

"What?"

"Some old coins from the 1620s and two coffins. One was very plain and semi-collapsed, but the other was lead-lined. Our theory is that Champlain, like other dignitaries, would have been buried in a lead-lined coffin."

"And this was where the original chapel stood, before the fire."

"You're not quite as ignorant as you pretend, Chief Inspector."

"Oh, my ignorance knows no bounds, Father."

"The dig was immediately shut down by the city. It was unauthorized and considered akin to grave robbing. But then Renaud went to the media and made a huge stink. Champlain finally found, the tabloids declared, but uptight, regulation-bound bureaucrats had stopped the excavation. The media decided to portray it as a David and Goliath fight. Little old Augustin Renaud, valiantly struggling to find the man symbolic of French Québec, and the official archeologists and politicians stopping him."

"Serge Croix must have loved that," said Gamache.

Père Sébastien chuckled. "The Chief Archeologist was livid. I had him in here dozens of times over that period, ranting and raving. It wasn't clear how much of his anger was directed at Renaud personally and how much was fear that Renaud might be right, and maybe this little amateur archeologist would make the biggest discovery of anyone's career."

"Champlain."

"The Father of Québec."

"But why is it important? Why're so many people so passionate about where Champlain might be buried?"

"Aren't you?"

"I'm curious, absolutely. And if he was found I'd visit the site and read everything I could about the discovery, but I don't take it personally."

"You think not? I wonder if that's true. I see a lot of people who don't realize they have a belief, a faith, until they're dying, and then they discover it buried deep inside them. There all along."

"But Champlain was a man, not a faith."

"Perhaps at first, but he's become more than that, to some. Come with me."

Père Sébastien stood, bobbed briefly toward the gold crucifix at the altar and hurried out of the vast church. Gamache followed. Up wooden stairs, through back halls and finally into a cramped office, piled high with books and papers. And on the wall two reproductions. One of Christ, crucified, the other of Champlain.

The priest cleared magazines off two chairs and they sat.

"Champlain was a remarkable man, you know, and yet we know almost nothing about him. Even his birthday is a mystery. We don't even know what he looked like. This painting? Does it look familiar?"

He motioned to the one on the wall. It was the image of Champlain every Quebecker knew, every Canadian knew. It showed a man about thirty wearing a green doublet, a lace collar, white gloves and a sword and hilt. His hair was in the style of the 1600s, long, dark and slightly curled. He had a trim beard and moustache. It was a handsome, intelligent face, a lean, athletic face with large, thoughtful eyes.

Samuel de Champlain. Gamache would pick him out of any lineup.

He nodded.

"That's not him," said Père Sébastien.

"It isn't?"

"Look at this." Sébastien pulled a book from the burdened bookcase. Flipping it open he handed it to the Chief Inspector.

"Look familiar?"

There was the painting of a man, slightly pudgy, standing in front of a window with a verdant scene behind him. He was about thirty, wearing a green doublet, a lace collar, white gloves and a sword and hilt. His hair was in the style of the 1600s, long, dark and slightly curled. He had a trim beard and moustache. It was a handsome, intelligent face, with large, thoughtful eyes.

"That's Michel Particelli d'Emery, an accountant for Louis XIII."

"But it's Champlain," said Gamache. "Slightly heavier, and turned in the other direction, but essentially the same man, even down to the clothing."

He handed the book back to the priest, stunned. Father Sébastien was smiling and nodding. "Someone lifted this image, tweaked it to make him look more courageous, more our image of a brave explorer, and called it Champlain."

"But why would anyone have to? If there're paintings of minor aristocrats and tradesmen, isn't there a portrait of Champlain?"

The priest leaned forward, animated. "There's not a single portrait of the man done during his life. We have no idea what he looked like. That's not all. Why wasn't

Champlain ever given a title, or land here? He wasn't even officially the Governor of Québec."

"Have we exaggerated his significance?" asked Gamache and immediately regretted it. Again the priest bristled as though the Chief Inspector had thrown dirt on his idol.

"No. Every document we do have confirms he was the father of Québec. The records were written at the time by the Récollets. They founded the mission and the chapel. Champlain left half his money to them. He had the church built to celebrate the return of Québec from the English. He hated the English you know."

"Hard not to hate an enemy. I suspect the English felt the same about him."

"Perhaps. But it wasn't just because they were enemies. He considered the English the real savages. Considered them cruel, especially to the natives. Reading Champlain's diaries it became clear he'd developed a special relationship with the Huron and Algonquins. They taught him how to live in this country, and gave him detailed information on the waterways.

"He hated the English because they were more interested in slaughtering the Indians than working with them. Don't get me wrong, Champlain saw the Indians as savages too. But he knew he could learn from them and he worried about their immortal souls."

"And their furs?"

"Well, he was a businessman," admitted Père Sébastien.

Gamache looked again at the painting on the wall next to the crucified Christ. "So we don't know what Champlain looked like, when he was born, or where he's buried. What do his diaries tell us about him?"

"That's interesting too. They tell us next to nothing. They're basically agendas about his travels and daily life here, but not his internal life, not his thoughts and feelings. He kept his private life private."

"Even in his own diaries? Why?"

Sébastien put his palms to the ceiling in a stupefied manner. "There're some theories. One is that he was a spy for the King of France, another is even more compelling. Some think he was actually the son of the King. Illegitimate, of course. But that might explain the mystery of his birth and the secrecy surrounding a man who should have been celebrated. It might also explain why he was sent here, to the middle of nowhere."

"You said Augustin Renaud found a lead-lined coffin beneath one of the sanctuaries along with some coins but that the dig was stopped. Could he have been right? Might it be Champlain?"

"Would you like to see?"

Gamache stood. "Please."

They walked back the way they came, each pausing to cross himself, and across the knave to a small grotto area with a tiny altar lit by votives.

"It's through here." Sébastien squeezed behind the altar and through a tiny archway. A flashlight balanced on a rough rock ledge and the priest turned it on, flooding the cramped area. The center of the beam played over the stones and came to rest on a coffin.

Gamache felt a thrill. Could this be him?

"Has it been opened?" Gamache dropped his voice.

"No," whispered the priest. "After all that publicity the city finally agreed to let Renaud continue the dig, under their supervision. Privately the official archeologists were furious, publicly they sounded happy with the compromise. But after more imaging was done and records pored over it was decided this wasn't Champlain but a much more recent coffin of a mid-level curate."

"Are they sure?" Gamache turned to Father Sébastien, barely visible in the gloom. "Are you sure?"

"I was the one who convinced the city to continue the dig. I actually respected Renaud. He didn't have a degree and he wasn't trained, but he wasn't a fool. And he'd found something no one else had, including me."

"But had he found Champlain?"

"Not here. I wanted to believe it was. It would've been a coup for the church, brought in more people, and yes, more money. But when we looked closer and added it all up, it just wasn't going to be Champlain."

"But the coins?"

"They were from the 1600s and confirmed this was once the site of the original chapel and the cemetery, but nothing more."

The two men emerged into the light of the little sanctuary.

"What do you think happened to Champlain, Father?"

The priest paused. "I think after the fire he was reburied. There's a reference to a reburial taking place, but they don't say where, and no official documents exist. This church has burned down a few times, taking valuable records with it each time."

"You've studied Champlain most of your life, what do you think?"

"You asked me earlier why he mattered,

why any of this mattered, and certainly why finding his body matters. It does. Champlain wasn't simply the founder of a colony, there was something different about him, something that separated him from every explorer who'd gone before. And that I think explains how he managed to succeed where others failed. And why he's remembered today, and revered."

"What made him different?"

"He never referred to Québec as New France, you know. In France they did. Later regimes did. But never Champlain. Do you know what he called this place?"

Gamache thought about that. They were in the body of the church again and he stared, almost unseeing, down the long empty path that ended in the golden altar and the saints and martyrs, angels and crucifixes.

"The New World," said Gamache at last.

"The New World," agreed Père Sébastien. "That is why he's loved. He's a symbol of all that is great, all that is brave, all that Québec could have been and might be again. He's a symbol of freedom and sacrifice and vision. He didn't just create a colony, he created a New World. And he's adored for it."

"By the separatists."

"By everyone," the priest eyed Gamache closely. "By yourself included, I think."

"It's true," admitted Gamache and thought of that painting of Samuel de Champlain, and realized it reminded him of someone. Not just the plump and prosperous accountant, but someone else.

Christ. Jesus Christ.

They'd made Champlain look like the savior. And now the man who would raise him was dead. Killed, if you believed the tabloids, by the English, who may very well be also hiding the body of Champlain.

"Could Champlain be buried in the Literary and Historical Society?"

"Not a chance," said Père Sébastien without hesitation. "That was wilderness in his day. They'd not have reburied him there."

Unless, thought Gamache, the founder wasn't quite the saint he'd become.

"Where do you think he is?" Gamache asked, again.

They were standing at the door, on the icy steps of the Basilica.

"Not far."

Before ducking back into the church the priest nodded. Across the street. To the Café Buade.

ELEVEN

It wasn't quite five in the afternoon and the sun was down. Elizabeth MacWhirter looked out the window. A small crowd had been milling outside the Literary and Historical Society all day. A bold few had come inside, almost daring the members to toss them out. Instead Winnie had greeted them, given them the bilingual brochures and invited them to join.

She'd even given some of the more brazen a brief tour of the library, pointing out the fine pillows on the walls, the collection of figs on the shelves and asking if any of them would like to become umlauts.

Not surprisingly few did. But three people actually paid twenty dollars and joined, shamed into it by Winnie's obvious kindness and handicap.

"Did you mention that the night is a strawberry?" Elizabeth asked when Winnie returned with a membership payment.

"I did. They didn't disagree. Ready?"

Before turning out the lights and locking up they checked the main library. More than once they'd locked poor Mr. Blake in, but his chair was empty. He'd already gone across to the rectory.

The crowd had disappeared, the dark and cold having killed curiosity. The two women walked cautiously over the path of hardened snow, planting their feet firmly and carefully. Watching their own steps, watching each other's.

In winter the very ground seemed to reach up and grab the elderly, yanking them to earth as though hungry for them. Shattering a hip or wrist, or neck. Best to take it slow.

Their destination wasn't far. They could see the lights through the windows of the rectory. It was a lovely stone building, gracious in proportions with tall windows to catch every ray of a miserly winter sun. Walking slowly, side by side, Elizabeth could feel her cheeks freeze in just this short stroll. Their feet squeaked on the snow, making a sound she'd heard for almost eighty years. A sound she'd never trade for waves lapping on a Florida shore.

Lights were appearing in homes and restaurants, reflecting off the white snow. It was a city that lent itself to winter, and to darkness. It became even cozier, more inviting, more magical, like a fairy-tale kingdom. And we're the peasants, thought Elizabeth with a wry smile.

As they crept up the walk they could see through the window the fire in the hearth and Tom handing around drinks. Mr. Blake and Porter were already there and Ken Haslam was sitting in an armchair, reading a newspaper.

He missed nothing, Elizabeth knew. It was a mistake to underestimate Ken, as people had all his life. People always dismissed the quiet ones, which was ironic in Ken's case, Elizabeth knew. She also knew why he was quiet. But she'd never tell a soul.

Elizabeth MacWhirter knew everything, and forgot nothing.

The two women entered the rectory without knocking, took off their coats and boots and before long they too were in front of the roaring fire in the large living room. Porter handed a Scotch to Winnie and a sherry to Elizabeth and the two women sat beside each other on the sofa.

It was a room they knew well from the intimate chamber music concerts, from the tea parties and cocktail parties. From the lunches and bridge parties and dinners.

Larger community events were held in the church hall just across the way, but this home had become the center of their more intimate gatherings.

Elizabeth noticed Ken's lips were moving. He smiled and she smiled.

Being with Ken was like being with a permanently foreign friend. It was impossible to understand them, but all you really needed to do was reflect back their own expressions. When Ken looked sad, they looked sad. When he looked happy, they smiled. It was actually very relaxing to be around him. Not much was expected.

"Well, I've had quite a day," said Porter, rocking on his feet in front of the fire. "Spent most of it giving interviews. Taped Jacquie Czernin's show for CBC Radio. It'll be on any minute. Want to hear it?"

He walked over to the stereo and turned on the CBC.

"I must've done ten interviews today," Porter said, guarding the radio.

"I did the crossword puzzle," said Mr. Blake. "Very satisfying. What's a six-letter word for 'idiot'?"

"Do proper names count?" asked Tom with a smile.

"Oh, here it comes." Porter turned up the volume.

"As we heard in the news," a melodious woman's voice said, "the amateur archeologist Augustin Renaud was found dead yesterday morning at the Literary and Historical Society. Police confirm he was murdered though they haven't made any arrests yet.

"Porter Wilson is the President of the Lit and His and he joins me now. Hello, Mr. Wilson."

"Hello Jacquie."

Porter looked around the rectory living room, expecting applause for his brilliance so far.

"What can you tell us about the death of Mr. Renaud?"

"I can tell you that I didn't do it."

Porter on the radio laughed. Porter in the rectory laughed. No one else did.

"But why was he there?"

"Frankly, we don't know. We're shocked, as you can imagine. It's tragic. Such a respected member of the community."

Porter, in the rectory, was nodding in agreement with himself.

"For God's sake, Porter, turn it off," said Mr. Blake, struggling out of his chair. "Don't be a horse's ass."

"No, wait," Porter stood before the stereo, blocking it. "It gets better. Listen."

255

"Can you describe what happened?"

"Well, Jacquie, I was in the office of the Lit and His when the telephone repairman arrived. I'd called him because the telephones weren't working. They should have been because, as you know, we're in the middle of a huge restoration of the library. In fact, you've helped us with the fundraisers."

What followed were five excruciating minutes of Porter plugging the fundraising and the interviewer desperately trying to get him to talk about anything other than himself.

Finally she cut off the interview and went to music.

"Is it over?" Tom asked. "Can I stop praying now?"

"What were you thinking?" Winnie asked Porter.

"What d'you mean? I was thinking this was a great chance to get more donations for the library."

"A man was murdered," snapped Winnie. "Honestly, Porter, this wasn't a marketing opportunity."

As they argued Elizabeth went back to reading the press. The papers were full of the Renaud murder. There were photographs of the astonishing-looking man, there were tributes, eulogies, editorials. He was barely cold and already he'd risen, a new man. Respected, beloved, brilliant and on the verge of finding Champlain.

In the Literary and Historical Society, apparently.

One paper, *La Presse,* had discovered that Renaud had approached the board shortly before his death and been turned down. Something that had seemed so reasonable, just following procedure, now seemed ominous, suspicious.

But the most disconcerting of all was the astonishment in all the French papers. Just as shocking as the discovery of Augustin Renaud's dead body was the discovery of so many live bodies, so many Anglo bodies, among them all this time.

Quebec City seemed to only now be awakening to the fact that the English were still there.

"How could they not know we're here?" said Winnie, reading over Elizabeth's shoulder.

Elizabeth had felt the sting too. It was one thing to be vilified, to be seen as suspects, as threats. Even to be seen as the enemy, she was prepared for all that. What she was unprepared for was not being seen at all.

When had that happened? When had they

disappeared, become ghosts in their home town? Elizabeth looked over at Mr. Blake who'd also lowered his newspaper and was staring ahead.

"What're you thinking?"

"That it must be dinner time," he said.

Yes, thought Elizabeth, going back to reading, best not to underestimate the English.

"I was also remembering 1966."

Elizabeth lowered her paper.

"What do you mean?"

"But you remember, Elizabeth. You were there. I was telling Tom about it just a week or so ago."

Elizabeth looked over at their minister, so young and vibrant. Laughing with Porter, charming the prickly old man. He hadn't even been born in 1966 but she remembered it as though it was yesterday.

The thugs arriving. The Québec flag waving. The insults. *Maudits Anglais. Têtes Carré* and worse. The singing outside the Literary and Historical Society. *Gens du Pays.* The separatist anthem, with such achingly beautiful words, hurled as an insult at the building and to the frightened Anglos inside.

Then the attack, the separatists racing through the doors and up the sweeping staircase, into the library itself. Into the very heart of the Lit and His. Then the smoke, the books on fire. She'd run, trying to stop them, trying to put out the fires, pleading with them to stop. In her perfect French, appealing to them. Porter and Mr. Blake and Winnie and others, trying to stop it. The smoke, the shouting, the breaking glass.

She'd looked over and seen Porter breaking the fine leaded glass windows, windows that had been in place for centuries, now shattered. And she saw him tossing books out, at random. Handfuls, armfuls. And Mr. Blake joining him. While the separatists burned the books, the Anglos threw them out the windows, their covers splaying as though trying to take flight.

Winnie, Porter, Ken, Mr. Blake and others, saving their history before saving themselves.

Yes. She did remember.

Armand Gamache got home just in time for Henri's dinner then they went for a walk. The streets of Québec were dark, but they were also clogged with revelers celebrating Carnaval. Rue St-Jean had been closed and filled with entertainment. Choirs, jugglers, fiddlers.

Man and dog wove in and out of the crowds, stopping now and then to appreciate the music, or to people watch. It was one of Henri's favorite things, after the Chuck-it. And bananas. And dinner time. Lots of people stopped and made a fuss of the young shepherd with the unnaturally large ears. Gamache, beside him, might as well have been a lamppost.

Henri lapped up the attention, then they went home where the Chief Inspector glanced at the clock. Past five. He made a call.

"Oui allô?"

"Inspector Langlois?"

"Ah, Chief Inspector, I was just about to call you with an update."

"Any news?"

"Not much, I'm afraid. You know what these things are like. If we don't find someone immediately then it becomes a slog. This is a slog. I'm just over at Augustin Renaud's home." He hesitated. "You wouldn't want to come, would you? It's not far from where you are."

"I'd love to see it."

"Bring your reading glasses and a sandwich. And a couple of beers."

"That bad?"

"Unbelievable. I don't know how people live like this."

Gamache got the address, played with

Henri for a few minutes, wrote a note for Émile, then left. On the way he stopped at Paillard, the marvelous bakery on rue St-Jean, and at a *dépanneur* for beer then headed up rue Ste-Ursule, pausing to check the address he'd been given, unconvinced he had it right.

But no. There it was. 93/4 rue Ste-Ursule. He shook his head. 93/4.

It would figure that Augustin Renaud would live there. He lived a marginal life, why not in a fractional home? Gamache walked down the short tunnel and into a small courtyard. Knocking, he waited a moment then entered.

He'd been in homes of every description in his thirty years of investigating crime. Hovels, glass and marble trophy homes, caves even. He'd seen hideous conditions, and uncovered hideous things and yet he was constantly surprised by how people lived.

But Augustin Renaud's home was exactly as Armand Gamache had imagined it would be. Small, cluttered, papers, journals, books piled everywhere. It was certainly a fire hazard, and yet the Chief had to admit he felt more at home here than in the glass and marble wonders.

"Anybody here?" he called.

"Through here. In the living room. Or maybe it's the dining room. Hard to say."

Gamache followed the trail cleared, like snow, through the paper and found Inspector Langlois bent over a desk reading. He looked up and smiled.

"Champlain. Every single scrap of paper's about Champlain. I didn't think this much had been written about the man."

Gamache picked up a magazine from the top of a stack, an old *National Geographic* detailing the first explorations of what is now New England. There was a reference to Champlain, whose name was on Lake Champlain in Vermont.

"My people are going through it all slowly," said Langlois. "But I estimate it will take forever."

"Would you like some help?"

Langlois looked relieved. "Yes, please. Could you?"

Gamache smiled and placing two bags on the desk he brought out an assortment of sandwiches and a couple of beers.

"Perfect. I haven't even had lunch yet."

"Busy day," said Gamache.

Langlois nodded, taking a huge bite from a roast beef, hot mustard and tomato sandwich on a baguette then took a swig of beer.

"We've only really had a chance to fingerprint and get DNA samples here. Even that's taken two days. The forensics people have been through and now the work begins." He glanced round.

Gamache pulled up a chair, grabbed a baguette filled with thick sliced maple-cured ham, brie and arugula and took a beer. For the next few hours the two men went through Augustin Renaud's home, organizing it, separating his original papers from photocopies of other people's works.

Gamache found reproductions of Champlain's diaries and scanned them. They were as Père Sébastien had said, little more than "to do" lists. It was a fascinating insight into everyday life in Québec in the early 1600s, but it could have been written by anyone. There was certainly no personal information. Gamache came away with no feeling for the man.

"Found anything?" Langlois wiped a weary hand across his face and looked up.

"Copies of Champlain's diary, but nothing else."

"Don't you think Renaud must have kept a journal or a diary himself?"

Gamache looked round the room and into the next, seeing stack after stack of papers. Bookcases stuffed to bursting, closets filled with magazines. "We might find some yet.

Have you found any personal papers at all?"
Gamache took off his reading glasses and
looked across the desk at Langlois.

"Some letters from people replying to
Renaud. I've made a file, but most seem to
just be telling him with varying degrees of
civility that he was wrong."

"About what?"

"Oh, different theories he had about
Champlain. That he was a spy, or the son of
the King, or even that he was Protestant. As
one said, if he was a Huguenot why give
most of his money to the Catholic Church
in his will? It was like all of Renaud's
theories. Close, but just a little wacky."

Gamache thought Langlois was being
charitable by calling Renaud "a little"
wacky. He glanced at his watch. Ten to eight.

"Are you still hungry?"

"Starving."

"Great. Let me take you to dinner. There's
a place just down the street I've been dying
to try."

On their way they stopped at a shop so
Langlois could pick up a nice bottle of red
wine then they carefully made their way just
a few steps down the slide that was rue Ste-
Ursule, to a hole-in-the-wall restaurant in
the basement.

As soon as they entered they were met by

warmth, by rich Moroccan spices and by the owner who introduced himself, took their coats and wine and led them to a quiet corner table by a wall of exposed stone.

He returned a moment later with the wine uncorked, two glasses and menus. After ordering they compared notes. Gamache told the Inspector about his day and his conversations with the members of the Champlain Society and Père Sébastien.

"Well, that dovetails nicely with my day. Among other things I spent much of it in the basement of the Literary and Historical Society with one very annoyed archeologist."

"Serge Croix?"

"Exactly. Not pleased to be called out on a Sunday, though he did admit it often happens. They're like doctors, I suppose. On call all the time in case someone suddenly digs up bones or an old wall or piece of pottery. Apparently it's quite common in Québec."

Their dinners arrived, steaming, fragrant plates of lamb tagine with couscous and stewed vegetables.

"Croix brought a couple of technicians and a metal-detector thing. But more sophisticated than anything I'd seen before."

Gamache tore a piece of baguette off the

loaf and dipped it in the tagine juices. "Did he think Renaud might have been right? That Champlain was there?"

"Not for a moment, but he felt they at least had to look, if only to tell reporters that Renaud was wrong, yet again."

"And never again," said Gamache.

"Hmm." Langlois was enjoying his dinner, as was Gamache.

"So you didn't find anything?"

"Potatoes and some turnips."

"It was a root cellar, I suppose that makes sense." Still, while Gamache was relieved for the English, he was a little disappointed. Part of him hoped Renaud had finally, perhaps fatally, gotten it right.

So why had he been killed? And why had he been at the Lit and His?

What did he want to talk to the board about?

But really, thought Gamache, whether Champlain was buried there or not was irrelevant. All that mattered was what Renaud believed. And what he could make others believe, which seemed was just about anything.

After dinner Langlois and Gamache parted ways, the Inspector to go home to his wife and family and the Chief Inspector to return to Renaud's home and sort through more papers.

An hour later he found them, hidden behind books two rows deep on the bookcase. The diaries of Augustin Renaud.

TWELVE

Jean-Guy Beauvoir got back to Three Pines by mid-afternoon after his visits to Olivier in prison and the antique shop in Montreal. He'd stopped at the Tim Hortons at exit 55 for a sandwich, a chocolate glazed doughnut and a double double coffee.

And now he was tired.

This was way more activity than he'd had since it had all happened, and he knew he needed to rest. At the B and B he had a long, luxurious bath and thought about what to do next.

Olivier had dropped a bombshell. Now he was saying the Hermit's name wasn't Jakob, and he wasn't even Czech. He'd only said that to spread round the guilt, put attention onto the Parras and the other Czech families in the areas.

Not only was that not very neighborly, it wasn't very effective. They'd still decided Olivier was the murderer and the courts had agreed.

OK. So. Beauvoir slipped deeper into the tub. Soaping himself he barely even noticed the ragged scar on his abdomen anymore. What he did notice was that his muscles were no longer toned. He wasn't fat, but he was flabby from inactivity. Still, he could feel his strength slowly returning, more slowly than he would have imagined.

He cleared his mind of those thoughts and instead concentrated on what the Chief had asked him to do. Quietly reopen Olivier's case.

Where do the day's findings leave us? he wondered.

But nothing came to mind except his large, inviting bed which he could see through the bathroom door, with its crisp white sheets and down duvet and soft pillows.

Ten minutes later the bath was drained, the *Do Not Disturb* sign was outside his door and Jean-Guy was fast asleep, warm and safe under the covers.

He awoke to darkness and rolling over contentedly he looked at the bedside clock. 5:30. He sat up. 5:30? A.M. or P.M.?

Had he been asleep for two hours or fourteen? He felt rested but it could be either.

Putting on the light he got dressed then stood on the landing outside his door. The B and B was quiet. A couple of lights were on, but they often were. Feeling disoriented, disconcerted, he went downstairs and looking out the bay window of the B and B he had his answer.

Lights were on at the homes around the village green and they glowed bright and cheery at the bistro. Happy that he was in for dinner and not breakfast Jean-Guy threw on his coat and boots and crunched across the green to be greeted inside by Gabri who was, unexpectedly, in his pajamas.

Beauvoir was back to his original question. Was it A.M. or P.M.? He was damned if he was going to ask.

"Welcome back. I hear you spent last night in the woods with the saint. Was it as much fun as it sounds? You don't look converted."

Beauvoir looked at the large man in pajamas and slippers and decided not to tell him what he looked like.

"What can I get you, *patron?*" asked Gabri when Beauvoir didn't respond.

What did he want? Scrambled eggs or a beer?

"A beer would be great, *merci.*" He took the micro-brewery ale and found a comfortable wing chair by the window. A paper lay on the table and picking it up, he read about the murder of Augustin Renaud in Quebec City. The mad archeologist.

"May I join you?"

He looked at Clara Morrow. She was also in pajamas and a dressing gown and, he glanced down, slippers. Could this be a new, and nightmarish, fashion trend? How long had he slept? While he knew flannel was an aphrodisiac to Anglos, it did nothing for Beauvoir. He'd never, ever worn it and didn't plan to start.

Glancing around he noticed every third or fourth person was in a dressing gown. He'd always secretly suspected this was not a village but an out-patient clinic from an asylum, now he had his proof.

"Here for your meds?" he asked as she sat.

Clara laughed and held up her beer. "Always." She nodded at his Maudite beer. "You too?"

Leaning forward he whispered, "What time is it?"

"Six." When he still stared she added, "In the evening."

"Then why . . ." He indicated her get-up.

"After Olivier was arrested it took Gabri a while to really function, so some of us

271

helped out. He didn't want to open on Sundays, but Myrna and I convinced him to and he finally agreed, on one condition."

"Pajamas?"

"You are clever," she smiled. "He didn't want to have to get dressed. After a while most of us started doing the same thing, showing up in our pajamas. It's very relaxing. I stay in them all day."

Beauvoir tried to look disapproving but had to admit, she did look comfortable. She completed the look by having bed-head, though that was nothing new. Her hair always stuck out in all directions, probably where she ran her hands through it. And that would also account for the crumbs in there, and the flecks of paint.

He tried to think of something friendly to say, something that would lead her to believe he was there because he liked their company.

"Do you have your art show soon?"

"A couple of months." She took a long haul of her beer. "When I'm not practicing my interview for the *New York Times* and *Oprah* I try not to think about it."

"Oprah?"

"Yes. It'll be a huge tribute show, to me. All the top art critics will be there, weeping of course, overwhelmed by my insight, by the power of my images. Oprah will buy a few pieces for 100 million each. Sometimes it's 50 million, sometimes 150 million."

"So she's getting a bit of a bargain today."

"I'm feeling generous."

He laughed, surprising himself. He'd never had an actual conversation with Clara. With any of them. The Chief had. Somehow he'd managed to become friends with most of them but Beauvoir had never been able to pass through that membrane, to see people as both suspects and human. He'd never wanted to. The idea repulsed him.

He watched her take some mixed nuts and sip on her beer.

"Can I ask you something?" he said.

"Sure."

"Do you think Olivier killed the Hermit?"

Her hand stopped on its way for more nuts. He'd dropped his voice as he spoke, making sure they weren't overheard. She lowered her hand and thought for a good minute before answering.

"I don't know. I wish I could say absolutely he didn't, but the evidence is so strong. And if he didn't then someone else did."

She casually looked around the room, and he followed her gaze.

There was Old Mundin and The Wife. The handsome young couple was dining with the Parras. Old, despite his name, wasn't yet thirty and was a carpenter. He also restored Olivier's antiques and had been among the last people in the bistro the night the Hermit was killed. The Wife, Beauvoir knew, had an actual name though he'd forgotten what it was as had, he suspected, most people. What had started as a joke, the young couple mocking their married state, had become reality. She was The Wife. They had a young son, Charlie, who had Down syndrome.

Glancing at the child Beauvoir remembered that had been one of the reasons people considered Dr. Vincent Gilbert a saint. His decision to abandon a lucrative career to live in a community of people with Down syndrome, to care for them. From that experience he'd written the book *Being*. It was by most accounts a book of staggering honesty and humility. Staggering because it had been written by such an asshole.

Well, as Clara often told them, great works of creation often were.

Sitting with Old and The Wife were Roar and Hanna Parra. They'd been among the main suspects. Roar was cutting the paths

274

through the woods and could have found the cabin with its priceless contents and shabby old occupant.

But why take the life and leave the treasure?

The same question held true for their son, Havoc Parra. Clara and Beauvoir glanced over at him, waiting a table by the other fireplace. He'd worked late in the bistro the night the Hermit had been killed and had closed up.

Had he followed Olivier through the woods and found the cabin?

Had he looked inside, seen the treasures, and realized what it meant? It meant no more tips, no more tables, no more smiling at rude customers. No wondering what the future held.

It meant freedom. And all he'd have to do was knock a solitary old man on the head. But, again, why were most of the priceless treasures still in the cabin?

Across the room were Marc and Dominique Gilbert. The owners of the inn and spa. In their mid-forties they'd escaped high-paying, high-pressure jobs in Montreal, to come to Three Pines. They'd bought the wreck on the hill and turned it into a magnificent hotel.

Olivier despised Marc and it was mutual.

Had the Gilberts bought the run-down old home because the Hermit and the cabin came with it? Buried in their woods?

And finally there was the asshole saint Dr. Vincent Gilbert, Marc's estranged father who'd appeared at exactly the same time as the body. How could that have been a coincidence?

Clara's gaze returned to Beauvoir just as the bistro door slammed shut.

"Goddamned snow."

Beauvoir didn't have to look round to know who it was. "Ruth," he whispered to Clara, who nodded. "Still crazy?"

"After all these years," Clara confirmed.

"Jeez," Ruth appeared at Beauvoir's chair, a scowl on her deeply wrinkled face. Her cropped white hair lay flat on her head, looking like exposed skull. She was tall and stooped and walked with a cane. The only good news was that she wasn't in her nightgown.

"Welcome to the bistro," she snarled, giving Clara the once over. "Where dignity goes to die."

"And not just dignity," said Beauvoir.

She gave a barking laugh. "You find another body?"

"I don't follow bodies, you know. I have a life outside of work."

"God, I'm bored already," said the old poet. "Say something smart."

Beauvoir was silent, looking at her with disdain.

"Thought so." She took a swig of his beer. "Blech, this is crap. Can't you drink something decent? Havoc! Get him a Scotch."

"You old hag," Beauvoir murmured.

"Oh, banter. Very clever."

She intercepted his Scotch and stomped away. When she'd gotten far enough Beauvoir leaned across the table to Clara, who also leaned forward. The bistro was noisy with laughter and conversation, perfect for a quiet talk.

"If not Olivier," said Beauvoir, keeping his voice down and a sharp eye on the room, "who?"

"I don't know. What makes you think it wasn't Olivier?"

Beauvoir hesitated. Should he cross the Rubicon? But he knew he already had.

"This must go no further. Olivier knows we're looking into it, but I've told him to keep quiet. And you too."

"Don't worry, but why're you telling me this?"

Why indeed? Because she was the best of a bad lot.

"I need your help. You obviously know

everyone way better than I do. The Chief's worried. Gabri keeps asking him why Olivier would move the body. It makes sense if he found the Hermit already dead but if you've just killed someone in a remote place you're almost certainly not going to advertise. The Chief thinks we might have gotten it wrong. What do you think?"

She was obviously taken aback by the question. She thought about it before slowly answering. "I think Gabri will never believe Olivier did it, even if he'd witnessed it himself, but I also think that's a good question. Where do we begin?"

We, thought Beauvoir, there is no "we." There's "me" and "you." In that order. But he needed her so he swallowed the retort, pasted a smile on his face and answered.

"Well, Olivier now says the Hermit wasn't Czech."

Clara rolled her eyes and ran her fingers through her hair which now stood out on both sides like Bozo. Beauvoir grimaced, but Clara neither noticed nor cared. Her mind was on other things. "Honestly, that man. Any other lies he's admitting to?"

"Not so far. He thought the Hermit was Québécois or perhaps English but completely fluent in French. All his books were English and the ones he asked Olivier to find for him were also English. But he spoke perfect French."

"How can I help?"

He thought for a moment then made a decision. "I've brought the case file. I'd like you to read it."

She nodded.

"And since you know everyone here I'd like you to sometimes ask questions."

Clara hesitated. She didn't like the idea of being a spy but if he was right then an innocent man was in prison and a murderer was among them. Almost certainly in the room with them at that moment.

Myrna and Peter arrived and Beauvoir joined them for a bistro dinner, ordering the filet mignon with cognac blue cheese sauce. They chatted about various events in the village, the ski conditions at Mont Saint-Rémy, the Canadiens game the night before.

Ruth came by for dessert, eating most of Peter's cheesecake, then she limped off alone into the night.

"She misses Rosa terribly," said Myrna.

"What happened to her duck?" asked Beauvoir.

"Flew off in the fall," said Myrna.

The duck was smarter than it looked, thought Beauvoir.

"I dread the spring," said Clara. "Ruth'll

be expecting her back. Suppose she doesn't come."

"It doesn't mean Rosa's dead," said Peter, though they all knew that wasn't true. Rosa the duck was raised from birth, literally hatched, by Ruth. And against all odds, Rosa had survived and thrived and had grown up, to follow Ruth everywhere she went.

The duck and the fuck, as Gabri called them.

And then last fall Rosa did what ducks do, what was in her nature to do. As much as she loved Ruth, she had to go. And one afternoon, as other ducks quacked and flew in formation overhead, heading south, Rosa rose up.

And left.

After dinner Beauvoir thanked them and got up. Clara walked him to the door.

"I'll do it," she whispered.

Beauvoir handed her the dossier and headed into the cold dark night. Walking slowly back to the B and B toward his warm bed, he stopped partway across the village green and looked at the three tall pine trees still wearing their multi-color Christmas lights. The colors bounced off the drifts of fresh snow. Looking up he saw the stars and smelled the fresh, crisp air. Behind him he heard people calling good night to each other and heard their scrunching steps in the snow.

Jean-Guy Beauvoir changed direction and arriving at the old clapboard home he knocked. The door was opened a crack.

"Can I come in?" he asked.

Ruth stepped back and opened her door.

Armand Gamache sat at Renaud's messy desk, bent over the diaries. For the past couple of hours he'd read them, making notes now and then. Like Champlain's diaries, Augustin Renaud's spoke of events but not feelings. They were really more of an agenda, but they were informative.

Sadly, while Renaud had made a note of the time of the Literary and Historical Society board meeting there was no indication why he was interested. And there was no mention of meeting anyone later in the day or that evening.

The next day was blank, though there was a notation for the following week. *SC at 1pm on the Thursday.*

The days stretched ahead, empty. Pages and pages, white and barren. A winter life. Not a lunch with a friend, not a meeting, not a personal comment. Nothing.

But what about his immediate past?

There were notations about books, page references, library references, articles. He'd made notes, done sketches of the old city, written addresses. Places, perhaps, he was considering for his next dig? All of them around the Notre-Dame Basilica.

It appeared he'd never considered any site outside a quite tight radius. Then what was he doing in the relative wilderness of the Lit and His? And if he was there simply to look for a book, as Émile had suggested, why was he in the basement, digging? And why ask to speak to the board?

Jean-Guy Beauvoir and Ruth Zardo stared at each other.

It felt like a cage match. Only one would emerge alive. Not for the first time in Ruth's company, Beauvoir felt an unpleasant retraction below his belt.

"What do you want?" Ruth demanded.

"I want to talk," snapped Beauvoir.

"Can't it wait, asshole?"

"No, it can't, you lunatic." He paused. "Do you like me?"

Her eyes narrowed. "I think you're anal, idiotic, cruel and perhaps slightly retarded."

"And I think the same of you," he said, relieved. It was as he thought, as he'd hoped.

"Well, glad we got that straight. Thank you

for coming by, now, nighty night." Ruth reached for the doorknob.

"Wait," Beauvoir said, his hand out, almost touching her withered arm. "Wait," he said again, almost in a whisper. And Ruth did.

Gamache leaned closer to the diary, a small smile on his face.

Literary and Historical Society.

There it was. Written as bold as could be in Renaud's diary. Not for the day of the board meeting, the day he died, but a week earlier. And above it the names of four people he'd planned to meet there.

A Chin, a JD and two people named S. Patrick and F. O'Mara. Beneath that was a number 18-something. Gamache slid the desk lamp over so that the light pooled on the page. 1800, or maybe 1869 or 8.

"Or is it 1809?" Gamache mumbled to himself, squinting and flipping to the next page to see if, from the back, it was any clearer. It wasn't.

He took off his reading glasses and leaned back in the chair, tapping the glasses absently on his knee.

1800 would make sense. That would be a time, six in the evening. Most Québécois used the twenty-four-hour clock. But —

The Chief Inspector stared into space. It actually didn't make sense. The Lit and His closed at five in the afternoon. 1700 hours.

Why would Renaud arrange to meet four people there an hour after closing?

Maybe, thought Gamache, one of them had a key and would let them in.

Or, maybe Renaud didn't realize the library would be closed.

Or, maybe he'd arranged to meet someone else there, a Lit and His volunteer not named who would open the door.

Had Augustin Renaud been to the Literary and Historical Society before the day he died? It seemed so. Not walking in like any normal patron, that didn't seem Renaud's style. No, the man needed something more dramatic, clandestine. This was a man, after all, who'd managed to break into the Basilica and start digging. The Literary and Historical Society would pose no physical or moral barrier. No door was locked to Augustin Renaud in his Quixotic quest for Champlain.

Gamache looked at his watch. It was after 11 P.M. Too late to call Elizabeth MacWhirter or any of the other board members, or to drop by. He wanted to see their faces when he asked the question.

He turned back to the diary. What wasn't

in question were Renaud's feelings about this rendezvous. He'd circled it a few times and even made a couple of exclamation marks.

The amateur archeologist seemed exult-ant, as though arranging the meeting had been a coup. Gamache found the phone book and looked up Chin. It sounded like a Chinese name and he remembered that Au-gustin Renaud had once, famously, dug through a wall looking for Champlain and ended up in the basement of a Chinese restaurant.

Could Chin be the name of the restaurant, or the owner?

But there was no Chin. Perhaps it was someone's first name. There weren't many Chinese in Quebec City, it wouldn't be hard to find out.

There were no O'Maras, but there was an S. Patrick living on rue des Jardins, in the old city. Gamache knew it. The small street wound along beside the Ursuline convent and ended right in front of the Notre-Dame Basilica.

And his address? 1809 rue des Jardins. 1809. Not a time then, but a street number. Were they to meet there first then head to the Lit and His?

There were a few other names in Renaud's

diary, mostly, it seemed, officials he was arguing with or editors who'd turned down his manuscripts. Serge Croix, the Chief Archeologist, was mentioned a few times, always with the word *merde* as though his name was hyphenated. Serge Croix-Merde.

Booksellers, mostly used, figured large in Augustin Renaud's life. It seemed if he had a relationship with anyone it was with them. Gamache jotted down their names then looked at his watch.

It was almost midnight, and Beauvoir was sitting on a plastic garden chair in Ruth's kitchen. He'd never been in her home before. Gamache had, a few times, but Beauvoir had always begged off those interviews.

He disliked the wretched old poet immensely which was why he was there.

"OK, dick-head, talk."

Ruth sat across from him, a pot of watery tea on the white pre-formed table, and one cup. Her thin arms were strapped across her chest, as though trying to keep her innards in. But not her heart, Beauvoir knew. That had escaped years before, like the duck. In time all things fled Ruth.

He needed to talk to someone, but someone without a heart, without compassion.

Someone who didn't care.

"You know what happened?" he asked.

"I read the papers you know."

"It wasn't all in the papers."

There was a pause. "Go on." Her voice was hard, unfeeling. Perfect.

"I was sitting in the Chief's office —"

"I'm bored already. Is this going to be a long story?"

Beauvoir glared at her. "The call came at 11:18 in the morning."

She snorted. "Exactly?"

He met her eyes. "Exactly."

He saw again the Chief's corner office. It was early December and Montreal was cold and gray through the windows. They'd been discussing a difficult case in Gaspé when the Chief's secretary opened the door. She had a call. It was the Inspector in Ste-Agathe. There'd been a shooting. An agent down and one missing.

But he wasn't missing, he was on the phone asking to speak to the Chief.

Things happened quickly after that, and yet seemed to go on forever.

Agents poured in, the tactical teams were alerted. Satellites, imaging, analysis. Tracing. All swung into action. Within moments there was a near frenzy of activity visible through the large window in the Chief's office. All going to a protocol Chief Inspector Gamache had designed.

But in his office there was quiet. Calm.

"I'm sorry, I'm so sorry," Agent Morin said, when connected to the Chief.

"It's not your fault. Are you hurt?" Gamache had asked.

By now Beauvoir was listening on the other line. For reasons he didn't yet understand they'd so far been unable to trace the call and the man who held Agent Morin and had shot the other agent seemed unconcerned. He'd handed the phone back to the young agent but not before making something clear.

He would neither let Morin go, nor would he kill him. Instead, he'd bind the young agent and leave him there.

"Thank you," said Gamache.

Through the glass Beauvoir could see agents at computers, recording, listening in, pin-pointing the location of the call. He could even see their fingers flying over the keys.

They'd know where Agent Morin was being held within moments. But Beauvoir felt a little uneasy. Why was it taking so long? This should be almost instantaneous.

"You'll follow me, I know you will," the farmer was saying. "So I need you not to."

"I won't," lied Gamache.

"Maybe," the man said in his broad country accent. "But I can't risk it."

Something stirred inside Beauvoir and he looked at Gamache. The Chief was standing, staring ahead, concentrating, listening, thinking. Trying not to make a mistake.

"What have you done?" Gamache asked, his voice hard, unyielding.

There was a pause. "I've tied your agent up and attached something to him."

"What?"

"It's something I made myself." The man's voice was defensive, weak, explaining. It was a fearful voice and that meant unpredictable and that meant trouble. The worst possible hostage-taker to deal with, they could panic at any moment. Their reason had fled and they were going on nerves not judgment.

"What is it?" Gamache asked.

Beauvoir knew what the Chief was doing. He was trying to become the sturdy center, the thing a weak, fearful man would move toward. Something firm, solid, predictable. Strong.

"From fertilizer. I didn't want to but it's the only way you'll leave me alone."

The voice was becoming more and more difficult to understand. The combination of the thick accent and words muffled by desperation.

"It's set to go off in twenty-four hours. At 11:18 tomorrow morning."

Beauvoir wrote that down, though he doubted he'd forget it. And he was right.

He heard the Chief inhale sharply, then pause, trying to control his anger.

"This is a mistake," he said, his voice steady. "You must dismantle that bomb. You're making this worse for yourself."

"Worse? How could it be worse? That other agent's dead. I killed a Sûreté agent."

"We don't know that."

"I do."

"Then you know we'll find you eventually. You don't want to spend your whole life running, do you? Wondering where we are?"

There was a hesitation.

"Give yourself up," said Gamache, his voice deep and calm and reasonable. A smart friend with a good idea. "I promise you won't be hurt. Tell me where to meet you."

Beauvoir stared at the Chief and the Chief stared at the wall, at the huge map of Québec. Both willing the man to see reason.

"I can't. I need to go. Good-bye."

"Stop," Gamache called into the phone, then contained himself with great effort.

"Stop. Wait. Don't do this thing. If you run you'll regret it the rest of your life. If you hurt Paul Morin you'll regret it."

His voice was barely more than a whisper, but even Beauvoir felt his skin grow cold from the threat in Gamache's voice.

"I have no choice. There's one other thing."

"What?"

Outside in the homicide offices more sophisticated equipment was being set up. Beauvoir could see Chief Superintendent Francoeur striding toward the Chief's door. Gamache also saw him and turned his back, fully focused on the voice at the other end of the line.

"I don't want you coming after me."

The door opened and Chief Superintendent Francoeur stepped in, his distinguished, handsome face determined. Gamache's back remained to him. Inspector Beauvoir took Francoeur by the arm.

"You need to leave, sir."

"No, I need to speak to the Chief Inspector."

They were outside the door now. "The Chief is on the line with the hostage-taker."

"With the murderer. Agent Bissonette died of his wounds five minutes ago."

He thrust his right hand into his jacket

pocket. It was a signal they all knew, a sign the Chief Superintendent was agitated, angry. The room, previously a buzz of activity, grew still and silent except for the two voices, loud and clear. The Chief, and the killer, over the monitors.

"I'm taking over here," said Francoeur and made for the door again but Beauvoir blocked him.

"You might take over, I can't stop you, but this is Chief Inspector Gamache's private office and he needs privacy."

As the two men stared at each other they heard Gamache's voice.

"You have to stop this," said the Chief. "Give yourself up."

"I can't. I killed that cop." Now his voice had risen almost to hysterics.

"Then even more reason to surrender yourself to me. I'll guarantee your safety." The Chief sounded reasonable, convincing.

"I have to get away."

"Then why didn't you just leave? Why call me?"

"Because I needed to."

There was a pause. Beauvoir could see the Chief in profile now. He saw his eyes narrow and his brows lower.

"What have you done?" Gamache almost whispered.

■ ■ ■ ■

Gamache packed up the diaries and left a scribbled receipt with his address and phone number on Renaud's desk, then he walked back through the streets.

It was past midnight and the revelers were just revving up. He could hear hoots on the plastic horns and unintelligible shouts a few streets over.

College kids, drunk and rowdy.

Gamache smiled. Some would end up in jail getting sober. It would make a great story one day, for disbelieving grandchildren.

A rowdy gang of young men rounded the corner and stumbled up rue Ste-Ursule. Then one spotted Gamache and stopped. The others, blind drunk, bumped into him and started shoving. A small skirmish broke out but the leader pulled them apart and nodded toward Gamache, who was standing in the middle of the road in front of them.

Watching.

They stared at each other, then Gamache smiled.

"Bonne nuit," he said to them, putting his large mittened hand on the leader's shoulder

as he passed.

"Really?" said Ruth. "You can make a bomb out of shit?" She seemed interested. "I don't believe it."

"Chemical fertilizer, not shit. And don't believe it. I don't care," said Beauvoir. In fact, he preferred it that way. There were times he didn't believe it himself. They were the best times. "Hag," he mumbled.

"Numb nuts," Ruth said, and poured him a cup of tea that looked like rancid water. She sat and rewrapped her torso with her arms. "So what was the other thing the crazy farmer said he'd done?"

Beauvoir still saw Gamache's face, would always see his face. The look of disbelief and surprise. Not yet dismay, not yet alarm. That would come in a moment.

"What have you done?" Gamache had asked.

"I've rigged it up."

"How?"

"I need you to be occupied, to give me time." Again the voice was wheedling, whiny, as though asking Gamache's permission, or understanding, or forgiveness.

Outside in the large common area of their division office, agents were bending over computer screens, tapping away, grabbing headphones. Giving and taking orders.

Chief Superintendent Francoeur stared at Beauvoir then turned and marched away. Beauvoir took a breath, unaware he'd been holding it, then quickly stepped back into the Chief's office.

"Tell me," said Gamache, his voice authoritative.

And the man did. Then he handed the phone back to Agent Paul Morin.

It was the last they ever heard from the man, though he might have been among the dead.

"I'm sorry," Agent Morin repeated. "I'm so sorry."

"It's not your fault. Are you hurt?" Gamache had asked.

"No." He sounded terrified and trying not to show it.

"Don't worry. We'll find you."

There was a pause. "Yes sir."

"But you still haven't answered my question," said Ruth, impatiently. "Do you think I have all night? What had the farmer done, besides the shit bomb?"

Jean-Guy Beauvoir looked down at the white, plastic garden table, feeling its rough edges. No doubt the demented old poet had found it by the side of some road or in a Dumpster.

Some piece of trash no one else wanted. She'd brought it home with her.

He stared for a very long time at the table, in a daze. No one had been told this, it hadn't been made public. And Beauvoir knew he shouldn't be saying anything now.

But he had to tell someone and who better than someone who didn't care? There'd be no sympathy, no pity, no real understanding. There'd be no awkwardness when they saw each other in the village, because while he'd bared his soul to her she wouldn't care.

"The bomb was wired to the phone line," he finally said, still staring at his hands and the expanse of white table. "It would go off if the line was cut."

"Okay," she said.

"And it would be cut if there was dead air. If they stopped talking for more than a few seconds."

There was silence then. "So you all took turns talking," said Ruth.

Beauvoir took a deep breath and sighed. There was something in the corner, by Ruth's chair, something he couldn't quite make out. A sweater she'd dropped or a dish towel.

"It didn't work that way. He needed Gamache tied to Morin, so he couldn't search for him."

296

"What do you mean, 'tied to Morin'?"

"There was voice recognition. It needed to be the two of them. Morin and the Chief."

"Oh, come on," laughed Ruth. "There's no such thing. You're making this up."

Beauvoir was silent.

"Well, okay, maybe you're not, but the farmer sure was. Are you telling me some backwoods bumpkin made a bomb, then a timer, then attached it to the phone line with, what did you call it? Voice recognition?"

"Would you risk it?" he growled, his eyes hard, daring her to go further. Hating her, as he knew he would, for seeing him so vulnerable. For not caring, for mocking. But he already hated her, what was a little more bile?

He pressed his lips together so hard he could feel his teeth cutting through.

In the office he watched his Chief as Gamache realized what this meant.

"I'm sorry, I'm so sorry," the young voice said down the phone line.

"I'm going to find you," the Chief promised.

"They talked the whole time?" Ruth asked.

"Every moment. For twenty-four hours.

Until 11:18 the next morning."

Beauvoir glanced into the corner and knew what was curled there. It was a blanket, a soft, flannel blanket made into a nest. Ready. Just in case.

Armand Gamache woke, groggy, and looked at the bedside clock.

Three twenty in the morning.

He felt the chill of the night air on his face and the warmth of the sheets and duvet around him. Lyng there, he hoped maybe this time he'd fall back asleep but eventually he got up. Slowly, stiffly. Putting on one light he dressed. As he sat on the side of the bed gathering himself he stared at the small pill bottle on the bedside table. Beside him Henri watched, his tail swishing back and forth, his eyes bright, a fluorescent yellow tennis ball in his mouth. Gamache gripped the bottle in his large hand, feeling it there. Then he placed it in his pocket and walked quietly downstairs, making sure not to waken Émile. Gamache put on his parka, his scarf, his toque and mitts. Lastly, he picked up the Chuck-it and they stepped out into the night.

Up the street they walked, their feet squeaking on the hard snow. At rue St-Louis they turned out the gate through the walls of the fortified and frozen city and past the ice palace. Bonhomme's palace.

Then onto the Plains of Abraham to toss the ball and contemplate a general's fatal mistakes. Henri, Chief Inspector Gamache and Agent Morin.

THIRTEEN

Armand Gamache slid the diary across the wooden table toward Émile Comeau.

"Look what I found last night."

Émile put on his reading glasses. As he examined the small book Gamache glanced out the window and patted Henri, sleeping beneath the table. They were having breakfast at Le Petit Coin Latin, a tiny restaurant on rue Ste-Ursule. It had been there forever and was a local favorite, with its dark wood interior, the fireplace, the simple tables. It was far enough off the main streets not to be found by accident. People went there on purpose.

The owner put their bowls of *café au lait* on the table and withdrew. Gamache sipped and watched the snow fall. It always seemed to snow in Quebec City. It was as though the New World was actually a particularly beautiful snow globe.

Finally Émile lowered the diary and removed his reading glasses.

"Poor man."

Gamache nodded. "Not many friends."

"None, as far as I can tell. The price of greatness."

"Greatness? You'd consider Augustin Renaud that? I was under the impression you and the other members of the Champlain Society considered him a kook."

"Aren't most great people? In fact, I think most of them are both brilliant and demented and almost certainly unfit for polite society. Unlike us."

Gamache stirred his coffee and watched his mentor.

He considered him a great man, one of the few he'd met. Great not in his singularity of purpose, but in his multiplicity. He'd taught his young protégé how to be a homicide investigator, but he'd taught him more besides.

Gamache remembered being shown into Chief Inspector Comeau's office his first week on the job, certain he was about to be fired for some mysterious transgression. Instead the wiry, self-contained man had stared at him for a few seconds then invited him to sit and told him the four sentences that lead to wisdom. He'd said them only once, never repeating them. But once had

301

been enough for Gamache.

I'm sorry. I was wrong. I need help. I don't know.

He'd never forgotten them and when he took over as Chief Inspector, Gamache passed them on to each and every one of his agents. Some took them to heart, some forgot them immediately.

That was their choice.

But those four statements had changed Armand Gamache's life. Émile Comeau had changed his life.

Émile was a great man because he was a good man, no matter what was happening around him. Gamache had seen cases explode around his Chief, he'd seen accusations thrown, he'd seen internecine politics that would stagger Machiavelli. He'd seen his Chief bury his own beloved wife, five years earlier.

Strong enough to grieve.

And when, a few weeks ago, Gamache had marched in the achingly slow cortege behind the flag-draped coffins he had with each halting step remembered his agents and with each step remembered his first Chief. His superior then, his superior now and always.

And when, finally, Gamache could take the pain no longer he and Reine-Marie had come here. Not to be healed, but to be helped.

I need help.

The owner of the bistro brought their breakfasts of *omelettes,* fresh fruit and a croissant each.

"I respect people who have such passion," Émile was saying. "I don't. I have a lot of interests, some I'm passionate about, but not to the exclusion of everything else. I sometimes wonder if that's necessary for geniuses to accomplish what they must, a singularity of purpose. We mere mortals just get in the way. Relationships are messy, distracting."

"He travels the fastest who travels alone," quoted Gamache.

"You sound as though you don't believe it."

"It depends where you're going, but no, I don't. I think you might go far fast, but eventually you'll stall. We need other people."

"What for?"

"Help. Isn't that what Champlain found? All other explorers failed to create a colony but he succeeded. Why? What was the difference? Père Sébastien told me. Champlain had help. The reason his colony thrived, the reason we're sitting here today, was exactly because he wasn't alone. He asked the natives for help and he succeeded."

"Don't think they don't regret it."

Gamache nodded. It was a terrible loss, a lapse in judgment. Too late the Huron and Algonquin and Cree realized Champlain's New World was their old one.

"Yes," said Émile, nodding slowly, his slender fingers toying with the salt and pepper shakers. "We all need help."

He watched his companion. He'd been heartened by Gamache taking an interest in this case. It was somewhere else to put his mind, other than that scalded spot. But then early that morning, while everyone else slept, he'd heard Armand and Henri, quietly leaving. Again.

"It's not your fault, you know. So many lives were saved."

"And lost. I made too many mistakes, Émile." It was the first time he'd talked about the events to his mentor. "Right from the start."

"Like what?"

The farmer's voice, with its broad country accent, played again in Gamache's head. All the clues were there, right from the start. "I didn't put things together fast enough."

"No one else even came close. Jesus, Armand, when I think what might have happened if you hadn't done what you did."

Gamache took a deep breath and looked down at the table, his lips tight.

Émile paused. "Do you want to talk about it?"

Armand Gamache looked up. "I can't. Not yet. But thank you."

"When you're ready." Émile smiled, took a sip of strong, aromatic coffee, and picked up Renaud's diary again. "I haven't read it all, of course, but what strikes me immediately is that there seems very little new in this. Certainly nothing we haven't heard a million times before. The places he'd marked as possible sites for Champlain's grave are all places we've known about. The Café Buade, rue de Trésor. But they've all been investigated and nothing's been found."

"Then why did he believe Champlain might be there?"

"He also thought Champlain was in the Lit and His, let's not forget. He saw Champlain everywhere."

Gamache thought for a moment. "There're bodies buried all over Québec from hundreds of years ago. How would you even know if you'd found Champlain?"

"That's a good question. It's had us worried for a long time. Would the coffin say

305

Samuel de Champlain? Would there be a date, an insignia perhaps? Maybe by his clothes. He apparently wore a quite distinctive metal hat, Renaud always thought that's how he'd know him."

"When he opened the coffin he'd see a skeleton in a metal hat and decide it's the father of Québec?"

"Genius might have its limits," admitted Émile. "But scholars think there might be a few clues. All the coffins made back then were wood, with a few exceptions. Experts believe Champlain would be an exception. His coffin was almost certainly lined in lead. And it's easier these days to date remains."

Gamache looked unconvinced. "Père Sébastien at the Basilica said there were mysteries surrounding Champlain and his birth. That he might be a Huguenot or a spy for the King of France or even his illegitimate son. Was that just romanticizing or is there more to it?"

"It's partly romantic, the noble bastard son. But a few things feed that rumor. One is his own near maniacal secrecy. For instance, he was married but only mentions his wife of twenty-five years a couple of times, and even then not by name."

"They didn't have any children, did they?"

Émile shook his head. "But others were

also pretty tight lipped about Champlain. A couple of the Jesuit priests and a Récollet lay brother mention him in their journals, but even then it was nothing personal. Just daily life. Why the secrecy?"

"What's your theory? You've studied the man most of your life."

"I think it was partly the time, less stress on the individual. There wasn't quite the culture of 'me' that there is now. But I also think there might've been something he was trying to hide and it made him a very private person."

"The unacknowledged son of a king?"

Émile hesitated. "He wrote prolifically, you know, thousands of pages. Buried in all those words, all those pages, was one sentence."

Gamache was listening closely, imagining Champlain bent over the paper with a quill pen and a pot of ink by candlelight in a Spartan home four hundred years and a few hundred yards away from where they were sitting.

"I am obligated by birth to the King," said Émile. "Historians for centuries have tried to figure out what that could mean."

Gamache rolled it around in his head. *I am obligated by birth to the King.* It was certainly suggestive. Then something occurred to him.

"If Champlain's body was found, and we knew beyond a doubt it was him, they could do DNA tests." He was watching Émile as he spoke. His mentor's eyes were on the table. Was it deliberate? Not wanting to make eye contact? Was it possible?

"But would it matter?" Gamache mused. "Suppose the tests proved he was the son of Henri IV, who cares today?"

Émile raised his eyes. "From a practical point of view it would mean nothing, but symbolically?" Émile shrugged. "Pretty potent stuff, especially for the separatists who already see Champlain as a powerful symbol of Québec independence. It would only add to his luster and the romantic vision of him. He'd be both heroic and tragic. Just how the separatists see themselves."

Gamache was quiet for a moment. "You're a separatist, aren't you Émile?"

They'd never talked about it before. It hadn't been exactly a dirty little secret, just a private subject they'd never broached. In Québec politics was always dangerous territory.

Émile looked up from his *omelette*. "I am."

There was no challenge, just acknowledgment.

"Then you might have some insight," said

308

Gamache. "Could the separatist movement use this murder?"

Émile was quiet for a moment then put down his fork. "It's slightly more than a 'movement' Armand. It's a political force. More than half the population say they're Québec Nationalists. Separatists have formed the government many times."

"I didn't mean to belittle it," smiled Gamache. "I'm sorry. And I'm aware of the political situation."

"Of course you are, I didn't mean to imply you weren't."

Already the atmosphere was becoming charged.

"I've been a separatist all my adult life," said Émile. "From the late sixties to this very day. Doesn't mean I don't love Canada. I do. Who couldn't love a country that allows such diversity of thought, of expression? But I want my own country."

"As you say, many agree with you, but there're fanatics on both sides of the debate. Ardent Federalists who fear and distrust the French aspirations —"

"And demented separatists who'd do whatever it took to separate from Canada. Including violence."

Both men thought about the October Crisis decades earlier when bombs were going off, when Francophones refused to speak English, when a British diplomat was kidnapped and a Québec cabinet minister murdered.

All in the name of Québec independence.

"No one wants to return to those days," said Émile, looking his companion square in the eye.

"Are you so sure?" asked the Chief Inspector, gently but firmly.

The air bristled between them for a moment, then Émile smiled and picked up his fork. "Who knows what's hidden below the surface, but I think those days are dead and buried."

"Je me souviens," said Gamache. "What was it René Dallaire called Québec? A rowboat society? Moving forward but looking back? Is the past ever really far from sight here?"

Émile stared at him for a moment, then smiled and resumed eating while Gamache gazed out the frosty window, his mind wandering.

If Samuel de Champlain was such a symbol of Québec nationalism, were the members of the Champlain Society all separatists? Perhaps. But did it matter? As Émile said, it was more common in Québec to be one than not, especially among the *intel-*

ligentsia. Québec separatists had formed the government more than once.

Then another thought occurred to him. Suppose Samuel de Champlain was found and found not to be the son of the King? He would become slightly less romantic, slightly less heroic, a less powerful symbol.

Might the separatists prefer a missing Champlain to one found and flawed? Perhaps they too wanted to stop Augustin Renaud.

"Did you notice the entry from last week?" Gamache decided to change the subject. He opened the diary and pointed. Émile read then looked up.

"Literary and Historical Society? So last Friday wasn't his first visit there. And it says 1800. The time of the meeting?"

"I was wondering the same thing, but the library would have been closed."

Émile looked at the page once again. The four names, the blurry, scribbled number. 18-. He squinted closer. "Maybe it's not 1800."

"Maybe not. I haven't found any of the others but I did find an S. Patrick at 1809 rue des Jardins."

"There's your answer." Émile called for the bill and stood up. "Shall we?"

Gamache downed the last of his *café au*

lait and stood. "I called and left a message on Monsieur Patrick's answering machine, saying we'd be there about noon. Before that I need to go to the Lit and His to ask them about that entry in Renaud's diary. Could you do something for me while I do that?"

"Absolument."

Gamache nodded out the window. "See that building?"

"9 3/4 rue Ste-Ursule?" said Émile, squinting at the building. "Does it really say that? What does a three-quarter apartment look like?"

"Want to see? It's Augustin Renaud's."

The two men paid up and with Henri they walked across the snowy street and into the apartment.

"Good God," said Émile. "It looks like a bomb went off."

"Inspector Langlois and I spent much of last night putting it in order. You should have seen it before." Gamache wound between the piles of research.

"All about Champlain?" Émile picked up a sheet at random and scanned it.

"Everything I've found so far is. His diaries were stuffed behind that bookshelf."

"Hidden?"

"It seems so, but I'm not sure we can read

312

much into that. He was pretty paranoid. Can you go through his papers while I go to the Lit and His?"

"Are you kidding?"

Émile looked like a kid loosed in the toy factory. Gamache left his mentor sitting at the dining table, reaching for a pile of papers.

Within minutes the Chief Inspector was at the old library, standing in the deserted hallway.

"May I tuna you?" Winnie asked from the top of the oak staircase.

"I was wondering if I could speak to you and whoever else is here." He spoke English in hopes the librarian would switch to her mother tongue.

"Meet we maybe in bookstore reunion?"

She hadn't taken the hint.

"Good idea," said Gamache.

"Bunny day," agreed Winnie and disappeared.

Gamache found Mr. Blake in the library and within minutes Winnie, Elizabeth and Porter had joined them.

"I have just a couple of questions," said the Chief. "We've found evidence that Augustin Renaud came here a week before he died."

He watched them as he spoke. To a person

they looked surprised, interested, a little disconcerted, but none of them looked guilty. And yet one of them had almost certainly lied to him. One of them had almost certainly seen, perhaps even met, Renaud here. Let him in.

But why? Why had Renaud wanted to come here? Why had he brought four others?

"What was he doing here?" Gamache asked and watched as they first stared at him, then at each other.

"Augustin Renaud came to the library?" asked Mr. Blake. "But I didn't see him."

"Neither did I," said Winnie, surprised into English.

Elizabeth and Porter each shook their heads.

"He might have come after the library closed," said Gamache. "At six o'clock."

"Then he wouldn't have gotten in," said Porter. "The place would've been locked. You know that."

"I know you all have keys. I know it would be easy for one of you to let him in."

"But why would we?" asked Mr. Blake.

"Do the names Chin, JD, Patrick and O'Mara mean anything to you?"

Again they thought and again they shook their heads. Like the Hydra. One body, many heads. But of a mind.

"Members, perhaps?" he pressed.

"I don't know about JD, but the others aren't members," said Winnie. "We have so few I know their names by heart."

It struck Gamache for the first time what an interesting English expression that was. To commit something to memory was to know it by heart. Memories were kept in the heart, not the head. At least, that's where the English kept their memories.

"May I have a list of your members?" he asked. Winnie bristled and Porter jumped in.

"That's confidential."

"A library membership list? Secret?"

"Not secret, Chief Inspector. Confidential."

"I still need to see it."

Porter opened his mouth but Elizabeth jumped in. "We'll get it for you. Winnie?"

And Winnie, without hesitation, did what Elizabeth asked.

As he left, membership list folded in his breast pocket, Gamache paused on the top step to put his heavy gloves on. From there he looked across to St. Andrew's Presbyterian Church and the rectory facing the old library.

Who would have the easiest time letting

someone into the Lit and His, unseen? And, if lights were turned on after closing time, who was most likely to see it?

The minister, Tom Hancock.

After first going to the stone home Gamache found the minister at his office in the church, a cluttered and comfortable back room.

"I'm sorry to disturb you, but I need to know if you saw Augustin Renaud at the Lit and His a week before he died."

If Tom Hancock was the one who'd let them in he would almost certainly deny it. Gamache wasn't expecting the truth, only hoping to surprise a fleeting look of guilt.

But he saw none.

"Renaud was there a week before he died? I didn't know that. How'd you find out?"

Alone among them Hancock hadn't tried to argue. He was simply, like the Chief, baffled.

"His diary. He was to meet four others there, after hours we think."

Gamache gave him the names but the minister shook his head. "Sorry, they mean nothing, but I can ask around if you like." He paused and examined Gamache closely. "Is there anything else I can help you with?"

Help. I need help. Gamache shook his head, thanked him, and left.

When he got back to 9¾ Ste-Ursule, Émile was still reading.

"Any luck?" He looked up.

Gamache shook his head and took off his coat, brushing snow from it. "You?"

"I was just wondering about these. Did you notice them?"

Gamache walked over to the table and looked down. Émile was pointing to the diary page, the one that mentioned the meeting at the Lit and His with the four men. At the bottom of the page, in very small but legible writing, were two numbers.

9-8499 and 9-8572.

"A bank account? A license plate maybe? They're not reference numbers," said Gamache. "At least, not Dewey Decimal numbers. I noticed them too, but he has so many numbers scribbled everywhere. The diary's littered with them."

They didn't seem to be phone numbers, certainly not for Québec. Map coordinates? Not like any he'd ever seen.

Gamache glanced at his watch. "I think it's time to visit Monsieur Patrick. Will you join me?"

Émile snapped the diary shut and stood, stretching. "It's amazing, all this paper and yet nothing new. All the research had been done by other people before him. You'd

317

think in all those years Augustin Renaud might have found something new."

"Maybe he did. People aren't usually murdered because nothing's happened. Something happened in his life."

Gamache locked up and they made their way along the narrow streets with Henri.

"All this was forest in Champlain's time?" said Gamache, as they walked along Ste-Ursule. Émile nodded.

"The main settlement stopped at about rue des Jardins but it wasn't all that long after Champlain's death that the colony expanded. The Ursulines built the convent and more settlers came once they realized it wasn't going away."

"And that fortunes could be made," said Gamache.

"True."

They stopped at rue des Jardins. Like most of the streets in the old city, this one curved and disappeared around a corner. There was nothing even approaching a grid system, just a higgledy-piggledy warren of tiny cobbled streets and old homes.

"Which way?" Émile asked.

Gamache froze. It took him a moment to remember where that came from. The last time someone asked him that question. Jean-Guy. Staring down the long corridor, first in one direction then the other, then at him. Demanding to know which way?

"This way."

It had been a guess then and it was a guess now. Gamache could feel his heart thumping from the memory and had to remind himself it was just that. It was past, done. Dead and gone.

"You're right," said Émile, pointing to a gray stone building with an ornate, carved, wooden door, and the number above. 1809.

Gamache rang the doorbell and they waited. Two men and a dog. The door was opened by a middle-aged man.

"Oui?"

"Mr. Patrick," said Gamache, in English. "My name is Gamache. I left a message on your machine this morning. This is my colleague Émile Comeau. I wonder if I might ask you some questions?"

"Quoi?"

"Some questions," said Gamache more loudly, since the man seemed not to have heard.

"Je ne comprends pas," said the man, irritated, and began to close the door.

"No, wait," said Gamache quickly, this time in French. *"Désolé.* I thought you might be English."

"Everyone thinks that," said the man,

exasperated. "My name's Sean Patrick." He pronounced it Patreek. "Don't speak a word of English. Sorry."

Once again he went to close the door.

"But, *monsieur,* that wasn't my question," Gamache hurried on. "It's about the death of Augustin Renaud."

The door stopped closing, then slowly opened again and Gamache, Émile and Henri were admitted.

Monsieur Patrick pointed them to a room.

Gamache ordered Henri to lie down by the front door then they took off their boots and followed Monsieur Patrick into the parlor, an old-fashioned word but one that fit. It certainly didn't seem to be a living room. Looking at the sofas Gamache could see no sign a body had ever touched those cushions, and weren't about to now. Monsieur Patrick did not invite them to sit down. Instead they clustered in the middle of the stuffy room.

"Lovely furniture," said Émile, looking around him.

"From my grandparents."

"Are those them?" asked Gamache, wandering over to the photos on the wall.

"Yes. And those are my parents. My great-grandparents lived in Quebec City too. That's them over there."

He waved to another set of photos and Gamache looked at two stern people. He always wondered what happened the instant after the shot was taken. Did they exhale, glad that was over? Did they turn to each other and smile? Was this who they really were, or simply a function of a primitive technology that demanded they stay still and stare sternly at the camera?

Though —

Gamache was drawn to another photo on the wall. It showed a group of dirty men with shovels standing in front of a huge hole. Behind them was a stone building. Most of the workers looked glum, but two were grinning.

"How wonderful to have these," said Gamache. But Patrick didn't look like it was wonderful, or terrible, or anything. Indeed, Gamache thought he probably hadn't looked at the sepia photos in decades. Perhaps ever. "How well did you know Augustin Renaud?" the Chief Inspector turned back into the room.

"Didn't know him at all."

"Then why did you meet him?"

"Are you kidding? Meet him? When?"

"A week before he died. He'd arranged to meet with you, Monsieur O'Mara and two others. A Chin and a JD."

"Never heard of 'em."

"But you do know Augustin Renaud," said Émile.

"Of him. I know of him. I don't know him."

"Are you saying Augustin Renaud never contacted you?" asked Gamache.

"Are you with the police?" Patrick had grown suspicious.

"We're helping the investigation," said Gamache, vaguely. Fortunately Monsieur Patrick wasn't very observant or curious, otherwise he might wonder why Gamache was there with an elderly man and a dog. A police dog, granted, but it was still unusual. But Sean Patrick didn't seem to care. Like most Quebeckers, he was simply fixated on Augustin Renaud.

"I hear the English killed him and buried him in the basement of that building."

"Who told you that?" asked Émile.

"That did." Patrick waved toward *Le Journalist* on the table in the front hall.

"We don't know who killed him," said Gamache firmly.

"Come on," insisted Patrick. "Who else but the Anglos? They killed him to keep their secret."

"Champlain?" asked Émile, and Patrick turned to him, nodding.

"Exactly. The Chief Archeologist says Champlain isn't there, but he's almost certainly lying. Covering up."

"Why would he do that?"

"The Anglos bought him off." Patrick was rubbing his two fingers together.

"They did no such thing, *monsieur,*" said Gamache. "Believe me, Samuel de Champlain is not buried in the Literary and Historical Society."

"But Augustin Renaud was," said Patrick. "You can't tell me *les Anglais* didn't have something to do with that."

"Why was your name in Monsieur Renaud's diary?" Gamache asked and saw a look of astonishment on Patrick's face.

"My name?" Now Patrick was making a face, something between disdain and impatience. "Is this a joke? Can I see some ID?"

Gamache reached into his breast pocket and brought out his ID. The man took it, read it, stared at the name, stared at the photo and looked up at Gamache. Stunned.

"You're him? That Sûreté officer? Jesus. The beard threw me off. You're Chief Inspector Gamache?"

Gamache nodded.

Patrick leaned closer. Gamache didn't move, but grew even more still. A more observant man might have taken warning.

"I saw you on TV of course. At the funerals." He examined Gamache as though he was an exhibit.

"*Monsieur —*" said Émile, trying to stop Patrick.

"It must have been horrible." And yet the man's eyes were gleaming, excited.

And still Gamache was silent.

"I kept the magazine, *L'actualité,* with you on the cover. You know, that photo? You can sign it for me."

"I will do no such thing."

Gamache's voice was low with a warning even, finally, Sean Patrick couldn't miss. Patrick turned at the door, an angry retort on his lips, and froze. Chief Inspector Gamache was staring at him. Hard. His eyes filled with contempt.

Patrick hesitated then colored. "I'm sorry. That was a mistake."

Silence filled the room and stretched on. Finally Gamache nodded.

"I have a few more questions," he said and Patrick, docile now, returned. "Has anyone mentioned Champlain to you or wanted to know the history of your home?"

"People are always interested in that. It was built in 1751. My great-grandparents moved here in the late 1800s."

"Do you know what was here before?"

324

Émile asked.

Patrick shook his head.

"And these numbers," Gamache showed him the numbers from the diary page. 9-8499 and 9-8572. "Do they mean anything to you?"

Again Patrick shook his head. Gamache stared at him. Why was this man's name in a dead man's diary? He could swear that while insensitive, Sean Patrick wasn't lying. He seemed genuinely baffled when told Augustin Renaud had an appointment to meet him.

"What do you think?" Gamache asked Émile as they left. "Was he lying?"

"I actually don't think so. So either Renaud meant another S. Patrick, or he planned to meet them but never actually set up the appointment."

"But he seemed so excited about it. Why not follow through?"

They walked quietly for a few minutes, then Émile stopped. "I'm meeting some friends for lunch, would you like to join us?"

"*Non, merci.* I think I'll go back to the Literary and Historical Society."

"More digging?"

"Of a sort."

FOURTEEN

A few sightseers, of the more gruesome type of tourism, still hung round outside the Lit and His. What did they hope to see?

Gamache realized as he listened to them talk about Augustin Renaud and Champlain, about conspiracy theories, about *les Anglais,* that human nature hadn't changed in hundreds of years. Two hundred years ago a similar crowd would have stood exactly where they were, huddled against the biting cold. Waiting to see the convict led to that large opening above the door, put on a small balcony, a noose around his neck, and thrown off. To swing, dead or dying, before the crowd that had gathered.

The only difference today was that the death had already occurred.

Was it an execution too?

Chief Inspector Gamache knew that most killers didn't consider their act a crime. They'd somehow convinced themselves the victim had to die, had brought it on themselves, deserved to die. It was a private execution.

Was that what Renaud's killer had believed? The power of the mind, Gamache knew, could not be underestimated. A murder was never about brawn, it began and ended in the brain and the brain could justify anything.

Gamache looked at the people around him. Men and women of all ages staring at the building as though it might get up and do something interesting.

But was he any better? After leaving Émile, he and Henri had strolled the narrow, snowy streets, thinking about the case. But also about why he was still on it. Surely his obligation was discharged? Inspector Langlois was a competent and thoughtful man. He'd solve the case, Gamache was sure of it, and he'd make sure the English weren't unfairly targeted.

So why was he still poking around into the murder of Augustin Renaud?

Now there is no more loneliness.

"Suzanne and I have a dog, you know."

"Really? What sort?"

"Oh, a mutt," said Agent Morin.

As he talked, and listened, Chief Inspector Gamache sat at his desk in front of his computer following the progress of the search, or lack of progress.

It had been six hours and they still hadn't traced the call. More and more sophisticated equipment, more experts, were brought in, and still nothing.

One team was trying to trace the call, another was analyzing the farmer's voice, teams were combing the countryside and following leads on the ground. All coordinated by Chief Superintendent Francoeur.

Though there was no love lost between the two men, Gamache had to admit he was grateful to the Chief Superintendent. Someone had to take charge and he clearly couldn't.

Gamache's voice with Morin was calm, almost jovial, but his mind was racing.

Something was very wrong. It didn't make sense, none of this did. As Morin talked about his puppy Gamache was thinking, trying to put it together.

Then he had it. Leaning into his computer he fired off an instant message.

The farmer isn't a farmer. It was an act. Get the voice analysts to verify his accent.

They have, came Agent Isabelle Lacoste's response. *The accent's genuine.*

She was in Ste-Agathe, gathering information at the scene of the shooting.

Get them to look harder. He's not the bump-kin he wanted us to believe. He can't be. So what is he? In his ear he heard Morin talking about dog food.

What are you thinking? Beauvoir joined in. He was outside in the Incident Room, helping the investigation.

Suppose this wasn't an accident? wrote the Chief, his fingers pounding the keyboard, typing quickly as his thoughts raced. *Suppose he wanted to kill an agent and kidnap another? Suppose this was the plan all along.*

Why? asked Beauvoir.

There was a pause on the telephone line.

"What's your dog's name?" Gamache asked.

"We call her Bois because she looks like a log." Morin laughed, as did the Chief.

"Tell me all about her."

I don't know, Gamache typed while Agent Morin told him about taking the dog home from the SPCA to Suzanne. *But let's say this is all planned, then that includes the timing. 11:18 tomorrow morning. They want us occupied until then. It's misdirection. They want us looking one way while they do something somewhere else.*

Something is planned to happen at 11:18 tomorrow morning? Both Beauvoir and Lacoste typed.

Or, typed the Chief, *something that ends at*

329

11:18 tomorrow morning. Something that's going on right now.

There was a pause. The cursor throbbed on Gamache's quiet screen while in his ears he heard about Bois's current habit of eating, and pooping, socks.

So what do we do? Beauvoir asked.

Gamache stared at his blinking cursor. What do they do?

You do nothing, appeared on the screen.

Who is this? typed Gamache quickly.

Chief Superintendent Francoeur, came the equally quick response. Gamache looked up and saw the Chief Superintendent in the Incident Room at a computer also staring at him through the window. *You, Chief Inspector, will continue to talk to your agent. That's your one and only job. Inspector Beauvoir and Agent Lacoste will continue to follow my orders. There can only be one leader of this investigation, you know that. We'll get your agent back, but you need to focus and follow a clear chain of command. Do not splinter off. That only helps the criminals.*

I agree, wrote Gamache. *But we need to consider other possibilities, sir. Including that this is all part of a well-organized plan.*

A plan? To alert every cop in North America? An agent's been killed, another kidnapped. Pretty crappy plan, wouldn't you say?

Gamache stared at the screen then typed. *This farmer isn't who he appears to be. We'd have found him by now. We'd have found Agent Morin. Something is going on.*

Your panicking isn't going to help, Chief Inspector. Follow orders.

He isn't panicking, wrote Beauvoir. *What he says makes sense.*

Enough. Chief Inspector Gamache, stay focused. We'll get Agent Morin back.

Chief Inspector Gamache watched the flashing cursor then looked over his screen. Francoeur was staring at him. Not angrily. Indeed, there seemed compassion in his stare, as though he had some idea how Gamache must be feeling.

And he might have. Gamache only wished the Chief Superintendent knew what he was thinking.

This was wrong. There were eighteen hours left to find Agent Morin and they were no closer. No ordinary farmer could bring all the resources and technology of the Sûreté to a halt. Therefore, this was no ordinary farmer.

Gamache nodded to the Chief Superintendent, who gave the Chief Inspector a grateful smile. This was not the time for the two leaders to clash and while Chief Superintendent Francoeur outranked Gamache, the Chief Inspector was the more respected.

No, a rift right now would be a disaster.

But so was ignoring what seemed to Gamache obvious. They were being led away from the truth. And with each passing minute they were getting further from it. From Agent Morin. From whatever larger plan was at work.

Gamache smiled back and paused. Should he do it? If he did, there was no going back. Careers and lives might be ruined. He stared through the window.

"You have a dog, don't you sir?"

"Yes. Henri. Also a foundling, like Bois."

"Funny how they get under your skin. I think there's something special about the ones we rescue."

"Yes," said Gamache decisively. He sat forward, jotted a note longhand and made eye contact with Inspector Beauvoir who got up, filled a pitcher with fresh water and wandered into the Chief's office, under the gaze of Chief Superintendent Francoeur.

Jean-Guy Beauvoir picked up the note and closed his hand over it.

Gamache's feet were growing numb with cold as he stared at the Literary and Historical Society. Beside him Henri was lifting first one paw then another. The snow and ice were so cold it actually, and ironically, burned.

Why was he still investigating the Renaud case? Was this his private misdirection? Was he trying to take his mind off something he might otherwise have to see? And hear? And feel? Was his whole career like that? Replacing one ghost with a fresher one? Racing one step ahead of his memory?

He yanked open the heavy wooden door and entered the Literary and Historical Society, where the Anglos kept and filed and numbered all their ghosts.

In the library Mr. Blake was just pouring himself a cup of tea and taking a cookie from the blue and white china plate on the long wooden table. He looked at Gamache and indicated the pot. Gamache nodded and by the time he'd taken off his coat and rubbed Henri's feet warm and dry there was a cup of tea and a cookie on the table for him.

Mr. Blake had gone back to reading and Gamache decided he might as well too. For the next hour he collected books, sipped the tea, nibbled his cookie and read, sometimes making notes.

"What're you reading?" Mr. Blake lowered his book, a slim volume on grasses in the Outer Hebrides. "Is it about the Renaud case?"

Armand Gamache marked his page with a slip of paper and looked across the sitting area to the elderly man, perfectly attired in gray flannels, a shirt, tie, sweater and jacket.

"No, I thought I'd give that a rest for an hour or so. This," he held up the book, "is just a curiosity of mine. It's about Bougainville."

Mr. Blake leaned forward. "As in bougainvillea? The flowering plant?"

"That's right."

They both imagined the exuberant, colorful plant, so common in the tropics.

"You're interested in botany too?" asked Mr. Blake.

"No, I'm interested in the Plains of Abraham."

"Not much bougainvillea there."

Gamache laughed. "Too true. But Bougainville was."

"Was what?"

"There," said Gamache. "At the Battle of the Plains of Abraham."

"Are we talking about the same man?" Mr. Blake asked. "The navigator? The one who brought bougainvillea back on one of his voyages?"

"The same. Most people don't realize he was one of Général Montcalm's *aides-de-camp.*"

"Wait a minute," Mr. Blake said. "One of the greatest cartographers and navigators of his time fought at the Plains of Abraham?"

"Well, fought is debatable. That's what I'm looking into." More ghosts, thought Gamache. My life is filled with them. Mr. Blake was looking at him, astounded. He had reason to be. This was a little known and curiously little acknowledged historical fact.

"There's more." Now Gamache leaned forward. "The French under Montcalm lost the Battle of the Plains of Abraham. Do you know why?"

"Because the English under General Wolfe scaled the cliffs. It's now considered a brilliant tactic." The elderly gentleman lowered his voice so that the ghosts and the wooden statue above them wouldn't hear. "Between us? I think Wolfe was doped up on medicine and didn't know what in the world he was doing."

Gamache laughed, surprised. General Wolfe, the Anglo hero of the battle, had indeed been ill in the days leading up to that day.

"You don't think it was a dazzling strategy?"

"I think he was demented and just got lucky."

Gamache paused. "Maybe. There is another factor in the English victory, you know."

"Really? Was Montcalm also doped up?"

"He made some mistakes," said Gamache. "But that wasn't one of them. No, I was thinking of something else. When Montcalm realized where the actual attack was coming from, he did two things. He hurried to meet them and he sent a message to his *aide-de-camp,* Bougainville, to come at once. Then Montcalm engaged the English."

"Too quickly, if I remember correctly. Don't people say he should have waited for reinforcements?"

"Yes. One of his mistakes. He rushed into battle without enough men."

Gamache paused, gathering himself. Watching him, Mr. Blake wondered why this long lost battle should affect his companion so strongly. But it did.

"It cost Montcalm his life," said Blake.

"Yes, he died, though not on the field. General Wolfe died on the field, but not Montcalm. He was hit several times and was taken to the Ursuline convent inside the walls, not far from here, actually. The nuns tried to save him but he died the next morning and was buried along with some of his men, in their basement."

Mr. Blake thought for a moment. "What about the *aide-de-camp?* Bougainville? Where was he?"

"Exactly," said Gamache. "Where was he? He was waiting for the English further upriver. Everyone expected the first wave to come from there. But when Montcalm sent for Bougainville, desperate for reinforcements, why didn't he come?"

"Why didn't he?"

"I don't know. No one knows. He came, but slowly, and when he finally arrived he held back. His official explanation was that by that time he judged the battle already lost. He didn't want to destroy his army in a losing cause."

"Sensible."

"I agree, but is it likely? His general had ordered him back. He could see the slaughter. Would he have really stopped? Some historians say if Colonel Bougainville had engaged the enemy he'd almost certainly have won. The English were in disarray, most of their senior commanders dead or wounded."

"What's your theory? You do have one?" Mr. Blake's eyes were sharp.

"It's not likely to be very popular, probably not very accurate either. But there was someone on the English side also in the battle, someone not often mentioned in the histories and yet he's the most famous of all those present. World famous."

"Who?"

"James Cook."

"Captain Cook?"

"The very same. He went on to map most of South America, Australia, New Zealand and the Pacific. He was the most famous cartographer alive and still famous today. But before all that he commanded a ship that let off the soldiers, who scaled the cliffs and took Québec once and for all for the English. Québec would never again be in French hands."

"So what's your theory?"

"In my line of work you grow suspicious of coincidences. They happen, but not often. And when you see one you ask questions."

"And this is a big one," agreed Mr. Blake. "Two world-famous mapmakers fighting on opposite sides of the same battle in a far-flung colony."

"And one of them hesitates, perhaps disastrously."

"You think he did it on purpose, don't you." It wasn't a question.

"I think it's possible they knew each other, had communicated. I think it's possible

Captain Cook, who was the more senior of the men, made a promise to Bougainville in exchange for a favor."

"A hesitation. A pause," said Mr. Blake. "It wouldn't seem much, but it cost the colony."

"And many lives, including Général Montcalm," said Gamache.

"And in exchange? What would Bougainville get?"

"Perhaps Cook pointed him toward the West Indies. Perhaps Cook turned his own blind eye and let Bougainville map and navigate some important places. I don't know. That's why I'm here." He held up his book. "I suspect I'm wrong and it really was just a coincidence."

"But it passes the time," said Mr. Blake. "And sometimes that's a blessing."

Avec le temps, thought Gamache. "And you?" he asked the elderly man.

Mr. Blake handed him the book on ancient Scottish grasses. "Ironically, now that I'm so near the end of my life I seem to have all the time in the world."

Gamache looked at the dry volume, trying to feign interest. Reading this would certainly make an hour seem an eternity. It would stretch, if not actually waste, time. He opened it. A first edition he noticed, but water damaged and so obscure it almost certainly wouldn't be worth anything. It was printed in 1845.

And there was something else, another number partly hidden beneath the library card.

"Do you know what this is?" He got up and showed it to Mr. Blake who shrugged.

"They're not important. This is the one that counts." Mr. Blake pointed to the Dewey Decimal catalog number.

"Still, I'd like to see the numbers underneath." Gamache looked round for assistance.

"Maybe we should get Winnie," said Mr. Blake.

"Good idea."

Mr. Blake picked up the phone and within minutes the librarian, tiny and suspicious, had arrived. After it was explained she turned to the Chief Inspector. "All right, come with me."

The three of them went through the corridors, twisting and turning, up some stairs, down others and finally they were in the large back office. Porter Wilson was there as was Elizabeth MacWhirter.

"Hello, Chief Inspector." Elizabeth came forward and shook hands, as did Porter.

Then, like a surgeon, Winnie bent over

the book and with an X-Acto knife pried up the top of the card holder, glued to place a hundred years before.

And below it were the numbers, undamaged, clear as the day they were placed on the dreary first edition.

6-5923

"What does that number mean?" Gamache asked.

There was silence as they took turns looking at it. Finally Winnie answered him.

"I think it's the old cataloging system, don't you, Elizabeth?"

"I think you're right," said Porter, who clearly didn't have a clue.

"What old system?" asked the Chief Inspector.

"From the 1800s. We don't use it anymore," said Elizabeth, "but back when the Literary and Historical Society was first established this is how they marked items."

"Go on."

Elizabeth gave an embarrassed little laugh. "It wasn't actually much of a system. The Literary and Historical Society was founded in about 1820 —"

"1824, actually," said Mr. Blake. "There's a charter somewhere around here."

He searched for it while Elizabeth talked.

"A call went out to the English community at the time to send in memorabilia, whatever people considered of historic importance," she laughed. "Apparently people took it as an excuse to empty their attics and basements and barns. They were given stuffed lizards, ball gowns, armoirs. Letters, shopping lists. Finally the Society refined its mandate so that it became mostly a library, and even then it was overwhelmed."

Gamache could imagine mountains of old, leather-bound books and even loose papers.

"As books came in they put on the year it arrived." She picked up the Scottish grasses volume and pointed. "That's the number 6 and the other was the number of the book. This one was the five thousandth, nine hundred and twenty-third."

Gamache was beyond baffled. "*Alors,* the first number, 6, means the year. But what decade? And was it the five thousandth book that year to arrive, or ever? I'm afraid I'm confused."

"Ridiculous system," sniffed Winnie. "Shocking. They obviously had no idea what they were doing."

"They were probably overwhelmed," said Elizabeth.

"And this sort of thing would just add to the confusion." Winnie turned to the Chief

Inspector. "It takes hard work and some guessing to figure out the code. Since this book was published in 1845 we can assume it was donated in 1846. Or '56, or '66 and so on."

"But what about the 5923?" Gamache asked.

"That's even worse," admitted Winnie. "They started at number 1 and just kept adding."

"So this was the five thousandth, nine hundred and twenty-third book?"

"That would make too much sense, Chief Inspector, so no. When they got up to 10,000 they started back at 1," she sighed. This seemed painful for her to admit.

"They cataloged everything. Some ended up on shelves and some were eventually given Dewey Decimal numbers, some not," said Elizabeth. "It was and is, a mess."

"Found it," said Mr. Blake, holding a worn folder. "This is the wording of the original mandate." He read, *"To discover and rescue from the unsparing hand of time the records which yet remain of the earliest history of Canada. To preserve, while in our power, such documents as may be found amid the dust of yet unexplored depositories, and which may prove important to general his-*

tory and to the particular history of this province."

Gamache listened to the old voice reading the old words and was deeply moved by the simplicity and the nobility of them. He suddenly felt an overwhelming desire to help these people, to help save them from the unsparing hand of time.

"What might these mean?" He showed them the numbers found in Augustin Renaud's diary.

9-8499 and 9-8572.

"Was there a Dewey Decimal number too?" Winnie asked. He had the impression if she could snort Dewey numbers she'd get high. But he had to disappoint her.

"Just those. Do they tell you anything?"

"We could look them up in the catalog."

Gamache turned and stared at Mr. Blake.

"There's a catalog?" he asked.

"Well, yes. That's what a catalog number's for," said Mr. Blake with a smile. "It's over here."

The "it" turned out to be eight huge volumes, handwritten, collected by decade. They each took one and began looking. The first "hit" was in 1839. There Porter found both a 9-8499 and a 9-8572.

"The first is a travel journal around the horn of Africa, written by a Colonel Ephram

Hoskins, and the 9-8572 is a book of sermons, donated by Kathleen Williams."

It didn't seem promising.

Gamache closed one catalog book and turned to another, his finger working down the long pages with the precise writing.

"Found one," said Elizabeth a few minutes later. "It's 9-8466 to 9-8594. Donated in 1899 by Madame Claude Marchand of Montreal."

"Nothing more specific?" Gamache asked, his heart sinking. Those were the only entries that might be what Augustin Renaud was interested in but he found it hard to believe a trip in the 1830s around Africa was of interest to the Champlain expert, or a collection of sermons. Even less promising was a lot of more than one hundred books given by a woman in Montreal. Still, it was the only lead.

"Are those books still in the library?"

"Let's see," said Winnie, taking the information over to their "modern" system. A card catalog. After a few minutes she looked up.

"The sermon book is in the library, though it hasn't been given a Dewey number yet. The horn of Africa one must still be in a box somewhere."

"And the Montreal lot?" Gamache asked.

"I don't know. All we have here is the lot number. It doesn't say what happened to the specific books."

"May I have the book of sermons, please?"

Winnie found it in the library and signed it out to him. He was the first to ever take it out. Gamache thanked them and left, walking with Henri back down the hill, their feet making prints side-by-side in the fluffy snow.

Once home he went onto his laptop and started searching. Émile returned and made a simple dinner of clay pot chicken and vegetables. After dinner Gamache went back to work, trying to track down Colonel Ephram Hoskins and Kathleen Williams. Colonel Hoskins died of malaria and was buried in the Congo. His book was considered important at the time then quickly fell into obscurity.

There was absolutely no connection to Champlain, Québec or Renaud.

Kathleen Williams turned out to be a steadfast benefactor of the Anglican Cathedral of Holy Trinity in old Québec. Her husband was a prosperous dry goods merchant and her son became a ship's captain. Gamache stared at the scant information, willing something to jump out at him, some connection he was missing.

Still sitting at the desk he scanned the book of sermons, a collection of stern Victorian lectures. Nothing about Québec, Champlain, or God as far as Gamache could tell.

Finally he searched Madame Claude Marchand of Montreal. It took him a while, even with the aid of the Sûreté computers but he finally found her.

"Coming to bed?" asked Émile.

Gamache looked up. It was almost midnight. "Not just yet. Soon."

"Don't strain your eyes."

Gamache smiled and waved good night, then went back to the search.

Madame Marchand was married to Claude Marchand. He died in 1925, she in 1937.

So why did they donate more than a hundred books back in 1899? Was it part of an estate? Had one of their parents died?

But why send the books to Québec? Surely that was a lot of trouble. And why to this little library? An English library when presumably the Marchands were French?

It was curious, Gamache had to admit.

After more searching through genealogical records he discovered neither Monsieur Marchand's parents nor Madame Marchand's parents died around 1899. So where did these books come from?

It had been a long time since the Chief Inspector had had to do research of this type. He generally assigned searches to agents or inspectors. It was the sort of thing Inspector Beauvoir in particular excelled at. Order, information.

They'd bring the facts to Gamache, scattered, disjointed often, and he'd try to make sense of it. See threads and connections, put them in order.

The Chief Inspector had almost forgotten the thrill of the information hunt, but as he tried this, then that, then the other lead he found himself getting lost in it, so that all else receded.

How did this couple come by the books? And why go to the effort and expense of having them shipped to Québec?

Gamache leaned back and stared at the screen, thinking.

The books were donated by her, not him, but he was alive at the time. What did that say? Gamache rubbed his still unfamiliar beard and stared.

What did it say?

It said that the books were hers to donate. They belonged not to them, but to her specifically. The census showed her as a housekeeper, though it didn't list her employer. But it did give her address.

A housekeeper, thought Gamache, in the late 1800s. There couldn't be that many who were literate, never mind owned a hundred books or more.

He leaned forward again and tapped on the keyboard, going here and there, trying to get information more than a century old on people who almost certainly had done nothing extraordinary. There was no reason for a record of them.

He tried down one route, then down another. The address wasn't very helpful. There were no phone books at the time, no electrical bills. Almost no paper trail, except, perhaps.

He started typing again. Insurance company records. And there he found it, the man who owned the home Madame Claude Marchand, housekeeper, had listed as an address in the census form.

Chiniquy. Charles Paschal Télesphore Chiniquy.

Who died in 1899.

Gamache threw himself back in the chair and grinned broadly.

He had it, he'd done it.

But what did it mean?

FIFTEEN

"You were up late last night."

Émile Comeau found Armand setting a pot of coffee on the table along with a plate of croissants and jams. He was looking happy, Émile noticed. A spring in his step.

"I was."

"What were you up to?" Émile sipped the strong, aromatic coffee and reached for a croissant. A few flakes hit the wooden table as he broke it in two.

"I think I've figured out what those numbers in Renaud's journal mean."

"Is that so? What?"

"You were right, he wasn't looking for Champlain's body in the Literary and Historical Society. I think he was looking for books. Those are catalog numbers. They refer to books given to the Lit and His in 1899."

Émile lowered his croissant, his eyes gleaming. Once an investigator it never left the blood. The need to know.

"What books?"

"I don't know." Gamache took a sip of his coffee. "But I do know they were in a lot donated to the Literary and Historical Society by a Madame Claude Marchand. She was a housekeeper for a family named Chiniquy. Charles Paschal Télesphore Chiniquy. He died in 1899. It seems likely the books belonged to him."

"Chiniquy," said Émile slowly. "An unusual name."

Gamache nodded. "Extremely. I looked it up. There're no Chiniquys here now. Right after breakfast I'm going to access the census information, see if there were Chiniquys in Quebec City in the past."

"There were." Émile looked distracted. Not worried, exactly, but perplexed.

"Really?" asked Gamache, waiting while Émile thought.

"This doesn't make sense," said Émile at last. "You say Renaud was looking for books that belonged to Chiniquy?"

"I think so. He had their catalog numbers in his diary."

Émile scratched his neck and his eyes took on a faraway look as he searched for a timid answer. "It doesn't make sense," he mumbled again.

"You know the name?" Gamache finally asked.

"I know the name, but it's odd."

"How so?"

"Well, that Augustin Renaud should be interested in anything belonging to Chiniquy."

There was a pause while Émile thought.

"Who was this Chiniquy?" Gamache pressed. "How do you know of him? Was he a member of the Champlain Society too?"

"No, not that I know of. Almost certainly not. As far as I know he had nothing to do with Champlain."

"So who was he?"

"A priest," said Émile. "A blip in Québec history, but a loud one at the time. Quite a character. Famous for his temperance campaigns. This was back in the 1860s or 70s. He hated alcohol, thought it led to all sorts of social and spiritual ills. From what I remember he had only the one interest, getting poor Québécois laborers to quit drinking. He became quite famous for a while, but he also alienated the Catholic Church. I can't remember the details but he quit the church and became a fervent Protestant. Used to hang around bars and brothels on Petit-Champlain in the Lower Town trying to convince the drunks to give it up. Had a

352

sanatorium outside the city for a while."

"Renaud was fixated on Champlain, and Chiniquy was fixated on temperance," said Gamache, almost to himself. Then he shook his head. Like his mentor he couldn't see a connection between the father of Québec in 1635, an 1800s teetotaler and a body three days ago in the Lit and His.

Except, maybe, the books. What were the books?

"Why would a Champlain scholar want books collected by a lapsed priest?" he asked, but got no answer. "Chiniquy showed no interest in Champlain?"

Émile shook his head and shrugged, flummoxed. "But I don't know much about the man and what I just told you might be wrong. Would you like me to look further?"

Gamache got up. "Please. But first, I'm going back to Renaud's apartment. Maybe the books are there. Would you like to come?"

"Absolument."

As they put on their heavy winter parkas Émile realized how natural it felt to follow this man. Chief Inspector Émile Comeau had seen Gamache arrive, an eager young agent in homicide. Had watched his wavy dark hair thin and turn gray, his body thicken, his marriage, his children, his rise through the ranks. He'd promoted him to Inspector, had seen the young man take command, naturally. Had watched as older, more experienced agents ceded their place, turning to him for his opinion, his leadership.

But Émile knew something else. Gamache wasn't always right. No one was.

As they walked up the hill, their breaths puffing into the crisp air, Émile glanced at Armand, Henri walking at his side. Did he seem better? Was he getting better? Émile thought so, but he also knew it was the internal injuries that did the most damage. The worst was always hidden.

A few minutes later they were once again in the cramped and stuffy apartment, negotiating their way between piles of magazines, stacks of correspondence, and furniture littered with books and journals.

The two men got to work quickly, taking off their coats and boots and each taking a room.

Two hours later Émile wandered into the dining room, which almost certainly had never seen a dinner party. The walls were lined with shelves, packed two and three books deep. Gamache was halfway around the room, having taken down each book, examined and replaced it.

He was exhausted. An activity he could have done easily two months earlier was now almost too much for him, and he could see Émile was also flagging. He was leaning against the back of a chair, trying not to look done in.

"Ready for a break?" Gamache asked.

Émile turned a grateful face to him. "If you insist. I could go on all day but if you'd like to stop I guess I could."

Gamache smiled. *"Merci."*

Still, it surprised him how weak he still felt. He'd managed to fool himself into believing he was back to full strength. And he had improved, his energy was better, his strength was returning, even the trembling seemed to have diminished.

But when pushed, he faded faster than he'd expected.

They found a table by the window at Le Petit Coin Latin and ordered beers and sandwiches.

"What did you find?" Gamache asked, biting into a baguette stuffed with pheasant terrine, arugula and cranberry sauce. A micro-brewery beer was in front of him with a slight head of foam.

"Nothing I didn't expect to find. There were a couple rare books on Champlain the Society would love to get its hands on, but since you were there I chose not to steal them."

"How wise."

Émile inclined his head and smiled. "You?"

"The same. There was nothing that didn't relate directly to Champlain or the early 1600s. There was nothing on Chiniquy, on temperance, on anything to do with the 1800s. Still, we need to keep looking. I wonder where he got all his books."

"Probably from used bookstores."

"That's true." Gamache brought Renaud's diary out of his satchel and flipped through it. "He made regular visits to the local secondhand bookstores and the flea markets in the summer."

"Where else do you find old books? What is it?" asked Émile.

Armand Gamache had tilted his head to the side and narrowed his eyes. "Where do those used bookstores get their books?"

"From people who're moving or cleaning house. From estate sales, buying them in lots. Why?"

"I think when we're finished in the apartment we need to visit a few shops."

"What're you thinking?" asked Émile, and took a long sip of his beer.

"I'm remembering something Elizabeth

MacWhirter told me." But now it was his turn to look at his companion. Émile Comeau was staring at the diary. Reaching out he turned it around so that it was right-side up for him. His slim finger rested on the page, below Augustin Renaud's clear printing. Below the words circled and underlined, below an assignation he had with a Patrick, and O'Mara, a JD and —

"Chin," said Gamache. "But there're no Chins in Quebec City. I thought I might ask at the Chinese restaurant on rue de Buade and find out if it's a —"

Gamache stared into the beaming eyes of his mentor. He closed his own eyes almost in pain. "Oh, no."

Opening them he looked down at the diary. "Is that it? Chin? Chiniquy?"

Émile Comeau was smiling and nodding. "What else?"

Jean-Guy Beauvoir took a soapy dish from Clara and dried it. He was standing in their large, open kitchen, doing the dishes. Something he rarely did at home, though he'd helped the Chief and Madame Gamache clean up a few times. It didn't seem like a chore with them. And it didn't, to his surprise, seem like a chore now. It was restful, peaceful. Like the village itself.

After lunch together, Peter Morrow had returned to his studio to work on his latest painting, leaving Clara and Jean-Guy to clean up after the soup and sandwiches.

"Did you get a chance to read the dossier?"

"I did," said Clara, handing him another dripping dish. "I have to say, it's a convincing case against Olivier. But let's say he didn't kill the Hermit, then someone else must have known the Hermit was hiding in the woods. But how would someone find him? We know he approached Olivier himself, to sell his things and because he wanted some companionship."

"And needed someone to do his errands, get things he needed from town," said Beauvoir. "He used Olivier and Olivier used him."

"A good relationship."

"People taking advantage of each other seems good to you?"

"Depends how you see it. Look at us. Peter's supported me financially all our married life, but I support him emotionally. Is that taking advantage of each other? I suppose it is, but it works. We're both happy."

Beauvoir wondered if that was true. He suspected Clara would be happy just about anywhere but her husband was another matter.

"Didn't seem equal to me," said Beauvoir. "Olivier brought the Hermit some groceries every two weeks and in exchange the Hermit gave Olivier priceless antiques. Someone was getting boned."

They carried their coffees into the bright living room. Unfiltered winter light streamed through the windows as they sat in large easy chairs by the hearth.

Her brow wrinkled as she looked into the mumbling fire. "But it seems to me the big issue, the only issue, is who else knew the Hermit was there? He'd been hiding in the forest for years, why was he suddenly killed?"

"Our theory was that Olivier killed him because the horse trail was getting close to the cabin. The Hermit and his treasure were about to be found."

Clara nodded. "Olivier didn't want anyone else discovering and maybe stealing the treasure, so he killed the Hermit. It was a spur of the moment thing, not planned. He picked up a menorah and hit him."

She'd heard it all at the trial and read it again last night.

She tried to imagine her friend doing that, and while her mind spun away from the image the truth was she could believe it. She didn't think Olivier would ever plan to kill someone, but she could see him doing it in a fit of rage and greed.

Olivier had then taken the menorah. Picked the bloody thing up from beside the dead man. He said he'd taken it because his fingerprints were all over it. He was afraid. But he also admitted the menorah was priceless. Greed and fear combined to drive him into a monumentally foolish act. An act of greed, not guilt.

Neither the judge nor the jury had believed him. But now Beauvoir had to at least consider the possibility Olivier had been stupid, but truthful.

"What changed?" Beauvoir mused. "Someone else must have found the Hermit."

"Someone who might've been looking for years, someone the Hermit stole from."

"But how'd he find him?"

"He either followed Olivier or followed the new horse trail," said Clara.

"That leads us to one of the Parras," said Beauvoir. "Either Roar or Havoc."

"Old Mundin could have done it. He's a carpenter and a carver, after all. He could have followed Olivier one night after picking up the broken furniture, and he could have carved that word, Woo, into the wood."

"But," said Beauvoir, "Old Mundin's a professional woodworker. I've seen his stuff. Woo was carved by an amateur, someone hacking away."

Clara thought. "Maybe it was someone new to the community, maybe that's what changed. The killer recently moved into Three Pines."

"The Gilberts," said Beauvoir. "They're the only new people."

Marc and Dominique Gilbert, Marc's mother Carole and his estranged father, Vincent. Saint Asshole, the famous doctor who now, curiously, lived in the Hermit's cabin. Beauvoir no longer wanted the murderer to be Dr. Vincent Gilbert but deep down he worried it might be.

"I think we need to talk to the suspects again," said Beauvoir. "I thought I might drop by the Mundins' place this afternoon, pretend I want to buy some furniture."

"Great, and I'll try to talk to some of the others." She hesitated. "There is another way the murderer could have found the Hermit."

"Yes?"

"Maybe he recognized the treasures when Olivier went to sell them. It says here," she tapped the manila file folder, "that Olivier sold a lot of the stuff on eBay. Well people all over the world could have seen it, including eastern Europe. Suppose someone recognized one of the items and tracked Olivier down."

"And followed him to the Hermit," said Beauvoir. "I'll look into it."

He was beginning to appreciate why the Chief Inspector insinuated himself into the communities they investigated. It had long perplexed Beauvoir and privately he didn't approve. It blurred the lines between investigator and investigated.

But he now wondered if that was such a bad thing.

As he stepped out of the small home the sun glared off the snow, blinding him. Beauvoir put his dark glasses on.

Ray-Ban. Old School. He liked them, made him look cool on cold days.

Getting in his car he let it warm up, feeling the heated seats grow warm under him. On a bitterly cold winter day it was almost as good as sex. Then he put the car in gear and headed up the hill and out of town.

Five minutes later he arrived at the old farm. The Sûreté team had last been there in late summer, when everything had been in bloom. Beyond bloom. It was going to seed, the leaves were turning color and the wasps fed drunkenly on over-ripe fruit.

But now it was all dead or dormant and the farm, once teeming with life, looked deserted.

But as he drove slowly up to the house the door opened and standing there was The Wife, holding little Charlie Mundin's hand.

As he got out of the car she waved and he noticed Old Mundin approaching the open door, wiping his large, expressive hands on a towel.

"Welcome," The Wife smiled, kissing him on both cheeks. He wasn't often greeted like that in a case, then he remembered, he wasn't on a case.

Like Old Mundin, The Wife was young, and like Old, she was stunning. Not in a *Vogue* sort of way, but her beauty came from her obvious good health and humor. Her dark hair was cut very short and her eyes were deep brown, large and warm. She smiled easily and readily, as did Old, as did Charlie.

"Come in, before you freeze," Old said, closing the door. "Would you like a hot chocolate? Charlie and I just got back from tobogganing and we sure could use one."

Charlie, his round face ruddy red from being outside, his eyes sparkling, looked up at Jean-Guy as though they'd known each other all their lives.

"I'd love one." Beauvoir followed them into their home.

"You'll have to excuse our place, Inspector," said The Wife, leading the way into the warm kitchen. "We're still renovating."

And the place certainly looked it. Some rooms weren't yet dry-walled, others had the plaster done, but no paint. The kitchen looked like something out of the 1950s, but not in a good way. Tacky, not retro-chic.

"It looks fine to me," he lied. What it did look, and feel, was comfortable. It felt like a home.

"You wouldn't know it," said Old, helping The Wife with the hot cocoa, "but we've actually done a lot of work. You should see the upstairs. It's wonderful."

"Old, I can't imagine the Inspector's come all this way to see our renovations," laughed The Wife. She returned to the kitchen table carrying steaming mugs of hot chocolate each with a large, melting, marshmallow.

"We saw you at the bistro the other night," said Old. "Gabri says you're here for a holiday. That's nice."

They looked at him with sympathy. It was gentle, it was meant to be supportive, but Jean-Guy wished it would stop, though he knew this young couple meant it kindly.

Fortunately, their sympathy also gave him the opening he needed.

"Yes, I haven't been back since the Hermit case. What a blow to the community."

"Olivier's arrest?" said The Wife. "We still can't believe it."

"You knew him quite well, as I remember," Beauvoir turned to Old. "Gave you your first job."

"He did. Restoring and repairing furniture."

"Show, show, show," said Charlie.

"Exactly," said The Wife. "*Chaud. Chocolat chaud.* He wasn't speaking six months ago but Dr. Gilbert's been coming once a week for dinner and working with him."

"Really? Vincent Gilbert?"

"Yes. You knew he used to work with children with Down syndrome?"

"Oui."

"Boo," said Charlie to Beauvoir, who smiled and tried to ignore the child. "Boo," Charlie repeated.

"Boo!" said Beauvoir back, thrusting his head forward in a way he hoped was more playful than terrifying.

"He means wood. *Bois,*" explained Old. "Yes Charlie, old son, we'll go soon. We whittle together in the evenings."

"Didn't Havoc Parra used to whittle toys

for Charlie?" Beauvoir remembered.

"He did," said Old. "I'm afraid he's wonderful at cutting down trees but not so good at carving them, though he enjoys it. Comes here sometimes to help me with the furniture. I pay him a little."

"What does he do? Restore it?"

"No, that's way too specialized. He helps when I have some furniture to make. Mostly staining."

They chatted about local events, about renovation projects and the antiques waiting to be restored. Beauvoir pretended to be interested in seeing Old Mundin's furniture and almost bought a bookcase thinking he could pass it off as his own creation. But he knew even Enid wouldn't believe that.

"Would you like to stay for dinner?" The Wife asked when Beauvoir said he had to go.

"*Merci,* but no. I just wanted to stop by and see your furniture."

They stood by the back door, waving to him. He'd been tempted to accept their invitation to join their little family. As he drove away he thought again about what Old had said so innocently about Havoc and his skill as a whittler, which rivaled Charlie's. On arriving back in Three Pines he went across to the bistro and ordered a *tarte au sucre* and a cappuccino. Myrna joined him with her *éclair* and *café au lait*. They chatted for a few minutes then Beauvoir made notes and Myrna read the London *Sunday Times Travel Magazine,* moaning occasionally over the *éclair* and over the descriptions of the spa getaways.

"Do you think it's worth a twelve-hour flight to go here?" She turned the magazine round and showed him soft white beaches, thatched huts, nubile young men, shirtless, carrying drinks with fruit in them.

"Where is it?"

"Mauritius."

"How much?"

Myrna checked. "Five thousand two hundred."

"Dollars?" Beauvoir almost gagged.

"Pounds. But it includes the flight. My budget today is five thousand pounds so it's a little over that."

"Book business must be good."

Myrna laughed. "I could sell every book in my place and still not be able to afford that." She put her large hand on the shiny picture. Outside the frosted window, kids were arriving home from school. Parents waited for them to come down the snowy, icy road from where the bus dropped them off, all red faced, bundled up, distinguish-

367

able only by the color of their bulbous snowsuits. They looked like giant, colorful balls cascading down the hill.

"This is fantasy money for a fictional trip. Cheap, but fun."

"Did someone say cheap but fun?" Gabri joined them and Beauvoir closed his notebook. "Where're we going this week?"

"He's also fictional, you know." Myrna indicated Gabri with her head.

"I am sometimes made-up," Gabri admitted.

"I'm considering Mauritius." She handed a magazine to Gabri and offered one to Beauvoir. He hesitated then noticed the icicles hanging from the homes, the snow piled on the roofs, the people bent against the wind and rushing for warmth.

He took one.

"Vacation porn," whispered Gabri. "Complete with rubber suits." He flashed an image of a muscular man wearing a tight scuba outfit.

Beauvoir gave himself a fictional budget of five thousand dollars then lost himself in Bali, in Bora-Bora, in St. Lucia.

"Have you been on a cruise?" he asked Myrna.

"Was on one earlier in the week. Upgraded to the Princess Suites. Next time I think I might upgrade all the way."

"I'm considering the owner's suite."

"Can you afford it?"

"True, I might go fake broke but I think it's worth it."

"God, I could use a cruise," said Gabri, lowering his magazine.

"Tired?" Myna asked. Gabri looked it.

"Très fatigué."

"It is true." Ruth plopped down in the fourth chair, knocking everyone with her cane. "He is a fatty gay."

The other two ignored her, but Beauvoir couldn't hide a small laugh. Before long the other two left, Myrna back to her quiet bookstore and Gabri to tend to a couple customers.

"So, why're you really here?" Ruth leaned forward.

"For your cheerful company, you old hag."

"Besides that, numb nuts. You never liked it here. Gamache does, I can tell. But you? You despise us."

Every hour of every day Jean-Guy Beauvoir searched for not just facts, but truth. He hadn't appreciated, though, how terrifying it was being with someone who spoke it, all the time. Well, her truth anyway.

"I don't," he said.

"Bullshit. You hate the country, you hate

nature, you think we're hicks, idiots. Repressed, passive-aggressive and English."

"I know you're English," he laughed. She didn't.

"Don't fuck with me. I don't have that much time left and I refuse to waste it."

"Then go away if you think I'm such a waste of time."

They glared at each other. He'd opened up to her the other night, told her things few others knew. He'd been afraid that might lead to some awkwardness but sure enough, when they'd met the next morning she'd looked at him as though he was a stranger.

"I know why you're here," he said at last. "For the rest of the story. You just want to hear all the gory details. You feed on it, don't you? Fear and pain. You don't care about me or the Chief or Morin or anyone else, all you want from me is the rest of the story, you sick old crone."

"And what do you want?"

What do I want? he thought.

I want to tell it.

SIXTEEN

Jean-Guy glanced round. The bistro was quiet. Placing his hands on the arms of his chair he hauled himself forward. The chair felt warm from the fire. In the grate the large logs popped, sending embers bouncing against the screen to glow on the stone hearth then slowly die away.

The maple logs smelled sweet, the coffee was strong and rich, the aromas from the kitchen familiar.

Not of home but of here.

He leaned forward and stared into the cold, blue eyes across from him. Winter eyes in a glacier face. Challenging, hard, impenetrable.

Perfect.

He paused and in an instant he was back there, since "there" was never far away.

"My favorite season is autumn, I think," Gamache was saying.

"I've always loved winter," came the

young voice over the monitors. "I think because I can wear thick sweaters and coats and no one can really see how skinny I am."

Morin laughed. Gamache laughed.

But that was all Inspector Beauvoir heard. He was out the door, through the Incident Room and into the stairwell. There he paused for a moment. Opening his fist he read the note Gamache had scrawled.

Find Agent Yvette Nichol. Give her this.

There was another note, folded, with Nichol's name on it. He opened it and groaned. Was the Chief mad? Because Yvette Nichol almost certainly was. She was the agent no one wanted. The agent who couldn't be fired because she wasn't quite incompetent or insubordinate enough. But she sure played around the cliff. And finally the chief had assigned her to telecommunications. Surrounded by things, not people. No interaction. Nothing major to screw up. No one to enrage. Just listening, monitoring, recording.

Any normal person would have quit. Any decent agent would have resigned. Like the witch trials of old. If she sank she was innocent, if she survived she was a witch.

Agent Nichol survived.

But still, he didn't hesitate. Down the stairs he ran, two at a time, until he was finally in the sub-basement. Yanking open a door he looked in. The room was darkened, and it took him a moment to make out the outline of someone sitting in front of green lights. On oval screens lines burst into a frenzy as words were spoken.

Then a face was turned to him. A green face, and eyes glowing green. Agent Yvette Nichol. He hadn't seen her in years and now he felt a tingling under his skin. A warning. Not to enter. This room. This person's life.

But Chief Inspector Gamache had wanted him to. And so he did. On the speaker he was surprised to hear the Chief's voice, talking now about various dog toys.

"Have you ever used a Chuck-it, sir?" Agent Morin asked.

"Never heard of it. What is it?"

"A stick thing with a cup on the end. It helps toss a tennis ball. Does Henri like balls?"

"Above all else," laughed Gamache.

"Idiotic conversation," came the female voice. A green voice. Young, ripe, filled with bile. "What do you want?"

"Have you been monitoring the conversation?" Inspector Beauvoir demanded. "It's on a secure channel. No one's supposed to have access to it."

"And yet you were about to ask me to start monitoring it, weren't you? Don't look so surprised, Inspector. Doesn't take a genius to figure that out. No one comes here unless they want something. What do you want?"

"Chief Inspector Gamache wants your help." He almost gagged on the words.

"And what the Chief Inspector wants, he gets. Right?" But she'd turned back into the room. Beauvoir felt on the wall and found the light switch. He turned it on and the room was flooded with bright fluorescent lights. The woman, who had seemed so menacing, so otherworldly, suddenly became human.

Staring at him now was a short, slightly dumpy, young woman with sallow skin marked by old blemishes. Her hair was dull and mousy and her eyes squinted to adjust to the sudden light.

"Why'd you do that?" she demanded.

"Sir," he snapped. "You're a disgrace but you're still a Sûreté officer. You'll call me 'sir' and the Chief Inspector by his full rank. And you'll do as you're ordered. Here."

He thrust the note at the agent who now looked very young, and very angry. Like a petulant child. Beauvoir smiled remembering his initial disquiet. She was pathetic. A sorry little person. Nothing more.

Then he remembered why he was there.

She might be a sorry little person, but Chief Inspector Gamache was risking his entire career in bringing her secretly into the investigation.

Why?

"Tell me what you know." She lowered the note and stared Beauvoir in the eye. "Sir."

It was a disconcerting look. Far smarter, far brighter, than he would have expected. A keen stare, and deep inside, still, a flash of green.

He bristled at her use of words. At that particular phrase. "Tell me what you know." It's what the Chief always asked when first arriving at a murder scene. Gamache would listen carefully, respectfully. Thoughtfully.

The antithesis of this willful, warped agent.

Surely she was mocking the Chief. But there were more important things than challenging her on that.

He told her what he knew.

The shooting, the kidnapping, the claims of the farmer to have attached a bomb. To go off the next morning at 11:18.

Instinctively they both glanced at the

clock. Ten past six in the evening. Seventeen hours left.

"Chief Superintendent Francoeur believes the kidnapper's a frightened backwoods farmer, probably with a small marijuana operation, who panicked. They think there's no bomb and no other plan."

"But Chief Inspector Gamache doesn't agree," said Agent Nichol, reading from the note. "He wants me to monitor closely." She looked up after a moment digesting the Chief's instructions. "They're monitoring closely upstairs I presume?"

She was unable, or unwilling, to rid her voice of bitterness. It was an annoying and annoyed little voice.

At a curt nod from Beauvoir she smiled and carefully folded the note. "Well I guess the Chief Inspector thinks I'm better."

Agent Nichol stared at Beauvoir, willing him to contradict her. He glared at her.

"Must be," he finally managed.

"Well, he's going to have to do more than talk about dog toys. Tell him to pause."

"Haven't you been listening? A pause and the bomb will go off."

"Does anyone really believe there's a bomb?"

"And you'd risk it?"

"Hey, I'm safe and warm here. Why not."

At a glare from Beauvoir she continued. "Look, I'm not asking him to go make a cup of coffee. Just a second here and there. Lets me record the ambient sound. Got it? Sir?"

Agent Yvette Nichol had started in homicide. Been chosen by Chief Inspector Gamache. Mentored by him. And had been a near complete failure. Beauvoir had begged the Chief to fire her. Instead, after many chances, he'd transferred her. To do something she needed to learn.

The one thing she clearly could not do.

Listen.

That was her job now. Her only job. And now Chief Inspector Gamache was putting his whole career, and perhaps Agent Morin's life, into these incompetent hands.

"Why haven't they traced the call yet?" Agent Nichol asked, swinging her seat back to the monitors and hitting some keys on her computer. The Chief's voice was crisper now, clear. As though he was standing with them.

"They can't seem to get a fix," said Beauvoir, leaning over her chair, staring almost mesmerized at the dancing waves on the screens. "When they do it shows Morin in a different place as though he's moving."

"Maybe he is."

"One moment he's by the U.S. border the next he's in the Arctic. No, he's not moving. The signal is."

Nichol made a face. "I think the Chief Inspector might be right. This doesn't sound like something rigged up by a panicked farmer." She turned to Beauvoir. "What does the Chief think it is?"

"He doesn't know."

"It would have to be something big," Nichol mumbled as she focused on the screen and the voices. "To kill an agent and kidnap another then to call the Chief Inspector."

"He needs to be able to communicate with us without Chief Superintendent Francoeur knowing," said Inspector Beauvoir. "Right now all his messages are monitored."

"No problem. Get me the code to his computer and I can set up a secure channel."

Beauvoir hesitated, examining her.

"What?" she demanded, then smiled. It was unattractive, and again Beauvoir felt a warning tingle. "You came to me remember. Do you want help or not? Sir?"

". . . Zora's a handful, apparently," came Gamache's voice. "Teething now. She loves the blanket you and Suzanne sent."

"I'm glad," said Morin. "I wanted to send

a drum set but Suzanne said maybe later."

"Marvelous. Perhaps you could also send some caffeine and a puppy," laughed Gamache.

"You must miss them, sir. Your son and grandchildren."

"And our daughter-in-law," Gamache said. "Yes, but they're enjoying Paris. Hard to begrudge them that."

"Damn it. He needs to slow down," snapped Nichol, annoyed. "He has to give me pauses."

"I'll tell him."

"Well, hurry up," said Nichol. "And get that code." She turned her back on Inspector Beauvoir as he strode out the door.

"Sir," he muttered as he bounded back up the stairs. "Sir. Shit-head."

At the eighth floor he wheezed to a stop and gasped for breath. Opening the door a little he could see Chief Superintendent Francoeur not far away. Over the monitors came the familiar voices.

"Has anybody spoken to my parents?" the young man asked.

"We're giving them regular updates. I've sent an agent to be with your family and Suzanne."

There was a longer pause.

"Are you all right?" Gamache jumped in.

"Fine," came the voice, though it was thin and struggling. "I don't mind for myself. I know I'm going to be all right. But my mother —"

There was silence again, but before it could go on too long the Chief Inspector spoke, reassuring the young agent.

Chief Superintendent Francoeur exchanged glances with the Inspector beside him.

Across the room Beauvoir could see the clock.

Sixteen hours and fourteen minutes left. He could hear Morin and the Chief Inspector discussing things they wished had gone differently in their lives.

Neither of them mentioned this.

Ruth exhaled. "This story you just told me, none of that was in the news."

She said "story" as though it was a fairy tale, a children's make-believe.

"No," agreed Beauvoir. "Only a few know it."

"Then why're you telling me?"

"Who'd believe you if you said anything? They'd all just think you're drunk."

"And they'd be right."

Ruth cackled and Beauvoir cracked a tiny smile.

Across the bistro Gabri and Clara watched.

"Should we save him?" Clara asked.

"Too late," said Gabri. "He's made a deal with the devil."

They turned back to the bar and their drinks. "So, it's between Mauritius and the Greek Islands on the *Queen Mary*," said Gabri. They spent the next half hour debating fantasy vacations, while several feet away Jean-Guy Beauvoir told Ruth what really happened.

Armand Gamache and Henri entered the third and last shop on their list, Augustin Renaud's list. The man while alive haunted the used bookstores in Quebec City buying anything that might have even a remote reference to Samuel de Champlain.

The little bell above the entrance tinkled as they entered and Gamache quickly closed the door before too much of the day crept in with him. It didn't take much, a tiny crack and the cold stole in like a wraith.

It was dark inside, most of the windows being "booked" off. Stacks of dusty volumes were piled in the windows, not so much for advertisement as storage.

Anyone suffering from claustrophobia would never get three steps into the shop.

The already narrow aisles were made all the more cramped by bookcases so stuffed they threatened to topple over, and more books were stacked on the floor. Henri picked his way carefully along behind Gamache. The Chief's shoulders brushed the books and he decided it might be best to remove his parka before he knocked over all the shelves.

Getting the coat off proved quite an exercise in itself.

"Can I help you?"

The voice came from somewhere in the shop. Gamache looked round, as did Henri, his satellite ears flicking this way and that.

"I'd like to talk to you about Augustin Renaud," called Gamache to the ceiling.

"Why?"

"Because," said Gamache. Two could play that game. There was a pause then a clambering of feet on a ladder.

"What do you want?" the bookseller asked, taking small, quick steps out from behind a bookcase. He was short and skinny, his fisherman's sweater was pilled and stained. An almost white T-shirt poked out of the collar. His hair was gray and greasy and his hands were dark from dust. He wiped them on his filthy pants and stared at Gamache then he noticed Henri looking out from behind the large man's legs.

Hiding.

Though Gamache would never say it to Henri's face, they both knew he wasn't the most courageous of dogs. Nor, it must be said, was Henri very bright. But he was loyal beyond measure and knew what mattered. Din-din, walks, balls. But most of all, his family. His heart filled his chest and ran to the end of his tail and the very tips of his considerable ears. It filled his head, squeezing out his brain. But Henri, the foundling, was a humanist, and while not particularly clever was the smartest creature Gamache knew. Everything he knew he knew by heart.

"Bonjour," the shopkeeper knelt in a totally involuntary movement and reached out to Henri. Gamache recognized it. He had it himself, as did Reine-Marie, when in the presence of a dog. The need to kneel, to genuflect.

"May I?" the man asked. It was the sign of an experienced dog owner, to always ask. Not only was it respectful, it was prudent. You never knew when a dog might not want to be approached.

"You run the risk of him never leaving, *monsieur,*" smiled Gamache as the shopkeeper produced a biscuit.

"Fine with me." He fed Henri the treat and rubbed his ears to groans from the dog.

It was then Gamache noticed the cushions on the floor and the name "Maggie" on the side of a food bowl. But no dog.

"How long ago?" Gamache asked.

"Three days," said the man, standing up and turning away. Gamache waited. He recognized this movement too.

"Now," the man finally said, turning back to Gamache and Henri. "You said you wanted to talk about Augustin Renaud. Are you a reporter?"

Gamache looked as though he might be, but not for the television or radio or even a daily paper. Perhaps for an intellectual, monthly magazine. One of those obscure university presses or journals specializing in dying ideas and the dead people who'd championed them.

He wore a shirt and tie under a cardigan the color of butterscotch. His slacks were charcoal gray corduroy. If the shopkeeper noticed the scar above Gamache's left temple he didn't mention it.

"*Non,* I'm not a reporter, I'm helping the police but in a private capacity."

Henri was now leaning against the little shopkeeper, whose hand was down by his side kneading the dog's head.

"Are you Alain Doucet?" Gamache asked.

"Are you Armand Gamache?" Doucet asked.

Both men nodded.

"Tea?" Monsieur Doucet asked. Within minutes the two men were sitting at the back of the tiny store in a cave of books, of words, of ideas and stories. And Monsieur Doucet, after pouring them fragrant cups of tea and offering his guest a digestive cookie, was telling his own story.

"Augustin came in once a fortnight at least, sometimes more often. Sometimes I'd call if I got in a book I knew he'd be interested in."

"What interested him?"

"Champlain, of course. Anything to do with the early colony, other explorers, maps. He loved maps."

"Was there anything he found here that particularly excited him?"

"Well, now, that's hard to say. Everything seemed to excite him, and yet he said almost nothing. I knew him for forty years but we never sat down like this, never had a conversation. He'd buy books and be animated and enthusiastic, but when I tried to ask him about it he'd get quiet, defensive. He was a singular man."

"He was that," said Gamache, taking a

bite of his digestive cookie. "Did you like him?"

"He was a good client. Never argued about price, but then I never tried to take advantage."

"But did you like him?" It was funny, Gamache had asked this question of all the used-bookstore owners and all had been evasive.

"I didn't know him but I'll tell you something, I had no desire to get to know him better."

"Why not?"

"He was a fanatic and they scare me. I think he'd do just about anything if he thought it would get him an inch closer to Champlain's body. So, I was civil, but kept my distance."

"Do you have any idea who might have killed him?"

"He had a knack for annoying people, but you don't kill someone just because they're annoying. The place would be littered with bodies."

Gamache smiled and took a leisurely sip of his strong tea, thinking.

"Do you know if Renaud had a current idea? Some new theory about where Champlain might be buried?"

"You mean the Literary and Historical

Society?"

"I mean any place."

Monsieur Doucet thought then shook his head.

"Did you buy books from them?"

"The Lit and His? Sure. Last summer. They had a big sale. I bought three or four lots."

Gamache put his mug down. "What was in them?"

"Frankly? I don't know. Normally I'd go through them but it was the summer and I was too busy with the flea market. Lots of tourists, lots of book collectors. I didn't have time to go through the boxes, so I just put them out at my stall. Renaud came by and bought a couple."

"Books?"

"Boxes."

"Did he go through them before buying?"

"No, just bought. People are like that, especially collectors. They want to go through them privately. I think that's part of the fun. I got another couple of lots from the Lit and His later, sometime this past fall, before they decided to stop the sale. I called Renaud and asked if he was interested. At first he said no then he showed up about three weeks ago asking if I still had them."

"Hmm." The Chief Inspector sipped and thought. "What does that tell you?"

Alain Doucet looked surprised. He had clearly thought nothing of it but now he did.

"Well, I guess it might mean he found something in that first lot and thought there might be more."

"Why the delay, though? If he bought the first couple boxes in the summer, why wait until after Christmas to contact you?"

"He's probably like most collectors. Buys loads of books meaning to go through them but they just sit there for months until he gets around to it."

Gamache nodded, remembering the rabbit warren that was Renaud's home.

"Do these numbers mean anything to you?" He showed Doucet the catalog numbers found in Renaud's diary. 9-8499 and 9-8572.

"No, but used books come in with all sorts of strange things written on them. Some are color-coded, some have numbers, some have signatures. Screws up their value, unless the signature is Beaudelaire or Proust."

"How'd he seem when he came by for the other lot?"

"Renaud? As always. Brusque, anxious. He was like an addict before a fix. Book freaks are like that, and not just old guys.

Look at kids lining up for the latest install-ment of their favorite books. Stories, they're addictive."

Gamache knew that was true. But what story had Augustin Renaud stumbled on? And where were the two books? Not in his apartment, not on his body. And what hap-pened to the other books in the lot? They weren't in the apartment either.

"Did he bring any books back?"

Doucet shook his head. "But you might ask the other used bookstores. I know he went to all of us."

"I've asked. You're the last, and the only one who bought the Literary and Historical Society books."

"Only one stupid enough to try to sell English books in old Quebec City."

The Chief's phone vibrated and he took it out. It was a call from Émile.

"Do you mind?" he asked and Doucet shook his head. "*Salut,* Émile. Are you at home?"

"No, I'm in the Lit and His. Amazing place. I can't believe I've never been before. Can you meet me here?"

"Have you found something?"

"I found Chiniquy."

"I'll be right there."

Gamache rose and Henri rose with him,

ready to go wherever Gamache went.

"Does the name Chiniquy mean anything to you?" he asked as they walked to the front of the store. It was almost four P.M. and the sun had set. Now the shop looked cozy, lit by lamps, the books merely suggestions in the shadows.

Doucet thought about it. "No, sorry."

Time, thought Gamache as he stepped once more into the darkness, it covered over everything eventually. Events, people, memory. Chiniquy had disappeared beneath Time. How long before Augustin Renaud followed?

And yet Champlain had remained, and grown.

Not the man, Gamache knew, the mystery. Champlain missing was so much more potent than Champlain found.

Picking up his pace, he and Henri wove between the revelers carrying their hollow plastic canes filled with Caribou, wearing their Bonhomme pins on their down-filled parkas. They wore smiles and huge mittens and joyful fluffy, warm toques, like exclamation marks on their heads. In the distance he heard the almost haunting blast on a plastic horn. A call to arms, a call to party, a call to youth.

Gamache heard it, but the call wasn't for

him. He had another calling.

Within minutes he and Henri were standing outside the brightly lit Literary and Historical Society. The small crowd of gawkers had given up, perhaps called away by the horns to something more interesting. Called to life, not to death.

Gamache entered and found his old mentor in the library surrounded by small stacks of books. Mr. Blake had emigrated from his armchair to the sofa and the two elderly men were chatting. They looked over as the Chief Inspector entered, and waved.

Mr. Blake stood and indicated his place.

"No, please," said Gamache, but it was too late. The courtly man was already standing next to his habitual chair.

"We've been having a terrific talk, you know," said Mr. Blake. "All about Charles Chiniquy. Remarkable man. But then, we're likely to think that," he said with a laugh.

"Found another one, Monsieur Comeau," Elizabeth MacWhirter called down from the balcony, then spying Gamache she waved.

Gamache caught Émile's eye and smiled. He'd made a few conquests here.

Soon all four were sitting round the coffee table.

"So," said Gamache, looking at the three

eager, elderly faces. "Tell me what you know."

"The first thing I did was call Jean," Émile said. "You remember him? He had lunch with us a few days ago at the Château Frontenac." Gamache remembered. The Laurel to René Dallaire's Hardy.

"A member of your Champlain Society."

"That's right, but he's also a student of Québec history in general. Most of the members are. He knew of Chiniquy, but not much more than I'd heard. Chiniquy was some sort of fanatic about temperance and had quit the Catholic Church and joined the Protestants. He's considered a bit of a nut. Did some good work then messed it up by going off the deep end himself.

"I was on my way home and just passing the Lit and His when I suddenly thought they might know Chiniquy here. After all, it is a Literary and Historical Society and presumably has links to Protestantism. So I came in."

Elizabeth picked up the thread. "He asked about Chiniquy. It's not a name I'm familiar with but I did find some books in our collection. He wrote quite a few. Then Mr. Blake came in and I directed Monsieur Comeau to him."

Mr. Blake leaned forward. "Charles Chiniquy was a great man, Chief Inspector. Much maligned and misunderstood. He should be considered one of the great heroes of Québec instead of forgotten or remembered only for his eccentricities."

"Eccentricities?"

"He was, it must be admitted, a bit of a showboat. Quite extravagant in his lifestyle and speeches. Charismatic. But he saved a lot of lives, built a sanatorium. At the height of his popularity tens of thousands took the pledge after listening to him speak. He was indefatigable. Ummm." Mr. Blake struggled a bit with the next part. "Then he went a bit far for the comfort of the Catholic Church. To be fair, they did give him a lot of warnings but finally he was stripped of his church. He quit in a rage and joined the Presbyterians."

"Didn't he claim Rome was conspiring to take over North America and had sent the Jesuits to kill Lincoln?" asked Émile.

"He might have mentioned that," said Mr. Blake. "Still, he did a great deal of good too."

"What happened to him?" asked Gamache.

"He moved to Illinois but annoyed so many people he soon left and ended his days in Montreal. Got married you know, and had two children, daughters I think. Died at the age of ninety."

"In 1899," said Gamache and when she looked surprised he explained. "I looked it up last night, but the file had just his dates, no real information about the man."

"There was a huge obituary in the *New York Times*," said Mr. Blake. "He was considered a hero by many people."

"And a nut by many too," admitted Elizabeth.

"Why would Augustin Renaud be interested in Chiniquy?"

All three shook their heads. Gamache thought some more.

"The big Presbyterian church is right next door, and the Lit and His has a number of his books, is it fair to assume there might have been a connection? A relationship?"

"Between Charles Chiniquy and the Lit and His?" asked Elizabeth.

"Well, there was James Douglas, he'd be a connection," said Mr. Blake.

"And who is that?" asked Gamache. Both Elizabeth and Mr. Blake turned in their seats and looked out a window. Gamache and Émile also looked but in the dark they saw only their own reflections.

"That's James Douglas," said Mr. Blake. Still they stared, and still all they saw were their own baffled faces.

"The window?" asked Gamache finally, after waiting long enough for Émile to ask the nonsensical question.

"Not the window, the bust," said Elizabeth with a smile. "That's James Douglas."

Sure enough, on the deep windowsill there stood a white alabaster bust of a Victorian gentleman. They always looked disturbing to Gamache. It was the white, empty eyes, as though the artist had sculpted a ghost.

"He was one of the founders of the Literary and Historical Society," said Mr. Blake.

Elizabeth leaned forward and said to Émile beside her, "He was also a grave robber. Collected mummies, you know."

Neither Gamache nor Émile did know. But they wanted to.

SEVENTEEN

"I'm afraid you'll have to explain yourself, *madame*," said Émile, with a smile. "Mummies?"

"Now, there was an original," Mr. Blake jumped in, warming to the subject. "James Douglas was a doctor, by all accounts a gifted physician. He could amputate a limb in less than ten seconds." On seeing their faces he continued, chastising them slightly. "It mattered back then. No anesthetic. Every moment must have been agony. Dr. Douglas saved a lot of people a lot of agony. He was also a brilliant teacher."

"Which is where the bodies come in," said Elizabeth, with more relish than they'd have expected. "He started off somewhere in the States —"

"Pittsburgh," said Mr. Blake.

"But was run out of town after he was caught grave robbing."

"It wasn't like it is today," said Mr. Blake.

"He was a doctor and they needed bodies for dissection. It was common practice to take them from paupers' graves."

"But probably not common practice for the doctors themselves to dig them up," said Gamache to Elizabeth's muffled laugh.

Mr. Blake paused. "That is, perhaps, true," he conceded. "Still, there was never any question of personal gain. He never sold them, only used the corpses to teach his students, most of whom went on to distinguished careers."

"But he got caught?" Émile turned to Elizabeth.

"Made a mistake. He dug up a prominent citizen and the man was recognized by one of the students."

Now everyone grimaced.

"So he came to Québec?" asked Gamache.

"Started teaching here," said Mr. Blake. "He also opened a mental hospital just outside the city. He was a visionary, you know. This was at a time when the deranged were tossed into places worse than prisons, locked up for life."

"Bedlam," said Elizabeth.

Mr. Blake nodded. "James Douglas was considered more than a little strange because he believed the mentally ill should be treated with respect. His hospital helped hundreds, maybe thousands, of people. People no one else wanted."

"Must have been an extraordinary man," said Émile.

"He was, by most accounts," said Mr. Blake, "a miserable, opinionated, arrogant man. Wretched. Except, when dealing with the poor and displaced. Then he showed remarkable compassion. Strange, isn't it?"

Gamache nodded. It was what made his job so fascinating, and so difficult. How the same person could be both kind and cruel, compassionate and wretched. Unraveling a murder was more about getting to know the people than the evidence. People who were contrary and contradictory, and who often didn't even know themselves.

"But where do the mummies come in?" asked Émile.

"Well, he apparently continued to take bodies from graves in and around Quebec City," said Elizabeth. "Again, just for teaching. He seems to have stayed clear of digging up the premier minister or any archbishops but his fascination with bodies does seem to have spread beyond just teaching."

"He was simply curious," said Mr. Blake, a slight defensiveness in his voice.

"He was that," agreed Elizabeth. "Dr.

Douglas was on vacation in Egypt and brought back a couple of mummies. Used to keep them in his home and would give talks in this very room on them. Propped them up against that wall," she waved to the far wall.

"Well," said Gamache slowly, trying to imagine it, "a lot of people were robbing graves back then. Robbing might be too strong a word," he said quickly, to assuage Mr. Blake's agitation. "It was the age when they were discovering all those tombs. King Tut, Nefertiti," he'd run out of Egyptian references. "And others."

Émile gave him an amused look.

"Show me a museum," said Mr. Blake, "and I'll show you treasures taken from graves. The British Museum stinks of tombs but where would we be without it? Thank God they took the things, otherwise they'd just be looted or destroyed."

Gamache remained silent. One civilization's courageous action was another's violation. Such was history, and hubris. In this case the famous Victorian ego that dared so much, discovered so much, desecrated so much.

"Whatever it was called," said Elizabeth, "it was strange. My grandparents went to Egypt on their Grand Tour and came back with rugs. Not a single body."

Émile smiled.

"One mummy was eventually sent to a museum in Ontario and then returned a few years ago to Egypt," Elizabeth continued, "when they discovered it was King Ramses."

"Pardon?" asked Gamache. "Dr. Douglas took the body of an Egyptian pharaoh?"

"Apparently," said Mr. Blake, struggling between embarrassment and pride.

Gamache shook his head. "So what does this remarkable Dr. Douglas have to do with Chiniquy?"

"Oh, didn't we say? They were good friends," said Mr. Blake. "While still a priest Chiniquy would go to Dr. Douglas's mental hospital to minister to the Catholics. It was Douglas who stirred Chiniquy to action. A number of the demented were also drunks. Dr. Douglas discovered if you locked them up, gave them good food and no alcohol they often returned to a state of sanity. But they had to stay sober or, better still, never have drunk to excess to begin with. He told Father Chiniquy about this and Chiniquy immediately grasped it. It became his life's work, his way to save souls, before they were damned."

"Temperance," said Gamache.

"The pledge," agreed Mr. Blake. "Get them to stop drinking, or never start. And tens of thousands did, thanks to Father Chiniquy. His public rallies became famous. He was the Billy Graham of his day, drawing people from all over Québec and the eastern United States. People couldn't sign up fast enough to take the pledge."

"All inspired by James Douglas," said Émile.

"They were lifelong friends," said Elizabeth.

A movement in the shadows caught Gamache's peripheral vision. He glanced up to the gallery but saw only the wooden statue of General Wolfe looking down on them, listening. But still, the Chief Inspector had the impression the General hadn't been alone. Someone else had been standing there, in the shadows. Hiding among the books, the stories. Listening. To the story of two inspired madmen, two old friends.

But there was another madman in the story. Augustin Renaud, who was also obsessed with the dead.

"The sale of books last year," Gamache began and immediately felt the shift in mood. Both Elizabeth MacWhirter and Mr. Blake became guarded. "I understand it wasn't very popular."

"No, within the English community it wasn't popular," admitted Elizabeth. "We eventually had to stop."

"Why?"

"Reactionaries," said Mr. Blake. "Perhaps not surprisingly the strongest opposition came from people who'd never even been in the Lit and His. They just hated the idea on principle."

"And what principle might that be?" asked Émile.

"That the Lit and His was created to preserve English history," said Elizabeth. "And any scrap of paper with English writing on it, every shopping list, every journal, every letter was sacred. By selling some off we were betraying our heritage. It just didn't feel right."

Feelings. As much as people tried to rationalize, tried to justify, tried to explain, eventually everything came down to feelings.

"Did anyone go through the books? How'd you decide what to sell?" Gamache asked.

"We started in the basement, ones that were deemed unimportant when they came in and so stayed in boxes. There were so many, I'm afraid we were overwhelmed and just sold them by the box load, happy to be rid of them."

"You had two sales?" asked the Chief.

"Yes. The first was in the summer, then we had a smaller, quieter one later. That was mostly to bookstores and people who seemed sympathetic to what we were doing."

"The books donated by Mrs. Claude Marchand back in 1899 were among the ones you sold," said Gamache.

"Is that right?" said Elizabeth.

"Is it significant?" asked Mr. Blake.

"We think so. Mrs. Marchand was Charles Chiniquy's housekeeper in Montreal. After his death they must have divided up his things and given her some of the books, or perhaps he asked that they be sent here. Either way, she must have known he had a relationship with the Literary and Historical Society and so sent them on. It seems when they arrived they were kept in boxes and probably put in your basement. People either didn't bother looking at them or didn't see their value."

"Are you saying we had a collection of Chiniquy's books and never even knew it?" asked Mr. Blake, getting quite agitated. "This is the very thing people were afraid of. That in our rush we'd sell off treasures. What were they?"

"We don't know," admitted Gamache. "But some were bought by Augustin Renaud and two books interested him in particular."

"Which ones?"

"Again, we don't know. We have the catalog numbers, but that's all. No titles, no idea what was in them."

"What could Father Chiniquy possibly have that Augustin Renaud would want?" Elizabeth asked herself. "Chiniquy wasn't interested in Champlain, at least not that we know of."

There were actually two questions, thought Gamache. What were those books? And why can't we find them?

Émile and Gamache paused outside the Lit and His.

"So, what do you think?" Émile asked, putting on his mitts and hat.

"I think if Chin is Chiniquy in Augustin Renaud's diary then JD must be James Douglas."

"And Patrick and O'Mara are long dead too," said Émile, his breath coming in puffs and his mouth already growing numb in the cold. Still the two men stood and talked.

Gamache nodded. "Renaud wasn't planning to meet those four men, he was making a note of a meeting they had. Here. More than a hundred years ago."

The men looked up at the building, rising behind them.

"And 18 whatever? The number in his diary?" Émile asked. "A time? A date?"

Gamache smiled. "We'll find out."

"We will," agreed Émile. It felt good to be working together again. "Coming?"

"I have a quick stop to make first. Can you take Henri home?"

Gamache watched Henri and Émile stepping carefully down rue St-Stanislas, making sure not to slip on the ice and snow.

The Chief Inspector walked the few meters to St. Andrew's Presbyterian Church. Trying the door he was somewhat surprised to find it unlocked. He poked his head into the church. The robin's egg blue ceiling was softly lit but the rest was in twilight.

"Hello," he called and his voice rattled round and finally disappeared. His intention was to speak to the young minister but he found himself drawn into the calm space. Taking his coat off he sat quietly for a few minutes, occasionally taking a deep breath and a long exhale.

Now there is no more loneliness.

Closing his eyes he let the voice loose, to

play. To run around in his head, to laugh and tell him once again about breaking his first violin, a tiny one lent by the school. Worth more money than they had and his mother mending it and handing it back to the distraught boy reassuring him.

Things are strongest where they're broken. Don't worry.

"What a kind thing to say," Gamache said and meant.

"To a clumsy boy," Morin agreed. "I broke everything. Violins, vacuums, glasses, plates, you name it. I once broke a hammer. If I didn't break it I lost it."

Morin laughed.

Gamache felt himself almost nodding off in the warmth and the peace and the soft laughter in his head, and when he opened his eyes he was surprised to find he was no longer alone. The young minister was sitting quietly at the other end of the pew, reading.

"You seemed amused just now," Tom Hancock said.

"Did I? Something came to me. What're you reading?" Gamache asked, his voice not more than a whisper.

Tom Hancock looked down at the book in his hand.

"Steer toward the third tall oak from the tip

of Fischer's Point," he read. *"Once halfway across you must adjust your course, taking into account the current, the winds, the ice. And always steer for the ice floes, never to open water."*

"A little known Gospel," said Gamache.

"Well, after the reforms they're harder to recognize," said the Reverend Mr. Hancock. He put a bookmark in, closed it and handed the old volume to his companion. Gamache accepted it and looked at the title.

DELIVERING THE MAIL ACROSS THE MIGHTY SAINT LAWRENCE, IN WINTER. A MANUAL.

Opening the cover he scanned the title page, and found the date. 1854.

"Obscure book." He handed it back. "Where'd you find it?"

"One of the perks of being so close to the Lit and His. You get to prowl the shelves. I think I'm the second person to take it out in 150 years."

"Have you found other interesting books there?"

"Some, most equally obscure. When I first arrived I'd check out books of old sermons, in the hopes some of my parishioners would be impressed but no one seemed to notice, so I stopped." He laughed. "This though is quite useful. Has strategies for crossing the river in winter."

"The ice canoe race? There must be easier pastimes."

"Are you kidding? Canoeing across a frozen river is a breeze compared to what I normally do."

Now Gamache shifted in the hard pew so that he was facing Tom Hancock. "That difficult?"

The young man grew somber. "At times."

"Have you heard of a Father Chiniquy?"

Tom Hancock thought then shook his head. "Who is he?"

"Was. He lived more than a hundred years ago. A famous Catholic priest who quit the church and joined the Presbyterians."

"Really? Chiniquy?" He thought about the name then shook his head. "Sorry. I should probably know who he was, but I'm not from here."

"Not to worry, not many know him now. I'd never heard of him."

"Is he important to the case?"

"I can't see how he can be, and yet his name's come up in Augustin Renaud's journal. Renaud seems to have bought a few of Chiniquy's books at the Lit and His sale."

The Reverend Mr. Hancock grimaced.

"That sale haunts us."

"Were you in favor of it?"

"It seemed obvious. The place was in disrepair, it was a question of losing a few unused books to save the many. It should have been an easy decision."

Gamache nodded.

That was often the equation, give up the few to save the many. From a distance it seemed so simple, so clear. And yet, from a distance you might see the big picture, but not the whole picture, you missed the details. Not everything was seen, from a distance.

"Did the opposition surprise you?" Gamache asked.

Tom Hancock hesitated. "I was disappointed more than surprised. The English community is shrinking, but it needn't die out. It's on the cusp. It could go either way. It's crucial right now to keep the institutions alive. They're the anchors of any community." He hesitated a moment, not happy with his choice of words. "No, not the anchors. The harbors. The places people go and know they're safe."

Safe, thought Gamache. How primal that was, how powerful. What would people do to preserve a safe harbor? They'd do what they'd done for centuries. What the French had done to save Québec, what the English had done to take it. What countries do to protect their borders, what individuals do to protect their homes.

They kill. To feel safe. It almost never worked.

But Tom Hancock was speaking again. "It's vital to hear your own language, to see it written, to see it valued. That's one of the reasons I was so glad to be asked to sit on the Literary and Historical Society board. To try to save the institution."

"Do they share your concern?"

"Oh yes, they all know how precarious it is. The debate is really how best to keep the institutions going. The Lit and His, the Anglican cathedral, this church, the high school and nursing home. The CBC. The newspaper. They're all threatened."

The young minister turned earnest eyes on Gamache. Not the burning eyes of a zealot, not Renaud or Champlain or Chiniquy eyes, but the eyes of someone with a calling greater than himself. A simple desire to help.

"Everyone's sincere, it's just a question of strategy. Some think the enemy is change, some think change is what will save them, but they all know their backs are to the cliff."

"The Plains of Abraham, replayed?"

"No, not replayed. It never ended. The English only won the first skirmish, but the French have won the war. The long-range plan."

"Attrition?" asked Gamache. "Revenge of the cradle?"

It was a familiar argument, and a familiar strategy. The Catholic Church and politicians for generations demanded the Québécois have huge families to populate the huge territory, to squeeze the more modest Anglos out.

But finally it wasn't simply the size of the French population that did the English in, but their own hubris. Their refusal to share power, wealth, influence with the French majority.

If their backs were to the cliff it was an abyss of their own making and an enemy they'd created.

"If the English community is going to survive," said Tom Hancock, "it's going to have to make some sacrifices. Take action. Adapt." He paused, looking down at the book clasped in his hand.

"Change course?" asked Gamache, also glancing at the book in the minister's hand. "They're making for the open water? Trying the easy way first?"

Tom Hancock looked at Gamache and the tension seemed to break. He even laughed a little.

"*Touché.* I guess we all do. I think people see me as this muscular, young guy. Stunningly handsome even." He stole a glance at his amused companion. "But the truth is, I'm not strong at all. Every day frightens me. That's why I'm doing the canoe race. Ridiculous thing to do, really, paddle and run across a half-frozen river in minus thirty degree temperatures. You know why I'm doing it?" When Gamache shook his head the younger man continued. "So that people will think I'm strong." His voice dropped, as did his eyes. "I'm not strong at all. Not where it counts. The truth is I'd rather be sweating and heaving a canoe over slush and ice than sitting one-on-one with a sick and dying parishioner. That terrifies me."

Gamache leaned forward, his voice as soft as the light. "What scares you about it?"

"That I won't know what to say, that I'll let them down. That I won't be enough."

I will find you. I won't let anything happen to you.

Yes sir. I believe you.

The two men stared into space, lost in their own thoughts.

"Doubt," said Gamache at last and the

412

word seemed to fill the huge empty space around them. He stared straight ahead, seeing the closed door. The wrong door.

Tom Hancock watched his companion, let him sit in silence for a few moments.

"Doubt is natural, Chief Inspector. It can make us stronger."

"And things are strongest where they're broken?" asked the Chief, with a smile.

"They better be, I'm counting on it," said the Reverend Mr. Hancock.

Gamache nodded, thinking. "But still you do it," he said at last. "You sit with parishioners who are sick and dying. It scares you, but you do it every day. You don't run away."

"I have no choice. I have to aim for the ice, not the open water if I'm going to get where I want to go. And so do you."

"Where do you want to go?"

Hancock paused, thinking. "I want to get to shore."

Gamache took a deep breath and a long exhale. Hancock watched him.

"Not everyone makes it across the river," said Gamache quietly.

"Not everyone's supposed to."

Gamache nodded.

I believe you, whispered the young voice.

Gamache leaned forward in the pew, placing his elbows on his knees and lacing his strong fingers together, one hand clasping the other, which trembled just a little. Then he rested his chin on them.

"I made some terrible mistakes," he said at last, staring into the half light. "Not seeing the full picture, though all the clues were there. Not grasping it all until it was almost too late and even then I made a terrible mistake."

The corridor, the closed door. The wrong door, the wrong way. The seconds ticking down. The race back toward the other door, heart pounding.

Don't worry, son. It will be all right.

Breaking through the door and seeing him sitting there, his thin back to them, facing the wall. Facing the clock. That ticked down.

Yes sir, I believe you.

To zero.

Bringing himself back to the silent church Gamache looked over to Tom Hancock.

"Sometimes life goes in a direction not of our choosing," said the minister, softly. "That's why we need to adapt. It's never too late to change direction."

Gamache remained silent. He knew the young minister was wrong, sometimes it was too late. Général Montcalm knew that. He knew that.

"They should have sold all those boxes of

414

books," said Tom Hancock, at last, lost in his own reverie. "Now, there's a symbol for you. The Lit and His cluttered with unwanted English words. Weighed down by the past."

"Je me souviens," whispered Gamache.

"It'll drag them under," said the Reverend Mr. Hancock, sadly.

Gamache was beginning to understand this community and this case.

And himself.

EIGHTEEN

"Ten more."

Clara groaned and lifted her legs in unison.

"Keep your back flat!"

Clara ignored the order. This wasn't pretty. It certainly wasn't perfect, but she was going to damn well do it.

"One, grunt, two, groan, three . . ."

"Did I tell you about my day skiing at Mont Saint-Rémy?"

Pina, the exercise instructor, apparently didn't need to breathe. Her legs and arms seemed independent of the rest of her, moving in military precision while she lay on the mat chatting away as though at a slumber party.

Myrna was swearing and sweating freely and sometimes making other noises while Ricky Martin sang "Livin' la Vida Loca." Clara was always happy to exercise close to Myrna since any number of sins, and sounds, could be blamed on her. And she was easy to hide behind. The entire class could hide behind Myrna.

Myrna turned to Clara. "If you hold her down, I'll kill her."

"But how? We'd never get away with it." Clara had been giving it some thought. So far she'd done twelve leg lifts of the ten Pina announced, and now Pina was complaining bitterly about snowboarders while her own pneumatic legs went up and down.

"No one would say anything," said Myrna, lifting her legs a millimeter. "And if they threaten to, we kill them too."

It was as good a plan as Clara had heard.

"Where are we with the leg lifts?" Pina asked. "Three, four . . ."

"OK, Bugsy, I'm in," snorted Clara.

"So'm I," said Dominique Gilbert on Clara's other side, her voice almost as unrecognizable as her purple face.

"Dear God," said The Wife, across the room, "do it soon."

"Do what?" asked Pina, starting to bicycle her legs in mid-air.

"Murder you, of course," snapped Myrna.

"Oh, that," laughed Pina, never totally ap-preciating how close it came every class.

Twenty minutes later the class was over, after a last Tai Chi movement in which

Clara meditated on murder. It was a good thing she adored Pina and needed the class.

Toweling off and rolling up her mat, Clara wandered over to the cluster of women who'd formed in the middle of the room. After a minute or so Clara managed to get the conversation around to where she wanted it.

"Did you see Inspector Beauvoir's back in the village?" she asked, nonchalantly, dabbing at a trickle of sweat down her neck.

"Poor guy," said Hanna Parra. "Still, he seems better."

"I think he's kinda cute," said The Wife. Her eyes were large, expressive and without guile. An earth mother, married to a carpenter.

"You don't," said Myrna with a laugh. "He's too skinny."

"I'd fatten him up," said The Wife.

"There's something about that Inspector. I want to save him," said Hanna. "Heal him, make him smile."

"Mr. Spock," said Clara, though this conversation wasn't exactly going as she'd hoped and she hadn't helped by just taking it off into outer space. "The Vulcan?" she explained when a few of the women looked perplexed. "Oh, for God's sake, you can't tell me you don't know *Star Trek?* Everyone had a crush on Mr. Spock because he was so cool and distant. They wanted to be the one to break down his reserve, to get into that heart."

"It's not his heart we want to get into," said Hanna and everyone laughed.

They put on their coats and ran across the snowy road to the inn and spa for the regular post-exercise tea and scones.

Clara was still amazed every time she entered the inn and spa, remembering it as the crumbling old Hadley house before Dominique and her husband Marc had bought it. Now their hostess sat relaxed and elegant, smiling and pouring tea.

Had Dominique killed the Hermit? Clara couldn't see it. No, if Clara was being honest, the most likely suspect months ago, and the most likely one still, was Marc Gilbert. Dominique's husband.

Clara brought the conversation around to murder once again.

"Hard to believe Olivier's been gone almost six months," she said, accepting a fragrant cup of tea from Dominique. Out the window she could see the clear blue day, always the coldest. Snow caught up in a whirlwind swirled by the window, making a slight sprinkling sound, like sand against the glass.

Inside the inn and spa it was peaceful. The room was filled with antiques, not cumbersome Victorian oak, but simple pine and cherry pieces. The walls were painted pastel shades and felt restful, serene. A fire was lit and the place smelled delicately of maple wood smoke, moisturizers and tisanes. Chamomile, lavender, cinnamon.

A young woman arrived with a plate of warm scones, clotted cream and homemade strawberry jam. This was Clara's favorite part of exercise class.

"How's Olivier doing?" The Wife asked.

"He's trying to adjust," said Myrna. "I saw him a few weeks ago."

"He still insists he didn't kill the Hermit," said Clara, watching everyone closely. She felt a fraud, pretending to be a homicide investigator, play-acting. Still, there were worse stages. Clara smoothed clotted cream on her warm scone, then strawberry jam.

"Well, if he didn't do it, who did?" Hanna Parra was a stout, attractive pillar. Clara had known her for decades. Could she be party to a murder? Might as well ask.

"Could you kill anyone?"

Hanna looked at her with some surprise, but no anger or suspicion.

"Now there's an interesting question. I know for sure I could."

"How can you be so sure?" asked Dominique.

"If someone broke into our home and threatened Havoc or Roar? I'd kill them in a second."

"Kill the women first," said The Wife.

"I beg your pardon?" asked Dominique. She sat forward and placed her delicate teacup on its saucer.

"It's a training booklet put out by the Mossad," said The Wife. Even the therapists who were giving Myrna and Hanna pedicures stopped what they were doing to stare at this lovely young woman who'd said the ugliest thing.

"How would you know that?" asked Myrna.

The Wife smiled fully. "Got you scared, don't I?"

They all laughed, but the truth was, they were thrown off a little. The Wife let them stew for a moment then laughed.

"I heard it on CBC Radio. A show on terrorism. The theory is that women almost never kill. It takes a great deal to get a woman to murder, but once she decides to, she won't stop until it's done."

There was silence as they thought about that.

"Makes sense to me," said Myrna, at last.

"When a woman commits to something she does it with both her heart and her head. Very powerful."

"That was the point of the interview," said The Wife. "Women rarely join terrorist cells, but Mossad agents are told if they raid a cell and there's a female terrorist, kill her first because she'll never surrender. She'll be the most vicious one there. Merciless."

"I really hate that thought," said Dominique.

"So do I," admitted The Wife. "But I think it might be true. Almost nothing could get me to hurt anyone, physically or emotionally, but I can see if I had to, I could. And it'd be awful."

The last sentence was said with sadness, and Clara knew it to be the truth.

Had one of these women killed the Hermit after all? But why? What could have driven them to it? And what did she really know about them?

"Did you know Charlie's speaking now?" said The Wife, changing the subject. "Thanks to Dr. Gilbert. He comes by once a week and works with him."

"How kind." A man's voice spoke from the doorway. They looked over.

Marc Gilbert stood there, tall, lanky, his blond hair was cut to his scalp and his blue eyes were intense.

"Charlie can now say 'boo' and 'shoo,' " said The Wife with enthusiasm.

"Congratulations," Marc smiled. There was sarcasm there, and amusement.

Clara felt her back go up. How easy it was to dislike this smiling man.

She'd tried to like him, for Dominique's sake, but it was a losing battle.

"I remember, my first word was 'poo,' " she said to The Wife, who was looking at Marc, perplexed.

"Poo?" asked Myrna, jumping into the awkward silence. "Should I ask?"

Clara laughed. "I was trying to say 'puppy.' Came out as 'poo.' Then it became my nickname, everyone called me that for years. My father still does, sometimes. Did your father have a nickname for you, growing up?" Clara asked Marc, trying to break some of the tension.

"He was never around. Then he took off and that was that. So, no."

The tension in the room rose.

"And now, it seems he's found another family." Marc stared at The Wife.

So that was it, thought Clara. Jealousy.

The Wife stared at Marc and Clara could see a flush spreading up her neck. Marc smiled, turned on his heels, and left.

"I'm sorry —" Dominique started to say to The Wife.

"It's all right, he has a point actually. Old worships your father-in-law. I think he sees him as a sort of surrogate grandfather for Charles."

"His own father doesn't visit?"

"No. He died when Old was a teenager."

"Must have been a fairly young man when he died," said Myrna. "An accident?"

"He walked out onto the river one spring. The ice wasn't as solid as he thought."

She left it at that and it was far enough. Everyone in the room knew what must have happened. The cracking underfoot, the web of lines, the man looking down. Stopping. Standing still.

How far away the shore must seem when you're on thin ice.

"Did they ever find him?" Myrna asked.

The Wife shook her head. "I think that's the worst. Old's mother's still waiting for him."

"Oh, God," moaned Clara.

"Does Old?" Myrna asked.

"Think he's still alive? No, thank God, but he doesn't think it was an accident."

Neither did Clara. It sounded deliberate to her. Everyone knew that walking on ice in spring was courting death.

And sure enough, the ice had broken under the father, as he knew it would, but his son had also lost his footing that day. And Vincent Gilbert had righted him. The Asshole Saint had stepped in and was helping Charlie, and helping Old. But at what cost?

Was that what she'd heard a few minutes ago in Marc Gilbert's voice? Not sarcasm, but a small crack?

"What about you Clara?" Dominique asked, pouring more tea. "Are your parents still alive?"

"My father is. My mother died a few years ago."

"Do you miss her?"

There was a question, thought Clara. Do I miss her?

"At times. She had Alzheimer's at the end." Seeing their faces she hurried to reassure them. "No, no. Strangely enough the last few years were some of our best."

"When she was demented?" asked Dominique. "I begin to see why they called you Poo."

Clara laughed. "It was actually a bit of a miracle. She forgot everything, her address, her sisters. She forgot Dad, she even forgot us. But she also forgot to be angry. It was wonderful," Clara smiled. "Such a relief.

She couldn't remember her long list of grievances. She actually became a delightful person."

She'd forgotten to love, but she also forgot to hate. It was a trade-off Clara was happy to accept.

The women in the room chatted about love, about childhood, about losing parents, about Mr. Spock, about good books they'd read.

They mothered each other. And by lunch they were ready to meet the winter's day. As Clara walked home, scone crumbs in her hair, the taste of chamomile on her lips, she thought of Old's father, frozen in time. And the look on Marc Gilbert's face as the crack had appeared.

Armand Gamache sat in the Paillard bakery on rue St-Jean and stared at Augustin Renaud's diary. Henri was curled up under the table while outside people were trudging head down through the snow and the cold.

How could Chiniquy, the fallen priest, and Augustin Renaud, the amateur archeologist be connected? Gamache stared at Renaud's excited markings, the exclamation marks, the swirls around the names of the four men. Chin, JD, Patrick, O'Mara. Swirls of ink so forceful the pen had almost ripped the paper. And below the entry were the catalog numbers.

9-8499

9-8572

Almost certainly the numbers related to books sold by the Literary and Historical Society and, equally certainly, they were from the lot donated by Chiniquy's housekeeper and left in their boxes in the basement for more than a century.

Until Augustin Renaud had bought them from the secondhand bookseller, Alain Doucet. In two lots. First in the summer, then the last lot just a few weeks ago.

What was in those books?

What did Chiniquy have that excited Augustin Renaud?

Gamache took a sip of hot chocolate.

It had to have something to do with Champlain, and yet the priest had shown absolutely no interest in the founder of Québec.

Chin, Patrick, O'Mara, JD. 18-something.

If Chiniquy was ninety when he died in 1899, that meant he was born in 1809. Could the number be 1809? Or 1899? Maybe. But where did that leave him?

Nowhere.

His eyes narrowed.

He looked at 1809 closely then snapping his notebook shut he drained his drink, put money on the table then he and Henri hurried into the cold. Taking long strides he saw the Basilica getting larger and larger as he approached.

At the corner he paused, in his own world, where snow and biting cold couldn't touch him. A world where Champlain was recently dead and buried, then reburied.

A world of clues over the centuries, as buried as the body.

He turned and walked briskly up des Jardins, stopping in front of the beautiful old door, with the wrought-iron numerals.

1809.

He rapped and waited. Now he felt the cold and beside him Henri leaned against his legs for warmth and comfort. Gamache was about to turn away when the door opened a crack, then all the way.

"Entrez," said Sean Patrick, stepping back quickly, out of the way of the biting wind as it invaded his home.

"I'm sorry to bother you again, Monsieur Patrick," said the Chief Inspector as they stood in the dark, cramped entrance. "But I have a couple of questions. May I?" He motioned toward the interior of the home.

"Fine," said Patrick, walking reluctantly

ahead. "Where to?"

"The living room, please."

They found themselves in the familiar room, surrounded by censorious Patricks past.

"These are your great-grandparents, correct?" Gamache looked at a couple posing in front of this home. It was a wonderful picture, two stern sepia people in what looked like their Sunday best.

"It is. Taken the year they bought this place."

"In the late 1800s you told us last time we talked."

"That's right."

"Do you mind?" Gamache reached to take the photo off the wall.

"Please yourself." It was clear Patrick was curious.

Turning the picture over Gamache found it was sealed at the back with brown paper. There was a photographer's shop sticker, but no date. And no names.

Gamache put his reading glasses on and peered closely at the photo. And there, poking out from under the frame in the lower right-hand corner was what he was looking for.

A date.

1870.

Replacing the photo, he moved down the wall and stopped in front of another picture of great-grandfather Patrick. In this one he was with a group of other laborers, standing in front of a big hole. The building behind was barely visible.

Great-grandfather Patrick was smiling and so was another man, standing next to him. But everyone else in the photo looked grim. And why not? Their lives, like their fathers' before them, would have been miserable.

Irish immigrants, they'd come to Canada for a better life only to die of plague in the crowded ships. Those that survived spent their lives in menial labor. Living in squalor in the Basse-Ville, the Lower Town, in the shadow of the cliffs, below the mighty Château Frontenac.

It was a life of near despair. So why were these two men smiling? Gamache turned the photo around. It too was sealed.

"I'd like to take this backing off. Do you mind?"

"Why?"

"I think it might help us with the case."

"How?"

"I can't tell you, but I promise not to harm the photo."

"Is this going to get me into trouble?"

Patrick searched Gamache's face and

rested on his thoughtful eyes.

"Not at all. Indeed, I'd consider it a favor."

After the briefest pause, Patrick nodded.

"*Bon, merci.* Can you turn on all the lights and get me your sharpest knife?"

Patrick did all that and the two men and a dog leaned over the table, the knife in Gamache's hand. It shook slightly and Gamache gripped it tighter. Patrick glanced at the Chief Inspector, but said nothing. Gamache lowered the knife and carefully pried the brittle old paper away from the frame. Little by little it came up.

Resisting the temptation to rip it off in one go, they carefully teased it up until it was off and the back of the photograph was exposed to sunlight for the first time since it was sealed more than a century earlier. And there, in precise, careful writing, were the names of the men, including the two who were smiling.

Sean Patrick and Francis O'Mara.

1869.

Gamache stared.

The note in Augustin Renaud's diary didn't say 1809. It said 1869.

Chiniquy met with this Patrick and this O'Mara and James Douglas in 1869.

Why?

Gamache looked over at the wall of ancestors standing outside this home. A great distance from the Basse-Ville, a universe away from there. Much further than the distance between Ireland and Canada, this was the unbridgeable gap between Us and Them.

A rough Irish laborer in a fine Upper Town home, in 1870. It should not have been. And yet, it was.

Gamache looked back down at the smiling men in the photograph, standing in front of a building. O'Mara and Patrick. What were they so happy about?

Gamache could guess.

NINETEEN

"Dr. Croix?"

Gamache saw the man's back stiffen. It was an eloquent little movement, involuntary and habitual. Here was a man engrossed in what he was doing, not pleased with the interruption. That, Gamache knew, was understandable. Who didn't feel that way occasionally?

What was even more telling, though, was the long pause. Gamache could almost see the armor going on, the plates snapping down the archeologist's back, the spikes and prickles and chains clicking into place. And then, after the armor, the weapon.

Anger.

"What do you want?" the stiff back demanded.

"I'd like to speak with you, please."

"Make an appointment."

"I don't have time."

"Neither do I. Good day." Serge Croix

leaned further over the table, examining something.

There was a reason, Gamache knew, Québec's Chief Archeologist chose to work with clay and shards of pottery, with arrowheads and old stone walls. He could question them and while they might, occasionally, contradict him it was never messy, never emotional, never personal.

"My name is Armand Gamache. I'm helping to investigate the murder of Augustin Renaud."

"You're with the Sûreté. You have no jurisdiction here. Go mind your own business."

Still the stiff back refused to move.

Gamache contemplated him for a moment. "Do you not want to help?"

"I have helped." Serge Croix turned round and glared at Gamache. "I spent an entire afternoon with Inspector Langlois digging in the basement of the Literary and Historical Society. Gave up my Sunday for that and you know what we found?"

"Potatoes?"

"Potatoes. Which is more than Augustin Renaud ever found when digging for Champlain. Now, I don't mean to be rude but go away, I have work to do."

"On what?" Gamache approached.

They were in the basement of the chapel of the Ursuline convent. It was lit with industrial lamps and long examination tables were set up in the center of the main room. Dr. Serge Croix stood beside the longest table.

"It's an ongoing dig."

Gamache looked into a hole by one of the rough stone walls. "Is this where Général Montcalm and his men were buried?"

"No, they were found over there." Croix motioned into another part of the basement and went back to his work. Gamache took a few strides and peered in. He'd never been in that basement before, but had read about it since he was a schoolboy. The heroic Général riding up and down on his magnificent horse, inspiring the troops. Then the fusillade, and the Général was hit, but still he clung to his mount. When it was clear the battle was lost, when it was clear Bougainville was not going to arrive, the French forces had retreated into the old city. Montcalm had ridden there, supported on either side by foot soldiers. Taken to this very spot, to die in peace.

He'd hung on, remarkably, until the next day when he finally succumbed.

The nuns, afraid the English might desecrate the body, afraid of reprisals, had buried the Général where he'd died. Then, at some later date, the sisters had dug up his skull and a leg bone and put it into a crypt in the chapel, to be protected and prayed to privately.

A relic.

These things had power in Québec.

Général Montcalm had only recently been reunited with the men he'd died with. His remains had been reburied in a mass soldiers' grave a few years ago, a grave that contained the bodies of all the men who died in one terrible hour on the fields belonging to the farmer Abraham.

French and English, together for eternity. Long enough to make peace.

Gamache watched the Chief Archeologist bend over a piece of metal, brushing the dirt free. Was this grave robbing? Could they never let the dead be? Why dig up the Général and rebury him with great ceremony and a huge monument a couple hundred yards away? What purpose was served?

But Gamache knew the purpose. They all did.

So that no one would ever forget, the deaths and the sacrifice. Who had died and who had done it. The city might have been built on faith and fur, on skin and bones, but it was fueled by symbols. And memory.

Gamache turned and saw that Dr. Croix was staring in the same direction, to where the Général had been buried and dug up.

"*Dulce et Decorum est,*" the archeologist said.

"*Pro patria mori,*" Gamache finished.

"You know Horace?" Croix asked.

"I know the quote."

"It is sweet and right to die for your country. Magnificent," said Croix, gazing beyond Gamache.

"You think?"

"Don't you, *monsieur?*" Croix turned suspicious eyes on the Chief Inspector.

"No. It's an old and dangerous lie. It might be necessary, but it is never sweet and rarely right. It's a tragedy."

The two men glared at each other across the dirt floor.

"What do you want?" Croix demanded.

He was tall and slender, hard and sharp. A hatchet. And he was aimed at Gamache.

"Why would Augustin Renaud be interested in some books belonging to Charles Chiniquy?"

Not surprisingly Dr. Croix looked at Gamache as though he was mad.

"What's that supposed to mean? I don't even understand the question."

"Not long before he was murdered Renaud found two books that excited him. Books that came from the Literary and Historical Society, but that had once belonged to Father Chiniquy. You know who I mean?"

"Of course I know. Who doesn't?"

The entire world out there, thought Gamache. It was funny how obsessed people believed others equally obsessed, or even interested. And for archeologists and historians, gripped by the past, it was inconceivable others weren't.

For them, the past was as alive as the present. And while forgetting the past might condemn people to repeat it, remembering it too vividly condemned them to never leave. Here was a man who remembered, vividly.

"What connection could Charles Chiniquy have had to Champlain?" Gamache asked.

"None."

"Think, please." Gamache's voice, while still pleasant, now held an edge. "Chiniquy possessed something that excited Augustin Renaud. We know Renaud had only one passion. Champlain. Therefore, in the late 1800s Charles Chiniquy must have found something, some books, about Champlain and when Renaud found them he felt they'd lead him to where Champlain is buried."

"Are you kidding? Birds led him there. Little voices in his little head led him there, rice pudding led him there. He saw clues and certainties everywhere. The man was a lunatic."

"I don't say the Chiniquy books really did answer the mystery of Champlain," Gamache explained. "Only that Renaud believed they did."

Croix's eyes narrowed but Gamache could see he was no longer dismissing the question. Finally he shook his head.

"I have another question," said the Chief Inspector. "Chiniquy and James Douglas were friends, correct?"

Croix nodded, interested in where this might be going.

"Why would they meet two Irish immigrant laborers in 1869?"

"The workers were either drunk or insane or both. No big mystery there."

"Except there is. They met at the Literary and Historical Society."

That gave Croix pause.

"Now, that is a mystery," he admitted. "The Irish hated the English. There's no way they'd have gone to the Literary and Historical Society voluntarily."

"You mean, it wouldn't have been their idea?"

"I frankly doubt they could even read and write. Probably didn't know the Literary and Historical Society existed and if they did, the last place they'd want to go is into the heart of the Anglo establishment."

"And yet they did. To meet with Father Chiniquy and Dr. James Douglas. Why?"

When no answer came Gamache fished into his breast pocket and brought out the old photograph.

"These are the workers, the ones smiling. Shortly after this was taken that man," Gamache placed his finger on the figure of Sean Patrick, "bought a home in the Upper Town, just around the corner from here on des Jardins."

"Impossible."

"Fact."

Croix searched Gamache's face then returned to the photograph.

"Do you know what digging work was going on at the time?"

"In 1869? Lots I'd imagine."

"It would be the summer, judging by what they're wearing and probably in the old city. Look at the stonework."

Croix examined the grainy photo and nodded.

"I can try to find out."

"Bon," said Gamache, holding out his hand for the picture. Croix seemed reluctant to let it go but eventually gave it back.

"How did you find out about this meeting between Chiniquy, Douglas and the laborers?" Croix asked.

"From Renaud's diary. I have no idea how he knew about it. Presumably it's in one of the books he found. He bought the Chiniquy collection from the Literary and Historical Society. There was something in them, but we can't find the books. Renaud seems to have hidden them. What could hundred-year-old books contain that someone was willing to kill for them?" Gamache wondered.

"You'd be surprised. Not everything buried is actually dead," said the archeologist. "For many the past is alive."

What putrid piece of history was walking among them? Gamache wondered. What had Augustin Renaud disturbed?

He remembered an entry in Renaud's diary. Not the one circled and exclaimed over but a quieter entry, a meeting he would never make. With an SC.

The Chief Inspector slowly returned the photograph to his pocket, watching Croix, who was walking back to his work table.

"Were you going to meet Augustin Renaud?"

Croix stopped, then turned and stared.

"What?"

"Thursday at one o'clock. Augustin Renaud had an appointment with an SC."

"SC? That would be anyone."

"With the initials SC, yes. Was it you?"

"Me, have lunch with Renaud? I wouldn't be seen in the same room with the man if I could help it. No. He was always asking, demanding, to meet with me, but I never agreed. He was a nasty little piece of work who thought he knew better than anyone else. He was vindictive and manipulative and stupid."

"And maybe, finally, he was right," said Gamache. "Maybe he found Champlain. Was that what you were afraid of? That he might actually succeed? Is that why you tried to stop him at every turn?"

"I tried to stop him because he was a bumbling idiot who was ruining perfectly good and valuable archeological digs with his fantasies. He was a menace."

Serge Croix's voice had risen so that the harsh words bounced and throbbed off the hard stone walls, coming back at the two men. Filling the space with rage that echoed and grew.

But the last sentence was rasped out. Barely audible, it scraped along the dirt floor and gave Gamache a chill.

"You tried to stop him. Did you finally succeed?"

"You mean did I kill him?"

They glared at each other.

"I didn't arrange to meet him, and I certainly didn't kill him."

"Do you know where Champlain is buried?" Gamache asked.

"What did you just ask?"

"Do you know where Samuel de Champlain is buried?"

"What do you mean by that?" Croix's voice was low and his look filthy.

"You know what I mean. The question is clear."

"You think I know where Champlain is buried and am keeping it a secret?"

Croix invested each and every word, every syllable, with scorn.

"I think it's almost inconceivable that we know where minor clerics, where war heroes, where farmers are buried," said Gamache, not taking his eyes off the archeologist. "But not the founder of this country, the father of this country. I think you and the archeological establishment heaped derision onto Augustin Renaud, not because he was so laughable, but because he wasn't. Was he getting close? Had he actually found Champlain?"

"Are you mad? Why would I hide the greatest archeological find in the nation? It would make my career, make my reputation. I'd be forever remembered as the man who gave the Québécois the one piece missing in their history."

"That piece isn't missing, *monsieur,* just the body. Why?"

"There was a fire, the original church burned, documents burned —"

"I know the official history but that doesn't explain it and you know that. Why hasn't his body been found? It makes no sense. So I ask myself the other question. Not why hasn't he been found, but suppose he has? Why cover it up?" Gamache moved closer to the Chief Archeologist with each word until they were almost nose to nose. And Gamache whispered, "To the point of murder."

They stared and finally Croix leaned back.

"Why would someone want to do that?" asked Croix.

"There's only one reason, isn't there," said Gamache. "Champlain wasn't what he seemed. He wasn't quite the hero, the father figure, the great man. Champlain's become

444

a symbol of the greatness of the Québécois, a potent symbol for the separatists of what the settlement might have been, had the English not taken over. Champlain hated the English, derided them as brutes. On every level Champlain is the perfect tool for Québec separatists. But suppose this wasn't true?"

"What're you saying?"

"A lot of what we know to be history isn't," said Gamache. "You know that, I know that. It serves a purpose. Events are exaggerated, heroes fabricated, goals are rewritten to appear more noble than they actually were. All to manipulate public opinion, to manufacture a common purpose or enemy. And the cornerstone of a really great movement? A powerful symbol. Take away or tarnish that and everything starts to crumble, everything's questioned. Can't have that."

"But what could be so bad about Champlain?" Croix asked.

"When was he born?"

"We don't really know."

"What did he look like?"

Croix opened his mouth then shut it again.

"Who was his father?"

Now Croix was silent, not even trying.

"Was he a spy? He was an expert map-maker and yet many of the maps showed ridiculous creatures and claimed events that were clearly lies."

"It was the style of the time."

"To lie? Is that ever a style? We know who would want him found, Dr. Croix, but who wants him to remain buried?"

As Gamache left he wished the meeting with the Chief Archeologist could have been more cordial, if such a thing was possible with Serge Croix. He'd have loved to poke around that storied basement, loved to ask about the Battle of the Plains of Abraham, about the cannonballs still found in trees in old Quebec City.

He'd have loved to ask him about the strange coincidence of Captain Cook and Bougainville fighting in the same battle, on opposite sides, and Bougainville's almost inconceivable decision not to help his Général.

But those were questions that would have to wait and for which there might be no answer.

Just before plunging back into the Québec winter he called Inspector Langlois and made an appointment. Ten minutes later he was walking through the corridors of police headquarters looking for Inspector Langlois's offices, a visiting professor perhaps, an academic called in to consult.

"Chief Inspector." Langlois advanced, his hand out. Others in the large room got to their feet as Gamache entered. He nodded to them and smiled briefly then Langlois showed him into his private office.

"You must be used to it by now," said Langlois.

"The staring? Goes with the position, so yes, I'm used to it." Gamache handed Langlois his coat. "But it's changed of course, since the kidnapping and the other events."

No use pretending otherwise.

Inspector Langlois hung up the Chief's parka.

"I've been following the fall-out from it all, of course. The main question seems to be why we didn't realize the attack was coming."

Langlois searched Gamache's face, anxious for an answer. But he'd find none there.

"The people who did this were patient. The plan a long time in the making," said the Chief at last. "It moved so slowly as to be invisible."

"But something that big —" Inspector Langlois's question was the same as everyone else's. How could they have missed it?

Misdirection. And cunning. And the ability of the attackers to adapt. That was how, thought Gamache.

He accepted the chair indicated but said nothing.

Langlois sat across from him. "When did you realize it was more than a simple kidnapping?"

Gamache was quiet. He saw again Inspector Beauvoir returning from seeing Agent Nichol in the basement of Sûreté headquarters. Where Chief Inspector Gamache had placed her a year or more ago. A job he knew she'd hate, but needed to learn. Listening to other people. And not talking.

She needed to learn to be quiet.

Beauvoir had not been happy at bringing Agent Nichol in. Neither had he, for that matter. But he could see no other option. Chief Superintendent Francoeur was off chasing the kidnappers, down paths Gamache was more and more convinced were being laid out by the kidnappers themselves. Leading the Sûreté here and there. Morin's transmissions appearing to pop up all over the vast province. The trace a farce.

No. They needed help. And the embittered young agent in the basement was the only one he could turn to.

Chief Superintendent Francoeur would

never think of her. No one ever did. And so Gamache could operate quietly, through her.

She says she needs the password for your computer, Beauvoir scrawled longhand. *So that nobody else will see our messages. She also wants you to pause as long as possible when speaking with Morin so she can get some ambient sound.*

Gamache nodded and without hesitation handed over his private password. He knew he was giving her access to everything. But he also knew he had no choice. They were blind. Not even Morin could help them. He was tied up facing a wall, and a clock. He'd done the best he could, describing his surroundings. The concrete floors, the dirt, the impression he had that wherever he was, it was abandoned. Paul Morin described the silence.

But he'd been wrong. The place wasn't abandoned. Nor was it silent. Not quite. He'd been fooled by the headset, which made clear Gamache's voice from miles away, but muffled any sound just feet away.

But Agent Nichol had found it. Slight sounds in the silence.

"The *premier* seems relieved it hasn't reached the political level, yet," said Langlois, crossing his legs. "The damage has

449

been contained."

Seeing Gamache's blank face he immediately regretted his comment.

"*Désolé,* I didn't mean that. I was in the funeral cortege. Far behind you, of course."

Gamache smiled slightly. "It's all right, it's hard to know what to say. I suspect there's no right thing. Don't worry about it."

Langlois nodded then, making up his mind, he leaned forward. "When did you realize what was going on?"

"You don't really expect me to answer that, do you?" It was said with some humor, just enough to cut the edge off the words.

"I suppose not. Forgive me. I know you've given your depositions but as a cop I'm just curious. How did we all miss it? Surely it was obvious? The planned attack was so," Langlois searched for a word.

"Primitive?" asked Gamache at last.

Langlois nodded. "So simple."

"And that's what made it effective," said Gamache. "We've spent years looking for a high-tech threat. The latest bomb. Bio-industrial, genetic, nuclear. We searched the Internet, used telecommunication. Satellites."

"But the answer was right there all along," said Langlois, shaking his head in amazement. "And we missed it."

I'll find you. I won't let anything happen to you.

I believe you, sir.

In the brief pauses Gamache provided in his conversation with Paul Morin they'd picked up distant sounds, like the whispers of ghosts deep in the background.

Agent Morin wasn't alone. The "farmer" hadn't abandoned him after all. Others were there, speaking softly, softly. Walking softly, softly. Making almost no noise. But some. Enough for the delicate equipment and surprisingly sensitive ears to find.

And the words they'd spoken? It had taken hours, precious hours, but Nichol had finally isolated one crucial phrase.

La Grande.

Over and over she'd played it for Beauvoir, examining each syllable, each letter. The tone, the breath. Until they'd reached a conclusion.

La Grande. The power dam that held back trillions of tons of water. The giant dam that was ten times the size of any other in North America. That provided hydroelectricity for millions, hundreds of millions, of people.

Without it much of Canada and the States would be plunged into a dark age.

The La Grande dam was in the middle of

nowhere, near impossible to get to without official permission.

Gamache had looked at his watch at that moment, when Beauvoir and Nichol had written him from the basement. Sent him the sound bite so he could hear what they'd found.

It was three in the morning. Eight hours left. He and Morin had been discussing paint samples and names. Banbury Cream. Nantucket Marine. Mouse Hair.

In a few strides Gamache was over at the huge ordinance map of Québec on his wall. His finger quickly found the La Grande River, and the slash across it that had diverted and dammed the flow, killing thousands of acres of old-growth forest, herds of caribou and deer and moose. Had stirred up mercury and poisoned native communities.

But it had also been a miracle of engineering and continued to provide power decades later. And if it was suddenly removed?

Chief Inspector Gamache's finger made its dreadful way south, tracing the torrent that would be created when all that water was suddenly released, all that energy suddenly released. It would be like nuclear bombs tumbling down the length of the province.

His finger hit Cree villages then larger and larger towns and cities. Val-d'Or. Rouyn-Noranda.

How far down would the water get before it petered out, before it dissipated? Before all its energy was spent? How many bodies would be swept down with it?

Now Paul Morin was talking about the family cat peeing in his father's printer.

Had Morin been taken there? Was he being held at the dam?

I'll find you.

I believe you, sir.

"Sir?"

Gamache looked up into the face of Inspector Langlois.

"Are you all right?"

Gamache smiled. "Just fine. My apologies."

"What can I do for you?"

"It's about the Renaud case. Have you found any boxes of books that might have belonged to Renaud that weren't in his apartment?"

"His ex-wife has some. He'd taken them over to her basement a few weeks ago. What is it?"

Gamache sat forward and brought out his notebook. "May I have her address please?"

"Certainly." He wrote the address down

and handed it to the Chief Inspector. "Anything else?"

"No, this is perfect. *Merci.*" Gamache folded the note, put on his coat, thanked the Inspector and left, his boots echoing with purpose down the long corridor and out the door.

Hopping into a cab he called Émile then had the cab swing by his home and together they drove out the old gates, along Grande-Allée with its merrily lit bars and restaurants. The cab turned right onto Avenue Cartier then right again onto a small side street. Rue Aberdeen.

From the taxi Gamache had called Madame Renaud to make sure she was home. A moment later she opened the door and the two men entered. It was a main-floor flat in the gracious old row houses, each with wrought-iron stairs outside, leading to the apartments above.

Inside, the floors were dark wood and the rooms were generous and beautifully proportioned. Wide original crown molding swept around where the walls met the high ceiling. Each chandelier had a plaster rosette. These were genteel homes in a much sought-after *quartier* of Québec. Not everyone wanted to live within the walls, where life tended to be cramped and dictated by planners long dead. Here the streets were wider, planted with soaring old trees and each home had a modest front garden, when not buried under feet of snow.

Madame Renaud was short and cheerful. She took their coats and offered them a cup of coffee which both men declined.

"We're sorry for your loss, *madame*," said Gamache, taking a seat in the inviting living room.

"*Merci*. He was unbearable, of course. A pig-headed man, totally self absorbed. And yet —"

Gamache and Émile waited while she composed herself.

"And yet now that he's gone life feels emptier, less vibrant. I envied him his passion. I don't think I've ever felt that strongly about anything. And he wasn't a fool, you know, he knew the price he paid, but he was willing to pay it."

"And what was that price?" Émile asked.

"He was mocked and ridiculed, but more than that, no one liked him."

"Except you," said Gamache.

She said nothing. "He was lonely, you know, in the end. But still he couldn't stop, couldn't trade a dead explorer for living friends."

"When did he bring these books to you?"

Gamache asked.

"About three weeks ago. There're four boxes. He said his apartment was too crowded."

Émile and Gamache exchanged a quick glance. Renaud's apartment was certainly cramped, but it was already a disaster, four more boxes would have made no difference.

No. He'd brought them to his wife for another reason. For safekeeping.

"Did he bring you anything else?" Émile asked.

She shook her head. "He was secretive by nature, some might say paranoid," she smiled. She was a woman of good cheer and Gamache wondered at Augustin Renaud, who'd chosen her as his wife. For a few bright years had he known happiness? Had that been his one shining attempt to change course? And find a place on the shore with this jovial, kind woman? But he couldn't, of course.

Gamache watched Madame Renaud chat with Émile. She still loved him, despite all that, thought Gamache. Was that a blessing or a curse?

And he wondered if that would go away, with time. Would the voice fade, the features blur? Would the memories recede and take their place with other pleasant, but neutral events from the past?

Avec le temps. Do we love less?

"Do you mind if we go through the boxes?" Gamache asked.

"Not at all. The other officers took a look but didn't seem very interested. What are you looking for exactly?"

"Two books," said Gamache. They'd walked to the back of the apartment, into the large, old-fashioned kitchen. "Unfortunately we don't know what they are."

"Well, I hope you find them here." She opened a door and turned on a light.

Gamache and Émile saw wooden steps going straight down into a dark cellar with a dirt floor. A slight musky aroma met them, and as they headed down the stairs it felt a bit like wading into water. Gamache could feel the cool air creep up his legs until it was at his chest, his head and he was submerged in the dank and the chill.

"Watch your heads," she called but both men were familiar with these old homes and had already ducked. "The boxes are over by the far wall."

It took a moment for Gamache's eyes to adjust, but finally they did and he saw the four cardboard boxes. Walking over he knelt at one while Émile took another.

Gamache's box contained a variety of

books in different sizes. First he checked their catalog numbers. All were from the Literary and Historical Society, a few even had the name Charles Chiniquy written in but none matched the numbers in the diary. He moved to another box.

That box was filled with bound sermons, reference books and old family bibles, some Catholic, some Presbyterian. He opened the first book and checked the number. 9-8495. His heart quickened. This was the box. Opening the next book and the next, the numbers mounted. 9-8496, 8497, 8498. Gamache brought out the next book, a black leather collection of sermons and opened it. 9-8500.

He stared at it, willing the numbers to change, then he carefully, slowly opened again and replaced each of the twenty books in the box. One was indeed missing.

9-8499.

It had sat between that book of sermons and Chiniquy's confirmation bible.

"Maudits," Gamache swore under his breath. Why wasn't it there?

"Any luck?" He turned to Émile.

"Nothing. The damned book should be right here," Émile shoved a finger between two volumes. "But it's gone. 9-8572. Do you think someone got here first?"

"Madame Renaud said only Langlois's team has been."

"Still, what is here might be helpful," said Émile.

Gamache peered into the box. It contained a series of black leather volumes, spine out, all the same size. Gamache took one out and examined it. It was a diary. Émile's box contained the diary and journals of Charles Paschal Télesphore Chiniquy.

"Each book is a year," said Émile. "The missing one is for 1869."

Gamache sat back on his haunches and looked at his mentor, who was smiling.

Even in the dim light of the basement Gamache could see Émile's eyes were bright. "Well, Chief?" said Émile, straightening up. "What next?"

"There's only one thing to do now, Chief," smiled Gamache. He picked up the box of Chiniquy journals. "Go for a drink."

The two men returned upstairs and with Madame Renaud's permission they left with the box. Just around the corner was the Café Krieghoff and a chilly minute later they were there, sitting at a corner table by the window, away from other patrons. It was six in the evening and the work crowd was just arriving. Civil servants, politicians from the nearby government offices, professors, writers and artists. It was a bohemian hangout, a separatist haunt, and had been for decades.

The waitress, clad in jeans and a sweater, brought them a bowl of nuts and two Scotches. They sipped, nibbled the nuts, and read from Chiniquy's journals. It was fascinating stuff, insight into a mind both noble and mad. A mind with absolutely no insight into itself, a mind filled with purpose and delusion.

He would save souls and screw his superiors.

Gamache's phone vibrated and he took the call.

"Chief?"

"*Salut* Jean-Guy. How are you?"

The question was no longer simply *politesse* but was asked with sincerity.

"I'm actually doing well. Better."

And he sounded it. There was an energy to the younger man's voice Gamache hadn't heard in months.

"You? Where are you? I hear lots of noise."

"Café Krieghoff."

Beauvoir's laugh came down the telephone line. "Deep into a case, I see."

"*Bien sûr.* And you?" He could hear sounds as well.

"The bistro. Research."

"Of course. Poor one."

"I need your help," said Beauvoir. "About the murder of the Hermit."

TWENTY

It took Chief Inspector Gamache a moment to tear himself away from the 1860s Québec of Charles Chiniquy's journals to the quaint village of Three Pines today.

And yet, it wasn't that much of a leap. He suspected Three Pines probably hadn't changed all that much in the last 150 years. Had Father Chiniquy chosen to visit the tiny hamlet he'd have seen the same old stone houses, the clapboard homes with dormers and smoking chimneys. He'd have walked across the village green to the shops made of faded rose brick, pausing perhaps to admire the trinity of trees at the very center of the community.

Only the people had changed in Three Pines in the past 150 years, with the possible exception of Ruth Zardo. Gamache could only imagine how Ruth would have greeted Father Chiniquy. He smiled at the thought of the drunken mad poet meeting the sober mad minister.

Well, take this then. *Ruth had written.*
Have some more body.
Drink and eat.
You'll just make yourself sick. Sicker.
You won't be cured.

Would Chiniquy have cured her? Of what? Her drinking, her poetry? Her wounds? Her words?

"How can I help?" he asked Beauvoir, picturing his second in command sitting in the bistro in front of the fire with a microbrewery beer and a bowl of salty chips.

"If Olivier didn't kill the Hermit it comes down to five other suspects," said Beauvoir. "Havoc Parra and his father Roar. Vincent Gilbert and his son Marc or Old Mundin."

"Go on." Gamache looked out the window of the Café Krieghoff to the cars crawling along the snowy evening street and the cheerful holiday lights still up. The capital had never looked prettier.

"There are two questions. Who had the opportunity and who had the motive? From what I can see, Roar, Havoc and Marc had the opportunity. Roar was cutting the trails that led right to the Hermit. The cabin was on Marc's land and he could have walked

463

those trails at any time and found it."

"*C'est vrai,*" said the Chief, nodding as though Beauvoir could see him.

"Havoc worked late every Saturday and could have followed Olivier to the cabin."

Gamache paused, remembering the case, remembering the night the Hermit had been killed. "But it wasn't just Havoc in the bistro, Old Mundin also came in every Saturday night around closing time to get furniture to repair. He was there the night of the murder."

"That's true," agreed Beauvoir. "Though he mostly went straight home before the bistro was locked up. But, yes, he's a possibility."

"So that's Roar and Havoc Parra, Old Mundin and Marc Gilbert. All could have found the cabin and killed the Hermit. So why is Vincent Gilbert still a suspect? As you say, he doesn't seem to have had the opportunity to find the cabin."

Beauvoir paused. "It just seems too pat. His son buys a derelict old home no one wanted. They move here, then the Hermit is murdered and Marc's estranged father shows up at almost exactly the same moment."

"But you have no proof," said Gamache, pushing slightly, "beyond a feeling."

464

He could sense his second in command bristle. Jean-Guy Beauvoir had no truck with "feelings," with "intuition." Gamache, on the other hand, did.

"But you might be right," said the Chief. "And what about motive?"

"That's more difficult. We know why Olivier might have wanted the Hermit dead, but why would anyone else? If the motive was robbery the killer made a pretty poor job of it. From what we can make out, nothing was stolen."

"What other motives could there be?" asked Gamache.

"Revenge. The Hermit did something terrible and the murderer found him and killed him for it. Might have been hunting him for years. That would also explain why the Hermit was a hermit. He was hiding. Those treasures had to come from somewhere. He almost certainly stole them himself."

"Then why didn't the murderer take them after he'd killed the Hermit? Why leave everything there?"

Gamache saw again the home buried in the wilderness. From the outside it seemed just a rustic log cabin, with window boxes of flowers and herbs, a vegetable garden, a fresh stream behind the home. But inside? Signed first editions, ancient pottery, tapestries, a panel from the famous Amber Room, leaded crystal and gold and silver candlesticks. And the violin.

And he saw young Agent Morin standing in the cabin, so awkward, like a wooden puppet, all gangly arms and legs. But as soon as he'd played that priceless violin his body had changed.

The haunting first notes of "Colm Quigley" returned to Gamache.

"There's another possibility," said Beauvoir. "The murder wasn't about the treasure but something else the Hermit had done."

"Your theory then is that the treasure distracted us. Distracted me."

"No one who walked into that cabin believed the motive was anything other than the treasure. It seemed so obvious."

But Gamache knew Beauvoir was being uncharacteristically tactful. He, Gamache, had been in charge of the investigation. He'd assigned the agents and investigators and he'd followed his own instincts, often in the face of strong protests on the part of Inspector Beauvoir who'd insisted all along both the murderer and the motive were in Three Pines.

Gamache now believed Beauvoir was right, and he'd been wrong. And perhaps had put an innocent man in prison.

"Okay, let's suppose the treasure had nothing to do with the murder," said the Chief Inspector. "Suppose the only thing of value the murderer wanted was the Hermit's life and once taken he left."

"So," said Beauvoir, slinging his leg over the side of the easy chair and burrowing into the wing. He was hidden from view of the rest of the bistro, only his casual leg visible. No one could see him, but neither could he see anyone. "Take away the treasure but that still leaves us with other clues. The repetition of the word 'Woo' whittled into that chunk of red cedar, and woven into the web. It must mean something. And Charlotte, that name kept popping up, remember?"

Gamache did remember. It had sent him rushing across the continent to a mist-covered archipelago in northern British Columbia, on what now appeared to be a fool's errand.

"There's something about your list of suspects," said Gamache after going over each one again in his head.

"*Oui?*"

"They're all men."

"Are you afraid the Equal Opportunity Bureau's going to complain?" laughed Beauvoir.

"I just wonder if we should be consider-ing some of the women," said Gamache. "Women have patience. Some of the most vicious crimes I've seen have been commit-ted by women. It's more rare than men, but women are more likely to bide their time."

"That's funny, Clara was saying the same thing this afternoon."

"How so?" Gamache leaned forward. Anything Clara Morrow had to say was, in the Chief's opinion, worth listening to.

"She spent the morning with a bunch of women from the village. Apparently Old's wife said something odd. She quoted some instruction manual that advised anti-terrorism squads to kill the women first."

"The Mossad," said Gamache. "I've read it."

Beauvoir was silent. The Chief Inspector often surprised him. Sometimes it was with incomprehensible bits of Ruth's poetry but mostly it was with things like this, with what he knew.

"So you know what it refers to," said Beauvoir. "A woman's capacity to kill."

"Yes, but mostly it's about her dedication. Once committed some women will never give up, they'll be merciless, unstoppable." Gamache was silent for a moment, staring out the window but no longer seeing the flow of people bundled against the biting cold. "In what context were they talking about this? Why did The Wife say it?"

"They were talking about the case. Clara had asked Hanna Parra if she could kill."

"Clara needs to be more careful," said the Chief. "Did anyone particularly respond to that?"

"Clara said they all did, but after some discussion they reluctantly agreed the Mossad might have had it right."

Gamache frowned. "What else did the women talk about?"

Beauvoir looked at his notes and told Gamache about the rest of the conversation. About fathers and mothers, about Alzheimer's, about Charlie Mundin and Dr. Gilbert.

"There was something else. Clara thinks Marc Gilbert is desperately jealous of Old Mundin."

"Why?"

"Apparently his father's spending a lot of time at the Mundins'. The Wife admitted Old has developed a sort of bond with Dr. Gilbert. A substitute father."

"Jealousy's a powerful emotion. Powerful enough to kill."

"But the wrong victim. Old Mundin isn't dead."

"So how could this play into the death of the Hermit?" the Chief asked and waited while there was a long pause. Finally Beauvoir admitted he didn't see how it could.

"Both Carole Gilbert and Old Mundin are originally from Quebec City. Could you ask around about them?" When the Chief agreed Beauvoir paused before asking his last question. "How are you?"

He hated to ask, afraid that maybe the Chief would one day tell him the truth.

"I'm at the Café Krieghoff with Émile Comeau, a bowl of nuts and a Scotch. How bad can it be?" Gamache asked, his voice friendly and warm.

But Jean-Guy Beauvoir knew exactly how bad it could be and had been.

Hanging up, an image stole into his mind, uninvited, unexpected, unwanted.

Of the Chief, gun in hand, suddenly being lifted off his feet, twisting, turning. Falling. To lie still on the cold cement floor.

Gamache and Émile hailed a cab and took the diaries home. As Émile prepared a simple supper of warmed-up stew Gamache fed Henri then took him for a walk to the bakery for a fresh baguette.

Once home the men sat in the living room, a basket of crusty bread on the table,

470

bowls of beef stew in front of them and the Chiniquy diaries piled on the sofa between them.

They spent the evening eating and reading, making notes, occasionally reading each other a particularly interesting, moving or unintentionally amusing passage.

By eleven Armand Gamache took off his reading glasses and rubbed his weary eyes. So far while historically fascinating the Chiniquy journals hadn't revealed anything pertinent. There was no mention of the Irish laborers, Patrick and O'Mara. And while he did talk about James Douglas in the earlier diaries, the later ones mentioned him only in passing. Eventually there was an entry Émile read Gamache about Douglas packing up his three mummies and heading down to Pittsburgh, to live with his son.

Gamache listened and smiled. Chiniquy had made it sound petty, like a kid picking up his marbles and going home. Had Father Chiniquy done that on purpose, to diminish Dr. Douglas? Had there been a falling out? Did it matter?

An hour later he glanced at Émile and noticed the older man had fallen asleep, a journal splayed open on his chest. Gently raising Émile's hand he removed the book, then put a soft pillow under Émile's head and covered him with a comforter.

After quietly placing a large cherry log on the fire Gamache and Henri crept to bed.

The next day, before breakfast, he found an email from the Chief Archeologist.

"Something interesting?" Émile asked.

"Very. Sleep well?" Gamache looked up from his message with a smile.

"Wish I could say that was the first time I'd nodded off in front of the fire," Émile laughed.

"So it wasn't my stimulating conversation?"

"No. I never listen to you, you know that."

"My suspicions confirmed. But listen to this," Gamache looked back down to his email. "It's from Serge Croix. I asked him to find out what digging work was being done in the old city in the summer of 1869."

Émile joined his friend at the table. "The year Chiniquy and Douglas met the Irish workers."

"Exactly, and the year covered in the missing journal. Dr. Croix writes to say there were three big digs. One at the Citadelle, to reinforce the walls, one to expand the Hôtel-Dieu hospital and the third? The third was to dig a basement under a local restaurant. The Old Homestead."

Émile sat for a moment then leaned back

in the chair and brought a hand up to his face, thinking. Gamache got to his feet.

"I think I'll treat you to breakfast, Émile."

Comeau got up, his eyes bright now too. "I think I know where."

Within twenty minutes they'd climbed the steep and slippery slope of Côte de la Fabrique, pausing for breath and to stare at the imposing Notre-Dame Basilica. Where the original little church had stood, built by the Jesuit priests and brothers and supported by Champlain. A modest New World chapel dedicated to the Virgin Mary to celebrate the return of Québec from the English in their see-saw battle for possession of the strategic colony.

This was where the great man's funeral had been held and where he'd been buried, albeit briefly. At one time Augustin Renaud had been convinced he was still there in the small chapel of St. Joseph, where the amateur archeologist had found a lead-lined coffin and some old coins. And had started digging without permission, igniting a storm that had engulfed even the church. Père Sébastien had sided with Renaud, to the fury of the Chief Archeologist.

Still, nothing had been found. No Champlain.

Though, strangely, that coffin had never

been opened. All had agreed it couldn't possibly be Champlain. It was a rare show of respect for the dead, by the archeologists, by Renaud and by a church more than happy to dig up Général Montcalm but not this anonymous corpse.

So, Gamache thought as he continued his walk, suppose Champlain hadn't originally been buried in the chapel but in the graveyard. The records showing the exact resting place of the father of Québec had been lost in the fire, even the exact position of the cemetery was just a guess. But if it was beside the chapel that could put the cemetery right about —

Here.

Gamache stopped. Above him loomed the Château Frontenac and off to the side Champlain himself, imposing and impossibly heroic, staring out across the city.

And in front of the Chief? The Old Homestead, now a restaurant.

Taking off his gloves he reached into his jacket and took out the sepia photo taken in 1869.

The Chief Inspector backed up a few paces, walked a couple to the right, then stopped. Looking from the photo to the reality and back again. His bare fingers were red and burning from the cold, but still he held the photo, to be sure.

Yes.

This was it, this was the exact spot where Patrick and O'Mara had stood 150 years earlier, on a sweltering summer day.

They'd been digging beneath the Old Homestead and something they found made the normally sullen men smile. Before it had been a restaurant the Homestead had been, as it sounded, a private home. And before that? It was a forest, or a field.

Or maybe, a graveyard.

The Old Homestead was now a greasy spoon. It had seen better days. Even bombardment by English cannons would have been better than what had become of it in recent years.

Waitresses, gamely wearing vaguely period costume, poured weak coffee into mass-produced white mugs. Hard, uncomfortable wooden chairs, made to look olde worlde, held tourists who'd hoped the charming exterior was a promise of a charming interior.

It wasn't.

Mugs with coffee slurping over the rims were placed in front of Émile and Gamache. They'd managed to get a banquette of worn red Naugahyde, rips and tears repaired with shiny silver duct tape.

Gamache caught Émile's eye. Both felt slightly ill as they looked at what had been done to a landmark. Old Quebec City had been fought over, the French valiantly defending their heritage, their *patrimoine*. They'd ripped it from the hands of the English time and again, only to ruin it themselves centuries later.

Still, it wasn't what was inside that mattered to them now. It wasn't even what was outside. What mattered to them was what lay beneath it. After ordering a simple breakfast of bacon and eggs the two men talked about the various theories. Their breakfast arrived, with a side order of home fries and baked beans. Surprisingly, the eggs were perfectly cooked, the bacon crispy and the *pain de ménage* actually homemade, warm and tasty. Once they'd finished and paid the waitress Gamache called her over again.

"I have one more request."

"What is it?"

She was impatient. She had her tip and needed to go work for another, and another and enough to put a modest roof over her head and feed her children. And these well-off men were delaying her, with their nice

476

clothes and aromas of soap and something else.

Sandalwood, she recognized. It was a nice fragrance and the larger man had kind eyes, thoughtful eyes, and was smiling at her. Still, she couldn't pay the landlord with smiles, though God knows she'd tried. Couldn't feed her kids the kindness of strangers. She needed these men gone and new bums on the seats.

"Can we speak to the manager, please." Gamache saw her alarm and hastened to reassure her. "No complaints, not at all. We have a favor to ask. In fact, perhaps you could help too. Did you know Augustin Renaud?"

"The Champlain guy, the one who was killed? Sure."

"But did you know him personally?"

"What's that supposed to mean?"

"Did he ever come into the restaurant?"

"A few times. Everyone knew him. I waited on him once, a few weeks ago."

"Was he alone, or was someone else with him?"

"Always alone."

"Do you remember all your customers?" Émile asked and was treated to her scrutiny.

"Not all," she said dismissively. "Only the memorable ones. Augustin Renaud was

477

memorable. A local celebrity."

"But he only started coming in recently?" asked Gamache.

"Last few weeks I guess. Why?"

"Did he ever speak to the manager?"

"You can ask her yourself." She pointed with the coffee pot to a young woman by the cash register.

Gamache gave her a twenty-dollar tip then they walked over to introduce themselves. The manager, a polite young woman, answered their questions. Yes, she remembered Augustin Renaud. Yes, he'd asked to see their basement. She'd been afraid he'd wanted to dig down there.

"Did you show it to him?" Émile asked.

"I did." Her eyes were wary, a naïve young woman afraid of doing the wrong thing and slowly realizing someone would always take exception.

"When was this?" Émile asked, his voice relaxed, disarming.

"A few weeks ago. Are you with the police?"

"We're helping with the investigation," said Gamache. "May we see your basement, please?"

She hesitated, but agreed. He was glad he didn't need to get a search warrant, or ask

Émile to fake a stroke while he snuck down unseen.

The basement was low and once again they had to duck. The walls were cinder block and the floor was concrete. Boxes of wine and cases of beer were piled in cool corners, broken furniture was stacked in the back rooms.

Like skeletons, but not skeletons. There was no sign that this had ever been anything other than the basement of a dreary restaurant. Gamache thanked her and as she disappeared upstairs and Émile was halfway up, he paused.

"What is it?" Émile asked.

Gamache stood quietly. For all the fluorescent light, for the smell of beer and cardboard and cobwebs, for the weary feel of the place, Gamache wondered.

Could this have been it? Was this where Champlain had been buried?

Émile came back down the stairs. "What is it?" he repeated.

"Can I speak to your Champlain Society?"

"Of course you can. We're meeting today at one thirty."

"Wonderful," said Gamache and headed for the stairs, energized. At the top, just before turning off the lights he looked down into the basement again.

"We meet in the room right beside the St-Laurent Bar, in the Château," Émile said.

"I didn't know there was such a room."

"Not many do. We know all the secrets."

Perhaps not all, thought Gamache as he snapped off the lights.

TWENTY-ONE

The men split up just outside the Old Homestead, with Émile going about his errands and Gamache turning right toward the Presbyterian church. He was tempted to go inside, to be in the calm interior and to speak with the young minister who had more to offer than he realized.

Gamache liked Tom Hancock. In fact, thinking about it as he walked, he liked everyone in this case. All the members of the Literary and Historical Society board, the members of the Champlain Society, he'd even liked, or at least understood, the Chief Archeologist.

And yet, one of them was almost certainly a murderer. One of them had taken a shovel to the back of Augustin Renaud's head, burying him in the basement in the hopes and expectation the body would be cemented over. If the phone line hadn't been severed Augustin Renaud might have disappeared as completely as Champlain.

Gamache paused for a moment to contemplate the façade of the Lit and His and think about the case.

Motive and opportunity, Beauvoir had said, and of course, he was right. A murderer had to have both a reason to kill and a chance to do it.

He'd been wrong in the Hermit case, had been blinded by the treasure, had seen just the façade of the case and had failed to see what was hiding beneath it.

Was he making the same mistake with this case? Was Champlain's grave the big, shiny, obvious motive, that was wrong? Maybe this had nothing to do with the search for the founder of Québec. But if not, what else was there? Renaud's life was consumed by only one thing, surely his death was too.

Walking up the steps he tried the door to the Lit and His only to discover it locked. He looked at his watch. It wasn't yet nine in the morning, of course it'd be locked. Now he was at a loss and, perversely, he felt even more strongly the need to get in.

Pulling out his phone he dialed. After the second ring a woman answered, her voice strong and clear.

"Oui allô?"

"Madame MacWhirter, it's Armand Gamache. *Désolé,* I hope I'm not disturbing you so early."

"Not at all, I was just sitting down to breakfast. What can I do for you?"

Gamache hesitated. "Well, it's a little embarrassing, but I'm afraid I've been overly ambitious with time. I'm outside the Literary and Historical Society but, of course, it's locked."

She laughed. "We've never had a member so anxious to get in. It's a novel experience. I have a key —"

"I don't want to disturb your breakfast."

"Well, you can't just stand on the stoop waiting, you'll freeze to death."

And Gamache knew that wasn't just a figure of speech. Every winter scores of people did just that. They were out in the cold too long, had exposed too much of themselves. And it killed them.

"Come over here, have a coffee and we'll head back together in a few minutes."

Gamache recognized a command when he heard it. She gave him her address, a home just around the corner on rue d'Auteuil.

When he arrived a couple minutes later he stood outside and marveled. It was as magnificent as he'd expected. In old Quebec City, "magnificent" wasn't measured in square feet, but in details. The blocks of gray stone, the carving over the doors and windows, the simple, clean lines. It was a gracious and elegant row of homes.

He'd walked up and down rue d'Auteuil many times in the past. It was a particularly beautiful street in a city thick with them. It followed the line of the old stone walls that defended the capital, but was set back, a ribbon of parkland between the street and the walls. And on the other side of the street, these homes.

This was where the first families of Québec lived, French and English. The *premier ministres,* the industrialists, the generals and archbishops, all lived in this row of elegant houses looking over the walls as though daring their enemies to attack.

Gamache had been to cocktail parties in some of the homes, a few receptions and at least one state dinner. But he'd never been into the one he stood in front of now. The stone was beautifully pointed, the wood painted, the iron work kept up and repaired.

As he stood on the stoop the door opened. He stepped in quickly, bringing the chill with him. It clung to him as he stood in the dark wood entrance but slowly the cold, like a cloak, slid off.

Elizabeth took his coat and he removed

his boots. A neat rank of velvet slippers, some for men, some for women, was lined up in the entrance.

"Take whichever fits, if you'd like."

He found a pair and wondered how many feet, over how many generations, had used the slippers. They looked Edwardian and felt comfortable.

The walls were papered in a William Morris print, rich, ornate, beautiful. Gleaming mahogany panels went a third of the way up the walls.

On the fine wood floors Indian rugs were scattered.

"Follow me. I eat in the morning room."

He followed her into a bright and airy room, a fire lit in the hearth, bookcases along a wall, *jardinières* filled with healthy ferns and Christmas cacti. And a breakfast tray on a hassock in front of the fire. Toast and jam and two bone china coffee cups.

"May I?" she asked.

"Please."

She poured him a cup and he added a touch of cream and sugar. As he sat in a comfortable chair across from the sofa where she sat, he noticed books on the floor and three newspapers. *Le Devoir, Le Soleil* and the *Gazette.*

"What brings you to the Lit and His so

early, Chief Inspector?"

"We're getting closer to knowing what the books were that Augustin Renaud got from your sale."

"That's a little awkward," she smiled slightly. "Our critics right. Most embarrassing. Did we sell books that should never have left us?"

Gamache looked into her eyes. They were steady, unwavering, dreading the answer, perhaps, but wanting to hear it anyway. As he watched her he noticed a few things, details that caught his eye. The faded and even frayed upholstery of the sofa and his own chair. A few floorboards heaved slightly, out of alignment. They could be easily nailed back to place. A handle missing from one of the doors of a cupboard.

"I'm afraid you did. They were Father Chiniquy's personal journals and diaries."

She closed her eyes but did not lower her head. When she opened them again a moment later her eyes were still steady but perhaps a little sad.

"Oh dear, that's not good news. The board will have to be told."

"They're evidence now but I suspect if you speak with Monsieur Renaud's widow she might sell them back at a reasonable price."

486

She looked relieved. "That would be wonderful. Thank you."

"But one is missing. From 1869."

"Really?"

"It was one of the books we were looking for, one of the books Augustin Renaud makes reference to in his own journals."

"Why 1869?"

"I don't know." And that was true, to a point. He actually had a very good idea why, but wasn't going to talk about it just yet.

"And the other book?"

"Missing too. We've found the lot it was bought with, but it could be anything." He put his cup down carefully on the tray. "Did you ever hear of a meeting in the Literary and Historical Society between Father Chiniquy, James Douglas and two Irish workers?"

"In the late 1800s?" She was surprised. "No. Irish workers you say?" Gamache nodded. She said nothing, but frowned.

"What is it?"

"It's just unlikely the Irish would have come to the Lit and His back then. Nowadays, yes, we have lots of members who are Irish. There isn't such a distinction, thank God. But I'm afraid back then there was a lot of animosity between the Irish and the English."

That was the weakness, Gamache knew, about New Worlds. People brought old conflicts.

"But feelings aren't so bad today?"

"No, with the passage of time things got better. Besides, we're too small, can't afford to fight."

"The lifeboat?" he smiled, picking up his coffee.

"You remember the analogy? Yes, that's exactly it. Who'd be foolish enough to rock a lifeboat?"

And what would the passengers do to keep the peace, wondered the Chief Inspector. He sipped his coffee and took in the room. It was faded and comfortable, a room he would choose to live in. Did she not notice, though, the worn fabric, the chipped paint? The small repairs adding up? He knew when people lived in a place for a long time, a lifetime, they stopped seeing it as it is, instead always seeing it as it was.

And yet, the outside of the home had been kept up. Painted, repaired.

"Speaking of small communities, do you know the Mundin family?"

"The Mundins? Yes, of course. He ran a successful antique shop on Petit-Champlain for years. Had beautiful things. I've taken a few things there."

Gamache looked at her quizzically.

"To sell, Chief Inspector."

It was said without flinching, without blushing, without apology. A statement of fact.

And he had his answer. She noticed everything but used her modest income to only repair the outside. The façade, the public face. The famous MacWhirter fortune had disappeared, become a fiction, one she chose to keep up.

This was a woman for whom appearances mattered, façades mattered. What would she be willing to do, to keep it in place?

"There was a tragedy, I hear," he said. "With the Mundin family."

"Yes, very sad. He killed himself one spring. Walked out onto the river and fell in. They called it an accident, but we all knew."

"Thin ice."

She smiled slightly. "Just so."

"And why did he do it, do you think?"

Elizabeth thought about it then shook her head. "I can't imagine. He seemed happy, but then things aren't always as they seem."

Like the gleaming paint, the pointed stones, the perfect exterior of this home.

"Had a couple of children though I only met the one. His son. Adorable, with curly blond hair. Used to follow his father every-where. He had a nickname for him. Can't remember it now."

"Old."

"Pardon?"

" 'Old' was the nickname."

"Yes, that's right. 'Old son,' his father would say. I wonder what became of the boy."

"He lives in a village called Three Pines, making and restoring furniture."

"The things we learn from our parents," said Elizabeth with a smile.

"My father taught me the fiddle," said Agent Morin. "Did your father teach you an instrument?"

"No, though he used to love to sing. My father taught me poetry. We'd go for long walks through Outremont and onto Mont Royal, and he'd recite poetry. I'd repeat it. Not well, most of the words meant nothing to me, but I remembered it all, every word. Only later did I realize what it meant."

"And what did it mean?"

"It meant the world," said Gamache. "My father died when I was nine."

Morin paused. "I'm sorry. I can't imagine losing my father, even now. It must have been terrible."

"It was."

"And your mother? It must have been awful for her."

"She died too. It was a car accident."

"I'm sorry," said the voice, small now, in pain for the large man sitting comfortably in his office while the young agent was all alone, tied to a hard chair, strapped to a bomb, facing a wall with a clock.

Counting down. Six hours and twenty-three minutes left.

And on Gamache's computer the rapid instant messages from his team, covertly following leads.

It was clear now the young agent wasn't being held at the La Grande dam. Agent Nichol and Inspector Beauvoir couldn't pick up the sounds of the massive turbines. But they could pick up other sounds. Trains. Some freight according to Nichol. Some passenger. Planes overhead.

Agent Nichol stripped back layer after layer of sound. Isolating bits and pieces.

We can't trace the call because it's embedded, her message had said.

What does that mean? Gamache had written.

It's like a hobo, riding along on a telecommunication line. Popping up here and there. That's why he seems to be everywhere at once.

Can you find which line?

Not enough time, Nichol replied.

Six hours left. Then two things would happen, simultaneously. A bomb would destroy the biggest dam in North America. And Agent Paul Morin would be executed.

As the moments ticked down Chief Inspector Armand Gamache knew a terrible decision was racing toward them. A choice.

"Is Mundin's son happy?" Elizabeth asked.

It took Gamache a moment, a heart beat, to come back. "I think so. Has a son of his own. Charlie."

"Charlie," she smiled. "I always think it's nice when a child is named for a parent."

Elizabeth got up, clearing the breakfast things. Gamache carried the tray to the old kitchen.

"There's someone else I wanted to ask you about," said Gamache, drying the dishes. "Do you know Carole Gilbert?"

"As in Vincent Gilbert?"

"Oui," though he couldn't believe Madame Gilbert would like to be defined by her estranged and exacting husband.

"I knew her slightly, we belonged to the same bridge club. But I think she's moved away. Quebec City is quite small, Chief Inspector. And old Québec even smaller, within the walls."

"And social circles smaller still?" smiled the Chief.

"Exactly. Some defined by language, some by economics and social standing, some by common interests. And often they overlap, and most people belong to more than one circle of friends and acquaintances. Carole Gilbert was an acquaintance, of the bridge variety."

She smiled at him warmly as they walked to the front hall. "But why do you ask?"

They put on their heavy winter coats, boots, hats and scarves, so that by the time they were finished there wasn't all that much to distinguish the Chief Inspector of homicide for Québec from the seventy-five-year-old woman.

"There was a case a few months back, in a village called Three Pines. Carole Gilbert lives there now. So does Old Mundin."

"Really?" But she didn't seem all that interested. Polite, but hardly riveted. Heading out into the sunshine they walked side-by-side down the middle of the narrow streets. Ahead they could see the young mountaineers strapped and harnessed thirty feet above the ground. They labored all winter shoveling snow from the steep metal roofs. It was harrowing to watch as they swung their axes and picks, hacking away at the feet of ice and snow that had accumulated, threatening to collapse the roofs.

Every winter roofs did collapse and every winter snow and ice slid off to the sidewalk below, crushing unfortunate pedestrians. There was a sound sliding ice made, a sound like no other, a cross between a slow, deep moan and a shriek. Every Québécois knew it, like buzz bombs in the Blitz.

But hearing it, and being able to do anything were two different things. The sound echoed off the old stone buildings, disguising location. It might be right above you, or it might be streets away.

True Québécois walked in the middle of the road. Tourists often thought the Québécois gracious, to cede the sidewalk to them, until the sound began.

"Would they have known each other here in Quebec City?" he asked.

"It's possible. She might have bought some antiques from Monsieur Mundin, or sold some I suppose. She had marvelous things, as I remember. An old Québec family, you know."

"The Gilberts?"

"No, Madame Gilbert's family. The Woloshyns."

They were approaching the Literary and

Historical Society.

"I always liked Carole. Very sensible," said Elizabeth as she brought out the key, warm from being carried in her glove. "It was a pleasure to play bridge with her. She'd never do anything foolish. Very patient, very calm, great strategist."

Once inside Gamache helped Elizabeth turn on the lights and turn up the heat, then she went to her office leaving the Chief Inspector alone in the magnificent library. He stood for a moment, like a miser at the bank. Then walking over to the circular iron staircase he hauled himself up. At the top he paused again. It was quiet, as only an old library can be and he was left alone with his thoughts.

"La Grande? Are you fucking kidding me?" Chief Superintendent Francoeur demanded.

Inspector Beauvoir had joined the Chief Inspector in his office, bringing with him the evidence he and Agent Nichol had collected. It was sparse, but enough. They thought. They hoped. Beauvoir had again taken the stairs two at a time, preferring to arrive unannounced, by the back way. From the stairwell door he'd once again seen the Chief Superintendent leading the search operations. Monitoring. Issuing orders. Giving every impression of doing his best.

And he probably was doing his best. But his best was not, Beauvoir knew, good enough.

He could hear over the speakers Chief Inspector Gamache talking about his days at Cambridge University. How he'd arrived with almost no English. Only the phrases he'd picked up off the English television programs beamed into Québec in the 1960s.

"Like what?" Paul Morin asked. His voice dragged, each word forced out.

"Fire on the Klingons," said the Chief Inspector.

Agent Morin laughed, perking up. "Did you actually say that to anyone?"

"Sadly, I did. It was either that or, 'My God, Admiral, it's horrible.' "

Now Agent Morin whooped with laughter and Beauvoir saw smiles on the faces of the men and women in the Incident Room, including Chief Superintendent Francoeur. Smiling himself Beauvoir turned his attention to the Chief Inspector.

Through the glass he saw the Chief. His eyes closed, gray stubble on his face. And then Gamache did something Beauvoir had never seen him do before. In all the years, all the cases, all the death and despair and exhaustion of past cases.

Chief Inspector Gamache lowered his head into his hands.

Just for a moment, but it was a moment Inspector Beauvoir would never forget. As young Paul Morin laughed, Chief Inspector Gamache covered his face.

Then he looked up, and met Inspector Beauvoir's eyes. And the mask reappeared. Confident. Energetic. In command.

Jean-Guy Beauvoir entered the Chief's office with the evidence. And at Gamache's request, invited Chief Superintendent Francoeur in and played him the tape.

"Are you fucking kidding?"

"Does it look like I'm kidding?"

The Chief was on his feet. He'd asked Paul Morin to carry the conversation, to keep speaking. And had whipped his headphone off, covering the microphone with his hand.

"Where'd you even get that recording?" Francoeur demanded. In the background Paul Morin was talking about his father's vegetable garden and how long it took to grow asparagus.

"It's background sound, from where Morin's being held," said Gamache.

"But where did you get it?" Francoeur was annoyed.

"It can't possibly matter. Are you listening?" Gamache replayed the fragment Agent Nichol had found. "They mention it two or three times."

"La Grande, yes I hear, but it could mean anything. It could be what they call whoever's behind the kidnapping."

"La Grande? As in La Grande Fromage? This isn't a cartoon." Gamache took a long breath and tried to control his frustration. On the speakers they could hear that Morin had moved on to a monologue on heirloom tomatoes.

"This is what I think, sir," said Gamache. "The kidnapping wasn't done by a frightened backwoods farmer with a marijuana crop. This was planned all along —"

"Yes, you've mentioned that before. There's no evidence."

"This is evidence." With a mighty effort Gamache stopped himself from shouting, instead lowering his voice to a growl. "The farmer has not left Morin alone as he said he would. In fact, not only is Morin clearly not alone, there're at least two, maybe three others with him."

"So, what? You think he's being held at the dam?"

"I did at first, but there're no turbine sounds in the background."

"Then what's your theory, Chief Inspector?"

"I think they're planning to blow the dam and they kidnapped Agent Morin to keep us occupied elsewhere."

Chief Superintendent Francoeur stared at Gamache. It was a scenario the Sûreté had practiced for, had protocols for. Dreaded. A threat against this mighty dam.

"You're delusional. Based on what? Two words barely heard far in the background. It might even be crossed wires. You think that in what" — Francoeur turned to look at the clock — "six hours someone's going to destroy the La Grande dam? And yet, they're not even there? They're sitting with your young agent somewhere else?"

"It's misdirection. They wa—"

"Enough," snapped Chief Superintendent Francoeur. "If it's misdirection it's one you've fallen for. They want you to hare off after a ridiculous clue. I thought you were smarter than that. And who are this mysterious 'they' anyway? Who'd want to destroy the dam? No, it's absurd."

"For God's sake, Francoeur," said Gamache, his voice low and hoarse with fatigue, "suppose I'm right?"

That stopped the Chief Superintendent as he made for the door. He turned and stared at Chief Inspector Gamache. In the long silence between the men they heard a small lecture on cow versus horse compost.

"I need more evidence."

"Agent Lacoste is trying to collect it."

"Where is she?"

Chief Inspector Gamache glanced quickly at Inspector Beauvoir. They'd dispatched Agent Lacoste two hours ago. To a remote Cree community. To the settlements closest to the great dam. Most affected by it going up. And most affected were it to suddenly, catastrophically, come down. There she'd been told to visit an elderly Cree woman Gamache had met years earlier. On a bench. Outside the Château Frontenac.

They'd hoped to have her evidence by now. To convince Chief Superintendent Francoeur to stop his high-tech search and lower his sights. To change course. To stop looking at the present and look to the past.

But so far, nothing from Agent Lacoste.

"I'm begging you, sir," said Gamache. "Just put a few people on it. Quietly alert security at the dam. See what the other forces might have."

"And look like a fool?"

"Look like a thorough commander."

Chief Superintendent Francoeur glared at Gamache. "Fine. I'll do that much."

He left and Gamache saw him speaking with his own second in command. While he suspected Francoeur of many things, the murder of tens of thousands of Québécois wasn't among them.

He slipped the headphones back on and rejoined Agent Morin, describing an argument he and his sister once had that resulted in fresh peas being thrown. His voice was once again slow, exhausted.

Gamache picked up the conversation, telling Morin about arguments between his own children, Daniel and Annie, when they were young. How Daniel was the more sensitive, more measured of the two. How Annie, young and bright, could always best her brother. And about the competition between them that had settled, with time, into a deep affection.

But as he spoke he knew two things.

In just under six hours, at 11:18, the La Grande Hydro Electric Dam would be blown up. And Agent Paul Morin would be executed. And Chief Inspector Gamache knew something else. If it was possible to stop only one of those acts, he knew which it would have to be.

"How's your friend?"

"Friend?" Gamache turned to see Elizabeth bringing a few books into the library and placing them on the "returns" cart.

"Monsieur Comeau," she said. "Émile." She leaned over the cart, sorting books, not looking at Gamache.

"Oh, he's fine. I'm seeing him in a few hours at the Château. There's a meeting of the Société Champlain."

"Interesting man," she said then left, leaving Gamache alone in the library once again. He waited until he heard her steps disappear then looked around at the acres of books. Where to start?

"Are you close? Are you going to make it?"

Fatigue had finally worn Morin down, so that his fear, contained for so long, boiled out through frayed nerves and down the telephone line.

"We'll make it. Trust me."

There was a pause. "Are you sure?" The voice was strained, almost squeaky.

"I'm sure. Are you afraid?"

There was no answer, just silence and then a keening.

"Agent Morin," said Gamache, standing up at his desk. He waited and still there was no reply, except the sound which said it all.

Gamache talked for a few minutes, soothing words about nothing in particular. About spring flowers and wrapping presents for his grandchildren, about lunches at Leméac Bistro on rue Laurier and his father's favorite song. And in the background was a wailing, a sobbing and coughing, a howling as Agent Morin finally broke down. It surprised Gamache the young man had been able to hold his terror in so long.

But now it was out, and fled down the phone line.

Chief Inspector Gamache talked about skiing at Mont Saint-Rémy and Clara Morrow's art and Ruth Zardo's poetry and slowly, in the background, the howling became a sob and the sob became a shuddering breath and the breath became a sigh.

Gamache paused. "Are you afraid?" he asked again.

Outside the office, through the large glass window, the agents, analysts, special investigators and Chief Superintendent Francoeur all stopped and stared at the Chief Inspector, and listened to the agent who had been so brave and was now falling apart.

Down in her dim studio Agent Yvette Nichol recorded it all and, glowing green, she listened.

"Are you with me, Agent Morin?"

"Yes sir." But the voice was small, uncertain.

"I will find you in time." Each word was

said slowly, deliberately. Words made of rock and stone, firm words. "Stop imagining the worst."

"But —"

"Listen to me," the Chief commanded. "I know what you're doing. It's natural, but you must stop. You're imagining the clock reaching zero, imagining the bomb going off. Am I right?"

"Sort of." There was panting, as though Morin had run a race.

"Stop it. If you have to look ahead think about seeing Suzanne again, think about seeing your mother and father, think of the great stories you can bore your children with. Control your thoughts and you can control your emotions. Do you trust me?"

"Yes sir." The voice was stronger.

"Do you trust me, Agent Morin?" insisted the Chief.

"Yes sir." The voice more confident.

"Do you think I'd lie to you?"

"No sir, never."

"I will find you in time. Do you believe me?"

"Yes sir."

"What will I do?"

"You'll find me in time."

"Never, ever forget that."

"Yes sir." Agent Morin's voice was strong,

as certain as the Chief Inspector's. "I believe you."

"Good." Gamache spoke and let his young agent rest. He talked about his first job, scraping gum off the Montreal Metro platforms and how he met Madame Gamache. He talked about falling in love.

Now there is no more loneliness.

As he spoke he followed all the instant messaging. The information. From Inspector Beauvoir and Agent Nichol as they isolated the recordings and reported on their findings. Sounds hidden in the background. Planes, birds, trains. Echoes. And things not heard. Cars and trucks.

Agent Lacoste finally reporting in from the Cree community. Leads she was following on the ground. Getting them closer to the truth.

He looked at the clock. Four hours and seventeen minutes left.

In his ear, in his head, Paul Morin talked about the Canadiens and their hockey season. "I think we finally have a shot at the cup this season."

"Yes," said Gamache. "I think we finally have a chance."

In the gallery of the Literary and Historical Society, Armand Gamache reached for the first book. Over the next few hours the library opened, the volunteers arrived and went about their work, Mr. Blake showed up and took his seat. A few other patrons appeared, found books, read periodicals, and left.

And all the while on the gallery the Chief Inspector pulled out books, examining them one at a time. Finally, just after noon he took his seat across from Mr. Blake. They exchanged pleasantries before both men subsided into their reading.

At one o'clock Armand Gamache rose, nodded to Mr. Blake then left, taking two books hidden in his satchel with him.

Twenty-Two

Myrna handed Clara a book.

"I think you'll like it. It's one of my favorites."

Clara turned it over. Mordecai Richler, *Solomon Gursky Was Here.*

"Is it good?"

"No, it's crap. I only sell crap here, and recommend it of course."

"So Ruth was right," said Clara. She tipped the book toward Myrna. "Thank you."

"Okay," said Myrna, sitting across from her friend. "Spill."

The woodstove was heating the bookstore and keeping the perpetual pot of tea warmed. Clara sipped from her favorite mug and read the back of the book as though she hadn't heard her friend.

"What's going on?" Myrna persisted.

Clara raised innocent eyes. "With what?"

Myrna gave her a withering look. "Something's up. I know you, what was all that at Dominique's yesterday after exercise class?"

"Sparkling conversation."

"It wasn't that." Myrna watched Clara. She'd been wanting to ask for several days, but the episode at the inn and spa convinced her.

Clara was up to something.

"Was it obvious?" Clara put the book down and looked at Myrna, her eyes worried.

"Not at all. I doubt anyone noticed."

"You did."

"True, but I'm very smart." Her smile faded and she leaned forward. "Don't worry, I'm sure no one else found it strange. But you were asking some unusual questions. Why were you talking about Jean-Guy and Olivier and all that?"

Clara hesitated. She hadn't expected to be asked and had no lie prepared. Foolish, really. What were her regular lies?

I'm busy that night. The art world's just too conservative to appreciate my work. The dog did it or, as a variation, it's Ruth's fault. That covered everything from smells, to missing food, to dirt through the house. To, sometimes, her art.

It didn't, however, seem to cover this.

"I think having the Inspector here just

508

reminded me of Olivier, that's all."

"Bullshit."

Clara sighed. She'd really messed up. The one promise she'd made to Beauvoir she was about to break. "You can't tell anyone."

"I won't."

And Clara believed Myrna but then, Beauvoir had believed her. Oh well, his mistake.

"Inspector Beauvoir's not here to recover from his injuries. He came down to unofficially reopen Olivier's case."

Myrna smiled. "I'd hoped that might be it. The only other explanation was that you'd lost your mind."

"And you weren't sure which it was?"

"It's so hard to tell." Myrna's eyes were bright. "This is the best news. So they think maybe Olivier didn't kill the Hermit? But then, who did?"

"That's the question. Seems it comes down to Roar, Havoc, Marc, Vincent or Old Mundin. And I have to say, what The Wife said about killing was pretty strange."

"That's true," said Myrna. "But —"

"But if she or Old were really involved she'd never have talked about killing. She'd have kept quiet."

"There you are."

The two women looked up with a guilty

509

start. Inspector Beauvoir was standing in the doorway that connected the bookstore to the bistro.

"I was looking for you." He gave them a mighty frown. "What're you talking about?"

Unlike Gamache, who could make an interrogation sound like a pleasant conversation, Beauvoir managed to make niceties sound like accusations.

Though, both women knew, he had good reason.

"Tea?" Myrna offered and busied herself pouring another cup and putting more hot water and another bag into the Brown Betty on the woodstove. This left Clara trying not to catch Beauvoir's eye. He sat beside Clara and glared at her.

The dog did it, the dog did it.

"I told Myrna everything." Clara paused. "It's Ruth's fault."

"Everything?" Beauvoir lowered his voice.

"So, I hear we still have a murderer among us," said Myrna, handing the mug to Beauvoir and taking her seat.

"Just about," said Clara.

Beauvoir shook his head. Still, it wasn't perhaps unexpected, nor was it necessarily a bad thing. Myrna had helped the Chief in the past and while Beauvoir had never, until now, wanted to ask for help from the villagers he suspected they actually had some to give. And now he had no choice.

"So what do you think?" he asked.

"I'd like to hear more. Have you found out anything new?"

He told them about his conversation with Gamache and what the chief had found out in Quebec City about Old Mundin's family and Carole Gilbert.

"Woloshyn?" Clara repeated. "Woo?"

"Perhaps," Beauvoir nodded.

"The inn and spa has a lot of antiques," said Myrna. "Could they have found them on rue Notre-Dame?"

"In the same store where Olivier sold the Hermit's things?" said Beauvoir. "You're thinking if they went in, they might have recognized some of Olivier's items?"

"Exactly," said Myrna. "All Carole Gilbert would have to do is casually ask how the owner got them. He would have directed her to Olivier and Three Pines, and *voilà*."

"No, it doesn't work," said Beauvoir.

"Of course it does. It's perfect," said Clara.

"Think about it," Beauvoir turned to her. "Olivier sold those things to the antique shop years ago. If Carole Gilbert found them why'd they wait almost ten years to buy the old Hadley house?"

The three sat there, thinking. Eventually

Clara and Myrna started batting around other theories, but Beauvoir remained lost in his own thoughts.

Of names. Of families. And of patience.

Armand Gamache folded back the sleeve of his parka so that he could see his watch.

Quarter past one. A little early for the meeting. He dropped his arm over the satchel, protecting it.

Instead of heading straight in to the Château Frontenac he decided to stroll along the Dufferin Terrace, the long wooden boardwalk that swept in front of the hotel and overlooked the St. Lawrence River. In the summer it was filled with ice cream carts and musicians and people relaxing in the pergolas. In the winter a bitter damp wind blew down the St. Lawrence River and hit pedestrians, stealing their breaths and practically peeling the skin off their faces. But still people walked along the outdoor *terrasse,* so remarkable was the view.

And there was another attraction. *La glissade.* The ice slide. Built every winter it towered above the promenade. As he turned the corner of the Château the wind hit Gamache's face. Tears sprung to his eyes and froze. Ahead, midway along the *terrasse,* he could see the slide, three lanes wide with stairs cut into the snow at the side.

Even on this brittle day kids were lugging their rented toboggans up the steps. In fact, the colder the day the better. The ice would be keen and the toboggans would race down the steep slope, shooting off the end. Some toboggans were going so fast and so far pedestrians on the *terrasse* had to leap out of their way.

As he watched he noticed it wasn't just kids climbing to the top, but adults as well including a few young couples. It was as effective as a scary movie to get a hug, and he remembered clearly coming to the slide with Reine-Marie early in their relationship. Climbing to the top, dragging the long toboggan with them, waiting their turn. Gamache, deathly afraid of heights, was still trying to pretend otherwise with this girl who'd stolen his heart so completely.

"Would you like me to sit in front?" she'd whispered as the people in front of them shoved off and plummeted down the slide.

He'd looked at her, a protest on his lips, when he realized here was a person he needn't lie to, needn't pretend with. He could be himself.

Their toboggan hurtled toward the Dufferin Terrace below, though it looked as though they were heading straight into the river. Armand Gamache shrieked and clutched Reine-Marie. At the bottom they laughed so hard he thought he'd ruptured something. He never did it again. When they'd brought Daniel and Annie it had been their mother who'd taken them while Dad waited at the bottom with the camera.

Now Chief Inspector Gamache stood and watched the kids, the couples, an elderly man and woman walk up the narrow snow steps and then shoot back down.

It comforted him slightly to hear that they too screamed. And laughed.

As he watched he heard another shout but this wasn't from the direction of the ice slide. This came from over the side of the terrace, from the river.

He wasn't the only one to notice. A few people drifted to the handrail. Gamache walked over and wasn't surprised to see teams of canoeists out on the ice practicing. The race was Sunday, two days away.

"Stroke, stroke," came the command. While there were three boats out there, only one voice was heard, loud and clear.

"Left, stroke, left, stroke." An English voice.

Gamache strained but couldn't make out which boat it was, nor did he recognize the voice. It wasn't Tom Hancock. Nor did he think it was likely to be Ken Haslam. A telescope was available, and though it was all but frozen, as was he, Gamache put some money in and trained it on the river.

Not the first boat.

Not the second, though he could see the leader's mouth moving he couldn't hear the words.

He trained the telescope on the furthest boat. Surely not. Not from so far away. Was it possible the piercing voice had traveled this far?

The boat was way out there in the middle of the river, six men sitting down, rowing. The boats could be paddled or rowed, could be in water or dragged over ice. This team was just clearing open water and heading upstream toward an ice floe.

"Stroke, stroke," came the command again. And now, because the racers were heading forward but facing backward, Gamache could see who it was.

He stared through the lens, not daring to touch his forehead to the metal telescope in case it froze there.

The booming, clear voice belonged to Ken Haslam.

Walking back to the Château, Gamache thought about that. Why would a man whisper all through his life, in every circumstance but be able, in fact, to shout?

Louder than anyone else out there. His voice had been piercing.

Was Haslam as surprised as Gamache? Had Haslam, in his sixty-eighth year, found his voice on the ice of Québec, doing something few others would attempt?

It was always a relief to get indoors, and even more wonderful when that indoors was the Château Frontenac. In the magnificent front lobby Gamache took off his mitts, coat, hat and scarf and checked them. Then, still protecting his satchel with his arm, he walked down the long, wide corridor to the double glass doors at the far end, with the light streaming through.

Inside the St-Laurent Bar he paused. Ahead of him was the circular wooden bar and around it tables and the huge windows. Open fires roared in the two hearths.

But this wasn't where he was expected.

Glancing to his right Gamache was surprised to see a door, one he'd never noticed before. Opening it he walked into a bright and airy side room, almost a solarium, with its own lit fireplace.

Whoever had been talking stopped as he entered. A dozen faces looked at him. All elderly, all white, all male. They were seated on the comfortable floral sofas and in wing

516

chairs and armchairs. He'd been expecting something more formal, a boardroom, a long table, a lectern.

He'd also been expecting that the meeting wouldn't have started. It was 1:25. Émile had said they started at 1:30 but it seemed clear the meeting was well under way.

Gamache glanced at Émile, who smiled then broke eye contact.

"Bonjour," said the Chief Inspector. "I hope I'm not disturbing you."

"Not at all." René Dallaire, as large and affable as the last time they met, greeted him. Others got to their feet as well. Gamache made the rounds, shaking hands, smiling greetings.

Everyone was cordial, pleasant, and yet he had the impression there was tension in the room, as though he'd interrupted an argument.

"Now, you wanted to speak with us?" Monsieur Dallaire said, indicating a large chair.

"Yes. It will come as no surprise that it's about the death of Augustin Renaud." Gamache sat down. There were sympathetic nods from some, others just stared, wary. While this wasn't exactly a secret society, it did seem secretive.

"Actually, I'd like to start off by talking

about Charles Chiniquy."

That brought the reaction he was expecting. A few sat up in their seats, more than a few looked at each other then back to Gamache with some annoyance.

Once again René Dallaire took the lead. "Forgive me, Monsieur Gamache, but you do realize we're not a general historical society?"

"*Oui, merci,* I know that you're the Société Champlain." As he said it something twigged. The Société Champlain. "But my story begins neither with Samuel de Champlain nor with Augustin Renaud, but somewhere in between. In 1869, to be exact, with Father Chiniquy."

"He was a nut," one elderly man said from the back.

"So you do know him," said Gamache. "Yes, he was a nut to some, a hero to others. He was something else entirely in our story."

Gamache glanced at Émile, who was looking out the window. Distancing himself from what was about to happen? Gamache wondered.

"Father Chiniquy was famous for one thing," said the Chief. "He wanted to save alcoholics. To do that he went to where he'd find them. In the Québec of the 1860s that was rue du Petit-Champlain, directly below us."

Indeed, if he could throw himself out that window with enough force he'd sail over the Dufferin Terrace and land on rue du Petit-Champlain below. Now a charming, cobbled street filled with lace stores and cafés and tourist shops, but back then it was the notorious Basse-Ville. Filled with drunks and blackguards and prostitutes, filled with sewage and disease.

Filled with poor French workers and Irish immigrants. And a fallen priest determined to save them and maybe himself.

"One summer's evening Chiniquy was in a bar scouting souls when he overheard a conversation between two Irishmen. Patrick and O'Mara. They'd been hired as diggers in the Upper Town to hack out a basement under an old building. There were more than twenty laborers on the site, but it was Patrick and O'Mara who made the discovery. They found something they believed might be valuable."

Despite themselves the members of the Société Champlain had grown interested. A few still looked annoyed and impatient but even they were listening. Only Émile continued to stare out the window.

What was he thinking? Gamache wondered. Did he see what was coming, know what was coming?

But it didn't matter. It was too late.

"Chiniquy listened to the two men and as he listened he grew more interested. Finally he joined them. The men, knowing who Chiniquy was, weren't overly welcoming at first but once the priest offered to buy them drinks they warmed up. And after a few more drinks they told him what they'd found.

"It was a coffin. At first Chiniquy was disappointed. Old Quebec City was practically built on coffins, built on bones. Not finding one would have been unusual. Surely these workers knew that. But this one was different, they said, it was heavy.

"The two men figured this was not only unusual but perhaps even valuable. They'd dragged it from the work site down the hill to Patrick's home. His wife refused to have it inside. He insisted, but knew he couldn't keep it there for long. The home was little more than a shack, and already crowded with Patrick, his wife and six kids. Now there was also a dead man."

Gamache examined his audience. They were all listening now, including Émile. They could see the scene, as could Gamache. The trampled and discouraged Irish woman. Having survived the harrowing voyage to her New World, she'd found it even worse than the humiliation and famine she'd fled and, as though life wasn't difficult enough, her husband had brought a corpse home from work.

"The men set about opening it, carefully prying the sealed lid off," Gamache continued the story. "Imagining why it was so heavy. It must, they felt, be filled with gold, with jewelry, with silver. This must be the coffin of a very rich person. But once opened, they were sorely disappointed. There was nothing inside except a ratty old book, a bible, and some remains. Bones and bits of clothing. It was heavy because it was lead-lined."

There was a small stir in the room. Did they know where this was headed?

"Patrick and O'Mara had been in the bar discussing how best to strip the lead, sell it then dump the body into the river, the bible with it. They couldn't read, so it was useless. Chiniquy asked to see the bible. At that stage the men grew wary. Then the priest tried another tack. If they would bring the coffin and the bible to the Literary and Historical Society the next night, Chiniquy could promise them a small reward.

"Why? the men had asked.

"Because they collect everything historic, especially books. This coffin might be old, Chiniquy reasoned.

"Patrick and O'Mara were already half drunk and didn't really care. If there was money they'd be there. The next night they showed up and were met by Father Chiniquy and another man. James Douglas."

"Is there a point to this?" one of the members of the Société Champlain asked.

"Please, Benoît," René Dallaire looked pained. "Civility."

"I'll be civil when he stops wasting my time."

"There is a point, *monsieur,* and we're almost there," said Gamache. He could feel his phone buzzing but couldn't very well look at it now. "I'm sure you've heard of Dr. Douglas?"

There were nods.

"He opened the coffin and examined the contents while Father Chiniquy looked at the bible. Then James Douglas made a mistake. He offered Patrick and O'Mara five hundred dollars each. Chiniquy was furious, but said nothing. The workers immediately knew something was up. That was a small fortune, way too much for the remains of some long-dead guy and a ratty old bible.

"They refused, insisting on one thousand dollars each, and they got it but only after Douglas had secured their pledge of secrecy and found out where they lived. The Irishmen, who hated the English, also feared them. They knew what lay behind the civilized veneer. They knew what an Englishman was capable of, if crossed. Patrick and O'Mara agreed, then carried the coffin to the basement and left."

His phone buzzed again. Still Gamache ignored it.

"How do you know all this?" someone asked.

"Because I found this."

Gamache bent down to his satchel and removed a black leather book. As he held it he looked at Émile who looked surprised, and something else. Was that a small smile? A grin or a grimace?

"It's Father Chiniquy's journal for the year 1869. Augustin Renaud found it and recognizing its significance he hid it."

"Where was it?" Émile asked.

"The library of the Literary and Historical Society," said Gamache, staring at his mentor.

"Augustin Renaud hid the journal in a library?" asked René Dallaire.

"No," clarified Gamache. "His murderer did."

"Why're you telling us all this?" Jean Hamel, slender and contained and sitting next to René Dallaire as always, asked.

"I think you know why," said Gamache, looking the man directly in the eyes until Hamel lowered his.

"Where did you say the Irish workers were digging?" a member asked.

"I didn't, but I can tell you. It was under the Old Homestead."

The room grew very quiet. Everyone stared at Gamache.

"You found the other book, didn't you," said Émile into the silence.

"I did."

Gamache reached into the satchel, now on his lap. The satchel he'd spent the last few hours protecting.

"Last year the Literary and Historical Society sold a number of boxes of books, boxes they hadn't bothered to examine. Augustin Renaud bought some of them. When he went to see what he had he found they were from the collection of Father Charles Chiniquy. Not very promising, for a Champlain scholar —"

The use of the word "scholar" brought some harrumphs.

524

"— so he didn't hurry to read them. But eventually, scanning them, he came across something extraordinary. He made mention of it in his own diary, but in true Renaud fashion he was" — Gamache searched for the word — "guarded."

"Don't you mean demented?" asked Jean Hamel. "Nothing he said or wrote can be trusted."

"No, I mean guarded. And he was quite right. What he'd found was staggering."

Gamache withdrew another black leather book. This one was larger, thicker than the first. Frayed and brittle, but in good condition. It had not seen the sun for hundreds of years then, dug up, it had sat anonymously on the bookshelves of Father Chiniquy's home for thirty years until his death.

"This," Gamache held up the book, "was Father Chiniquy's secret, and in the end the secret had died with him so that when his housekeeper packaged up his books and sent them to the Lit and His more than a century ago, no one knew what treasures they contained.

"In reading Chiniquy's journals Augustin Renaud found the report of the fateful encounter one July evening in 1869. And among the many religious books, the hymnals, the sermons, the family bibles in the box of used books he found this."

Gamache laid his large hand on the plain leather cover, barely recognizable for what it was.

Once again his phone buzzed. It was his private line. Few knew the number, but it hadn't stopped ringing for the past ten minutes.

"May I?" Émile reached out.

"Oui." Gamache stood and handed the book to his mentor and watched as Émile did exactly what he himself had done an hour earlier. Exactly what he imagined Augustin Renaud had done a month ago. What Father Chiniquy had done a century ago.

Émile opened the simply tooled leather book to the inscription page.

There was a sharp intake of breath then Émile sighed and with the sigh two words escaped. *"Bon Dieu."*

"Yes," said the Chief. "Good God."

"What is it?" Jean Hamel asked, stepping out from the convenient shadow of his friend René. It was clear now who was the real leader of the Société Champlain.

"They'd found Champlain," said Émile, staring at Gamache. It wasn't a question, it was beyond question. "It was Champlain's coffin the Irish workers found beneath the Old Homestead."

"Ridiculous," said the ornery member. "What would Champlain be doing buried under the Old Homestead? We all know he was either buried in the chapel, which burned, or in the cemetery, not hundreds of yards away in a field."

"Champlain was a Huguenot," said Émile, his voice barely audible. "A Protestant." He held out the book. A bible.

"But that's impossible," snapped Jean. There was a hubbub of agreement. Hands snatched at the bible and the uproar subsided as it made the rounds and the men saw the evidence.

Samuel de Champlain, inscribed in ink. The date, *1578.*

It was an original Huguenot bible, a rare find. Most had been destroyed in the various Inquisitions, burned along with their owners. It was a dangerous book, to the church and to whoever possessed it.

Champlain must have been a devout man indeed to have kept such a thing, and to have been buried with it.

The room was quiet, just the mumbling and crackling of the fire. Gamache took the bible back and replacing it in his satchel along with Chiniquy's journal he said, *"Excusez-moi,"* to the group lost in their own thoughts, and left the room.

Outside he took the call and noticed there'd been twenty-seven calls from a variety of people. Reine-Marie, his son Daniel and daughter Annie. From Superintendents Brunel and Francoeur and Agent Isabelle Lacoste. From various friends and colleagues, and from Jean-Guy Beauvoir whose call was now coming in.

"*Bonjour,* Jean-Guy. What's happened?"

"Chief, where've you been?"

"In a meeting, what's going on?"

"There's a video, gone viral on the Internet. I just heard about it from Peter Morrow, then Lacoste called and a few friends. More calls are coming in. I haven't seen it yet."

"What is it?" But even as he asked he could guess, and felt a sickening feeling in his stomach.

"It's from the tapes, the ones recorded at the raid."

Everyone had worn tiny cameras integrated into their headsets, to record what happened. Investigators had long realized a verbal debrief wasn't enough. Even well-intentioned cops would forget details, especially in the heat of the moment, and if things went badly, as they often did, cops could stop being "well intentioned" and start lying.

This made lying harder, though not impossible.

Each camera showed what each officer saw, and what each officer did, and what each officer said. And, like any film, it could be edited.

"Chief?" Beauvoir asked.

"I see." He felt like Beauvoir sounded. Upset, suddenly exhausted, bewildered that anyone would do this and that anyone would want to see such a thing. It was a violation, especially for the families. His officers' families.

"I'll call," he said.

"I can, if you'd like."

"No, *merci*. I'll do it."

"Who would do this?" Beauvoir asked. "Who even has access to the tapes?"

Gamache lowered his head. Was it possible?

He'd been told there were three gunmen. But there'd been more, many more. Gamache had assumed it was a mistake. Dreadful, but unintentional.

He'd doubled the number of suspects, and assumed instead of three there were six.

Knowing that to be on the safe side.

He'd been wrong.

He'd brought six agents with him. Chosen them. Handpicked. And he'd brought Inspector Beauvoir. But not Agent Yvette

529

Nichol. She'd stood there, her tactical vest already on. Her pistol on her belt. Her eyes keen. She would go with them into the factory. The place she'd found by following the sounds. By listening more closely than she'd ever listened in her life.

To the trains. To their frequency. To their cadence. Freight trains. A passenger train. A plane overhead. A hoot in the background. A factory.

And whispers. Ghosts in the background.

Three of them, she'd said.

With Inspector Beauvoir's furious help they'd narrowed and narrowed. Winnowed, whittled. Pored over train timetables, over flight paths, over factories old enough to still use whistles.

Until they knew where Agent Paul Morin was being held.

But there was another goal. The La Grande dam. To save the young agent would be to alert the suspects that their plot against the dam had been discovered. And if they realized that they might destroy it right away, before the tactical squad could be moved into place.

No. A choice had to be made. A decision had to be made.

Gamache could see Agent Nichol standing by the door. Ready. And her rage when told his decision.

"Are you going to watch?" Beauvoir asked.

Gamache thought. "Yes. You?"

"Maybe." He also paused. "Yes." There was a silence as both men considered what that meant. "Oh, God," sighed Beauvoir.

"When you do, don't be alone," said Gamache.

"I wish —"

"So do I," said Gamache. They both wished the same thing. That if they had to relive it, they could at least be together.

Sitting heavily in one of the leather wing chairs of the St-Laurent Bar, Chief Inspector Gamache asked for a glass of water and called Reine-Marie.

"I was trying to get you." She sounded stressed, upset.

"I know, I'm sorry, I've been in a meeting. Jean-Guy just told me. How did you hear?"

"Daniel called from Paris. A colleague told him. Then Annie called. It apparently appeared about noon and has gone wild. Journalists have been calling for the past half hour. Armand, I'm so sorry."

He heard the strain in her voice and he could have happily killed whoever had done this. Forcing Reine-Marie to relive it, forcing Annie and Daniel and Enid Beauvoir.

And worse. The families of those who died.

He wanted to reach down the line and hold Reine-Marie, hug her to him. Rock her and tell her it would be all right, that this was just a phantom from the past. The worst was over.

But was it?

"When will you be home?"

"By tomorrow."

"Who would do this, Armand?"

"I don't know. I need to watch it, but you don't. Can you wait until I come home? If you still want to see it we can watch together."

"I'll wait," she said. She could wait.

She remembered fragments of that day. Armand hadn't been home. Isabelle Lacoste had contacted her and explained the Chief was working on a case and couldn't even, in fact, speak with her. Not for a day.

She'd never gone twenty-four hours without hearing her husband's voice. Not once, in more than thirty years together. Then, next morning, at just after noon a coworker at the Bibliotheque Nationale arrived at work, her face stricken.

A bulletin on Radio-Canada. A shootout. Officers of the Sûreté among the dead, including a senior homicide officer. The race to the hospital, not listening to the reports.

Too afraid. The world had collapsed to this imperative. To get there. To get there. Get there. Seeing Annie in the emergency room, just arrived.

The radio said Dad —
I don't want to hear it.

Comforting each other. Comforting Enid Beauvoir, Jean-Guy's wife, in the waiting room. And others arriving she didn't know. The grotesque pantomime, strangers comforting each other while secretly, desperately, shamefully praying the other will be the one with bad news.

A paramedic appearing through the swinging doors from the emergency room, looking at them, looking away. Blood on his uniform. Annie grabbing her hand.

Among the dead.

The doctor, taking them aside, away, separating them from the rest. And Reine-Marie, light-headed, steeling herself to hear the unbearable. And then those words.

He's alive.

She didn't really take in the rest. Chest wound. Head wound. Pneumothorax. A bleed.

He's alive was all she needed to know. But there was another.

Jean-Guy? she'd asked. Jean-Guy Beauvoir?

The doctor hesitated.

You must, tell us, Annie said, far more insistent than Reine-Marie expected.

Shot in the abdomen. He's in surgery now.

But he'll be all right? Annie demanded.

We don't know.

My father, you said a bleed, what does that mean?

From the head wound, a bleed into his head, the doctor had said. A stroke.

Reine-Marie didn't care. He's alive. And she repeated that to herself now as she had every hour of every day since. It didn't matter what the damned video showed. He's alive.

"I don't know what could be on it," Gamache was saying. And that was the truth. He'd forced himself to remember, for the inquiry, but mostly what he was left with were impressions, the chaos, the noise, the shouting and screams. And gunmen, everywhere. Far more than expected.

The rapid gunshots. Concrete, wood exploding from the bullets all around. Automatic weapons fire. The unfamiliar feel of his tactical vest. An assault weapon in his hands. The people in his sights. The report as he fired. Aiming to kill.

Scanning for gunmen, issuing orders. Keeping order even in the storm.

Seeing Jean-Guy fall. Seeing others fall.

He woke at night with those images, those sounds. And that voice.

"I'll find you in time. Trust me."

"I do. I believe you, sir."

"I'll be home tomorrow," Gamache said to Reine-Marie.

"Be careful."

That was also something she never said before. Before all this happened. She'd thought it, he knew, every time he left for work, but never said it. But now she said it.

"I will. I love you." He hung up, pausing to gather himself. In his pocket he felt the bottle of pills. His hand went to it, closing over it.

He closed his eyes.

Then taking his empty hand from his pocket he started calling the officers who'd survived, and the families of those who hadn't.

He talked to their mothers, their fathers, their wives and a husband. In the background he could hear a young child asking for milk. Over and over he called, and listened to their rage, their pain, that someone could release a video of this event. Not once did they blame him, though Armand Gamache knew they could.

"Are you all right?"

Gamache looked up as Émile Comeau lowered himself into the seat opposite.

"What's happened?" Émile asked, seeing the look on Gamache's face.

Gamache hesitated. For the first time in his life he was tempted to lie to this man who had lied to him.

"Why did you say the Société Champlain meets at one thirty when it clearly meets at one?"

Émile paused. Would he lie again? Gamache wondered. But instead the man shook his head.

"I'm sorry about that Armand. There were things we needed to discuss before you came. I thought it was better."

"You lied to me," said Gamache.

"It was just half an hour."

"It was more than that, and you know it. You made a choice, chose a side."

"A side? Are you saying the Champlain Society is on a different side than you?"

"I'm saying we all have loyalties. You've made yours clear."

Émile stared. "I'm sorry, I should never have lied to you. It won't happen again."

"It already has," said Gamache getting to his feet and putting down a hundred dollars for the water and the use of the quiet table by the fireplace. "What did Augustin

Renaud say to you?"

Émile got to his feet too. "What do you mean?"

"SC in Renaud's journals. I'd taken it to mean an upcoming meeting with someone, maybe Serge Croix. A meeting he'd never make because he was murdered. But I was wrong. SC was the Société Champlain, and the meeting was for today at one. Why did he want to meet the Society?"

Émile stared, stricken, but said nothing.

Gamache turned and strode down the long corridor, his phone buzzing again and his heart pounding.

"Wait, Armand," he heard behind him but kept walking, ignoring the calls. Then he remembered what Émile had meant to him and still did. Did this one bad thing wipe everything else out?

That was the danger. Not that betrayals happened, not that cruel things happened, but that they could outweigh all the good. That we could forget the good and only remember the bad.

But not today. Gamache stopped.

"You're right. Renaud wanted to meet with us," said Émile, catching up to Gamache as he retrieved his parka from the coat check. "He said he'd found something. Something we wouldn't like but he was willing to bury, if we gave him what he wanted."

"And what was that?"

"He wanted to join the Société and have all the credibility that went with it. And when the coffin was found he wanted us to admit he'd been right all along."

"That was all?"

"That's it."

"And did you give it to him?"

Émile shook his head. "We decided not to meet him. No one believed he'd actually found Champlain, and no one believed he'd found anything compromising. It was felt that having Augustin Renaud in the Société would cheapen it. He was blackballed."

"An elderly man comes to you wanting acceptance, just acceptance, and you turn him away?"

"I'm not proud of it. That's what we needed to discuss privately. I wanted them to tell you everything and said if they didn't I would. I'm so sorry Armand. I made a mistake. It's just that I knew it couldn't matter to the investigation. No one believed Renaud. No one."

"Someone did. They killed him."

The meeting of the Société Champlain had been filled with elderly Québécois men. And what held them together as a club? Certainly their fascination with Champlain and the early colony, but did that explain a lifetime's loyalty? Was it more than that?

Samuel de Champlain wasn't simply one more explorer, he was the Father of Québec, and as such he'd become a symbol for the Québécois of greatness. And freedom. Of New Worlds and new countries.

Of sovereignty. Of separation from Canada.

Gamache remembered the extremes of the late 1960s. The bombs, the kidnappings, the murders. All done by young separatists. But the young separatists of the 1960s became elderly separatists, who joined societies and sat in genteel lounges and sipped aperitifs.

And plotted?

Samuel de Champlain was found and found to be a Protestant. What would the church make of that? What would the separatists make of that?

"How did you find the books?" Émile asked, dropping his eyes to the bag at Gamache's side.

"It was his satchel. Why carry it just for a small map? There must have been something else in it. Then when we couldn't find the books I realized he probably kept them with him. Augustin Renaud would have refused to let them out of his possession, even for a moment. He must have taken them to the Literary and Historical Society when he met his murderer. But they weren't on his body. That meant the killer must have taken them. And done what?"

Émile's eyes narrowed, his mind moving along the path Armand had laid out. Then he smiled. "The murderer couldn't take them home with him. If they were found in his possession they'd incriminate him."

Gamache watched his mentor.

"He could have destroyed them, I suppose," Émile continued, thinking it through. "Thrown them into a fireplace, burned the books. But he couldn't bring himself to do that. So what did he do?"

The two men stared at each other in the crowded hall of the hotel. People swirled around them like a great river, some bundled against the cold, some in formal wear off to a cocktail party. Some in the colorful, traditional sashes of the Carnaval, *les ceinture fléchée.* All ignoring the two men, standing stock-still in the current.

"He hid them in the library," said Émile, triumphantly. "Where else? Hide them among thousands of other old, leather, unread, unappreciated volumes. So simple."

"I spent this morning looking and finally found them," said Gamache.

The two men walked out of the Château, gasping as the cold hit their faces.

"You found the books, but what happened to Champlain?" Émile asked, blinking his eyes against the freezing cold. "What did James Douglas and Chiniquy do with him?"

"We're about to find out."

"The Lit and His?" Émile asked, as they turned left past the old stone buildings, past the trees with cannonballs still lodged in them, past the past they both loved. "But why didn't the Chief Archeologist find Champlain when he looked a few days ago?"

"How do you know he didn't?"

TWENTY-THREE

When the Chief Inspector and Émile Comeau arrived at the Literary and Historical Society, Elizabeth, Porter Wilson, tiny Winnie the librarian and Mr. Blake were assembled in the entrance hall, waiting.

"What's going on?" Porter launched right into it before Gamache and Émile had even closed the door behind them. "The Chief Archeologist is back with some technicians and that Inspector Langlois is also there. He's ordered us to stay away from our own basement."

"Had you planned to go down there?" Gamache asked, taking off his coat.

"Well, no."

"Do you need to go down there?"

"No, not at all." The two men stared at each other.

"Oh, for God's sake, Porter, this is embarrassing," said Elizabeth. "Let the men do their work. But," she turned to Armand Gamache, "we would appreciate some information. Whatever you can give us."

Gamache and Émile exchanged glances. "We think Augustin Renaud might have been right," said the Chief Inspector.

"About what?" snapped Porter.

"Don't be a fool," said Mr. Blake. "About Champlain, what else?" When Gamache nodded Mr. Blake frowned. "You believe Samuel de Champlain is in our basement and has been all this time?"

"For the last 140 years anyway, yes. *Pardon.*"

The men squeezed past the gathering and made their way through the now familiar halls to the trap door into the first basement, then down another steep metal ladder to the final level.

Through the floorboards of the level above they could see glaring light, as though the sun was imprisoned down there. But once down they recognized it for what it was, a series of brilliant industrial lamps trained, once again, on the dirt and stone basement.

The Chief Archeologist was standing in the center of the room, his long arms hugging his chest perhaps trying, unsuccessfully, to contain his anger. The same two technicians who'd accompanied him before were there again, as was Inspector Langlois, who immediately took Gamache aside.

"I can explain," Gamache began before being interrupted.

"I know you can, it's not that. Let Croix stew for a while, he's an asshole anyway. Have you heard?"

Langlois searched the Chief Inspector's face.

"About the video? *Oui.* But I haven't seen it." Now it was Gamache's turn to examine his companion. "Have you?"

"Yes. Everyone has."

It was, of course, an exaggeration but not, perhaps, by much. He continued to examine Langlois's face for clues. Was there a hint of pity?

"I'm sorry this has happened, sir."

"Thank you. I'll be watching it later this afternoon."

Langlois paused, as though he wanted to say something, but didn't. Instead he turned swiftly to look back at the Chief Archeologist.

"What's this all about, *patron?*"

"I'll tell you," smiled Gamache, touching the man on the arm and guiding him back to the larger room and the gathering. He spoke to Serge Croix.

"You were here almost a week ago, I know, to see if maybe Augustin Renaud's wasn't

544

the only body in this basement. To see if the man you considered a menace might actually have been right, that Champlain was buried here. Not surprisingly, you found nothing."

"We found root vegetables," said Croix to the snickers of the technicians behind him.

"I'd like you to look again," said the Chief, smiling too, and staring at the archeologist. "For Champlain."

"Not here I'm not. It's a waste of time."

"If you don't, I will." Gamache reached for a shovel. "And you must know, I'm even less of an archeologist than Renaud."

He took his cardigan off and handed it to Émile then, rolling up his sleeves, he looked around the basement. It was pocked with fresh-turned earth, where holes had been dug and filled back in.

"Maybe I'll start here." He put the shovel in the earth and his boot on it.

"Wait," said Croix. "This is absurd. We searched this basement. What makes you think Champlain would be here?"

"That does."

Gamache nodded to Émile, who opened the satchel and handed the old bible to Serge Croix. They watched as the Chief Archeologist's life changed. It began with the tiniest movement. His eyes widened, fractionally, then he blinked, then he exhaled.

"Merde," he whispered. "Oh, *merde."*

Croix looked up from the bible and stared at Gamache. "Where did you find this?"

"Upstairs, hiding where you'd hide a precious old book. Among other old books, in a library no one used. It was almost certainly put there by the murderer. He didn't want to destroy it, but neither could he keep it himself, so he hid it. But before that it was in Renaud's possession and before that it belonged to Charles Chiniquy."

Gamache could see the man's mind racing. Making connections, through the years, through the centuries. Connecting movements, events, personalities.

"How'd Chiniquy find this?"

"Patrick and O'Mara, those two Irish laborers I told you about, found it and sold it to Chiniquy."

"You asked me to find out about digging sites in 1869, is this what that was about? They were working at one of the sites?"

Gamache nodded and waited for Croix to make the final connection.

"The Old Homestead?" the Chief Archeologist finally asked, then brought his hand to his forehead and tilted his head back. "Of course. The Old Homestead. We'd always dismissed it because it was outside the range we considered reasonable for the original hallowed ground. But Champlain wouldn't have been buried in hallowed ground. Not if he was a Huguenot."

Croix gripped the bible and seemed himself in the grip of something, a great excitement, a sort of fugue.

"There'd been rumors, of course, but that's the thing with Champlain, so little's known about the man, there were rumors about everything. This was just one more, and a not very likely one, we thought. Would the King put a Protestant, a Huguenot in charge of the New World? But suppose the King didn't know? But no, it's more likely he did and this would explain so much."

The Chief Archeologist was now like a teenager with his first crush, giddy, almost babbling.

"It would explain why Champlain was never given a royal title, why he was never officially recognized as the Governor of Québec. Why he was never honored for his accomplishments, while others were honored for much less. That's always been a mystery. And maybe it explains why he was sent here in the first place. It was considered almost a suicide mission and maybe Champlain, being a Huguenot, was expendable."

"Would the Jesuits have known?" one of the technicians asked. It was a question that had puzzled Gamache as well. The Catholic Church played a powerful role in the establishment of the colony, in converting the natives and keeping the colonists in line.

The Jesuits were not famous for tolerance.

"I don't know," admitted Croix, thinking. "They must have. Otherwise they'd have buried him in the Catholic cemetery, not outside it."

"But surely the Jesuits would never have allowed him to be buried with that." Gamache pointed to the Huguenot bible, still in Croix's grip.

"True. But someone must have known," said Croix. "There're all sorts of eyewitness accounts of Champlain being buried in the chapel, a chapel he himself had supported. Left half his money to them."

The Chief Archeologist stopped, but they could see his mind racing.

"Could that be it? Was the money a bribe? Did he leave half his fortune to the church here so they'd give him a public burial in the chapel then later, let him be reburied beyond the Catholic cemetery, in a field? With this?" He held up the bible.

Gamache listened, imagining this great leader dug up in the dead of night, his remains lugged across the cemetery, across hallowed ground, and beyond.

Why? Because he was a Protestant. All his deeds, all his courage, all his vision and determination and achievements finally stood for nothing. In death he was only one thing.

A Huguenot. An outsider, in a country he'd created, a world he'd built. Samuel de Champlain, the humanist, had been lowered into the New World, in ground unblessed, but unblemished too.

Had Champlain come here hoping it would be different? Gamache wondered. Only to find the New World exactly like the Old, only colder.

Samuel de Champlain had lain in his lead-lined coffin with his bible until two Irish workers, living in squalor and despair had dug him up. He'd made their fortune. One, O'Mara, had left the city. The other, Patrick, had left lower Québec, buying a home on des Jardins among the affluent.

Had he been happier there?

"And now you think he's here?" Serge Croix turned to Gamache.

"I do." And Gamache told them the rest of the story. Of the meeting with James Douglas, of the payoff.

"So Chiniquy and Douglas buried him

here?" Croix asked.

"That's what I think. Champlain was too powerful a symbol for French Québec, a rallying point. Better never found. 1869 was only two years after Confederation. A lot of French Québec wasn't happy about joining Canada, there were calls for separation even then. Finding Champlain would do no good to the Canadian cause, and might do a great deal of harm. Chiniquy probably didn't care greatly, but I suspect Dr. Douglas did. He was aware of the political forces, and a conservative by nature, the less fuss the better."

"And the remains of Champlain would cause a fuss," said Inspector Langlois, nodding. "Better to bury the dead, and leave it be."

"But the dead had a habit of leaving the grave," said Croix. "Especially around James Douglas. You're familiar with his activities?"

"As a grave robber?" said Gamache. "Yes."

"And the mummies," said Croix.

"Mummies?" Langlois asked.

"Another time," said the Chief Inspector. "I'll tell you all about it. Now we have another body to find."

For the next hour the archeologist and his technicians searched the basement again, finding more tin boxes, more vegetables.

But under the stairs, exactly where the metal steps landed, they found something else. Something dismissed in their first sweep earlier in the week as just the blip from the stairs themselves but now, examined closer, proved to be something else.

Digging carefully but without enthusiasm or conviction, the technicians hit something, something larger than the tin boxes. Something, indeed, not tin at all but wood.

Digging more carefully now, excavating, taking photographs and recording the event, they slowly, painstakingly, uncovered a coffin. The men gathered round and by rote crossed themselves.

The Inspector called his forensics team and within minutes the investigators had arrived. Samples were taken, more photographs, prints.

Cameras recording, the coffin was raised and the Chief Archeologist and his head technician pried up the nails, long and rusty red. With a slow shriek they came out of the wood, reluctant to leave, reluctant to reveal what they'd hidden for so long.

Finally freed of the nails the lid was ready to be lifted. Serge Croix reached out then hesitated. Looking over at Gamache he gestured, beckoning him forward. Gamache declined, but when the Chief Archeologist

551

insisted he agreed.

Armand Gamache stood before the worm-eaten coffin. A simple maple wood, made from the ancient forests hacked down to build Québec four hundred years earlier. Gamache could feel the tremble in his right hand, and knew it showed.

He reached out and touched the coffin, and the tremble stopped. Resting his hands there he considered what was about to happen. After centuries of hunting, after lifetimes spent in the singular search for the Father of Québec, after his own childhood spent reading about it, dreaming about it, reenacting it with friends. A stick in his hand, he'd stood astride rocks in Parc Mont Royal, commanding the great ship, fighting noble battles, surviving terrible storms. Valiant. Along with every other school child in Québec his hero had been Samuel de Champlain.

Exploring, mapping. Creating. Québec.

Gamache looked down at his large hands, resting gently on the old wood.

Samuel de Champlain.

Gamache stepped aside and gestured to Émile to take his place. The elderly man shook his head but Gamache walked over and led him to the coffin then stepped back and smiled at his mentor.

"Merci," Émile mouthed. Together he and the Chief Archeologist slowly, carefully, raised the heavy, lead-lined lid.

A skeleton lay there. Finally, found.

After a long silence the Chief Archeologist, gazing into the coffin, spoke.

"Unless Champlain had another big secret, this isn't him."

"What do you mean?" Gamache asked.

"It's a woman."

Something had changed. Jean-Guy Beauvoir could feel it. It was the way people looked at him. It was as though they'd seen him naked, as though they'd seen him in a position so vulnerable, so exposed it was all they could see now.

Not the man he really was. An edited man.

They'd seen the video, all of them. That much was obvious. He was the only one in Three Pines who hadn't, he and maybe Ruth, who was barely out of the stone ages.

But while the people of Three Pines might know something about him, he knew something about them, something no one else knew. He knew who'd killed the Hermit.

It was late Friday afternoon. The sun had long since set and the bistro was clearing out, people heading home for dinner after a drink.

Beauvoir looked round. Clara, Peter and Myrna were sitting with Old Mundin and The Wife, who held a sleeping Charles. At another table Marc and Dominique Gilbert sipped beer while Marc's mother, Carole, had a white wine. The Parras were there, Roar and Hanna. Their son Havoc was waiting tables.

Ruth sat alone and Gabri stood behind the bar.

The door opened and someone else blew in, batting snow off his hat and stomping his feet. Vincent Gilbert, the asshole saint, the doctor who'd been so tender with Beauvoir and so cruel with others.

"Am I late?" he asked.

"Late?" said Carole. "For what?"

"Well, I was invited. Weren't you?"

Everyone turned to Beauvoir then to Clara and Myrna. Old and The Wife had been invited for drinks by the two women, as had the Parras. The Gilberts had come at Beauvoir's invitation and Ruth was just part of the décor.

"Patron," said Beauvoir, and Gabri locked the front door then closed the side entrances from the other shops.

"What's all this about?" Roar Parra asked, looking perplexed but not alarmed. He was short and squat and powerful and Beauvoir was glad he wasn't alarmed. Yet.

They stared at Beauvoir.

He'd quietly had a word with Gabri earlier and asked him to ask the other patrons to leave, discreetly, so that only these few remained. Outside snow was falling and beginning to blow about, visible in the glow from the homes. The cheery Christmas lights on the three pine trees on the village green bobbed in the wind. They'd be battling a small blizzard by the time they left.

Inside, it was snug and warm and though the wind and snow swirled against the windows it only increased their sense of security. Fires were lit in the hearths and while they could hear the wind outside the sturdy building never even shuddered.

Like the rest of Three Pines, and its residents, it took what was coming and remained standing. And now, together, they stared at him.

With just a touch of pity?

"OK, numb nuts, what's all this about?" asked Ruth.

Armand Gamache sat in the library of the Literary and Historical Society marveling that a week ago he barely knew it, barely knew the people, and now he felt he knew them well.

The board had assembled one more time.

Tense, suspicious Porter Wilson at the head of the table, even if he wasn't a natural leader. The real leader sat beside him and had all their lives, quietly running things, picking up pieces dropped and broken by Porter. Elizabeth MacWhirter, heir to the MacWhirter shipyard fortunes, a fortune long faded away until all that remained were appearances.

But appearances mattered, Gamache knew, especially to Elizabeth MacWhirter. Especially to the English community. And the truth was, they were at once stronger and weaker than they appeared.

The English community was certainly small, and diminishing, dying out. A fact lost on the Francophone majority who, despite every evidence, still saw the Anglos, if they saw them at all, as threats.

And why not, really? Many of the Anglos still saw themselves as wielding, and deserving, of power. A manifest destiny, a right conferred on them by birth and fate. By General Wolfe, two hundred years earlier on the field belonging to the farmer Abraham.

Like whites in South Africa or the Southern states who knew that things had changed, who even accepted the changes, but who couldn't quite shake the certainty deeply, diplomatically, hidden, that they should still be in charge.

There was Winnie, the tiny librarian who loved the library and loved Elizabeth and loved her work among things and ideas no longer relevant.

Mr. Blake was there, in suit and tie. A benign older gentleman, whose home had shrunk from the entire city, to a house, and finally to this one magnificent room. And what, Gamache wondered, would someone do to defend their home?

Tom Hancock sat quietly, watching. Young, vital, wise, but not really one of them. An outsider. But that gave him clarity, he could see what was only visible from a distance.

And finally, Ken Haslam. Whose voice was either silent or shrieking.

No middle ground, a man of extremes, who either sat quietly in his chair or fought his way across a frozen river.

A man whose wife and daughter were buried in Québec but who was not considered a Québécois, as though even more could be expected.

They'd adjourned to the library once the coffin had been removed and the others had gone, leaving Émile, Gamache and the board.

Gamache looked at the board members, resting finally on Porter Wilson. Expecting an outburst, expecting a demand for information, tinged perhaps with a slight accusation of unfairness.

Instead they all simply looked at the Chief Inspector, politely. Something had changed, and Gamache knew what.

It was the damned video. They'd seen it, and he hadn't. Not yet. They knew something he didn't, something about himself. But he knew something they didn't, something they wanted to know.

Well, they'd have to wait.

"You were out practicing this afternoon, I believe," said Gamache to the Reverend Mr. Tom Hancock.

"We were," he agreed, surprised by the topic.

"I saw you." The Chief turned to Ken Haslam.

Haslam smiled and mouthed something Gamache couldn't make out. There was a nodding of heads. The Chief turned to the others.

"What did Mr. Haslam just say?"

Now several faces blushed. He waited.

"Because," he finally said, "I didn't hear a word and I don't think you did either." He turned again to the upright, distinguished man. "Why do you whisper? In fact, I don't think it can even be called a whisper."

Gamache had spoken respectfully, quietly, without anger or accusation but wanting to know.

Haslam's lips moved and again no one heard anything.

"He speaks —" began Tom Hancock before Gamache put up a hand and stopped him.

"I think it's time Mr. Haslam spoke for himself, don't you? And you, perhaps uniquely, know he can."

Now it was the Reverend Mr. Hancock's turn to blush. He looked at Gamache but said nothing.

Gamache leaned forward, toward Haslam. "I heard you out on the ice calling the strokes. No other crew could be heard, no other person. Just you."

Ken Haslam looked frightened now. He opened his mouth, then shook his head, practically in tears.

"I can't," he said, his voice barely registering. "All my life I've been told to be quiet."

"By whom?"

"Mother, Father, brothers. My teachers, everyone. Even my wife, God bless her, asked me to keep my voice down."

"Why?"

"Because."

The word was spoken clearly, too clearly. It wasn't so much piercing as all enveloping, filling the space. It was a voice that carried, boomed, and drove all before it. No other voice could exist, but that one. An English voice, drowning out all others.

"And so you learned to be silent?" asked Gamache.

"If I wanted friends," said Haslam, his words slamming into them. Was it some quirk of palate and brainpan and voice box so that the sound waves were magnified? "If I wanted to belong, yes, I learned never to raise my voice."

"But that meant you could never speak at all, never be heard," said Gamache.

"And what would you choose?" Haslam asked, his loud voice turning a rational question into an attack. "To speak up but chase people away, or to be quiet in company?"

Armand Gamache was silent then, looking down the long table at the solemn faces, and he knew Ken Haslam wasn't the only one who'd faced that question, and made the same choice.

To be silent. In hopes of not offending, in hopes of being accepted.

But what happened to people who never

spoke, never raised their voices? Kept everything inside?

Gamache knew what happened. Everything they swallowed, every word, thought, feeling rattled around inside, hollowing the person out. And into that chasm they stuffed their words, their rage.

"Perhaps you could explain the coffin in our basement," Elizabeth broke the silence.

It seemed a reasonable request.

"As you know I came here to recover from my wounds." Beauvoir wouldn't let them think he didn't know what they knew. A few villagers lowered their eyes, a few blushed as though Beauvoir had dropped his pants, but most continued to look at him, interested.

"But there was another reason. Chief Inspector Gamache asked me to look into the murder of the Hermit."

That caused a stir. They looked at each other. Gabri, alone among them, stood up.

"He sent you? He believed me?"

"Hasn't that case been solved?" said Hanna. "Haven't you caused enough harm?"

"The Chief wasn't satisfied," said Beauvoir. "At first I thought he was wrong, that perhaps he'd been persuaded by the wishful thinking of Gabri here, who every day since Olivier was arrested sent the Chief a letter, containing the same question. Why did Olivier move the body?"

Gabri turned to Clara. "It was my query letter."

"And we all know you're quite a query," said Ruth.

Gabri was bursting, beaming. No one else was.

"The more I investigated the more I began to think Olivier might not have killed the Hermit. But if not Olivier, then who?"

He stood with his hands on the back of a wing chair for support. Almost there. "We believed the motive had to do with the treasure. It seemed obvious. And yet, if it was the motive, why hadn't the murderer taken it? So I decided to take a different tack. Suppose the treasure had very little to do with the killing of the Hermit? Except for one crucial feature. It led the murderer here, to Three Pines."

They all stared at him, even Clara and Myrna. He hadn't shared his conclusions with them. This close to trapping the killer he couldn't risk it.

"If he hid all those things in his cabin, how could they lead anyone to Three Pines?" Old Mundin asked from the back of the room.

"They didn't stay hidden," Beauvoir explained. "Not all of them. The Hermit began to give some to Olivier in exchange for food and company and Olivier, knowing what he had, sold them. Through eBay, but also through an antique shop in Montreal on rue Notre-Dame."

He turned to the Gilberts. "I understand you bought some things on rue Notre-Dame."

"It's a long street, Inspector," said Dominique. "A lot of stores."

"True, but like butchers and bakers, most people develop a loyalty for a specific antique shop, they go back to the same one. Am I right?"

He looked around. Everyone, except Gabri, dropped their eyes.

"Well, not to worry. I'm sure the owner will recognize your photographs."

"All right, we used the Temps Perdu," said Carole.

"Les Temps Perdu. Popular place. It happens to be where Olivier sold the Hermit's things." Beauvoir wasn't surprised. He'd already spoken to the owner about the Gilberts.

"We didn't know that's where he went," said Dominique, her voice sounding squeezed, sharp. "It just had nice things. Lots of people go there."

"Besides," said Marc. "We only bought the home here in the last year. We didn't need antiques before that."

"You might have gone in to look. People window-shop up and down rue Notre-Dame all the time."

"But," said Hanna Parra, "you said the Hermit wasn't killed for his treasure. Then why was he killed?"

"Exactly," said Beauvoir. "Why? Once I set aside the treasure other things took on more importance, mostly two things. The word 'Woo,' and the repetition of another word. 'Charlotte.' There was *Charlotte's Web,* Charlotte Brontë, the Amber Room was made for a Charlotte, and the violin's maker, his wife and muse was named Charlotte. We might, of course, be reading more into it than it deserved, but at the very least it deserved another look."

"And what did you find?" The Wife asked.

"I found the murderer," said Beauvoir.

Armand Gamache was tired. He wanted to go home to Reine-Marie. But now wasn't the time to show weakness, now wasn't the time to flag. Not when he was so close.

He'd told them about Chiniquy, he'd told

564

them about James Douglas. About Patrick and O'Mara. And he showed them the books, the ones they'd unwittingly sold from their collection.

Including perhaps the most valuable volume in Canada today.

An original Huguenot bible belonging to Samuel de Champlain.

That had brought groans from the board members, but no recriminations. They were beginning to band together, to shore up their differences.

Things are strongest when they're broken, Agent Morin had said, and Armand Gamache knew it to be true. And he knew he was witnessing a broken community, fractured by unkind time and events, and a temperament not, perhaps, best suited to change.

But it was pulling together, mending, and it would be very strong indeed because it was so broken. As Ken Haslam had been broken, by years of hushing. As Elizabeth MacWhirter had been worn down by years of polishing the façade. As Porter Wilson and Winnie and Mr. Blake had been shattered watching family, friends, influence, institutions disappear.

Only young Tom Hancock was unscathed, for now.

"So when Augustin Renaud came to speak to us a week ago he wanted to dig?" asked Mr. Blake.

"I believe so. He was convinced Champlain was buried in your basement, put there by James Douglas and Father Chiniquy."

"And he was right," said Porter, all bravado gone. "What'll they do to us when they find out we've been hiding Champlain all these years?"

"We didn't hide him," said Winnie. "We didn't even know he was there."

"Try convincing the tabloids of that," said Porter. "And even if most believe us, the fact is, it was still an Anglo conspiracy."

"A conspiracy of two," said Mr. Blake. "More than a hundred years ago. Not the whole community."

"And you think if James Douglas had asked the community they'd have disagreed?" demanded Porter, making a more coherent argument than Gamache had thought him capable of. One thing was certain, he knew his community, as did Mr. Blake, who accepted that Porter, finally, was right.

"This is a disaster," said Winnie and no one contradicted her, except Gamache.

"Well, not entirely. The coffin was Champlain's, but the body inside wasn't."

Now they gaped at him. Dying men thrown a rope, a slender hope.

They were hushed. And finally Ken Haslam spoke, his voice filling the room, squeezing them all into the corners.

"Who was he?"

"She. The body in the coffin appears to be female."

"She? What was she doing in Champlain's coffin?" Haslam shouted.

"We don't know, but we will."

Beside him Émile's eyes slid from Haslam to Elizabeth MacWhirter. She looked sad and frightened. Her veneer cracking. Émile smiled at her slightly. An encouraging look from someone who knew what it felt like to be shattered.

"Things are strongest where they're broken," Agent Morin laughed. "Good thing too, since I'm always dropping things. Suzanne's pretty clumsy too, you know. We're going to have to put our babies in bubble wrap. Babies bounce, right?"

"Not twice," said Gamache and Morin laughed again.

"Oh well, I guess we'll have strong kids."

"Without a doubt."

"I started with the assumption that the killer

had found one of the Hermit's treasures in the antique shop," said Beauvoir, "and traced it back here to Three Pines."

The only sounds now in the bistro were the crackling of the log fire and snow hitting the windows.

Inside, the fireplaces threw odd shadows against the walls but none of them threatening. Not to Beauvoir, but he suspected at least one person in this room was beginning to find it close, tight, claustrophobic.

"But who could it be? The Gilberts had bought a lot of antiques from that very store. The Parras? They'd inherited a lot of things from their family in the Czech Republic and managed to get them out when the wall came down. By their own admission, they'd sold most of it to pay for their new home. Perhaps they sold the things through Les Temps Perdu. Old Mundin? Well, he restores antiques. Wouldn't he also be drawn to the terrific shops on rue Notre-Dame?

"It hardly seemed to narrow the suspects, so I looked at another clue. Woo. Olivier had described the Hermit whispering the word when he was particularly distressed. It was upsetting to him. But what did 'woo' mean? Was it a name, a nickname?"

He looked over to the Gilbert table. Like

568

the rest they were staring, entranced and guarded.

"Was 'woo' short-form for a name that was hard to say, particularly for a child? That's when most nicknames are given, isn't it? In childhood. I was at the Mundins' and heard little Charlie speaking. Shoo, for *chaud.* Kids do that, trying to get their tongues around hard words. Like Woloshyn. Woo."

Clara leaned in to Myrna and whispered, "That's what I was afraid of. As soon as I heard her maiden name was Woloshyn."

Myrna raised her brows and turned, with the rest of them, to look at Carole Gilbert.

Carole didn't move but Vincent Gilbert did. He rose to his full height, his towering personality filling the room.

"Enough with these insinuations. If you have something to say come out with it."

"And you," Beauvoir rounded on him. "Sir. The magnificent Dr. Gilbert. The great man, the great healer." As he spoke he knew the Chief Inspector would be handling this differently, would never employ sarcasm, would rarely lose his temper, as Beauvoir could feel himself doing. With an effort he pulled back from the edge. "One of the great mysteries of this case has always been why the murderer didn't steal the treasure.

Who could resist it? Even if it wasn't the motive for murder, it was just sitting there. Who wouldn't pick up a trinket? A rare book? A gold candlestick?"

"And what was your brilliant conclusion?" Dr. Gilbert asked, his voice filled with contempt.

"There seemed only one. The killer had no need of it. Did that apply to Olivier? No. He was about as greedy as they come. Marc, your son? Same thing. Greedy, petty. He'd have stripped the cabin."

He could see Marc Gilbert struggling, wanting to defend himself, but recognizing that these insults actually helped clear him of suspicion.

"The Parras? A landscaper, a waiter? Not exactly rolling in money. Even one of the Hermit's pieces would make a huge difference in their lives. No, if one of them had killed the Hermit they'd have stolen something. Same with Old Mundin. A carpenter's income is fine for now, but what happens when Charlie gets older? He'll need to be provided for. The Mundins would have stolen the treasure if not for themselves then for their son."

Now he turned back to Vincent Gilbert.

"But one person, sir, didn't need the treasure. You. You're already wealthy. Besides, I don't think money's important to you. You have another motivation, another master. Money was never the currency that counted. No. It's compliments you collect. Respect, admiration. You collect the certainty that you're better than anyone else. A saint, even. It's your ego, your self-esteem that needs feeding, demands feeding, not your bank account. You alone among all the suspects would have left the treasure, because it meant nothing to you."

If Dr. Gilbert could have ripped Beauvoir's life away with a look, the young Inspector would have dropped dead right there. But instead of dying, Inspector Beauvoir smiled and continued his story, his voice suddenly calm, reasonable.

"But there was another mystery. Who was the Hermit? Olivier started off saying he was Czech and his name was Jakob but he's since admitted he was lying. He had no idea who the man was except that he wasn't Czech. More likely French or English. He spoke perfect French, but seemed to prefer to read English."

Beauvoir noticed Roar and Hanna Parra exchange relieved glances.

"The only clue we had led us back to the antiques and antiquities in his cabin. I don't know antiques, but people who do said these were amazing. He must have had an eye for it. He didn't pick the stuff up at flea markets and garage sales."

Beauvoir paused. He'd seen Gamache do this time and again, reeling in the suspect then letting him run, then reeling some more. But doing it subtly, carefully, delicately, without the suspect even realizing it. Doing it steadily, without hesitation.

It would be terrifying for the murderer when it dawned on him what was happening. And that terror was what the Chief counted on. To wear the person down, to grind them down. But it took a strong stomach, and patience.

Beauvoir had never appreciated how difficult this was. To present the facts in such a way so that the murderer would eventually know where it was heading. But not too soon as to be able to wiggle away, and not too late to have time to fight back.

No, the point was to wear the murderer's nerves wire thin. Then give him the impression he wasn't a suspect, someone else was. Let him breathe, then move in again when his guard was down.

And do that, over and over. Relentlessly.

It was exhausting. Like landing a huge fish, only one that could eat the boat.

And now Beauvoir moved in again, for the

last time. For the kill.

"The truth, for we know it now, is that the treasure played a role. It was the catalyst. But what drove the final blow wasn't greed for a treasure lost but for something else lost. Something more personal, more valuable even than treasure. This wasn't about the loss of family heirlooms, but the family itself. Am I right?"

And Beauvoir turned to the murderer.

The killer stood and everyone in the room stared, bewildered.

"He killed my father," said Old Mundin.

TWENTY-FOUR

The Wife pushed away from the table and gaped.

"Old?" she whispered.

It was as though the bitter wind had found a way in and frozen everyone in place. Had Beauvoir accused the mantelpiece of murder they could not have been more astonished.

"Oh, God, Old, please," The Wife begged. But a hint of desperation had crept into her eyes, slowly replacing disbelief. Like a healthy woman told she had terminal cancer, The Wife was in a daze. The end of her life was in sight, her simple life with a carpenter, making and restoring furniture, living in the country in a modest home. Raising Charles, and being with the only man she ever wanted to be with, the man she loved.

Over.

Old turned to her and his son. He was impossibly beautiful and even the vile accusation couldn't tarnish that.

"He killed my father," Old repeated. "I came to Three Pines to find him. He's right," he jerked his head toward Beauvoir. "I was working in Les Temps Perdu, restoring furniture when a walking stick came in. It was very old, handmade. Unique. I recognized it right away. My father had shown it to me and pointed out the inlaying, how the woodworker had designed it around the burling. It appeared to be just a simple, rustic walking stick, but it was a work of art. It had been my father's and had been stolen after he died. Had been stolen by his murderer."

"You found out from the shop records who had sold it to Les Temps Perdu," said Beauvoir. This was supposition now, but he needed to make it sound as though he knew it to be true.

"It was from an Olivier Brulé, living in Three Pines." Old Mundin breathed deeply, prepared to take the plunge. "I moved here. Got a job repairing and restoring Olivier's furniture. I needed to get close to him, to watch him. I needed proof he'd killed my father."

"But Olivier could never do that," said Gabri, quietly but with certainty. "He could never kill."

"I know," said Old. "I realized that the more I got to know him. He was a greedy man. Often a little sly. But a good man. He could never have killed my father. But someone did. Olivier was getting my father's things from someone. I spent years following him all over the place, as he did his antiquing. He visited homes and farms and other shops. Bought antiques from all over the place. But never did I see him actually pick up one of my father's things. And yet, they kept appearing. And being sold on."

Perhaps it was the atmosphere, the warm and snug bistro. The storm outside. The wine and hot chocolate and lit fires, but this felt unreal. As though their friend was talking about someone else. Telling them a tale. A fable.

"Over the years I met Michelle and fell in love," he smiled at his wife. No longer The Wife. But the woman he loved. Michelle. "We had Charles. My life was complete. I'd actually forgotten about why I'd come here in the first place. But one Saturday night I was sitting in the truck after picking up the furniture and I saw Olivier close up and leave the bistro. But instead of heading home he did something strange. He went into the woods. I didn't follow him. I was too surprised. But I thought about it a lot and the next Saturday I waited for him, but he just went home. But the following week he went into the woods again. Carrying a bag."

"Groceries," said Gabri. No one said anything. They could see what was happening. Old Mundin in his truck. Watching and waiting. Patient. And seeing Olivier disappear into the woods. Old quietly getting out of the vehicle, following Olivier. And finding the cabin.

"I looked in through the windows and saw —" Old's voice faltered. Michelle reached out and quietly laid her hand on his. He slowly regained himself, his breathing becoming calmer, more measured, until he was able to continue with the story.

"I saw my father's things. Everything he'd kept in the back room. The special place for his special things, he'd told me. Things only he and I knew about. The colored glass, the plates, the candlesticks, the furniture. All there."

Old's eyes gleamed. He stared into the distance. No longer in the bistro with the rest of them. Now he was back at the cabin. On the outside looking in.

"Olivier gave the bag to the old man and they sat down. They drank from china my father let me touch, and ate off plates he said came from a queen."

"Charlotte," said Beauvoir. "Queen Charlotte."

"Yes. Like my mother. My father said they were special because they would always remind him of my mother. Charlotte."

"That's why you named your son Charles," said Beauvoir. "We thought it was after your father, but it was your mother's name. Charlotte."

Mundin nodded but didn't look at his son. Couldn't look at his son, or his wife now.

"What did you do then?" Beauvoir asked. He knew enough now to keep his voice soft, almost hypnotic. To not break the spell. Let Old Mundin tell the story.

"I knew then I was looking at the man who'd killed my father fifteen years ago. I never believed it was an accident. I'm not a fool. I know most people think it was suicide, that he killed himself by walking onto the river. But I knew him. He would never have done that. I knew if he was dead he'd been killed. But it was only much later I realized his most precious things had been taken. I talked to my mother about it but I don't think she believed me. He'd never shown her the things. Only me.

"My father had been murdered and his

priceless antiques stolen. And now, finally, I'd found the man who'd done it."

"What did you do, Patrick?" Michelle asked. It was the first time any of them had heard his real name. The name she reserved for their most intimate moments. When they were not Old and The Wife. But Patrick and Michelle. A young man and woman, in love.

"I wanted to torment the man. I wanted him to know someone had found him. One of our favorite books was *Charlotte's Web*, so I made a web from fishing line and snuck into the cabin when he was working on his vegetable garden. I put it in the rafters. So that he'd find it there."

"And you put the word 'Woo' into it," said Beauvoir. "Why?"

"It was what my father called me. Our secret name. He taught me all about wood and when I was small I tried to say the words but all I could say was 'woo.' So he started calling me that. Not often. Just sometimes when I was in his arms. He'd hug me tight and whisper, 'Woo.' "

No one could look at the beautiful young man now. They dropped their eyes from the scalding sight. From the eclipse. As all that love turned into hate.

"I watched from the woods, but the Hermit didn't seem to find the web. So I took the most precious thing I own. I kept it in a sack in my workshop. Hadn't seen it in years. But I took it out that night and took it with me to the cabin."

There was silence then. In their minds they could see the dark figure walking through the dark woods. Toward the thing he had searched for and finally found.

"I watched Olivier leave and waited a few minutes. Then I left the thing outside his door and knocked. I hid in the shadows and watched. The old man opened the door and looked out, expecting to see Olivier. He looked amused at first, then puzzled. Then a little frightened."

The fire crackled and cackled in the grate. It spit out a few embers that slowly died. And Old described what happened next.

The Hermit scanned the woods and was about to close the door when he saw something sitting on the porch. A tiny visitor. He stooped and picked it up. It was a wooden word. Woo.

And then Old had seen it. The look he'd dreamed of, fantasized about. Mortgaged his life to see. Terror on the face of the man who'd killed his father. The same terror his father must have felt as the ice broke underneath him.

The end. In that instant the Hermit knew

the monster he'd been hiding from had finally found him.

And it had.

Old separated himself from the dark forest and approached the cabin, approached the elderly man. The Hermit backed into the cabin and said only one thing.

"Woo," he whispered. "Woo."

Old picked up the silver menorah and struck. Once. And into that blow he put his childhood, his grief, his loss. He put his mother's sorrow and his sister's longing. The menorah, weighed down with that, crushed the Hermit's skull. And he fell, Woo clutched in his hand.

Old didn't care. No one would find the body except Olivier and he suspected Olivier would say nothing. He liked the man very much, but knew him for what he was.

Greedy.

Olivier would take the treasure and leave the body and everyone would be happy. A man already lost to the world would be slowly swallowed by the forest. Olivier would have his treasure, and Old would have his life back.

His obligation to his father discharged.

"It was the first thing I ever made," said Old. "I whittled Woo and gave it to my father. After he died I couldn't bear to look at it anymore so I put it in the sack. But I brought it out that night. One last time."

Old Mundin turned to his family. All his energy spent, his brilliance fading. He placed his hand on his sleeping son's back and spoke.

"I'm so sorry. My father taught me everything, gave me everything. This man killed him, shoved him onto the river in spring."

Clara grimaced, imagining a death like that, imagining the horror as the ice began to crack. As it did now beneath The Wife.

Jean-Guy Beauvoir went to the bistro door and opened it. Along with a swirl of snow two large Sûreté officers entered.

"Can you leave us, please?" Beauvoir asked of the villagers, and slowly, stunned, they put their winter coats on and left. Clara and Peter took The Wife and Charles back to their home, while Inspector Beauvoir finished the interview with Old Mundin.

An hour later the police cars drew away, taking Old. Michelle accompanied him, but not before stopping at the inn and spa to hand Charles over to the only other person he loved.

The asshole saint. Dr. Gilbert. Who tenderly took the boy in his arms and held him for a few hours, safe against the bitter cold world pounding at the door.

■ ■ ■ ■

"Hot toddy?"

Peter handed one to Beauvoir, who sat in a deep, comfortable chair in their living room. Gabri sat on the sofa in a daze. Clara and Myrna were also there, drinks in their hands, in front of the fireplace.

"What I don't get," said Peter, perching on an arm of the sofa, "is where all those amazing antiques came from in the first place. The Hermit stole them and took them into the woods, but where did Old's father get them to begin with?"

Beauvoir sighed. He was exhausted. Always happier with physical activity, it constantly amazed him how grueling intellectual activity could also be.

"For all that Old Mundin loved his father, he didn't know him well," said Beauvoir. "What kid does? I think we'll find that Mundin made some trips to the Eastern Bloc, as communism was falling. He convinced a lot of people to trust him with their family treasures. But instead of keeping them safe, or sending people the money, he just disappeared with their treasures."

"Stole them himself?" Clara asked.

Beauvoir nodded.

"The Hermit's murder was never about the treasure," said Beauvoir. "Old Mundin could care less about it. In fact, he came to hate it. That's why it was left in the cabin. He didn't want the treasure. The only thing he took was the Hermit's life."

Beauvoir looked into the fire and remembered his interrogation of Old, in the deserted bistro, where it had all begun months ago. He heard about the death of Mundin's father. How Old's heart had broken that day. But into that crack young Old had shoved his rage, his pain, his loss but that wasn't enough. But once he placed his intention there his heart beat again. With a purpose.

When Olivier had been arrested Old Mundin had wrestled with his conscience, but had finally decided this was fate, this was Olivier's punishment for greed, for helping a man he knew very well was at best a thief and at worst, worse.

"You play the fiddle?" Beauvoir had asked Old, when they were alone in the bistro, after the others had left. "I understand you perform at the Canada Day picnics?"

"Yes."

"Your father taught you that too?"

"He did."

Beauvoir nodded. "And he taught you

about antiques and carpentry and restoration?"

Old Mundin nodded.

"You lived in old Quebec City, at number sixteen rue des Ramparts?"

Mundin stared.

"And your mother used to read *Charlotte's Web* to you and your sister, as children?" Beauvoir persisted. He didn't move from his seat, but it felt as though with each question he was approaching Mundin, getting closer and closer.

And Mundin, baffled, seemed to sense that something was approaching. Something even worse than what had already happened.

The lights flickered as the blizzard threw itself against the village, against the bistro.

"Where did you get your name?" Beauvoir asked, staring at Old Mundin across the table.

"What name?"

"Old. Who gave you that name? Your real name is Patrick. So where did Old come from?"

"Where everything I am came from. My father. He'd call me old son. 'Come along, old son,' he'd say. 'I'll teach you about wood.' And I'd go. After a while everyone just called me Old."

Beauvoir nodded. "Old. Old son."

Old Mundin stared at Beauvoir, his face blank then his eyes narrowed as something appeared on the horizon, very far off. A gathering. Terror, the Furies. Loneliness and Sorrow. And something else. Something worse. The worst thing imaginable.

"Old son," Beauvoir whispered again. "The Hermit used that expression. Called Olivier that. 'Chaos is coming, old son.' Those were his words to Olivier. And now I say it to you."

The building shuddered and cold drafts stole through the room.

"Chaos is coming, Old son," Beauvoir said quietly. "The man you killed was your father."

"He killed his own father?" Clara whispered. "Oh, dear God. Oh my God."

It was over.

"Mundin's father faked his death," said Beauvoir. "Before that he'd built the cabin and moved the treasures. Then he returned to Quebec City and waited for spring, and a stormy day to cover his tracks. When the perfect conditions came he put his coat by the shore and disappeared, everyone assumed into the St. Lawrence River. But in fact, into the forest."

There was silence then, and in that silence they imagined the rest. Imagined the worst.

"Conscience," said Myrna, at last. "Imagine being pursued by your own conscience."

And for a terrible moment they did. A mountain of a conscience. Throwing a lengthening shadow. Growing. Darkening.

"He had his treasure," said Clara, "but finally all he wanted was his family."

"And peace," said Myrna. "A clear and quiet conscience."

"He surrounded himself with things that reminded him of his wife and kids. Books, the violin. He even carved an image of what Old might look like as a young man, listening. It became his treasure, the one thing he could never part with. He carved it, and scratched 'Woo' under it. It kept him company and eased his conscience. A bit. When we first found it we thought the Hermit had made a carving of Olivier. But we were wrong. It was of his son."

"How's Old?" Clara asked.

"Not good."

Beauvoir remembered the look of rage on the young man's face when the Inspector had told him the Hermit was in fact his father. He'd murdered the very man he meant to avenge. The only man he wished was alive, he killed.

And after the rage, came disbelief. Then horror.

Conscience. Jean-Guy Beauvoir knew it would keep Old Mundin company in prison for decades to come.

Gabri held his head in his hands. Muffled sobs came from the man. Not great dramatic whoops of sorrow, but tired tears. Happy, confused, turbulent tears.

But mostly tears of relief.

Why had Olivier moved the body?

Why had Olivier moved the body?

Why had Olivier moved the body?

And now, finally, they knew. He'd moved the body because he hadn't killed the Hermit, only found him already dead. It was a revolting thing to do, disgraceful, petty, shameful. But it wasn't murder.

"Would you like to stay for dinner? You look exhausted," Beauvoir heard Clara say to Gabri. Then he felt a soft touch on his arm and looked up.

Clara was talking to him.

"It'll be simple, just soup and a sandwich, and we'll get you home early."

Home.

Perhaps it was the fatigue, perhaps it was the stress. But he felt his eyes burning at the word.

He longed to go home.

But not to Montreal.

Here. This was home. He longed to crawl under the duvet at the B and B, to hear the blizzard howl outside and do its worst and to know he was warm, and safe.

God help him, this was home.

Beauvoir stood and smiled at Clara, something that felt at once foreign and familiar. He didn't smile often. Not with suspects. Not at all.

But he smiled now, a weary, grateful grin.

"I'd like that but there's something I have to do first."

Before he left he went into the washroom and splashed cold water onto his face. He looked into the reflection and saw there a man far older than his thirty-eight years. Drawn and tired. And not wanting to do what came next.

He felt an ache deep down.

Bringing the pill bottle out of his pocket he placed it on the counter and stared at it. Then pouring himself a glass of water he shook a pill into his palm. Carefully breaking it in half he swallowed it with a quick swig.

Picking up the other half from the white porcelain rim of the sink he hesitated then quickly tossed it back in the bottle before he could change his mind.

Clara walked him to the front door.

"Can I come by in an hour?" he asked.

"Of course," she said and added, "bring Ruth."

How did she know? Perhaps, he thought as he plunged into the storm, he wasn't as clever as all that. Or perhaps, he thought as the storm fought back, they know me here.

"What do you want?" Ruth demanded, opening the door before he knocked. A swirl of snow came in with him and Ruth whacked his clothing, caked in snow. At least, he thought that was why she was batting away at him, though he had to admit the snow was long gone and still she hit him.

"You know what I want."

"You're lucky I have such a generous spirit, dick-head."

"I'm lucky you're delusional," he muttered, following her into the now familiar home.

Ruth made popcorn, as though this was trivial. Entertainment. And poured herself a Scotch, not offering him one. He didn't need it. He could feel the effects of the pill.

Her computer was already set up on the plastic garden table in her kitchen and they sat side-by-side in wobbly pre-formed plastic chairs.

Ruth pressed a button and up came the site.

Beauvoir looked at her. "Have you watched it?"

"No," she said, staring at the screen, not at him. "I was waiting for you."

Beauvoir took a deep ragged breath, exhaled, and hit play.

"Too bad about Champlain," said Émile as they walked down St-Stanislas and across rue St-Jean, waiting for revelers to pass like rush-hour traffic.

It was beginning to snow. Huge, soft flakes drifted down, caught in the street lamps and the headlights of cars. The forecast was for a storm coming their way. A foot or more expected overnight. This was just the vanguard, the first hints of what was to come.

Quebec City was never lovelier than in a storm and the aftermath, when the sun came out and revealed a magical kingdom, softened and muffled by the thick covering. Fresh and clean, a world unsullied, unmarred.

At the old stone home Émile got out his key. Through the lace curtains on the door they could see Henri hiding behind a pillar, watching.

Gamache smiled then brought his mind

591

back to the case. The curious case of the woman in Champlain's coffin.

Who was she, and what happened to Champlain? Where'd he go? Seemed his explorations didn't end with his death.

Once inside Gamache took Henri for a walk and when he returned Émile had set the laptop on the coffee table, put out a bottle of Scotch, lit the fire and was waiting.

The elderly man stood in the center of the room, his arms at his side. He looked formal, almost rigid.

"What is it, Émile?"

"I'd like to watch the video with you."

"Now?"

"Now."

All through the walk the Chief Inspector had been preparing himself for this. The cold flakes on his face had been refreshing and he'd stopped and tilted his face up, closing his eyes and opening his mouth, to catch them.

"I love doing that," Morin said. "But the snow has to be just right."

"You were a connoisseur?" the Chief asked.

"Still am. The flakes have to be the big, fluffy kind. The ones that just drift down. None of the hard, small flakes you get in storms. That's no fun. They go up your nose and get in your ears. Get everywhere. No it's the big ones you want."

Gamache knew what he meant. He'd done it himself, as a child. Had watched Daniel and Annie do it. Children didn't need to be taught, it seemed instinctive to catch snowflakes with your tongue.

"There's a technique, of course," said Morin in a serious voice, as though he'd studied it. "You have to close your eyes, otherwise the snow gets in them, and stick out your tongue."

There was a pause and the Chief Inspector knew the young agent was sitting, bound to the chair, his head tilted back, his eyes closed, his tongue out. Catching snowflakes.

"Now," agreed Gamache and after bending down to release Henri, he walked to the sofa and sat before the laptop.

"I found the site." Émile sat and looked over at Armand in profile. The trim beard suited the man, now that Émile had gotten used to it. Gamache's eyes were steady, staring at the screen, then he turned and looked directly at his mentor.

"Merci."

Émile paused, taken by surprise. "What for?"

"For not leaving me."

Émile reached out and touched Gamache on the arm, then clicked the button and the video started to play.

Beauvoir stared at the screen. As he suspected, the images were cobbled together from the tiny cameras attached to the headsets of each Sûreté officer. What he hadn't expected was the clarity. He'd thought it'd be grainy, hard to distinguish the players, but it was clear.

As were their voices.

"Officer down!" Gamache called above the gunfire.

"Go, go, go," Beauvoir shouted, pointing to a gunman on the gallery above. Rapid fire shots, the camera swinging wildly, then dropping. Then another view, of the officer on the ground. And blood.

"Officer down," shouted one of the team. "Help him."

Two forms moved forward, automatic weapons firing, laying down cover for a third. Someone grabbing the downed officer, dragging him away. Then a cut to a corridor, racing, chasing the gunmen down darkened halls and into cavernous rooms. Explosions, shouts.

The Chief leaning against a wall, wearing a black tactical vest, automatic rifle in his hands. Firing. It looked so strange to see Gamache with a gun, and using it.

"We have at least six shooters," someone called.

"I count ten," said Gamache, his voice clipped, precise, clear. "Two down. That leaves eight. Five on the floor above, three down here. Where're the medics?"

"Coming," came Agent Lacoste's voice. "Thirty seconds away."

"We need a target alive," the Chief ordered. "Take one alive."

All hell was breaking loose as bullets slammed into walls, into bodies, into the floor and ceiling. Everything became gray, the air filled with dust and bullets. Shouts and screams. The Chief issuing orders as they pushed the gunmen from one room into another. Cornering them.

Then Beauvoir saw himself.

He stepped out from the wall and shot. Then he saw himself stagger, and fall.

Hitting the floor.

"Jean-Guy!" the Chief yelled.

He saw himself splayed on the ground, legs collapsed beneath him. Unmoving.

Gamache ran, calling, "Where are those medics!"

"Here, Chief, here," called Lacoste. "We're coming."

Gamache grabbed Beauvoir's jacket, dragging him behind the wall, shots ringing out. Now, with the sounds of explosions all round, the scene was suddenly intimate. The Chief's worried face, in close up, staring down.

Armand Gamache watched, unblinking, though all he wanted to do was look away. Close his eyes, cover his ears, curl into a ball.

He could smell again the acrid gunpowder, the burning, the concrete dust. He could hear the violent report of the weapons. Feel the rifle in his own hands, pounding out bullets. And weapons firing at him.

Bang, bang, bang, exploding all round. The bullets hitting and bouncing, ricocheting, thudding. The riot of sensations. It was near impossible to think, to focus.

And for an instant he felt again the jolt of seeing Beauvoir hit.

On the screen he saw himself staring down at Beauvoir, searching his face. Feeling for a pulse. The camera catching not just the events, but the sensations, the feelings. The anguish in Gamache's face.

"Jean-Guy?" he called and the Inspector's eyes fluttered and opened, then rolled closed.

Bullets splayed their position and the Chief ducked over Beauvoir, pulling him further behind the wall and propping him up. He opened Jean-Guy's vest, his eyes sweeping down the Inspector's torso, stopping at the wound. The blood. Ripping open a pocket in his own vest he brought out a bandage and pressed it into Beauvoir's hand then pressed the hand to the wound.

Leaning forward he whispered in Beauvoir's ear.

"Jean-Guy, you have to hold your hand there, can you do it?"

Beauvoir's eyes fluttered open again, fighting for consciousness.

"Stay with me," the Chief commanded. "Can you stay conscious?"

Beauvoir nodded.

"Good." Gamache looked up, at the fighting ahead and overhead, then looked back down. "Medics are on their way. Lacoste's coming, she'll be here in a moment." He paused and did something not meant to be seen by anyone else, and now seen by millions. He kissed Beauvoir on the forehead. Then smoothing Beauvoir's hair, he left.

Beauvoir watched the screen through his fingers clutched to his face, his eyes wide. He'd expected the video to have captured, imperfectly, the events. It hadn't occurred to him it would also capture how it felt.

The fear and confusion. The shock, the pain. The searing pain as he clutched at his abdomen. And the loneliness.

On the screen he saw his own face watching, pleading, as Gamache left him. Bleeding and alone. And he saw Gamache's agony, at having to do it.

The view changed and they followed the team, chasing gunmen through corridors. Exchanging fire. A Sûreté officer wounded. A gunman hit.

Then Gamache taking the stairs two at a time, in pursuit, the man turning to fire. Gamache throwing himself at him and the two struggling, fighting hand to hand. From the screen came a confusion of arms and torsos, gasps, as they fought. Finally the Chief grabbed for the weapon that had been knocked out of his hand. Swinging it at the terrorist he caught him with a terrible crunch to the head. The man dropped.

As the cameras watched, Gamache collapsed to his knees beside the man and felt for a pulse, then he cuffed him and dragged him down the stairs. At the bottom the Chief staggered a bit, catching himself. Struggling to stand upright, Gamache turned. Beauvoir was sprawled against the wall across the room. A bloody bandage in one hand and a gun in the other.

There was a rasping, gasping.

"I . . . have . . . one," Gamache was saying, trying to catch his breath.

Émile hadn't moved since the video began. He'd only twice in his career had to fire his gun. Both times he'd killed someone. Hadn't wanted to, but he'd meant to.

And he'd taught his officers well. It was an absolute, you never, ever take out your gun unless you mean to use it. And when you use it, aim for the body, aim to stop. Dead, if need be.

And now he watched Armand, his face bloody from the fight, sway a bit, then step forward. From his belt he grabbed his pistol. The gunman was unconscious at his feet. Shots continued all round. Émile saw the Chief Inspector turn, react to shooting above him. Gamache took another step forward, raised his gun and took shots in quick succession. A target was hit. The shooting stopped.

For a moment. Then there was a rapid fire.

Gamache's arms lifted. His whole body lifted. And twisted. And he fell to the ground.

■ ■ ■ ■

Beauvoir held his breath. It was what he'd seen that day. The Chief lying, unmoving, on the floor.

"Officer down," Beauvoir heard himself rasp. "The Chief's down."

It seemed forever. Beauvoir tried to move, to drag himself forward, but he couldn't. Around him he heard gunfire. In his headphones officers were calling to each other, shouting instructions, locations, warnings.

But all he saw was the still form in front.

Then there were hands on him and Agent Lacoste kneeling, bending over him. Her face worried and determined.

He saw her eyes move down his body, to his bloody hand clutching his abdomen. "Here, over here," she shouted and was joined by a medic.

"The Chief," Beauvoir whispered and motioned. Lacoste's face fell as she looked.

As medics leaned over Beauvoir, putting pressure bandages on his wound, sticking needles into him, calling for a stretcher, Beauvoir watched Lacoste and a medic run to the Chief. They moved toward him but shooting erupted and they had to take cover.

Gamache lay motionless on the concrete

floor just beyond their reach.

Finally Lacoste raced up the stairs and from her camera they saw her trace the shots to a gunman in a doorway above. She engaged him, eventually hitting him. Grabbing his gun she shouted, "Clear!"

The medic ran to Gamache. Across the floor Beauvoir strained to see.

Émile watched as the medic leaned over Gamache.

"*Merde,*" the medic whispered. Blood covered the side of the Chief Inspector's head and ran into his ear and down his neck.

The medic looked up as Lacoste joined him. The Chief was coughing slightly, still alive. His eyes were half closed, glazed, and he gasped for breath.

"Chief, can you hear me?" She put her hands on either side of his head and lifted it, looking into his eyes. He focused and struggled to keep his eyes open.

"Hold this." The medic grabbed a bandage and put it over the wound by Gamache's left temple. Lacoste pressed down, holding it there, trying to stop the bleeding.

The Chief stirred, tried to focus, fighting for breath. The medic saw this, his brow furrowed, perplexed. Then he ripped open the Chief's tactical vest and exhaled.

"Christ."

Lacoste looked down. "Oh, no," she whispered.

The Chief's chest was covered in blood. The medic tore Gamache's shirt, exposing his chest. And there, on the side, was a wound.

From across the room Beauvoir watched, but all he could see were the Chief's legs, his polished black leather shoes on the floor moving slightly. But it was his hand Beauvoir stared at. The Chief's right hand, bloody, tight, taut, straining. And in the headset he heard gasping. Struggling for breath. Gamache's right arm outstretched, fingers reaching. His hand grabbing, trembling, as though the breath was just out of reach.

As medics lifted Beauvoir onto a stretcher he whispered over and over again, pleading, "No, no. Please."

He heard Lacoste shout, "Chief!"

There was more coughing, weaker. Then silence.

And he saw Gamache's right hand spasm, shudder. Then softly, like a snowflake, it fell.

And Jean-Guy Beauvoir knew Armand Gamache was dying.

On the uncomfortable plastic chairs, Beauvoir let out a small moan. The video had moved on. Shots of the squad engaging the remaining gunmen.

Ruth stared at the screen, her Scotch untouched.

"Chief!" Lacoste called again.

Gamache's eyes were open slightly, staring. His lips moved. They could barely hear what he was saying. Trying to say.

"Reine . . . Marie. Reine . . . Marie."

"I'll tell her," Lacoste whispered into his ear and he closed his eyes.

"His heart's stopped," the medic called and leaned over Gamache, preparing for CPR. "He's in cardiac arrest."

Another medic arrived and kneeling down he grabbed the other's arm.

"No wait. Get me a syringe."

"No fucking way. His heart's stopped, we need to start it."

"For God's sake do something," Lacoste shouted.

The second medic rifled through the medical kit. Finding a syringe he plunged it into the Chief's side and broke the plunger off.

There was no reaction. Gamache lay still, blood on his face and chest. Eyes closed.

The three stared down. He didn't move. Didn't breathe.

Then, then. There was a slight sound. A small rasp.

They looked at each other.

Émile finally blinked. His eyes felt dry as though they'd been sandblasted and he took a deep breath.

He knew the rest of the story, of course, from calls to Reine-Marie and visits to the hospital. And the Radio-Canada news.

Four Sûreté officers killed, including the first by the side of the road, four others wounded. Eight terrorists dead, one captured. One critically wounded, not expected to survive. At first the news had reported the Chief Inspector among the dead. How that leaked out no one knew. How any of it leaked out no one knew.

Inspector Beauvoir had been badly hurt.

Émile had arrived that afternoon, driving straight from Quebec City to Hôtel-Dieu hospital in Montreal. There he found Reine-Marie and Annie. Daniel was on a flight back from Paris.

They looked wrung out, nothing left.

"He's alive," Reine-Marie had said, hugging Émile, holding him.

"Thank God for that," he'd said, then

seen Annie's expression. "What is it?"

"The doctors think he's had a stroke."

Émile had taken a deep breath. "Do they know how bad?"

Annie shook her head and Reine-Marie put her arm around her daughter. "He's alive, that's all that matters."

"Have you seen him?"

Reine-Marie nodded, unable now to speak. Unable to tell anyone what she'd seen. The oxygen, the monitors, the blood and bruising. His eyes closed. Unconscious.

And the doctor saying they didn't know the extent of the damage. He could be blind. Paralyzed. He could have another one. The next twenty-four hours would tell.

But it didn't matter. She'd held his hand, smoothed it, whispered to him.

He was alive.

The doctor had also explained the chest wound. The bullet had broken a rib which had punctured the lung causing it to collapse and collapsing the second. Crushing the life out of him. The wound must have happened early on, the breathing becoming more and more difficult, more labored, until it became critical. Fatal.

"The medic caught it," the doctor said. "In time."

He hadn't added "just," but he knew it to

be the case.

Now the only worry was the head wound.

And so they'd waited, in their own world of the third floor of Hôtel-Dieu. An antiseptic world of hushed conversations, of soft fleet feet and stern faces.

Outside, the news flew around the continent, around the world.

A plot to blow up the La Grande dam.

It had been a decade in the planning. The progress so slow as to be invisible. The tools so primitive as to be dismissed.

Canadian and American government spokesmen refused to say how the plan was stopped, citing national security, but they did admit under close questioning that the shootout and deaths of four Sûreté officers had been part of it.

Chief Superintendent Francoeur was given, and took, credit for preventing a catastrophe.

Émile knew, as did anyone who'd had a glimpse inside the workings of major police departments, that what was being said was just a fraction of the truth.

And so, as the world chewed over these sensational findings, on the third floor of Hôtel-Dieu they waited. Jean-Guy Beauvoir came out of surgery and after a rocky day or so, began the long, slow climb back.

And after twelve hours Armand Gamache struggled awake. When he finally opened his eyes he saw Reine-Marie by his side, holding his hand.

"La Grande?" he rasped.

"Safe."

"Jean-Guy?"

"He'll be fine."

When she returned to the waiting room where Émile, Annie, her husband David and Daniel sat, she was beaming.

"He's resting. Not dancing yet, but he will."

"Is he all right?" Annie asked, afraid yet to believe it, to let go of the dread too soon in case it was a trick, some jest of a sad God. She would never recover from the shock of being in her car, listening to Radio-Canada and hearing the bulletin. Her father . . .

"He will be," said her mother. "He has some slight numbness down his right side."

"Numbness?" asked Daniel.

"The doctors are happy," she assured them. "They say it's minor, and he'll make a full recovery."

She didn't care. He could limp for the rest of his days. He was alive.

But within two days he was up and walking, haltingly. Two days after that he could make it down the corridor. Stopping at the rooms, to sit by the beds of men and women he'd trained and chosen and led into that factory.

Up and down the corridor he limped. Up and down. Up and down.

"What are you doing, Armand?" Reine-Marie had asked quietly as they walked, hand in hand. It had been five days since the shooting and his limp had all but disappeared, except when he first got up, or pushed too hard.

Without pausing he told her. "The funerals are next Sunday. I plan to be there."

They took another few paces before she spoke. "You intend to be at the cathedral?"

"No. I intend to walk with the cortege."

She watched him in profile. His face determined, his lips tight, his right hand squeezed into a fist against the only sign he'd had a stroke. A slight tremble, when he was tired or stressed.

"Tell me what I can do to help."

"You can keep me company."

"Always, *mon coeur.*"

He stopped and smiled at her. His face bruised, a bandage over his left brow.

But she didn't care. He was alive.

The day of the funerals was clear and cold. It was mid-December and a wind rattled down from the Arctic and didn't stop until it slammed into the men, women and children who lined the cortege route.

Four coffins, draped in the blue and white fleur-de-lys flag of Québec, sat on wagons pulled by solemn black horses. And behind them a long line of police officers from every community in Québec, from across Canada, from the United States and Britain, from Japan and France and Germany. From all over Europe.

And at the head, walking at slow march in dress uniform, were the Sûreté. And leading that column were Chief Superintendent Francoeur and all the other top-ranking officers. And behind them, alone, was Chief Inspector Gamache, at the head of his homicide division. Walking the two kilometers, only limping toward the very end. Face forward, eyes determined. Until the salute, and the guns.

He'd closed his eyes tight then and raised his face to the sky in a grimace, a moment of private sorrow he could no longer contain. His right hand clamped tight.

It became the image of grief. The image on every front page and every news program and every magazine cover.

Ruth reached out and clicked the video

closed. They sat in silence for a moment.

"Well," she finally said. "I don't believe a word of it. All done on a soundstage I bet. Good effects, but the acting sucked. Popcorn?"

Beauvoir looked at her, holding out the plastic bowl.

He took a handful. Then they walked slowly through the blizzard, heads bowed into the wind, across the village green to Peter and Clara's home. Halfway across, he took her arm. To steady her, or himself, he wasn't really sure.

But she let him. They made their way to the little cottage, following the light through the storm. And once there, they sat in front of the fireplace and ate dinner. Together.

Armand Gamache rose.

"Are you all right?" Émile got up too.

Gamache sighed. "I just need time alone." He looked at his friend. *"Merci."*

He felt nauseous, physically sickened. Seeing those young men and women, shot. Killed. Again. Gunned down in dark corridors, again.

They'd been under his command. Handpicked by him against Chief Superintendent Francoeur's protests. He'd taken them anyway.

And he'd told them there were probably six gunmen in the place. Doubling what he'd been told. What Agent Nichol had told him.

There're three gunmen, the message had said.

He'd taken six officers, all he could muster, plus Beauvoir and himself.

He thought it was enough. He was wrong.

"You can't do this," Chief Superintendent Francoeur had said, his voice low with warning. The Chief Superintendent had burst into his office as he'd prepared to leave. In his ear Paul Morin was singing the alphabet song. He sounded drunk, exhausted, at the end.

"Once more please," Gamache said to Morin then whipped off his headset and Chief Superintendent Francoeur immediately stopped talking.

"You have all the information you need," the Chief Inspector glared at Francoeur.

"Gleaned from an old Cree woman and a few sniff-heads? You think I'm going to act on that?"

"Information gathered by Agent Lacoste, who's on her way back. She's coming with me, as are six others. For your information, here are their names. I've alerted the tactical squad. They're at your disposal."

"To do what? There's no way the La Grande dam is going to be destroyed. We've heard nothing about it on the channels. No one has. Not the feds, not the Americans, not even the British and they monitor everything. No one's heard anything. Except you and that demented Cree elder."

Francoeur stared at Gamache. The Chief Superintendent was so angry he was vibrating.

"That dam is going to be blown up in one hour and forty-three minutes. You have enough time to get there. You know where to be and what to do."

Gamache's voice, instead of rising, had lowered.

"You don't give me orders," Francoeur snarled. "You know nothing I don't and I know no reason to go there."

Gamache went to his desk and took out his gun. For an instant Francoeur looked frightened, then Gamache put the pistol on his belt and walked quickly up to the Chief Superintendent.

They glared at each other. Then Gamache spoke, softly, intensely.

"Please, Sylvain, if I have to beg I will. We're both too old and tired for this. We need to stop this now. You're right, it's not my place to give you orders, I apologize.

Please, please do as I ask."

"No way. You have to give me more."

"That's all I have."

"But it doesn't make sense. No one would try to blow up the dam this way."

"Why not?"

They'd been over this a hundred times. And there was no time left.

"Because it's too rough. Like throwing a rock at an army."

"And how did David slay Goliath?"

"Come on, this isn't biblical and these aren't biblical times."

"But the same principle applies. Do the unexpected. This would work precisely because we won't be expecting it. And while you might not see it as David and Goliath, the bombers certainly do."

"What are you? Suddenly an expert in national security? You and your arrogance, you make me sick. You go stop that bomb if you really believe hundreds of thousands of lives are at stake."

"No. I'm going to get Paul Morin."

"Morin? You're saying you know where he is? We've been looking all night," Francoeur waved to the army of officers in the outer office, trying to trace Morin. "And you're telling me you know where he is?"

Francoeur was trembling with rage, his

voice almost a scream.

Gamache waited. In his peripheral vision he could see the clock, ticking down.

"Magog. In an abandoned factory. Agent Nichol and Inspector Beauvoir found him by listening to the ambient sound."

By listening to the spaces between words they'd found him.

"Please, Sylvain, go to La Grande. I'm begging you. If I'm wrong I'll resign."

"If we go there and you're wrong I'll bring you up on charges."

Francoeur walked out of the office, out of the incident room. And disappeared.

Gamache glanced at the clock as he made for the door. One hour and forty-one minutes left. And Armand Gamache prayed, not for the first time that day, or the last.

"It could've been worse," said Émile. "I mean, who knows who made this video? They could've made the entire operation look like a catastrophe. But it doesn't. Tragic, yes. Terrible. But in many ways heroic. If the families have to watch, well . . ."

Gamache knew Émile was trying to be kind, trying to say the editing could have made him out to be a coward or a bumbling idiot. Could have looked like those who died had squandered their lives. Instead everyone had looked courageous. What was the word Émile used?

Heroic.

Gamache slowly climbed the steep stairs, Henri at his heels.

Well, he knew something Émile didn't. He suspected who had made the video. And he knew why.

Not to make Gamache look bad, but to make him look good, too good. So good the Chief would feel as he did. A fraud. A fake. Lionized for nothing. Four Sûreté officers dead and Armand Gamache the hero.

Whoever had done this knew him well. And knew how to exact a price.

In shame.

TWENTY-FIVE

The storm blew in to Quebec City a few hours later and by two in the morning the capital was lashed by high winds and blowing snow. Highways were closed as visibility fell to zero in white-out conditions.

In the garret of the old stone home on St-Stanislas, Armand Gamache lay in bed, staring at the beamed ceiling. Henri, on the floor beside him, snored, oblivious to the snow whipping the windows.

Quietly, Gamache rose and looked out. He couldn't see the building across the narrow street and could just barely make out the street lamps, their light all but blotted out by the driving snow.

Dressing quickly, he tiptoed down the stairs. Behind him he heard the clicking of Henri's nails on the old wooden steps. Putting on his boots, parka, toque, heavy mitts and wrapping a long scarf around his neck Gamache bent down and petted Henri.

"You don't have to come, you know."

But Henri didn't know. It wasn't a matter of knowing. If Gamache was going, Henri was going.

Out they went, Gamache gulping as the wind hit his face and took away his breath. Then he turned his back and felt it shoving him.

Perhaps, he thought, this was a mistake.

But the storm was what he needed, wanted. Something loud, dramatic, challenging. Something that could blot out all thought, white them out.

The two struggled up the street, walking in the middle of the deserted roads. Not even snow plows were out. It was futile to try to clear snow in the middle of a blizzard.

It felt as though the city was theirs, as though an evacuation notice had sounded and Gamache and Henri had slept through it. They were all alone.

Up Ste-Ursule they trekked, past the convent where Général Montcalm had died. To rue St-Louis, then through the arched gate. The storm, if possible, was even worse outside old Quebec City. With no walls to stop it, the wind gathered speed and snow and slammed into trees, parked cars, buildings, plastering itself against whatever it hit.

Including the Chief Inspector.

He didn't care. He felt the cold hard flakes hit his coat, his hat, his face. And he heard it pelting into him. It was almost deafening.

"I love storms," Morin said. "Any kind of storm. Nothing like sitting in a screen porch in summer in the middle of a thunderstorm. But my favorite are blizzards, as long as I don't have to drive. If everyone's safe at home, then bring it on."

"Do you ever go out in them?" Gamache asked.

"All the time, even if it's just to stand there. I love it. Don't know why, maybe it's the drama. Then to come back in and have a hot chocolate in front of the fire. Doesn't get any better."

Gamache trudged forward, his head down, looking at his feet as he plowed his way slowly through the knee-high drifts. Excited, Henri leapt up and down in the trail made by Gamache.

They made slow progress but finally found themselves in the park. Lifting his head the Chief was briefly blinded by the snow, then squinting he could just make out the shapes of ghostly trees reeling against the wind.

The Plains of Abraham.

Gamache looked behind and noticed his boot prints had filled in, disappearing almost as quickly as he made them. He wasn't lost, not yet, but he knew he could be if he went too far.

Henri abruptly stopped his dancing and stood still, then he started to growl and slunk behind Gamache's legs.

This was a sure sign nothing was there.

"Let's go," said Gamache. He turned and came face-to-face with someone else. A tall figure in a dark parka also plastered with snow. His head was covered in a hood. He stood quietly a few feet from the Chief.

"Chief Inspector Gamache," the figure spoke, his voice clear and English.

"Yes."

"I hadn't expected to find you here."

"I hadn't expected to find you either," Gamache shouted, struggling to make himself heard above the howling wind.

"Were you looking?" the man asked.

Gamache paused. "Not until tomorrow. I was hoping to speak to you tomorrow."

"I thought so."

"Is that why you're here now?"

There was no answer. The dark figure just stood there. Henri, emboldened, crept forward. "Henri," Gamache snapped. *"Viens ici."* And the dog trotted to his master's side.

"The storm seemed fortuitous," said the man. "It makes it easier, somehow."

"We need to talk," said Gamache.

"Why?"

"I need to talk. Please."

Now it was the man's turn to pause. Then he indicated a building, a round stone turret built on the knoll, like a very small fortress. The two men and one dog trudged up the slight hill to the building and trying the door Gamache was a bit surprised to find it unlocked, but once inside he knew why.

There was nothing to steal. It was simply an empty, round, stone hut.

The Chief flicked a switch, and an exposed light bulb overhead came on. Gamache watched as his companion lowered his hood.

"I didn't expect to find anyone out in this storm." Tom Hancock whacked his snow-caked hat against his leg. "I love walking in storms."

Gamache raised his head and stared at the young minister. It was almost exactly what Agent Morin had said.

Looking round he noticed there were no seats but he indicated the floor and both men sat, making themselves comfortable against the thick stone walls.

They were silent for a moment. Inside, without a window, without an opening, they could have been anywhere, anytime. It could have been two hundred years earlier, and outside not a storm but a battle.

"I saw the video," Tom Hancock said. His cheeks were brilliant red and his face wet with melted snow. Gamache suspected he looked the same only, perhaps, not quite so young and vital.

"So did I."

"Terrible," said Hancock. "I'm sorry."

"Thank you. It wasn't quite as it looked, you know. I —" Gamache had to stop.

"You?"

"It made me look heroic and I wasn't. It was my fault they died."

"Why do you say that?"

"I made mistakes. I didn't see the magnitude of what was happening until it was almost too late. And even then I made mistakes."

"How so?"

Gamache looked at the young man. The minister. Who cared so much for hurt souls. He was a good listener, Gamache realized. It was a rare quality, a precious quality.

He took a deep breath. It smelled musky in there, as though the air wasn't meant to be breathed, wasn't meant to sustain life.

Then Gamache told this young minister everything. About the kidnapping and the long and patient plot. Hidden inside their own hubris, their certainty that advance technology would uncover any threat.

They'd been wrong.

Their attackers were clever. Adaptable.

"I've since discovered that security people call it an 'asymmetrical approach,' " Gamache smiled. "Makes it sound geometric. Logical. And I guess in some ways it was. Too logical, certainly too simple for the likes of us. The plotters wanted to destroy the La Grande dam, and how would they do it? Not with a nuclear bomb, not with cleverly hidden devices. Not by infiltrating the security services or using telecommunications or anything that left a signature that could be found and traced. They did it by working where they knew we wouldn't look."

"And where was that?"

"In the past. They knew they could never compete with us when it came to modern technology, so they kept it simple. So simple it was invisible to us. They relied on our hubris, our certainty that state-of-the-art technology would protect us."

The two men's voices were low, like conspirators, or storytellers. It felt as it must have millennia ago, when people sat together across fires and told tales.

"What was their plan?"

"Two truck bombs. And two young men willing to drive them. Cree men."

Tom Hancock, who had been bending forward toward the story and the storyteller, leaned slowly away. He felt his back against the cold stone wall. A wall built before the Cree knew of the disaster approaching. A disaster they would even assist, guiding the Europeans to the waterways. Helping them collect the pelts.

Too late, the Cree had realized they'd made a terrible mistake.

And now, hundreds of years later some of their descendents had agreed to drive huge trucks filled with explosives along a perfectly paved ribbon of road through a forest that had once been theirs. Toward a dam thirty stories high.

They would destroy it. And themselves. Their families. Their villages. The forests, the animals. The gods. All gone. They would unleash a torrent that would sweep it all away.

In the hopes that finally someone would hear their calls for help.

"That's what they were told, anyway," said the Chief, suddenly weary, wishing now he could sleep.

"What happened?" whispered Tom Hancock.

"Chief Superintendent Francoeur got there in time. Stopped them."

"Were they — ?"

"Killed?" Gamache nodded. "Yes. Both shot dead. But the dam was saved."

Tom Hancock found himself almost sorry to hear that.

"You said these young Cree men were used. You mean this wasn't their idea?"

"No, no more than it was the truck's idea. Whoever did this chose things ready to explode. The bombs made by them and the Cree made by us."

"But who were they? If the two Cree men were used by the bombers, then who planned all this? Who was behind it?"

"We don't know for sure. Most died in the raid on the factory. One survived and is being questioned but I haven't heard anything."

"But you have your suspicions. Were they native?"

Gamache shook his head. "Caucasian. English speaking. All well trained. Mercenaries, perhaps. The goal was the dam, but the real target seems to have been the eastern seaboard of the United States."

"Not Canada? Not Québec?"

"No. In bringing down La Grande they would have blacked out everything from

Boston to New York and Washington. And not just for an hour, but for months. It would have blown the whole grid."

"With winter coming too."

They paused to imagine a city like New York, millions of frightened, angry people freezing in the dark.

"Home-grown terrorists?" asked Hancock.

"We think so."

"You couldn't have seen this coming," said Hancock at last. "You speak of hubris, Chief Inspector. Perhaps you need to be careful yourself."

It was said lightly, but the words were no less sharp.

There was a slight pause before Gamache responded. It was with a small chuckle. "Very true. But you mistake me, Mr. Hancock. It wasn't the threat I should have seen coming, but once it was in motion I should have known the kidnapping wasn't so simple much sooner. I should have known the backwoods farmer wasn't that. And —"

"Yes?"

"I was in over my head. We all were. There was almost no time and it was clear something massive was happening. As soon as Agent Nichol isolated the words 'La Grande' I knew that was it. The dam is in

Cree territory so I sent an agent there to ask questions."

"Just one agent? Surely you should have sent everyone." Only then did Hancock stop himself. "If you need any more suggestions on tactics, come to me. They teach it, you know, at the seminary."

He smiled and heard a small guffaw beside him. Then a deep breath.

"The Cree have no love of the Sûreté. Nor should they," said Gamache. "I judged one smart agent was enough. We have some contacts there, among the elders. Agent Lacoste went to them first."

As the hours passed her reports had started to come in. She moved from community to community, always accompanied by the same elderly woman. A woman Chief Inspector Gamache had met years ago, sitting on a bench in front of the Château Frontenac. A woman everyone else had dismissed as a beggar.

He had helped her then. And she helped him now.

Agent Lacoste's reports started to form a picture. Of a generation on the reserves without hope. Drunk and high and lost. With no life and no future and nothing to lose. It had all been taken. This Gamache already knew. Anyone with the stomach to look saw that.

But there was something he didn't know. Lacoste had reports of outsiders arriving, teachers. White teachers, English teachers. Insinuating themselves into the communities years earlier. Most of the teachers were genuine, but a few had an agenda that went far beyond any alphabet or times table. Their curriculum would take time to achieve. The plan had started when the young men were boys. Impressionable, lost, frightened. Hungry for approval, acceptance, kindness, leadership. And the teachers had given them all that. Years it had taken to win their trust. Over those years the teachers taught them how to read and write, how to add and subtract. And how to hate. They'd also taught their students that they need not be victims any longer. They could be warriors again.

Many young Cree had toyed with the attractive idea, finally rejecting it. Sensing these were simply more white men with their own aims. But two young men had been seduced. Two young men on the verge of doing themselves in anyway.

And so they would go out in glory. Convinced the world would finally take notice.

At 11:18.

The La Grande dam would be destroyed.

Two young Cree men would die. And, miles away, a young Sûreté agent would be executed.

Armed with this evidence Gamache had presented it, yet again, to Chief Superintendent Francoeur. But when Francoeur had again balked, instead of reasoning with the man Gamache had allowed his temper to flare. His disdain for the arrogant and dangerous Chief Superintendent to show.

That had been a mistake. It had cost him time. And maybe more.

"What happened?"

Armand Gamache looked over, almost surprised to find he wasn't alone with his thoughts.

"A decision had to be made. And we all knew what that was. If Agent Lacoste's information was right we had to abandon Agent Morin. Our efforts had to go into stopping the bombing. If we tried to save Morin the bombers would be warned and might move sooner. No one could risk that."

"Not even you?"

Gamache sat still for a very long time. There was no sound outside or inside. How many others had hidden in there against a violent world? A world not as kind, not as good, not as warm as they wished. How many fearful people had huddled where they sat? Taken refuge? Wondering when it might be safe to go out. Into the world.

"God help me, not even me."

"You were willing to let him die?"

"If need be." Gamache stared at Hancock, not defiantly but with a kind of wonder that decisions like that needed to be made. By him. Every day. "But not before I'd tried everything."

"You finally convinced the Chief Superintendent?"

Gamache nodded. "With a little under two hours to go."

"Good God," exhaled Hancock. "That close. It came that close."

Gamache said nothing for a moment. "We knew by then that Agent Morin was being held in an abandoned factory. Agent Nichol and Inspector Beauvoir found him by listening to the sounds and cross-referencing plane and train schedules. It was masterful investigating. He was being held in an abandoned factory hundreds of kilometers from the dam. The plotters kept themselves at a safe distance. In a town called Magog."

"Magog?"

"Magog. Why?"

The minister looked bemused but also slightly disconcerted. "Gog and Magog?"

Gamache smiled. He'd forgotten that

biblical reference.

"You will make an evil plan," the minister quoted.

Once again Gamache saw Paul Morin at the far end of the room, bound to the chair, staring at the wall in front of him. At a clock.

Five seconds left.

"You found me," said Morin.

Gamache took off across the room. Morin's thin back straightened.

Three seconds left. Everything seemed to slow down. Everything seemed so clear. He could see the clock, hear the second hand thud closer to zero. See the hard metal frame chair and the rope strapped around Paul Morin.

There was no bomb. No bomb.

Behind Gamache, Beauvoir and the team rushed in. Gunshots exploded all round. The Chief leapt, to the young agent who sat up so straight.

One second left.

Gamache gathered himself. "I made one final mistake. I turned left when I should have turned right. Paul Morin had just described the sun on his face, but instead of heading to the door with light coming through, I headed for the darkened one."

Hancock was silent then. He'd seen the video and now he looked at the solemn, bearded man sitting on the cold stone floor with him, his dog's head with its quite extravagant ears resting on Gamache's thigh.

"It's not your fault."

"Of course it's my fault," said Gamache angrily.

"Why are you so insistent? Do you want to be a martyr?" said Hancock. "Is that why you came out in a blizzard? Are you enjoying your suffering? You must be, to hold on to it so tightly."

"Be careful."

"Of what? Of hurting the great Chief Inspector's feelings? If your heroism doesn't put you beyond us mere mortals then your suffering does, is that it? Yes it was a tragedy, it was terrible, but it happened to them, not you. You're alive. This is what you've been handed, nothing's going to change that. You have to let it go. They died. It was terrible but unavoidable."

Hancock's voice was intense. Henri lifted his head to stare at the young minister, a slight growl in his throat. Gamache put a calming hand on Henri's head and the dog subsided.

"It is sweet and right to die for your country?" asked the Chief.

"Sometimes."

"And not just to die, but to kill as well?"

"What does that mean?"

"You'd do just about anything to help your parishioners, wouldn't you?" said Gamache. "Their suffering hurts you, almost physically. I've seen it. Yes, I came out into the blizzard in hopes it would quiet my conscience, but isn't that why you signed up for the ice canoe race? To take your mind off your failings? You couldn't stand to see the English suffer so much. Dying. As individuals, but also as a community. It was your job to comfort them but you didn't know how, didn't know if words were enough. And so you took action."

"What do you mean?"

"You know what I mean. Despite a city filled with people he'd alienated, only six people could have actually murdered Augustin Renaud. The board of the Literary and Historical Society. Quite a few volunteers have keys to the building, quite a few knew the construction schedule and when the concrete was to be poured, quite a few could have found the sub-basement and led Renaud there. But only the six board members knew he'd visited, knew he'd demanded to speak with them. And knew why."

The Reverend Mr. Hancock stared at Gamache in the harsh light of the single, naked bulb.

"You killed Augustin Renaud," said Gamache.

There was silence then, complete and utter silence. There was no world outside. No storm, no battlefield, no walled and fortified and defended city. Nothing.

Only the silent fortress.

"Yes."

"You aren't going to deny it?"

"It was obvious you either knew already or would soon find out. Once you found those books it was all over. I hid them there, of course. Couldn't very well destroy them and couldn't risk having them found in my home. Seemed a perfect place. After all, no one had found them in the Literary and Historical Society for a hundred years."

He looked closely at Gamache.

"Did you know all along?"

"I suspected. It could really only have been one of two people. You or Ken Haslam. While the rest of the board stayed and finished the meeting you headed off for your practice."

"I went ahead of Ken, found Renaud and told him I'd sneak him in that night. I told him to bring whatever evidence he had, and if I was convinced, I'd let him start the dig."

"And of course he came."

Hancock nodded. "It was simple. He started digging while I read over the books. Chiniquy's journal and the bible. It was damning."

"Or illuminating, depending on your point of view. What happened?"

"He'd dug one hole and handed me up the shovel. I just swung it and hit him."

"As simple as that?"

"No it wasn't as simple as that," Hancock snapped. "It was terrible but it had to be done."

"Why?"

"Can't you guess?"

Gamache thought. "Because you could."

Hancock smiled a little. "I suppose so. I think of it more that no one else could. I was the only one. Elizabeth never could do it. Mr. Blake? Maybe, when he was younger, but not now. Porter Wilson couldn't hit himself on the head. And Ken? He gave up his voice years ago. No, I was the only one who could do it."

"But why did it need to be done?"

"Because finding Champlain in our basement would have killed the Anglo community. It would have been the final blow."

"Most Québécois wouldn't have blamed you."

"You think not? It doesn't take much to stir anti-Anglo sentiment, even among the most reasonable. There's always a suspicion the Anglos are up to no good."

"I don't agree," said Gamache. "But what I think doesn't matter, does it. It's what you believe."

"Someone had to protect them."

"And that was your job." It was a statement, not a question. Gamache had seen that in the minister from the first time he'd met him. Not a fanaticism, but a firm belief that he was the shepherd and they his flock. And if the Francophones harbored a secret certainty the Anglos were up to no good, the Anglos harbored the certainty the French were out to get them. It was, in many ways, a perfect little walled society.

And the Reverend Tom Hancock's job was to protect his people. It was a sentiment Gamache could understand.

But to the point of killing?

Gamache remembered stepping forward, raising his gun, having the man in his sights. And shooting.

He'd killed to protect his own. And he'd do it again, if need be.

"What are you going to do?" Hancock asked, getting to his feet.

"Depends. What are you going to do?" Gamache also rose stiffly, rousing Henri.

"I think you know why I came here tonight, to the Plains of Abraham."

And Gamache did. As soon as he knew it was Tom Hancock in the parka he'd known why he was there.

"There would at least be a symmetry about it," said Hancock. "The Anglo, slipping back down the cliff, two hundred and fifty years later."

"You know I won't let you do that."

"I know you haven't a hope of stopping me."

"That's probably true and, it must be admitted, this one won't be any help," he indicated Henri. "Unless the sight of a dog whimpering frightens you into surrendering."

Hancock smiled. "This is the final ice floe. I have no choice. It's what's been handed me."

"No, it isn't. Why do you think I'm here?"

"Because you're so wrapped up in your own sorrow you can barely think straight. Because you can't sleep and came here to get away, from yourself."

"Well, that too, perhaps," smiled Gamache. "But what are the chances we'd meet in the middle of the storm? Had I come ten minutes earlier or later, had we walked ten feet apart, we'd have missed each other. Walked right by without seeing, blinded by the blizzard."

"What are you saying?"

"I'm saying, what are the chances?"

"Does it matter? It happened. We met."

"You saw the video," Gamache said, lowering his voice. "You saw what happened. How close it came."

"How close you came to dying? I did."

"Maybe this is why I didn't."

Hancock regarded Gamache. "Are you saying you were spared to stop me from jumping over the cliff?"

"Maybe. I know how precious life is. You had no right to take Renaud's and you have no right to take your own now. Not over this. Too much death. It needs to stop."

Gamache stared at the young man beside him. A man, he knew, drawn to seawalls and jagged cliff faces and to the Anglos of Québec, standing just off shore where the ice was thinnest.

"You're wrong you know," Gamache finally said. "The English of Québec aren't weak, aren't frail. Elizabeth MacWhirter and Winnie and Ken and Mr. Blake, and yes, even Porter, couldn't kill Augustin Renaud, not because they're weak but because they know there's no need. He was

637

no threat. Not really. They've adapted to the new reality, to the new world. You're the only one who couldn't. There'll be Anglos here for centuries to come, as there should be. It's their home. You should have had more faith."

Hancock walked up to Gamache.

"I could walk right by you."

"Probably. I'd try to stop you, but I suspect you'd get by. But you know I'd follow you, I'd have to. And then what? A middle-aged Francophone and a young Anglo, lost in a storm on the Plains of Abraham, wandering, one in search of a cliff, the other in search of him. I wonder when they'd find us? In the spring, you think? Frozen? Two more corpses, unburied? Is that how this ends?"

The two men looked at each other. Finally Tom Hancock sighed.

"With my luck, you'd be the one to go over the cliff."

"That would be disappointing."

Hancock smiled wearily. "I give up. No more fight."

"Merci," said Gamache.

At the door Hancock turned. Gamache's hand, with a slight tremble, reached for the latch. "I shouldn't have accused you of trading on your grief. That was wrong."

"Perhaps not so far off," smiled Gamache. "I need to let it go. Let them go."

"With time," said Hancock.

"*Avec le temps*," Gamache agreed. "Yes."

"You mentioned the video just now," said Hancock, remembering another question he had. "Do you know how it got onto the Internet?"

"No."

Hancock looked at him closely. "But you have your suspicions."

Gamache remembered the rage on the Chief Superintendent's face when he'd confronted him. Theirs was a long battle. An old battle. Francoeur knew Gamache well enough to know what would hurt him most wouldn't be criticism over how he handled the raid, but just the opposite. Praise. Undeserved praise, even as his people suffered.

Where a bullet had failed to stop the Chief Inspector, that might.

But he saw, now, another face. A younger face. Eager to join them. And denied, yet again. Sent back into her basement. Where she monitored everything. Heard everything. Saw everything. Recorded everything.

And remembered, everything.

TWENTY-SIX

"Give Reine-Marie my love," said Émile.

He and Armand stood by the door. Gamache's Volvo was packed with his suitcase and assorted treats from Émile for Reine-Marie. Pastries from Paillard, paté and cheese from J.A. Moisan, chocolate made by the monks, from the shop along rue St-Jean.

Gamache hoped most of it made it back to Montreal. Between him and Henri, he had his doubts.

"I will. I'll probably be back in a few weeks to testify, but Inspector Langlois has all the evidence he needs."

"And the confession helps," said Émile with a smile.

"True," agreed Gamache. He looked around the home. He and Reine-Marie had been coming for many years, since Émile had retired and he and his wife moved back to Quebec City. Then, after Alice died, they came more often, to keep Émile company.

"I'm thinking of selling," said Émile, watching Armand look around.

Gamache turned to him and paused. "It's a lot of house."

"The stairs are getting steeper," agreed Émile.

"You're welcome to come live with us, you know."

"I do know, *merci,* but I think I'll stay here."

Gamache smiled, not surprised. "You know, I suspect Elizabeth MacWhirter is finding the same thing. Difficult living in a large home alone."

"Is that right?" said Émile, looking at Gamache with open suspicion.

Armand smiled and opened the door. "Don't come out, it's cold."

"I'm not that frail," snapped Émile. "Besides, I want to say good-bye to Henri."

At the sound of his name the shepherd looked at Émile, ears forward, alert. In case there was a biscuit involved. There was.

The sidewalk was newly plowed. The blizzard had stopped before dawn and the sun rose on a white, unblemished landscape. The city glowed and light sparkled off every surface making it look as though Québec was made of crystal.

Before opening the car door Gamache scooped up some snow, pressed it into his fist and showed Henri the snowball. The dog danced, then stopped, intent, staring.

Gamache tossed it into the air and Henri leapt, straining for the ball, believing this time he'd catch it, and it would remain perfect and whole in his mouth.

The snowball descended, and Henri caught it. And bit down. By the time he landed on all fours he had only a mouthful of snow. Again.

But Henri would keep trying, Gamache knew. He'd never give up hope.

"So," said Émile, "who do you think the woman in Champlain's coffin was?"

"I'd say an inmate of Douglas's asylum. Almost certainly a natural death."

"So he put her into Champlain's coffin, but what did he do with Champlain?"

"You already know the answer to that."

"Of course I don't. I wouldn't be asking if I did."

"I'll give you a hint. It's in Chiniquy's journals, you read it to me the other night. I'll call you when I get home, if you haven't figured it out I'll tell you."

"Wretched man." Émile paused, then reached out and laid his hand briefly on Gamache's as it held the car door.

"Merci," said Gamache. "For all you've done for me."

"And you for me. So you think Madame MacWhirter might need a little help?"

"I think so." Gamache opened the car door and Henri jumped in. "But then, I also think the night might be a strawberry."

Émile laughed. "Between us? So do I."

At home three hours later, Gamache and Reine-Marie sat in their comfortable living room, a fire crackling away in the grate.

"Émile called," said Reine-Marie. "He asked me to give you a message."

"Oh?"

"He said 'Three mummies.' Does that mean anything to you?"

Gamache smiled and nodded. Three mummies were taken to Pittsburgh but Douglas had only brought two back from Egypt.

"I've been thinking about that video, Armand."

He took off his half-moon glasses. "Would you like to see it?"

"Would you like me to?"

He hesitated. "I'd rather not, but if you need to I'd watch it with you."

She smiled. "*Merci,* but I don't want to see it."

He kissed her softly then they went back to reading. Reine-Marie glanced over her book at Armand.

She knew all she needed to know.

Gabri stood behind the bar of the bistro, dish towel in hand, wiping a glass clean. Around him his friends and clients chatted and laughed, read and sat quietly.

It was Sunday afternoon and most were still in their pajamas, including Gabri.

"I'd love to go to Venice," said Clara.

"Too many tourists," Ruth snapped.

"How do you know?" Myrna asked. "Have you been?"

"Don't need to go. Everything I need is here." She took a sip of Peter's drink and screwed up her face. "Dear God, what is that?"

"Water."

The friends drifted over to the fireplace to chat to Roar and Hanna Parra while Gabri took a handful of licorice allsorts from the jar on the bar and scanned the room.

His eyes caught a movement outside the frosted window. A familiar car, a Volvo, drove slowly down du Moulin into the village. The sun gleamed off the fresh snow banks and kids skated on the frozen pond on the village green.

The car stopped halfway through the village and two men got out.

Jean-Guy Beauvoir and Armand Gamache. They paused beside the car then the back door opened.

Clara turned at the sound of soft thudding at the bar. Allsorts were spilling from Gabri's hand. The conversation in the bistro dropped then disappeared as patrons first looked at Gabri, then out the window.

Gabri continued to stare.

Surely not. He'd imagined, fantasized, pretended so many times. Had seen it clearly only to have to come back, alone, to the real world. Not taking his eyes off the sight, he walked from behind the bar. Patrons parted, making way for the large man.

The door opened, and Olivier stood there.

Gabri, unable to speak, opened his arms and Olivier fell into them. The two men hugged and rocked and wept. Around them villagers applauded and cried and hugged each other.

After a time the two men parted, wiping tears from each other's faces. Laughing and staring at each other, Gabri afraid to look away in case it was taken away, again. And Olivier overwhelmed by all that was so familiar and beloved. The faces, the voices, the sounds he knew so well and hadn't heard in what seemed a lifetime. The scent of maple logs in the fire, and buttery croissants, and roasted coffee beans.

All the things he remembered, and ached for.

And Gabri's scent, of Ivory soap. And his strong, certain arms around him. Gabri. Who'd never, ever stopped believing in him.

Gabri dragged his eyes from Olivier and looked behind his partner to the two Sûreté officers.

"Thank you," he said.

"Inspector Beauvoir deserves the thanks," said the Chief Inspector. The place was quiet again. Gamache turned to Olivier. He needed to say this for everyone to hear. In case there were any lingering doubts.

"I was wrong," Gamache said. "I'm so sorry."

"I can't forgive you," Olivier rasped, struggling to keep his emotions in check. "You have no idea what it was like." He stopped, regained his composure then continued. "Maybe, with time."

"Oui," said Gamache.

As everyone celebrated, Armand Gamache walked out into the sunshine, into the sound of children playing hockey, and snowball fights, and tobogganing down the hill. He paused to watch but saw only the young man in his arms. Bullet wounds through his back.

Found, but too late.

Armand Gamache hugged Paul Morin to him.

I'm so sorry. Forgive me.

There was only silence then and, from very far away, the sound of children playing.

ABOUT THE AUTHOR

Louise Penny is an award-winning journalist who worked for many years for the Canadian Broadcasting Corporation. Her bestselling first mystery, *Still Life*, was the winner of the New Blood Dagger, Arthur Ellis, Barry, Anthony, and Dilys awards; and her second, *A Fatal Grace*, won the 2007 Agatha Award for Best Novel. She lives in a small village south of Montréal where she writes, skis, and volunteers. This is her sixth novel.